One-String Guitar

A novel

by Mona de Vestel

Harvard Square Editions
New York
2016

One-String Guitar

Copyright © 2016 Mona de Vestel

Cover design by Megan McDonagh © 2016
Photo credit: Adam Jones, Ph.D./Wikimedia
Commons Personal website:
adamjones.freeservers.com
Bio photograph by John Dowling Photography

ISBN 978-1-941861-29-5
Printed in the United States of America

Published in the United States by
Harvard Square Editions
www.harvardsquareeditions.org

Praise for *One String Guitar*

"*One-String Guitar* tells stories so embedded in sensations and rhythms of everyday consciousness that when it takes us across the boundaries of identities and cultures, we travel there with open hearts and minds. From the Pine Ridge Reservation of South Dakota, to the rust-belt Central New York town that becomes a refuge from the genocide in Rwanda, to the borderland of transgender identity, we are taken on a journey of pain but also of hope and love for these characters in crisis. de Vestel is an astute interpreter of historical trauma, addiction, and mental illness who conveys an understanding of home and the notion of a socially-constructed family from the perspective of the displaced."

—Rebecca Garden, Associate Professor of Bioethics & Humanities, SUNY Upstate Medical University

"Akin to Leslie Marmon Silko's weaving, *One-String Guitar* is at once a personal, political and poetic novel, that draws the reader into lives beyond the borders of geography, culture, and even biology. de Vestel is a skilled storyteller, traversing multiple landscapes, and contending with the charged political consequences of genocide and complex intersections of class, race and queer identity. Her treatment of relationships is reminiscent of Maggie Nelson's *The Argonauts:* sensitive, revealing and finely-attuned. You won't want to put *One-String Guitar* down."

—Amy King, author of *The Missing Museum*

"*One-String Guitar* is a revelation. It's also a novel you should give yourself plenty of time to read so that you can savor its many depths, both personal and political. Earlier in her career, Mona de Vestel was a spoken word poet and performance artist of magnetic power, all her incandescence is right there on the page where you have been waiting for it all your life."

—Nancy Keefe Rhodes, arts writer & editor

"Congratulations are in order to Mona for the achievement. Here you will find a compelling narrative of grace rare in an inaugural work. This is a meticulously crafted text that still somehow manages to sprawl across characters, cultures, continents, and an impressive array of emotional registers. It is a sophisticated work, polished, crafted, deeply layered while never forgetting what makes literature literature – it is a good read, reeking of authority. The text facilitates unique character intimacy before reforging it in the horrific genocides of Rwanda and the First Nations without ever sliding into easy sentiment or sensationalism. This is a journey both disturbing and revelatory, and ultimately beautiful as only meaningful literature can be. This inaugural work establishes Mona de Vestel as a contender and true voice. This one she can be proud of. Forever."

—Arthur Flowers, novelist

"HEDLEY: You watch. One string make plenty, plenty music. Now when I was a little boy I asked my grandfather where his mother was. He say she was long gone far away. Say when he play this he could hear her pray, I asked him, 'How?' He say, 'Listen.' (He plucks the string.)"

— *Seven Guitars,* August Wilson

To the people of the Oglala Lakota Nation and the Tutsi, Hutu and Twa people of Rwanda, Burundi and the Congo. To all of my ancestors and my family across and beyond bloodlines.

Part I

Chapter 1 – Edgar Owl Feather

Pine Ridge Reservation, South Dakota, 1998

They come at dawn to tell me she's dead. When I open the door, two half-breed cops walk into my house like they're home. I feel disoriented, it being dark outside and having them stand there on my doorstep. One of the cops looks at me with his freckled face. Must have Irish or French blood in him and I think how his white side makes his Indianness look strange. He is wearing his black hair cropped short, in a crew cut. His cheekbones, no doubt about it, are Lakota. For a moment, I wonder if we're related. I pray we aren't. Don't want no goons in the family.

Even before they spoke, I knew she was dead. But knowing it only took me to the places I remembered. I paid no mind to the goons standing in my house and I just let my mind take me to the dead zone. I walked in the desert where nothing grows. I closed my eyes and made myself fall, a tumbling rock at the foot of the black hills. *Fallen rock*, I said to myself. *You are now a fallen rock.* I went to the foot of the mountains where my ancestors were born and waited for gravity to turn on me but nothing happened. I even waited for Felicia to come to me to say: "Our child is dead now. Our child is dead." She never did.

"Edgar Owl Feather?"

"Yes, that's me."

"Can you come with us to the station?"

"What's this about?"

"A young woman was found dead at the New Hope Rehabilitation Center; we believe it is Maya Owl Feather. We need you to come identify the body.

There is a point when a man realizes he's got no reason left to live. I reached this moment the second they tell me Bird Girl's dead.

Just last week, she was sitting no more than two feet away from me. I could have done something to save her. I should have done something, but I didn't.

She had the narrow face of a goldfinch in late spring the way she cocked her head to the side, listening to the leaves rustling. Could she hear them? Voices. That's all I hear. Everyone blaming someone else. No one taking responsibility. Outside, the wind is howling. Spring's full of anger, always, rageful. I don't know why we try to make it seem like spring is cute and cuddly, pink and white, blue like they're announcing the birth of a boy. Spring is messy, pushes the earth out of the way. Young shoots tear open by themselves for a chance at light.

On the day Bird Girl arrived at the rehab center, her eyes were haggard and sunken, her hands scratched as if a cat had attacked her. I wanted to save her, maybe I even wanted to hold her the way I held her when she was a baby and her mama was already gone. But Mary, the rehab director and one of the many white BIA staff members just wouldn't have it.

"You know you can't work with your own daughter," she said, grabbing me aside as I was walking with Bird Girl.

"Since when do you care about the well-being of Indians, Mary?" I asked her. She rang her hands nervously.

"I can help her." I was whispering now, glancing over in Bird Girl's direction every few seconds.

"Not like this. You can't help her as her counselor. And you know it."

Deep down, I knew that Mary was right, but I couldn't let Bird Girl go.

"I can help her," I heard myself expressing a little more of my own despair than I'd have liked.

"And how do you plan on doing that?" Mary was angry now. She'd never really liked me in the first place.

I didn't know exactly what I meant by this, and I suspected that she didn't either. Our feet were touching now and I realized that if I leaned, our faces would brush together. I saw that her eyes were changing into the blossoming of a strange flower and I prayed that she would change her mind.

"How can you help her overcome her grief?"

"I know I can help her," I whispered, placing my hands on her shoulders. I had never touched her before. She stood very still and then leaned forward.

"OK. You get one chance. One chance is all you get. But if you screw it up, consider yourself fired." I was surprised by the part about being fired but I really didn't give a shit. I wanted to save my baby girl.

The truth is that I'd lost Bird Girl a long time before the cops marched into my home. When she was 13, I caught her drunk in the back of our shed with a pint of gin. I sat her down real quiet and told her about her mama. I talked to her about Felicia, but that only made it worse. One day I realized, *you can't save them all. Sometimes you got to cut the noose to save yourself.* I reckon that's what I did with my own daughter.

When I last saw Bird Girl a week ago, she wasn't talking in group. It was her silence that tipped me off. She'd usually be like the others, rambling on. Complaining. But on that last day, she was quiet. I liked to call her that. I'd been calling her "Bird Girl" since the day she was born. And that's a good thing. Birds are free. Sometimes I see her like those young meadowlarks just out of the nest, flying into window panes in early summer. They're full of life, flying into their own distorted reflections. It takes a certain kind of bird to stay on course. There are many shiny things out in the world. You just have to stay on course.

New Hope, that's the name of our drug and alcohol rehab center, got these chairs from a broken down school they closed in the southern part of the county. They said there was no more funding for the school and we needed chairs. So we got 'em.

Rony was still talking about the white man. *The white man this, the white man that.* That's all they talk about. All of their energy goes into talking about the white man. When they're not flying into the glass pane, they're looking for it.

"Rony, why'd you punch him, anyway?"

"You know why I punched him. He was calling me names. How long are we going to take this shit?"

"What do you think about what Rony is saying, Maya?"

Bird Girl stopped scraping the paint on her chair. The sound slipped out of earshot. She looked up at me with those eyes that reminded me of her mother's.

She was young. But her face looked ancient, like somebody up in the spirit world had doubled her 28 years with suffering.

"You got nothing to say about it? You always have something to say, how come you're quiet today?"

Everyone laughed. Bird Girl looked down again. I'd just lost her. Didn't mean to get the group to turn on her. This pack of wolves often turn on each other—on themselves even. They don't even know it. Time was up anyway.

"You should have clocked him harder. I heard you can kill someone if you punch 'em right. Like in that soft part, right above the nose" Jeffrey piped in. He pointed to the third eye— that one place to get the white man down.

"Let's wrap it up here. Anyone got anything else they wanna add?"

They were all quiet. Bird Girl had gone back to scraping the chair with her nails. We stood up and the sound stopped. We gathered round and held each other by the hand.

"God, grant me the strength to accept the things I cannot change, the courage to change the things I can, and the wisdom to know the difference."

Everyone hugged and then it was over. Gary, a big bear of a guy, came over, grabbed me by the arm, and pulled me to him. He'd been doing this after every meeting for six months now.

"Thanks, man."

"You good?" I asked him.

"Yeah, I'm OK. You know. One day at a time."

"Uh huh. Yeah."

I pulled away, looked around and Bird Girl was gone. After group, there's an hour of quiet time alone. People go off and write, they walk outside, they read a book, they talk, play a game of cards. I like to call this "center time." It's a moment for them to figure out who they are. For most, this is the hardest time. Growing up on the res, all they have is time and they spend their energy trying to kill it with booze, with sex, dope, and anything else they can find. Now that they were in rehab, they had to learn to figure out who they were all over again. Like a kid learning to walk. With the booze gone, everything's got an edge. Like someone turned up all the lights real bright and is shining them in your face. After a while, you wanna look away: you wanna find that shield again, something to take the edge off.

I remember thinking that I should have gone to find my Bird Girl, to talk to her, and see if she was OK, but I didn't. It's funny to think about the way we make decisions. One moment, I'm standing in the dark, hand reaching. Moon's out, a full moon, all round and pregnant. I like to imagine that moment right before everything changes; it reminds me I'm alive. But then I don't move like that night with Felicia. I stayed still in the dark, feet buried in the snowdrift, I looked, and then it happened. This is what it all comes down to. Choosing to move or standing still.

The rehab center had a stench. Always did. A cross between chlorine and urine. Not quite urine, but an afterthought of dirty bathrooms. Sometimes I slip back into the past, to escape. The past is my glass pane, it's my booze, it's what keeps me off balance. I slip into it sometimes, or just plain fall in it.

It's like the day Jessie that new girl, came into group last winter with her big belly. She was ready to pop. And I remembered my wife, Felicia. The way she looked the day I left. Everything they say about pregnant women shining like a brand new fruit was true about Felicia. There was this light that came from deep inside her. If I took her in the dark with me she'd lead the way. Felicia's face was smooth, so young, so full of the life in her belly. Two babies.

Sometimes I get stuck on that day, that very last day before I left. It's not even a day, it's a moment. A static picture, motionless. But I can hear everything. I remember the breeze. Days had gotten warmer by then; it was an early spring day in the camp. We were all hungry as fuck. The Feds had cut off our food supplies. It was up to the warriors to get the people some food. This is what I told her. I remember standing there; she was scared. She looked real scared and I told her not to worry.

"If they catch me, they got nothing on me," I told her. "They got nothing."

She was holding her belly, placed her hand on the top of the mound knowing she needed to protect them. Her hair was long, real long having grown so much during the pregnancy. She had it pulled back in a twist, to keep it off her neck. And I remember her glistening face and the wind brushing up against her hair. In her eyes, her deep black, piercing eyes, I saw the fear, but more than that, I saw her strength. She knew she had to be strong for the babies. And then I was gone.

The problem with the past is that it keeps me from moving forward, like a giant rock tied up around my ankles. Sometimes I want to cut it loose, but the rock is the only thing that keeps me connected to gravity: it's the only thing that keeps me standing. If I get rid of it, what will I have left?

I like to keep to myself. I don't mingle much. Ain't no point in it. No point in creating more rocks to tie around myself. I like my work. I try to help. Try to make a difference. In the end, it's not for me to judge how well I did down here. One day, I'll leave this sad, fucking place, and Tunkašila will judge how much I helped, how much I didn't.

There is so much space around me now. Don't have too many friends. I like to think I have more friends than enemies. On a good day, I'd say that's true. And then sometimes, everything just crashes, and I wonder if I've done anything to help my people. But like I said, it's not for me to judge.

But now Maya's dead and I've got two cops in my house. I keep saying this in my head over and over again. *Bird Girl's dead.* I try to stir, but my body is slow. *Bird Girl's dead.* Funny how the body protects itself from the mind, coils on itself like a snake under attack so the mind can't get to it with its poison. All I can think of is the sound of Maya's fingernails scraping that old chair. I'm stuck on the smallest detail, on the smallest piece of life.

"How did she die?" I hear myself asking the cops. What am I going to do with that information? Why am I asking this?

"We're not sure yet. The counselor on duty just found her an hour ago in the bathroom. She'd been drinking."

Everything is moving really fast in my head now. Like I just got thrown into the eye of the storm. My mind begins to leak its poison into my body. *Should have gone to find her after group. I should have gone.*

Outside, I hear the wind. A nasty wind is coming from the West. I didn't move and now she's dead. I pull on my old jacket and slip on some shoes. Sandals I use in the house. I can't think straight.

The goons and I ride in the dark. On the horizon, the sun's peeking, getting ready to do its show. Ain't nothing left to shine on in this res. Reminds me of the shows my grandfather used to do for the tourists. Made them feel like they were a part of a myth or something. The old west with the good Indian. The tamed Indian, the broken tiger in the zoo.

I don't talk to the cops. And when they speak, I keep it simple. Words make me fall into their traps. They like to drag out things you say to them, stupid things about the weather and shit like that, so they can use it against you. Like the time my friend Jimmy told a cop he didn't like the rain. Made him feel sad. I knew that about him too. He told me about it one day. Anyway, he told the cops in passing about not liking the rain. After they took him in, they'd put him outside every time it rained. It was shit like that bad cops liked to remember. Some say that's what makes a good cop. Someone who can use you against yourself. Like I said, the worse kind of traps are your own.

The cops say nothing. Must be tired or something because they usually like to talk. But these leave me alone. When we get to the station, they take me to this empty room and the same two cops ask me a bunch of questions. The whole time they're asking me questions, I keep thinking how strange they're making such a fuss over one of us being dead. I put both feet down on the ground. Keep myself grounded with mother earth. I try to remember that I know the way. To remind myself not to get lost.

"I understand you were Maya Owl Feather's counselor, is that right?"

"Yes, it is."

"You were also her father?" I nodded. This is when it hit me. This is why they had me. They wanted to break me.

"How long have you been working at New Hope?"

"Two years." I try to keep the answers short and to the point. Nothing more, nothing else. If you answer less, they end up asking more and that's a good way to get lost. If you end up answering more, they'll end up using it against you, like with Jimmy.

"What hours did you work yesterday?"

"I worked 8 to 6."

"Is that your usual shift?"

"Yes. Sometimes I work nights on Saturdays."

"Are the people at New Hope allowed to keep alcohol on the facility?"

"No. It's a rehab center." I could smell the trap in the making. I could feel them reining me in like a wild horse. I tapped my feet on the ground to remind me of the earth.

"Maya was found with two empty bottles of whisky. Can you tell me where she might have found them?"

"No. I can't."

"So you have no idea where Maya could have gotten the whisky?"

"No."

"And you were not aware that she had it?"

"No, of course not." I cursed myself for that last bit "of course not" makes cops mad when you express emotion, riles them up, and makes them wanna break you. When they can feel the life force in you. Gets them going.

"Yet you are responsible to keep the people of New Hope alcohol free, are you not?" Trick question. If I tell the truth, they'll get me; if I lie, I'm screwed.

"Patients at New Hope are responsible for their own actions. If they end up drinking, it's no one's responsibility but their own."

"So then, would you say your job is useless?"

"You can't save everyone." That seemed to satisfy him. Sometimes if the answer is short, strange, or vague enough, it throws them off balance and they either take a different turn or they stop.

"I think that does it for now, Mr. Owl Feather. Let's just walk over to the morgue so you can identify the body of your daughter."

Chapter 2 – Elbe

Syracuse, New York, 1998

I didn't know they were coming. Later, my mother said she didn't want me to fuss regarding their visit. I knew the moment she walked in the door that she had something to tell me. My mother would also say it wasn't a secret that she had never kept secrets from me. But I knew that this too was a lie.

I was forcing my way into consciousness when Wolf began to bark fiercely. The advantage of having a dog is the advance notice he affords. He barked and then the bell rang. Since I'd taken leave from school, I'd slipped into a strange and diluted world of blurred visions and nauseous mornings with my brand-new prescription of antidepressants. This was my new shield against the world. I rolled to the edge of the couch and sat up slowly. Sudden movement always made my head spin. I'd found that lying still kept the world perfectly bearable, like a nice static image in a diorama.

The bell sounded again, this time with more insistence. Maybe I knew before I opened the door that my parents had traveled the distance from Vermont to see me. On some plane, in some dimension of reality, I already knew of their visit. I even knew what they had come to tell me.

I saw them standing in the cold, blustery gusts of winter. I watched my mother through the thick glass of the storm door as she held herself, wrapping her arms around her own body as if she were trying to find comfort from within. She looked small, fragile, with my father standing next to her in his perfectly poised composure, his removed stance from the world. I remember seeing the blue of my mother's eyes bleeding through the thickness of the glass door. The oval of her face accentuated by the magnifying effect of the glass into an almost replica of Munch's terrifying scream.

Even before I opened the door, I recognized the strange urgency in my mother's blue eyes, the same urgency she'd shown on the day she told me about my birth.

When I opened the door, I noticed something in my mother's face had changed. I wondered for a moment if she had aged, somehow, in the few short months since I'd last seen her. The distance between Montpelier, Vermont and Syracuse, NY is not as far as one would think, but geography and the miles between us had nothing to do with the distance that had always separated my mother and me.

"What are you doing here?" A cold gust of wind blew into the house as I propped my body against the open door. Wolf growled behind me.

"You know grandma and grandpa! Wolf, stop growling." I said addressing the dog as he pushed his way between my legs to sniff my mother's thigh. He stopped growling. A tentative tail wag later and he was off into the house in absolute indifference.

"I thought he was going to bite us for a moment. He doesn't bite does he?"

"Mother, of course he doesn't bite! You know Wolf doesn't bite."

I quickly closed the door behind them. My mother looked older since I'd last seen her only months earlier. Her face was worn, the usual elegance in her movements dulled.

"I can't believe you're here!" My heart was racing now. I hadn't moved or walked around in two days, except for a couple of trips to the kitchen for food and to the bathroom to relieve myself.

We walked into my apartment and I suddenly noticed the chaos of my cocooned life since taking a leave of absence from school. I felt awkward with my parents in my home, reduced to a perpetual state of childishness in their presence. The simplest task became insurmountable. Making tea: boil water, find cups, choose tea. Each task equally puzzling. I asked myself: is it the depression or is it their presence that reduces me to this paralyzed state? I had no words; I had lost language. Fallen echoes in a strange vast space of emptiness. I recognized their faces. I knew them by heart. Now they were aging, and even this I was unable to measure, to notice, to accept. I had lost track of what my parents looked like: even they had become invisible. I tried to see them as they were. I tried to see myself as I was. In their presence, small and girl-like. Docile and perfectly nimble. I became flexible like a reed in the wind.

I looked at my mother. Maybe I was looking at her for the first time. She wore a red shawl on her shoulders that offset the paleness of her face. I'd always admired my mother's paleness. The way her face reflected the slightest bit of light, like a field of white bringing light out onto itself. I looked at her in search of comfort. How many times had I searched for answers in the chiseled lines of her aristocratic lineage?

I thought about the time my mother told me about my birth. I remembered the pink of her skin, the lines of constricted blood in her palms as she wrung her hands. I don't remember her words, except for one: *adopted*. I just remember watching her hands for the first time and realizing that we were not the same color. Afterwards, she held me close and cried. I put my head on her lap and watched my own sandy-bronzed arm resting against her pale and pinkish skin. It seems odd for me now to think that I'd never noticed my difference before that day. And maybe I'd always known it but I had never needed to name it before. When my mother said *adopted*, I bit my cheeks and tasted metal in my mouth. I thought about the taste of my own blood as I held out my arm against hers trying to name the difference between us for the first time. That's when I started counting and measuring everything around me. I remember the world before she uttered the words of what I'd always known, out loud: *adopted*. I remember everything being less sharp around me, more blurred, without so many lines to count. 43 steps between my bedroom and the bathroom. 43 steps as long as I walked in a straight line and didn't have to step over anything along the way. 42 steps to the bathroom if I wore my big fuzzy bear slippers. I couldn't stand the difference; I walked barefoot every time. I grew up hearing my mother yelling at me about my feet and *catching my own death*. I imagined death, a strange wolverine-like creature, all crumpled and wet, shaggy like a dog at the bottom of my butterfly net. I'd caught my death.

Each time my mother held me, everything shifted and I pushed my own difference outward like a shield. "I am not white!" I wanted to scream at the top of my lungs, even though I'd been reminded of that fact a thousand times by my classmates growing up. They'd called me everything from *squaw* to *nigger* and everything else along the way. I remember mimicking Jennie Jones' every speech pattern, her every gesture. She was blond and the most popular girl in school. All the boys wanted her and I was determined to be Jennie Jones in every possible way. I'd learned to blow my bubble gum the way she did, to flip a small piece of my hair in between sentences looking away annoyed the way she did. I'd learned how to intonate with a strange question-like tone at the end of every sentence I uttered. I was Jennie Jones.

One day in gym class, Jennie Jones spoke to me. It was the only time she ever addressed me directly. She stood next to me by the mirror as I was brushing my hair and she said: "It's too bad your hair is so black and your eyes are so brown, otherwise you wouldn't look like such a squaw."

And then she walked away. I remembered the contrast between the two of us standing next to each other, her talking to my reflection in the mirror, and me looking at the light of her blond hair and the blue of eyes reflected back to me. I remember feeling like an opaque black hole that sucked the world's energy.

Early on, I learned to make an inventory of my past: one Lakota mother, one unknown father, one birth on a reservation. These were the facts that contained me, like the four corners of a box. I wanted more than that; I wanted so much less. A clean slate onto which I could have raised myself from the ground up. A clean slate and a white body, pink hands like my mother's, dirty blond hair like my father's, blue eyes, or even green. An insipid past encroached in the comfort of my family's Quaker religion. Settlers and well meaning middle-class teachers who approached everything in the world with good measure.

"I can make the tea," my mother said to me when they had finally settled on the couch in the living room. I looked around and saw the mess, the residues of my own life, this part of me exposed to my parents. I felt myself shift uneasily on the couch. I caught my father watching me; he watched me without seeing.

My father has always been like a ghost, now more so that his hair had turned white. I was used to the way he pulled back into his quietude. The way he gazed at everything and rarely spoke. I wanted to see my father's hands. He always said he had the hands of a farmer, like his parents before him. I knew that I could find my father again in the callous of his hands, in the thickness of his fingers. But he was standing by the bookshelf in my living room examining each title like he'd found a hidden treasure. My mother smiled. She looked tired. I visualized the distance they had traveled to see me. The miles they had covered to erase the distance between us, a distance that had always existed since birth.

"I'll make the tea," I answered rhetorically.

This is my territory. I thought. *This is my turf.* I was determined to stand my ground, to not lose any of it in their presence. I was still able to make tea in my home. I got up, shakily, uneasily. The medication they had prescribed had buried me inside the bottom of a barrel. Sometimes it felt like the ocean, or a tunnel, a place of confinement.

Suddenly, memories of childhood came flooding in. I remembered my mother telling me how she began speaking her native French to me when I was old enough to see. I never understood why she waited until I could see to speak her native tongue to her brand-new baby girl. I imagined myself cooing to the sound of my mother's voice, to its nasal and glottal stops, to the guttural R in French. I'd read somewhere that babies have the latent capacity to speak all languages at birth. How many languages had I heard by the time I'd reached my mother's arms?

But the woman who became my mother spoke French.

Ne pleure pas mon bébé. Mon bébé. My mother must have whispered in my ear. "Don't cry, my baby." I was her baby then. To whom do we belong when we are born?

Behind me, I heard her footsteps. The kitchen appeared small. My kitchen had never looked so small. So remotely removed from anything I knew. This place was paltry, dingy, and dark. I felt sorry for the person who lived here. I thought of myself in the third person now. I had become a third being, removed from all of this. I filled the kettle with water.

"You don't use filtered or mineral water?" My mother's voice called me back to this moment.

"The water is clean here. The best water in the state." Here I was, making up statistics about water quality. I found myself defending the water source; I wanted to defend all water sources around me.

My mother dreamt of birthing babies of her own. Long before my birth, Marie bought a pram. The old-fashioned style, a pram with thin, pretty white wheels and shiny silver rims. A pram with the high handles and the beautiful white hood to protect her new baby. The pram was bought when I was still elsewhere, in that place between worlds, in this hovering before birth. I tried to imagine the place again, the warmth of it, my knowing of its impermanence. And I thought: *all babies are bred to die*. We come into the world wired with the knowledge of change, wired with the understanding that the warmth and darkness from which we come has been altered into a world of noise and light and chaos. When we're born, we become imprinted with the shock of this change, we become experts in impermanence. One passage to another; this is the way of the body.

My mother began opening cabinets at random in my kitchen.

"Where do you keep your tea?"

"Here," I answered, pointing to an overcrowded cupboard packed with tea boxes and expired snacks. She rummaged through the cabinet. My mother was known to organize any content in alphabetical order. I began counting the different items inside the cupboard: chamomile, mint and hibiscus, two types of honey, two large bags of sugar, one bag of flour, four cans of corn.

The kettle was whistling now. In the distance, I heard the sound calling me out of the tunnel. My mother was pouring the water in the cup. One cup. Only one cup.

"You're not having tea?" I asked.

"No, none for me." My water was not clean enough. The water quality in my life was not good enough for my mother. We sat at the kitchen table. Where was my father? I glanced at him from the kitchen door and saw him standing in the living room; he was standing by my bookcases and looking through my library. Not a single business book. How would he find his way home?

Long ago, my mother had told me about her family and about the day my father, Rowan, had met my grandparents. My mother came from a dwindling aristocratic family in France. She met my father in Paris, where he was doing a semester abroad. She held him, like the way someone grabs a blanket before running out of a burning house, and she never let go.

Marie's parents, the grandparents I never met, were horrified by the idea of their daughter marrying an American. Maybe if he had come from an old family, it would have been less shameful. After all, *old* in America is nothing more than a parenthesis in French history.

Marie, born Marie Françoise de Peussy, was the only daughter out of three children—two sons and one wayward girl. My grandparents come from a long line of *ducs* and *duchesses* dating all the way back to the Middle Ages. There is an entire village in the Limousin named after them. The small castle south of the village, hidden in the hills was the home of their ancestors.

My mother spoke of her family as one speaks of ghosts. Their presence among us was a constant and yet it was their absence from our lives that defined her. Born Marie Françoise, my mother dropped the second half of her first name when she moved to the United States. This severance was a symbol of what she had left behind. My mother told me she had never really liked her name and when she turned the page on her past, she severed a part of herself she no longer needed, like a piece of her residual tail or losing a wisdom tooth one night. Wisdom is not what she lost when she traveled to Vermont where my father grew up. She didn't know then that this was a permanent change, that turning her back on her parents—the divine de Peussys—would not be an alterable condition.

At first, my mother felt at home in the rolling green hills of Vermont. She felt as though she had traveled to an unknown part of France or maybe, at worst, to a remote place in Ireland. Vermont's resemblance to Ireland had been one of the reasons why my father Rowan's parents had moved to the luscious hills of this forgotten state. My mother liked to say that my father's parents differed from her own as a pig differs from a peacock. Over the years, I often wondered which family was the pig and which was the peacock.

Rowan's parents were each spawned from a family of farmers. Farming was in their blood: tending to the earth, watching the crops grow, or die, depending on the season. Rowan had grown up with stories about ruined crops, crops that rotted in the muck of a violent spring. He'd been lulled by stories of late frosts killing all young plants or the sudden visit of a scorching sun, devilish and queer, in that part of the world where the sun had little business. Marie, on the other hand, grew up with the presence of social rules, oppressive directives of conduct that molded and shaped her every action. In the de Peussy family, there were the aristocrats like themselves and then there was the rest of the world. My mother grew up with her two siblings in the city of Limoges. She was the only daughter, and her defining characteristic had more to do with the nature of her sex than with her own disposition. Having grown up around boys, Marie Françoise developed a rambunctious sort of boldness that her mother liked to define as "vulgar."

My grandmother, Marguerite Marie, confused my mother's bold and free ways with a lack of refinement. For years, she tried to teach her daughter the ways of the feminine world. She showed her how to hold a wine glass, how to delicately wipe her mouth after each bite, or how to laugh without crossing over into depravity and coarseness, long before my mother was out of childhood. And then there were the things my mother learned from her mother indirectly, in a symbiotic way—an osmosis of knowledge, like how to smile to those who are by nature, "lesser than they were," how to indicate disapproval of behavior in a social setting without uttering a single word and most importantly, how to discern the *faux-upper class* from the *nouveaux riches*. This was of course the most important and the easiest. It had always been expected that my mother would grow up to marry within the realms of her ranks.

Contrary to most people's belief about the aristocrats, my mother's family was not rich. Their wealth had long dwindled through the generations and vanished in political foibles that sometimes resulted in beheadings or in miscalculated choices of partnership. Marrying outside of one's ranks was by far the worst offense anyone in my mother's family could commit. This is what my mother chose to do. Not only had she chosen a common man, but he wasn't even French; worse yet, he was American. For my grandparents, as is the case for many aristocratic French and even commoners, Americans are by far the most debased and common people one could ever choose. There was, of course, the innate vulgarity of Americans, their almost childlike naiveté, *niaiserie,* as my grandmother had said to her daughter—this *niaiserie* that some people somehow found charming. There was also the problem of Americans' inherent dilution of culture, with their constant intermarriages so predominant in their upbringing. Not one culture ever remained intact and whole.

When my mother brought my father home for lunch to meet her parents, Marguerite Marie later told her daughter that Americans are the symbol of bastardization, everything the de Peussy family abhorred and rejected. My mother recounted that first and final encounter between my father and his future in-laws many times. I'd heard about Rowan's transgressions countless times, so much so that I'd convinced myself that I had been there that day.

Marie brought Rowan home on a Sunday afternoon. She had not bothered to tell her parents about his presence, an unconscious foible on her part, most probably out of fear of what she knew would happen. The weekly Sunday gathering was sacred ground; it was not to be missed under any circumstance by any of the three grown children in the de Peussy family. They knew, as they did with with many of the unspoken rules of the family, that missing such an occasion could only mean one of three things: a life-threatening illness, an accident, or death itself. Bringing an outsider to these gatherings required a great deal of planning, unless that person had already been accepted into the clan by their own clear lineage.

Rowan walked into this battlefield like an innocent lamb. Marguerite Marie opened the door knowing right away that something was terribly wrong. Each of her three children had a key to the house, so she did not understand why Marie Françoise had rung the bell in the first place. My mother had not wanted to force Rowan into the family completely; she thought that by allowing her mother to open the door and admit him herself she could ease his presence in the family. My parents were greeted by Marguerite Marie's best scornful look. A wry smile with a piercing gaze and the absence of a handshake. Rowan, who had learned that only business people shook each other's hands was not at all alarmed by this first sign of trouble. My grandfather, Jean, was decanting the wine in the dining room when they walked in.

"Maman, this is Rowan. I told you so much about him. I decided to bring him to lunch so you could all meet him."

Marguerite Marie may have heard certain things about Rowan but nothing that she cared to remember. When she had first heard about "the American," she had allowed everything her daughter told her to slip past her into oblivion. Marguerite Marie wanted to know nothing of this boy. My grandmother did not believe in friendship between men and women and so she never considered the possibility of anything but a tragic romance between her daughter and this American farmer's son.

Frédérique, Marie's brother was already there. He stood up intrigued and eager to witness the carnage that was about to take place. He smiled at Rowan and extended his hand, giving him a firm shake. This, perhaps, was the first sign in Rowan's mind that something had gone terribly wrong when he'd walked in a few seconds earlier. Should he have shaken her mother's hand? The moment had passed. In a matter of seconds, the room was swarmed with the de Peussy family.

Jean François walked in with his well-accepted fiancée, Sylvie, on his arm. Her family came from the long line of the de Ségur family, a prominent family in Limoges; there was no doubt in anyone's mind that the upcoming wedding in the spring would be a complete success.

My grandfather came in, carrying a half-opened wine bottle in one hand. He looked at my parents and said: "I would shake your hand, but as you can see they are occupied at the moment. Shall we seat ourselves for lunch?"

My mother knew in these first few minutes that nothing she or my father could ever say or do would alter her parents' decision to reject his presence from the family permanently. Rowan seated himself next to my mother when in fact this was Frédérique's place, and had been since childhood. The honored spot for a guest had always been at the head of the table across from my grandfather, but that spot was not set and had to be prepared catastrophically at the last minute. Rowan did not drink wine, a transgression worse than stealing. He kept his napkin and elbow on the table and occasionally rested his hand on his lap. He had never tasted any of the Rocamadour or Cantal cheeses they were savoring, and worse yet, he'd never heard of Limoges or the Limousin region. My grandmother grew very silent while my grandfather made strange and uncomfortable references to the poverty in Ireland, as soon as he heard about my father's roots. My uncles asked Rowan a million questions, which only led him faster to his demise.

"What do you think of Notre Dame?" He had not had a chance to visit it.

"Where did you grow up?" In rural Vermont, his parents were farmers. "If you don't eat escargot, then what do you eat, hamburgers?" Rowan had been killed and buried in one easy afternoon lunch.

My mother never said she missed her family, and yet it was in the way she evoked them that I knew their absence defined her. When I was a little girl, she liked to speak of the long, endless afternoons spent at her mother's family chateau, sitting outside with the entire family; the adults sipping cool drinks: Pastis, Absinthe, or Cointreau; watching the light shift as an afternoon lingered on into a sweet evening. Cool air would descend on the family as darkness approached, and everyone would move into the house to make a fire in the fireplace. There would be naps and long strolls through the long and narrow alleyways of around the chateau. In the fall, they picked *girolles* mushrooms and made a feast in the kitchen. Weekends were spent in the company of a good wine, aged at least ten years, and conversations about art. Art was, by definition, was something that had been created by someone who had died long ago. It was something that lived in a museum; art connected us to God and the higher plane of our existence; art did not exist within.

From the tunnel of my thoughts, I looked at my mother standing in my kitchen. Her face was not as I had remembered it. She looked older, more fragile, and vulnerable. I noticed a new line on her face. Right between the eyes. In the third eye. The place that sees all. She has gained wisdom there.

"I wish you had called me earlier. I could have taken care of you."

"I'm OK. It's not like I'm sick or anything. I just got a little tired. That's all."

"I know, it's just that I hate to think of you up here all alone. The reason I'm here is that I really want you to come home with us. It would do you some good. And with your leave from school, you have no obligations holding you back."

I was trying to count the number of hours since my last dose. Where was my medication?

"Did you hear me?" My mother interrupted my thoughts.

"Yes, I heard." I answered coldly. "I can't come with you. I have things to do."

"Things? Like what things?"

My mother had always been the expert on the scales of importance in everyone else's life. Work came at the top of the list, even though my mother did not work. And second were community activities.

"I'm a volunteer interpreter for African refugees from Rwanda." My mother perked up. I noticed her sit up straight in my tiny and rusted metal chair, the one I bought at Walmart four years earlier when I'd moved into the apartment. It had spent an entire winter rusting on my porch long after barbeque season ended.

"An interpreter? That's wonderful! They speak French, then?"

"Yes, they're from Rwanda."

"Oh, that's that terrible place where they started killing each other, isn't it, a few years ago? What are the tribes' names again?"

"Yes, the Hutus and Tutsis. The Hutus killed one million Tutsis by hacking them to death in just 100 days. Did you know that the weapons were supplied by the government of France?" This last bit had slipped out of me.

"Well, no. Are you sure? I mean, why would France do such a thing?"

"Why wouldn't they? There is a lot of money to be made in giving people a chance to kill each other."

"When did you become so cynical?" My mother's body looked strangely overgrown sitting at my narrow kitchen table. She was keeping her arms and hands away from the table sitting perfectly straight. It reminded me of my childhood dolls, stiff and straight-legged, in their perfect lifeless postures.

"I'm not being cynical. I'm just telling you how it is."

I thought about how I was beginning to sound like my college friend Joey and it brought on a feeling of uneasiness. Calling something out required sticking my neck out and I'd spent my whole life learning how to blend in, how to live my life unnoticed. Somehow, I knew in that moment of clarity that

I had—not with much conscious thought, however—planned out my entire life as one long rehearsal of absolute homogeneity. My genetics had always betrayed me; simply walking into a room sometimes became a political statement, rocking the sometimes pastoral, quiet atmosphere of a room filled with whites; when suddenly I was *the Indian girl*, filling the quotas, spotting the social landscape of a world otherwise uniform in color. I was sick of being colorful. I had never asked for the difference that marked me. I just wanted to confound myself in the voice of the masses; I wanted my narrow, angular "bird face" (as my mother liked to say) and the color of my skin to suddenly smooth into the paleness of pink champagne. I wanted my looks to round out into the palette of my father's Irish ancestry, into the aristocratic lines of my mother's family. Why had I been placed with them if I could never, no matter how hard I tried be just like them? How cruel.

And then there was Joey. Joey and I were twins of opposition. Joey pushed his way through life, sticking his neck out in every place nameable and taboo. Joey was loud, brash; he cut his way through silence brutally, and he enjoyed watching people squirm. I remembered meeting Joey in college, in a political science class. He had just started to take testosterone and transition from being a girl to becoming male. Like everything else in Joey's life, being trans was not something he ever tried to hide.

"Hi, my name is Joey I used to be called Michele when I lived in a body without a dick," he announced to our Poly Sci class on the first day of class. A friendship with Joey was not for the faint of heart. Knowing about Joey's gender of origin had left little impact on me. I hadn't changed the way I perceived him. Joey was a guy and that was that.

Joey was the voice that never stopped. He raged through the semester, slamming his ideas into our classroom, pounding his way into the professor's own limitations. He finished the semester with a C minus.

"Bullshit patriarchal reminder of white male domination and the mediocrity that ensues when trying to come against it. In other words, the asshole is trying to put me back in my place. Yes massa', yes massa'." I'd never really heard anyone use the word "patriarchy" on a regular basis. Joey had a staple of words he pulled out of his militant hat. They were his tattoos, his scars, his birthmarks of choice. There was something about Joey that I envied. It was the same thing that made me recoil and sometimes frightened me. This passionate, almost suicidal nature that pushed Joey to the edge of everything he encountered. Joey was, by definition, a fearless creature, actually, a fearless man. There was nothing creature-like about him except his marginal nature and the way he liked to drag people to the edge with him. Some came kicking and screaming only to marvel at the depth of the precipice, the void to which he had brought them. Others—like me—came quietly, almost catatonically, like moths drawn to light. The disorientation that came with such a compliant response to Joey's rants could lead to one thing and one thing only: absolute metamorphosis or complete destruction. What if the moth mutated and suddenly became light? What if it no longer craved the single ray of light that always led it to its own death? This was the solution.

In our Poly Sci days, Joey wore his hair in a mass of brown curls that framed his pretty face. Joey was *the androgyne* at its best. His body was angular, muscular, and lean, without any trace of the femaleness of his birth. He worked as a bicycle messenger delivering packages to the biggest corporations in the city. He liked to sneak what he called *propaganda leaflets* into his customer's deliveries and slip back into oblivion "with the rest of the proletariat," as he liked to call himself. Joey had a face full of freckles sprinkled on his amber skin, offset by two jet black eyes. Being white, black, and Lakota, Joey referred to himself as *multiracial*. Joey had always been proud of being able to name his exact Native American ancestry.

My father came into the kitchen interrupting the flow of my memories. He paced around, examining every corner absentmindedly. He looked like a disinterested tourist in a bad museum.

"Where shall we go for dinner?" He asked, finally stopping by the kitchen counter.

"Oh, Rowan, she's not well enough to go to dinner," my mother said. "We're going to order something to be delivered here."

The thought of my being ill was something I could not tolerate and yet I knew that if we went out, we risked running into school colleagues. After all, I was on sick leave and couldn't exactly be seen gallivanting around town.

"What's a good place where we could order food? Do you have a Chinese place, or Mexican restaurant in the area? I can't bear to do pizza. Too much grease."

We ordered Chinese food from the place on the corner. I tried not to look at my mother who held her breath in between syllables, as if she were holding back a piece of herself.

We were pushing back the inevitable. Keeping the distance between us at bay. If we could lose ourselves in the everyday details of life, in the mundane connecting us to each other by a thread, then I wouldn't have to listen to what she had to say.

Growing up, I remember my father like a shadow in our lives. He came home from work and listened to NPR news. He read the paper and worked in his office for hours, even on the weekends. My parents rarely argued, but when they did, it was always my mother who yelled and cried. And when it was over, my father looked as he always did: impassive and still. I came to fear my father. When I was a baby, my mother later told me that I sought my father's attention. But unable to find warmth, I began to drift away from him. An absent and silent man is all I know and remember of this man who adopted me. I don't remember the years when I sought him out. I don't remember wanting anything from him. Or maybe the wanting is so large and omnipresent that I don't see it anymore. I came to fear him like one fears stillness in a place of great noise. My childhood was still and quiet in his presence. I showed him my grades and talked to him about my classes. Not about school per se or anything outside of the realm of academics. I didn't tell him about my friends or my fights with people. I didn't tell him about people calling me names in school or why my shirt was torn. I just learned that the grades and my successful performance in school were all that he was interested in. Maybe I learned to excel because I knew that it was the only thing that could link me to my father. I remember bringing a C home one day. My father stared at the grade and said nothing. He returned to reading his paper and didn't scold or lecture me on mediocrity, the way I'd heard other parents do. He just retreated into his silence again. That was the last time I ever got a low grade. When I brought him As and Bs, he would smile and praise me. He would see me. He even took me for ice cream at Dairy Queen behind my mother's back because she said soft ice cream was *unclean*. When I was in second grade, he bought me an enormous dictionary. These moments of sharing excellence is what I remember best about my father. The rest of the time, we both retreated back into his silence.

My father taught business to MBA students. I grew up watching him work in his office. He'd have countless piles of papers and well-labeled files. I knew early on, that I would never go into business. My mother was also a teacher. She was the one who connected me to the world, with emotions. She was a thread that pulled me back into something vaster than my father's silence. Growing up with these two distinct people, I was always pulled between the two worlds: the realm of feelings and the realm of silence. I think of myself as a sociable hermit. I am perfectly well versed in the social rules and the ways to smile and carry on civil conversations. But at the same time, the sound of the phone sends me into a panic. I could remain for days without seeing anyone for long stretches of time. In the end, both worlds completely terrified me. People could not be contained, even if that is all they tried to do with me, to push through the vast erasure of myself, an infinite landscape of barrenness that always called for something external in the end. This was an endless loop; a sociable hermit like myself always would need to go back to the world of people only to find that silence is the only soothing element that makes relationships bearable.

We shooed Wolf away from the steamy plates of Chinese food. He shook his blond mane and trotted away in a huff, in the way dogs can sometimes be more expressive than people. My mother ordered the food without asking us what we wanted. I didn't have the energy for combat. I could feel myself slipping into a more and more malleable place. It reminded me of the *plasticine* my mother brought me back from France when I was about five years old. Fancy French Play-Doh where I tried to shape myself, to shape my family. To create their faces and mine so I could see us from the outside. But all I could manage was rolling us all into tiny faceless blobs of clay. We were faceless and I knew it, even then.

After the meal, we almost held our breath. I was afraid to move. I could read in my mother's body language that the moment had come. She had begun wrapping her arms around her own shoulders again. She held her breath in between syllables, as if she were holding back a piece of herself.

"We received some news, in the mail. About your birth family." She was looking down into her plate where a pile of congealed Chinese food was already beginning to dry. My father sat still, docile like a child. His eyes had a watery quality that gave him an air of nostalgia. Was he crying? I had never seen my father cry before. I wanted to move, but I couldn't. My body was trapped under the weight of the medication. I had taken it so it would pin me down, so I could be restrained from feeling anything. Suddenly, I wanted to be free again. But I'd given myself away to it and now I couldn't walk away so easily. My mind was now trapped underwater like a lifeless form at the end of rope, tightly secured by boulders.

"This is not easy to say," my mother said, pulling a letter out of her purse. She was looking at me now. She had unfolded her arms slightly, placing her elbows on the table, holding the letter between her palms, as if she were trying to keep the paper warm. This simple infraction of my mother's elbows on the table, this cultural transgression of manners only emphasized the gravity of the situation. If Marie Françoise de Peussy was placing her elbows on the table, all bets were off.

"Apparently, you have a sister. A twin sister. And she wants to know about you." My mother handed me the letter. I couldn't look at it right away. I needed to let the words sink inside my brain. I let them settle in the fertile murky earth of my muddled mind. *Twin.* I tried to replicate an image of myself, only to find that I could not remember what I looked like. I tried moving my hand. If I held out my hand, if I could move in the direction of seeing myself, any part of myself, then maybe I could begin to see this other person. I finally looked at the letter. It was postmarked from Pine Ridge, South Dakota. The name of the sender was written in a choppy, childlike handwriting: *Maya Owl Feather.*

"She recently found out about your existence. She'd been searching for years and now she found you. It's up to you. If you want contact, then I can give you her address."

I looked at my father again. His eyes were dry. Maybe I had imagined the presence of tears. Memory cannot be trusted. What I hold to be true cannot be trusted.

"You're not speaking." My mother's voice was pulling at me again. She wanted something now. She wanted me to give her something. I tried to stir myself to think.

Think, think about what you have to give this woman who saved your life.

Like a puppy, like a stray dog, Marie de Peussy saved my life. The medication was making me cynical. She was right.

"When did she write?" I looked down at the postmark date again, five weeks earlier: *August 6, 1998.*

My father perked up. He was looking directly at me now. It was as if my asking a factual question had suddenly brought him back to a piece of himself.

"The letter arrived a month ago. You were fragile. We didn't want to upset you."

One month and this strange piece of myself, this other half of me was waiting for an answer. I wanted to measure the world. Not just this room. Two cups, one glass, for my milk. My mother always gave me milk when she thought I was about to break. The breaking point had passed now. And she was still standing at the corner, waiting with her handkerchief in hand, waving at me from the corner as I rode away on the school bus. If I could measure the world, I could find my way home. I understood my father all of a sudden. Twenty-eight years of silence, and suddenly this man and I were closer to each other than we'd ever been. Closer than destiny, closer than fate and love and everything else that splits the heart open leaving it exposed. This solitary man with a mind for clarity came to me; he came to my rescue.

"You don't have to respond. There is nothing that forces you to respond. Your mother and I just wanted you to know. To give you the option."

I found comfort in the idea of waiting. Waiting is what I knew. I had waited for a family my whole life. Not this family. Not this life. I had waited for my real life to start. Soon it would happen. My life would start soon.

Chapter 3 – Francine

Syracuse, New York, 1998

Francine rested her open palm on the frozen window. She liked the feel of the cold against her flesh. It reminded her that she was still alive; that her brain was sending signals through her body. Cold = pain = life. She pressed her index finger into the frost and watched the thin layer of ice melt under the pressure of her body heat. The melted spot formed a circle, a tiny opening onto the outside world. She could see the gray dawn hanging like a veil above the world. *This place is dead,* she thought. *Winter kills everything.* Her fingers formed additional circles, tiny windows until she could finally see them: her children standing in the crisp air, waiting for the school bus.

Francine watched the blue parka, electric blue piercing through the blandness around Boy, her boy, her son. He looked small standing there next to the others. He was the smallest. The youngest. He was the one hanging by a thread. He was only four. Boy stood very still next to the others.

Francine closed her eyes and imagined running naked through the snow. She pictured this over and over again, like one imagines jumping off a bridge. She knew the cold would kill her, eventually. She liked to think of the slow death. The deliberate detachment the frigid temperatures would enforce on her body.

Distant voices of approaching children pierced the silence. Their voices were muffled by the walls of the house surrounding Francine, and by the thick snow encircling all of them. Francine first saw the girl. She was walking ahead of them. They were all marching towards her children, waiting at the bus stop. The girl must have been nine or maybe she was a small ten-year-old. A pack of boys was chasing her, laughing, taunting her. One boy wearing a small wool hat quickly made a snowball with the newly fallen, untouched snow on the sidewalk. He bent quickly and then thrust his small frame forward. His pale face opened like a flower. "Get this!"

Francine could barely hear them. Their voices falling in the distance, as if speaking from the bottom of a well. The boys were laughing wolfhounds. The small girl was trying not to run. Her face held fear, but she was forcing a smile. Francine felt her stomach tighten. A sharp pain shot through her abdomen. She could not take her eyes from the pack of children. The boys were nearing now. Her long blond locks cascaded down her back. Her face was pristine, the tiny symmetrical figurine features. Porcelain skin. She reminded Francine of the European dolls of her childhood. *One day she will be beautiful*, Francine thought. *Their paths will diverge.* When the boys will have become wasted men, bald and unshapely. When their bodies will have fallen under the pull of gravity, their guts pulling downward, their skulls exposed, she will attract older men with sinewy bodies. The alpha wolves with large bank accounts. The muscled men with golden skin and silver hair. One day these boys will remember her. The girl they used to taunt. The small mermaid with golden locks they only touched with tainted snow.

The children reached the bus stop. Boy ignored them playing with a tiny pile of snow he had formed with his foot. Sylvie, Francine's second-eldest stared at the blond girl with great interest. *My daughter has never seen a child so blond.* Angélique, Devota and Sophie were busy talking with each other, busying themselves with the small of life. The wolfhound pack of boys did not even glance at Francine's children. Instead, they had encircled their victim and were now taunting her with a refrain they were repeating over and over again in a sing-song tone.

The bus came and Francine pulled away from the window, as if she had seen a ghost. She did not want to watch her children disappear into a bus. She couldn't bear seeing them leave, even if she told herself they would be back later that day.

After the children vanished, Francine usually allowed herself an hour or two on the couch where she lay wrapped in a blanket, wishing away the perpetual cold of this land. She preferred taking these pseudo naps in the living room far from the bed she shared with her new husband, Jean de Dieu, even though he had left for work long before the children awoke. Francine did not have the luxury of sleeping all day until the children came home from school. But an hour or two away from the world was the gift she gave her brain from having to think about the others and the muck of her life.

By midday, Francine would rise from the couch, and hurl herself into the cadence of the daily chores; six loads of laundry, a trip to the grocery store, cooking a pot of rice, with *lenga lenga* greens and chicken, cleaning the bathroom, and sweeping the floor. With so many children in the house, the work was never done.

That afternoon, the kids came home and filled the house with the ruckus of their childhood. She watched their resilient limbs running and playing carelessly, as if no blood had ever been shed on their land. She listened to the giggles of her oldest daughter, Devota, as she tried to run from Boy chasing her through the house. When Jean de Dieu came home, he was tired. His job at the box factory, where he worked on the assembly line, kept him exhausted and quiet—sedated like a caged animal. One peck on the cheek as he walked through the door, and Francine and her husband had finalized the last bit of physical contact they would have for the rest of the day.

When night fell, the children were fed and coaxed into bed. Jean de Dieu liked to retreat at the same time as the children, leaving Francine to sit at the kitchen table in the blue glow of the hot water heater. This was the time when Francine would find the quiet inside her and wrap it around herself like a shawl. She would sit until sleep found and trapped her with the heaviness of her limbs and the closing of her eyes. That is when she would drag herself to bed and tumble into sleep from which she accessed no dreams. In the middle of darkness and the quiet of the muffled silence of the snowy streets, Francine was was roused again into thought and consciousness by the cries of her son, Boy. Francine sat in bed for a long time in the blue glow of the room and listened to her son's cries. She sat very still and waited for the child to stop crying. She could feel Jean de Dieu's warmth next to her. The rise and fall of his heavy, labored breathing after a long day of work. Francine knew he would not be woken by the tiny whimpers of her son. In between cries, Francine heard the house creaking and moaning. The boiler rumbled like a monster hidden in the basement; it was coughing hot air into the house, desperately trying to fight the cold outside.

"Mama, it hurts!" he cried. Francine felt she was hurling herself out of bed. She thought of the violence it required to extricate her body from the warm sheets to walk through the cold dark house in order to check on a child whose death she had prayed for a long time.

"Where?" Francine asked curtly. "Where does it hurt?" she asked standing by the child's bed.

Boy pointed to his head, and then to his belly. His small finger rigid, a frail twig, a tiny stick leading to the truth.

"Wait here," Francine whispered and then she was gone into the dark house in search of warm milk. This house was larger than any home she had ever lived in and yet it was shabbier. Francine was accustomed to the comfort of her modern home in Kigali, and the ease that comes with the work of servants to keep the house clean. That home was gone now, as was everything else that had been taken away.

When she returned, Francine handed Boy a cup with frothy hot milk. Boy shook his head. *No.* "No, Mama. My stomach hurts."

She thought of death and how it resembled an old toothless woman trailing around the house.

"Tomorrow, when the sun comes up, we will go see the doctor." Francine placed the cup of milk on the nightstand next to Boy's bed. Angélique and Sylvie were sound asleep in their beds nearby. She walked over to each girl and pulled the blanket up to their chins and then walked out of the room.

Francine stood by the window of her bedroom and watched the night sky filled with stars. *Africa.* She thought. *Rwanda. There is nothing left for me there.* Francine thought about the ghosts wandering the streets of Kigali at night. *They must wander not knowing they are dead,* Francine wanted to cry. She wanted to cry for the dead; she wanted to cry for Boy and for everything he needed, for everything she could not give him, but she had no tears left to cry.

Chapter 4 – Elbe

Syracuse, New York, 1998

The next morning after my parents had gone, I forced myself to dial the number for my volunteer gig. Everything had become an effort. The smallest task, a mountain climb, a trek through a hot and humid forest on a scorching day. It was ringing on the other end. Three rings and then a machine.

"Hello, you've reached Catholic Charities. We're not here at the moment, so please leave a message." The beep sounded. Holding my breath as if under water, I forced myself to speak.

"Hi, my name is Elbe McEwan." I heard myself, a third party, floating somewhere above the room, by the ceiling. What kind of name was *Elbe McEwan?* Some hippy name maybe, a white chick with liberal parents. I was still speaking. "I am a medical interpreter volunteering with refugees. I am calling to see if you need me this week…um because I am available. If you need to reach me, my number is 315-723-1415." I was on automatic pilot. Whenever, I made professional calls, it was as if I wasn't even the one talking. I hung up. After my parents had left, I had made a pact to do something productive with my time, to stay connected to the world somehow.

I looked around. The bedroom was a mess. I hadn't made the bed in a week. I simply lay in it all day and all night, with intermittent visits to the kitchen and the bathroom. Each time I returned to the sheets, I tried to brush the accumulating animal hair off the pillow and the top of the bed. I pulled on the blankets trying to bring order without exerting energy. Everything required so much effort. Drinking, eating, defecating, and urinating. The body required constant care. I had never noticed this before. Staying alive was a full time job.

I had gone to see my doctor. I'd had a cough for a few days, which didn't seem serious, but what if it was? What if I required serious care? My doctor had listened to me. He'd reached for his stethoscope and placed it gently in the middle of my back, the soft and vulnerable place where the lungs were hiding. *Are they this low?* I wondered. I realized that I didn't even know the placement of my own organs in my body. *How can I get better if I don't even know where my spleen is?*

I had felt strangely comforted by his touch. This anonymous hand on my body. How he had pressed the stethoscope against my back. With this simple gesture, I had felt attachment, or even love. I wondered about love for a moment. What it really was. Could it be measured in a certain kind of touch? This stranger did not love me. I knew this rationally, and yet for a moment, I had felt held. Contained. Maybe containment was a form of love.

"You don't have bronchitis, not even a cold, really," he said, moving back as if he wanted to see me more clearly, more fully.

"Let me ask you a few questions. Do you mind?" he asked scratching his bald head.

I acquiesced with a nod.

"OK, so do you do things slowly?"

What did he mean? I had no idea. "No," I answered blankly.

"OK." He jotted my answer quickly on a sheet of paper clipped to a board. "Does your future seem hopeless?"

I considered the question closely. "Hopeless, as in uncertain?" I asked.

"Hopeless, yes, without any hope."

I could tell he did not want to have a philosophical discussion with me about the nature of hope. *Stick to the facts, Elbe.* I told myself. *Stick to the facts.*

"Yes, it does."

"OK."

He gave me the same reaction as when I had answered no. There seemed to be no correlation between his reaction and the type of answer I provided.

"Do you have trouble making decisions?"

"Yes."

"Do you feel like a failure?"

"Yes." The list went on and on and each time, I found myself answering *yes*.

"It sounds like you might be suffering from depression," he said, stepping away from me with an air or scrutiny, as if he were trying to discern whether the depression could be visible from the outside.

Before I left the office, the doctor said, "did you know that lungs are associated with sadness?" He smirked and shrugged. I noticed the worry lines on his forehead. The baldness made him look more vulnerable. *Who cared for this man?* I wondered. *Who held him at night?*

Sadness. A trail of the past came back in a strange mist. A wafting smell. This was the second time I had pneumonia. Although the last part about pneumonia was my own leap of faith. The good bald doctor had never pronounced those words. Not exactly. I liked how it sounded, however. It gave weight to my listlessness. It gave credibility to my inability to get out of my bedroom, except to perform the rudimentary bodily functions.

When I got home, I opened a can of vegetable lentil soup. Wolf followed me into the kitchen, his blond shaggy body strangely attached to the shadow I cast around the house. There was a magnetic pull between me and the dog. He could see right through me. I knew this and sometimes feared him for all that he could see in me. My transparency. His eyes reflected mine. He was sad. I hadn't taken him for a walk in a week. I would only put him on the extendable leash every four or five hours and let him out and waited as he defecated and urinated right outside the house. I always hated this halted moment. Having to stand there, my life in suspension. In the end, the two of us were reduced to the same functions.

Upstairs, I noticed the fetid smell of the room. A faint putrid odor of the previous meal—a veggie sub with salad dressing and something else, some strange hidden body secretions. The cats were curled up on the bed. They barely opened their eyes when I entered, stretched and then curled up again in the middle of the crumpled blanket on the bed. I brushed the hair off my pillow half-heartedly and watched Wolf as he climbed up on the mattress I had set up for him next to my bed.

I felt the old pang in the chest. My parents were gone and I thought about how in the end, I had to ask them to leave. I had pressed my mother for my twin sister's address and then I had sent them back out into their world, into the borrowed places where I spent years growing.

I looked outside. It had begun to snow. I thought about the vulnerability of my parents out in the cold. I imagined them, small and wrinkled and old, and I asked myself if I had a heart. The words still hung in the air like a stench, like an unshakable stench: *Twin—a twin, another one of me—another.* I tried to see myself; I tried to close my eyes. I listened to the wind outside, the howling wind in the eye of the brewing storm and I tried to see myself. My hair, long brown hair, *straight as a sheet.* This is what Dana had said to me once in our third-grade recess: "You can't play with us. Your hair is as straight as a sheet."

And I remember trying to understand her words. Even now, I don't quite get it, beyond her singling out my *otherness.* But it was her eyes I understood that day, the blue of her eyes squinting when she said it. As if she wanted to close the deal, to mark her words with movement of change. And the girls around her cackled. They giggled and laughed and then their backs were turned on me. I tried to stand straight and walk the other way. I went into the bathroom because I could feel the sting in my eyes and the involuntary tears getting ready to come. I passed the mirror and I caught my reflection. It startled me. I saw myself as a ghost, hovering, trying to hold on to a place that no longer existed. I no longer existed. My people no longer existed—or did they? And yet I stood in this bathroom with my stinging eyes and my yellow dress. And the ribbon in my hair. The ribbon Marie put in my hair to match my dress because she said: "Yellow is beautiful on you, it glows with your color."

Your *color. My color.* What color was I? I tried to see what others saw. I stared at myself in the mirror, through the blur of the tears and all I could see where the run of the colors, the black of my hair, and the yellow of my dress whirling in my head until the bell went off.

I called Leon. Suddenly I wanted to see him. I wanted to hold his calloused hand and smell his scent. I wanted to bury my nose in the nape of his neck. His scent is like no other: musky and bitter, soft and biting, eucalyptus and pine, arid soil and salty marshes. I wanted him to hold me. The line rang. He answered. His voice cracked through the phone. I visualized the distance between us. The miles between here and the nation. The snow standing in our way. The wind blurring our own footsteps.

"Hey, sweet girl. I thought you were going to rest tonight."

"My parents came, from Vermont, out of the blue."

"That's good, then. Maybe I can meet them."

"They just left." I felt a pang of relief. They would never meet. Their words would never collide. Relief and regret.

"Already? I thought you said they just came out of the blue."

"They did, long story." I didn't want to explain.

"I need you." The way I spoke those words startled me. Rattled me, as if the words had fallen out of me like coins out of my pocket. I tried to backtrack.

"If you want. I mean, I know it's snowing, and…"

"I'll come right over."

I'd never asked Leon anything and he'd never had to grant or refuse me. But suddenly the urgency had made my head spin. Wolf was staring at me. He looked as though he wanted to speak. He wanted to tell me that I scared him a little that he loved me and that he understood, but that my sadness was taking up too much room in the house.

Outside, the streets were quiet. A few cars passed slowly the sound of their tires muffled by the thick blanket of snow. I thought of the strings of people in my life moving their way through the storm. Moving towards me, away from me. Moving. I heard the growling sound of Leon's car cut through the silence and then stop. His car door slammed and then silence again. I ran to the door and opened it. I felt like a child at Christmas. He was my Santa Claus. He was here to deliver a piece of myself to me. He would tell me who I was. He would know.

When I opened the door, I was struck by his presence. His ponytail had come loose and long strands of black hair draped his broad shoulders. Hundreds of snowflakes were now melting on the top of his head.

"Hey, baby." I stood on my tiptoes to kiss him, my bare toes stepping delicately on the monstrosity of his cold and wet boots. I buried my nose in his neck. His scent had shifted. A subtle shift of pine and marshy waters and a faint smell of whisky. When I kissed him, it wasn't just whisky, but bourbon. Black Bourbon, he later told me. I searched for myself in him. In the broad open palms of his hands, in the tangled knots in his hair, in the way he held his head slightly off to the right, like a bird listening to a forest fire. I watched him move in the space I had claimed. I watched him smile. I watched him moving his lips, in the way he kissed me, in the way he held me without holding me captive. In the way he stood as if he would never move again and in the way he moved. He never asked me about the sadness. He never asked me about my parents.

And I never told him. The world closed in on us that night. The muffled sound of winter unraveling itself for the first time. The first storm is the most violent. The most ravaging. It is rarely the storm that kills. We're not willing to pull ourselves together in the face of what we know can annihilate us.

We found our way into the bedroom because words no longer carried meaning. I tripped on myself over and over again. In my invisibility. I tried to etch myself in the motion of Leon's hands on my body. We slipped under the covers, first cool—the cool of the sheets—and then warm again. Blood against blood, hidden in folds of our flesh and bones. Leon's body is angular. It breaks in places, likes waves against the roundness of the land, against the curves of my waist. He held on to my breasts, one in each hand like he had finally found his way home. He squeezed them, causing pain and then pleasure. I pushed away the absence, filling me up all the way to my nose. I pushed away the blurred vision of the third-grade yellow dress and the black of my hair. His tongue found his way inside me, between my legs. He first moved quickly, like a reptile or like a quiet monster, and then he became motionless, his body resting between my legs like a fallen tree. I entered a world of light with his tongue. Gold, aqua and jewels at the bottom of the ocean with each stroke of his hunger for me. I slipped and slid and fell inside the cavern of this strange pleasure. This luminous world of pearls and coins. I heard myself, the small whimpers, the shallow breathing like a fugitive fox, cutting through the woods at the speed of light. A silver fox crouching in the hills. I spread my legs wider. I wanted him to crawl inside me. His body whole. First his tongue and then the rest of him, leaving nothing behind. The shallow breaths were pushed out of me, turning into grunts. A loud grunt and then a bang. His body shifted and he was deeper inside me. The golden sparks and the aqua from before shifted—a ray of light, an explosion; he was moving against me, pushing his way home, lapping against the shore of my stomach. I began seeing myself from the inside out, an inverted image. First filled at the center. He was drawing me, one line at a time. With each push, the contour of my body became firmer, more definite. Charcoal lines of my waist. Of my hands pushing against the flanks of his buttocks pushing him deeper inside me. The harbor of my legs opened wide, darker lines for the chiseled form of my arms now entangling him, unraveling him, tangled branches around his shoulders. His breath brushed against me, the wind of his panting. The bitterness was gone now. He'd pushed his hair back into a tight ponytail. I tried to find his eyes; I tried to latch on to his gaze. A compass, a midway point between absence and the definition of light. With each push, my body became clearer. I could almost see myself whole. I felt myself tighten around him. I was holding him, holding him inside me. I could not lose my way home. I watched my arms around the square of his shoulders. The red of his skin, the red of mine. We formed a human tree. The ancient tree of life. But when he left my apartment that night, I felt invisible again.

**

After Leon left, I remained with the trails of our love, his scent on my body. I could still feel him on me: the scent of man, of smoke and eucalyptus—or was it mint? Or pine with a trail of whisky? He always had the lingering smell of alcohol. I said nothing about being adopted, about my mother being French. I did not speak of my father's ancestry in Ireland, of his devotion to the land in Vermont, of the shattered history of my ancestors. We are bound by silence and by what we leave behind.

This is what I liked best: tracing back the past. I should have been an archaeologist, not a history teacher. I would have liked to have measured the world in the traces of the past, in counting bones and piecing them back vertebrae after vertebrae. Pulling them out of the sand, unearthing the human body: whitened bones, whitewashed in late summer sun. I would have liked to have seen the centuries on the broken fragments of the past. One tiny, shattered teacup; one clay pot, two molars and a fractured skull. These are the only ways we can measure the world.

I found comfort in yesterday's imprint, in what others have left behind. The past was washed out with nothing but remaining trails. We have all been washed out, and one day nothing will remain but our bones.

**

When I first saw Leon, all I saw were his piercing black eyes, a riveting night sky without any stars. And his hair, his long flowing hair, smoothly groomed. I've watched him after we make love, brushing his hair with a hundred strokes, but his hands move like a man's, not a woman's. The way he holds his shoulders square. The sharp angles of his jaw offset the fluidity of the sheen of his hair. This is what I noticed first when I saw him at the Westcott Street Fair, a community event held once a year to connect the neighborhood with its various businesses and organizations—an excuse to play live music and eat good food on the streets. We saw each other across the crowds of golden-haired heads, across the sea of liberal white faces and the few scattered brown children running around pushing their way through the crowds to sing songs. He saw me too. I was holding a small basil plant I'd bought at the organic herbs and garden stand. He was passing through as he later told me, marching away from the crowd in a straight line. And then we saw each other. There we were: two Indians. He said he knew from the second he saw me that there was something different about me. And for a while, I told myself I didn't know what he meant by this. He never explained it. But secretly we both knew that he was talking about my "ways." A white woman in an Indian costume— *an apple*, as they call us—white on the inside, red on the outside. From the moment I met him. I wanted saving; I wanted him to save me. I felt a pull, this strange magnetic tug, and before I knew it, we were standing next to each other. We said nothing; we both smiled.

"I'm Leon."

I extended my hand. "I'm Elbe." Maybe this was the first transgression on my part. *Is this what Indians do?* I thought. Do *they* shake hands? He took mine and kept smiling. I waited for something to happen. Something momentous. Something that would shape and alter me. This is what I wanted, alteration like a misshapen sculpture going into the hands of an artist for perfection. I remember the sun. The early autumn afternoon light. The same light with the same canopy sky I'd seen on that street five years earlier when I'd moved there. Low and cloudless almost touching the roofs of the red brick buildings of the neighborhood. I remember feeling safe there in Leon's presence, in the presence of this shifting light. Autumn in Syracuse, in this part of the state is a passionate season—a crossroads between richness, abundance and ease: summer warmth still lingering and the impending, violent transformation of winter. I could feel the warmth of the sun on my face as he smiled. I loved the heat of this transitory season, and in this moment I could almost forget that winter was on its way and that I had never been held in the arms of a mother, a woman who resembled me. I could almost forget that I could not really see myself in the mirror, and that Leon was just a man and that he did not have the magical powers of someone who would be able to save me from my mangled past.

The phone rang, interrupting my memories.

"Hello," a stranger's voice said tentatively on the other line. "My name is Sam, I am the coordinator with Catholic Charities." I listened to the "case" of this new family of refugees from Rwanda who needed me to take a woman and her son to the doctor the next day. I heard myself agreeing to the appointment and hung up.

What had made me sign up for this volunteer work? Why did I need to help refugees from Africa make sense of the world around them? I did not even know myself. When I spoke, I could hear myself from a distance. I was split into two equal parts. One part listened to the facts, jotted down names, addresses, times, and locations, and the other measured the span of my decision. Did I really want to help? I wanted to fill the void with more obligations, with fewer meaningful ties. If I could turn to strangers, I wouldn't have to turn to those I knew.

The next day, I drove across town to a poor neighborhood on the south side. I never drove in this poverty-striken area unless I was passing through to a wormhole, to another world waiting for me on the other side of myself. I was stepping out of my ivory tower. Stepping into the other side of humanity. When I parked, I noticed that the house was large, once an elegant one-family home at the turn of the last century, now it was three tenement apartments on the wrong side of town. I rang the bell: 2B.

I heard commotion on the other side. Voices clamoring in a foreign language—it wasn't French. Then, a young girl of maybe eight opened the door. I later learned she was actually ten but had suffered from malnutrition. Her poignant eyes were fixed on me; I lost myself in the pain within her gaze.

Bonjour, I greeted her in French. James, the coordinator, had told me that this family didn't speak a word of English. The child didn't smile when I looked into her eyes; instead she looked away.

"Bonjour," she answered. "My name is Elbe. I am here to take your mother to see the doctor."

The girl pulled away from the door and indicated I should step inside. She yelled something in a language I didn't understand. I waited in the hallway with her; as she seemed obligated to keep me company. I could feel the forced smile on my face and I wondered how alienating I must seem. I looked away.

A woman in her early thirties approached the doorway. We appeared to be the same age, but her face reflected a kind of suffering I had only read about. She was beautiful, the way felines are beautiful with their long and narrow lines. Her cheekbones carved out in lines of symmetry offset perfectly by a fine nose and generous lips.

"My name is Francine," she said, extending her hand in mine. She smiled tiredly. Her face drawn. "*Umuhuˆungu!*" she yelled, glancing behind her. A little boy came walking slowly to the door. He was small and frail, a tiny chipmunk. I felt the urge to take him into my arms and carry him, but instead I stood by the door smiling.

Francine put on her coat and walked quietly to the car. I waited for the boy to follow us. He grabbed a worn coat and made his way with us outside. The child looked at me intermittently, turning his head away quickly each time I tried to make eye contact with him. It was important I not let the silence pull us into permanent awkwardness. I wanted to find out the boy's name but instead I asked Francine: "How long have you been here?"

I knew all of the basic facts about them through the organization. They had arrived two months ago to the day, but I was trying to make conversation. Francine rubbed a crucifix like a charm, as she answered my questions. I noticed the long, drawn-out circles under her eyes.

We drove to the east side of town where Francine's Medicaid doctor was located. The waiting room was busting at the seams with people, every single one of them a varying shade of brown. Where were the white faces of my world? There was one open seat; I offered it to Francine and her son. She sat and left him standing by her side. I wanted to reach for the child and hold him, but I reminded myself that he was not my child to comfort. Staring down at his feet, the little boy stood on one foot and then the other as if playing some kind of game of hopscotch. Francine did not seem to notice him. Francine and I were relieved of the feeling of having to talk to each other. One baby cried nonstop, her face visibly flushed and warm. I counted the people in the waiting room: 23.

23 people, two doctors who walked in and out. 22 chairs, two piles of books, ten books in each. I made the count in my head. I was multiplying the world, making an inventory of reality.

We waited for an hour, watching the faces shift in the waiting room as more people entered while a few left. I got a seat across the waiting room from Francine. Every once in a while, I looked across the room and smiled at her and the boy. Their faces remained impassive as if they were unable to notice anything but their own internal world. I watched the little boy's hands, how small they were as he pretended each finger was a tiny person talking to the other. I tried to discern his imaginary conversation, to catch a word here and there, but the bustle of the waiting room overpowered his secret whispers.

We were called into the examination room. I walked ahead, showing them the way. I was the beacon. The nurse took us into a large white room.

"Hi, my name is Betty. How are you today?" She asked looking only at me. I glanced at Francine as she scanned the room lingering on the white and silver of the instruments shining brightly around us. Francine carried the little boy up on the examining table and sat down next to him. I sat on a small stool.

"Can you please ask her to remove her coat?" The nurse asked. Her face was small and perfectly formed, without a single wrinkle. Wisps of blond hair dangled loosely around the line of her jaw, beyond the confines of the ponytail holding a small mass of limp, shoulder-length hair. She had not glanced at either of them once.

"How old is the child?" Nurse Betty asked pen in hand. I translated and Francine answered each question mechanically.

"Four. He just turned four."

"What kind of symptoms has he had? What is the reason for their visit today?" Betty asked with feigned interest.

"Belly ache, fever, chills at night. Difficulty sleeping."

I thought about Francine's vulnerability. How she needed to expose herself to strangers. She folded her coat and placed it on her lap. Her body was smaller than I would have expected. She was thin, brittle almost, or was it that she was wearing clothes too large for her? I suddenly felt strange being responsible for this stranger who would need to peel layers of herself in front of me.

The nurse began firing questions. *Does this hurt, what about this? Does he have an appetite? How often does the child have a bowel movement? How many times a night does he wake?* I translated. Francine glanced at me and then down at her coat on her lap. The nurse and I shared a common bond: I translated the world she measured: weight, age, height, blood pressure, temperature. These were the statistics of Francine's physical realm. Her body was pumping blood, it was a living machine. Inside, wrapped around the vessels of blood and muscles, behind the bones, existed the spirit of Francine.

"I am going to need to draw some blood from both of them." Blondie addressed me. They were invisible. I told Francine what to expect. She nodded and looked down again. As the nurse approached the child with her needle, she addressed him for the first time.

"What's your name?" she asked in an overly high-pitched voice.

No one answered. In a normal tone, and now without a faux smile, Blondie asked me almost annoyed. "Do *you* know what his name is?"

"No, I don't," I told her the nurse before asking Francine the name of her child.

"His name is Innocent," Francine answered.

"Innocent." I translated.

"Innocent, as in not guilty?" asked the nurse laughing.

"Yes, I giggled nervously."

Francine looked up and scanned my face trying to understand the nature of my laugh. I was not laughing *at* her.

How could I explain? Seeing the needle in Blondie's hand, Innocent began to cry.

"It's OK. Sweetheart. This won't hurt. I promise." She was back to her high-pitched voice resembling a dog whistle.

Innocent stared at the woman through his tears letting his cries turn into a wail.

Blondie whose surface patience had suddenly vanished turned to me. "Can you tell him that it won't hurt? I have to draw this blood, otherwise, we won't be able to figure out what's wrong with him."

I knelt by Innocent who was sitting in a chair next to his mother.

"Do you like ice cream?"

He stopped crying and listened to me intently. Then, in between sniffles, he nodded yes.

"Good, because after we're done with this place, we'll go get some ice cream." Innocent sat very quietly and looked at Blondie stoically, waiting for her to do her job.

"He's very warm. I'm certain he has a fever," she said as she placed her hand on his little arm and held it straight as she drew the blood. Innocent did not budge. He kept his eyes on me, as if keeping my promise required him maintaining eye contact.

"All done," she said, putting a BandAid on Innocent's arm.

"OK, now for your temperature," she held a thermometer under his tongue until it beeped.

"104.3. The doctor is going to want to look at him."

I told Francine, who continued to sit very still on the chair with her coat neatly folded.

Blondie drew blood from Francine and then disappeared. The three of us waited in silence. I wanted to say something to this woman whose experience I was translating, but I had nothing to offer. Innocent's legs dangled in the air. He moved them back and forth, two small pendulums swaying.

The door opened. Blondie had returned with a doctor.

"This is Doctor Schneider, he will examine the child." Before leaving the room, she gave Innocent a lollipop. The boy took the small treasure in his hand and examined it as if he had never seen candy in his life.

"What seems to be the problem?"

I translated every word Francine gave me.: *fièvre, vomissement, mal de ventre, il ne dort pas la nuit.*

"He has trouble sleeping at night."

The doctor glanced at Innocent, who was sucking on his lollipop very slowly.

"And how long has this been going on?"

"Since he was born."

"*Tout a commencé quand il est né,*" Francine had said to me. *Everything began when he was born.* She had spoken the words like it had been a jail sentence.

The doctor knelt by Innocent's side.

"Innocent's physical health is not good. He is severely dehydrated. We will have to conduct more tests. I'd be more comfortable if we kept him overnight for observation."

"Is his life in any danger?" Francine asked.

The doctor cleared his throat. "It's too soon to tell. We'll know more once we've run a number of tests. He's extremely dehydrated. I'd like to keep him overnight, so we can get some fluids back in him. You can probably pick him up tomorrow after we've run some tests." I translated the flow of words determining her child's fate: *Innocent doit rester à l'hôpital.*

Her stance was tense but she said nothing. She nodded. She hadn't touched or looked at Innocent once. She sat while the doctor examined her in turn. He prodded her, told her to open her mouth, he listened to her heart. Innocent continued to lick his lollipop ever so slowly as if he were alone in the room.

"Everything seems OK, although you do appear very tired. Are you getting the rest you need?" Like most doctors, he was not listening. Without translating, I answered him directly. "She is not sleeping. The boy is not sleeping either."

"Well, I can prescribe some sleeping pills, which can help her get to sleep at night." I was getting angry.

"How will she help her child, if she is sleeping through his cries?"

"Que dit-il?" Francine wanted to know what the doctor was saying.

"He wants to know if you want some pills so that you can sleep at night."

"Yes, tell the doctor to give me the pills."

I felt angry but translated her request.

"Good, I will write the prescription." It was an easy fix. The doctor shook Francine's hand and then mine.

"The nurse will come back to take the child to Pediatrics. You can call tomorrow to see if he can be picked up." He turned to Innocent who was almost done with his lollipop. Francine began putting on her coat slowly. Innocent looked at me with the same look as when I'd told him about the ice cream.

"Ice cream?" he finally said in a small voice.

I was such a shit. Why had I promised something I could not deliver? I spoke quickly, barely looking at Innocent. "You can get ice cream tomorrow. First, you have to stay with the doctors for one night," I told the child in French. I hated myself for not knowing how to talk to children. *Stay with the doctors?* This was no way to talk to a child. Innocent stood very still, he looked at me as tears began to well. His little arm was stiff as he held the lollipop stick in the air. I did not know which hurt him more, not having ice cream or having to stay behind.

Nurse Betty came back. "If you're not going to carry him, it would be best to put him in a wheelchair. He should be quite weakened by his dehydration and fever."

I translated the nurse's words for Francine, who stood impassive, as if she had not understood a word I'd said.

"I'll carry him," I said, leaning down to Innocent.

"Je peux te porter?" May I carry you? I asked him. He nodded solemnly still trying to process the absence of ice cream in his near future. I reached to take his hand, but he was still holding the lollipop stick. "Would you like to throw this away?" I asked him. He shook his head no. I scooped him into my arms allowing him to hold on to the precious lollipop. Francine walked beside us in silence. She depended on me. I was showing her the way. I watched the dark chestnut of Francine's skin, smooth like parchment. I wanted to touch her hand and unite her to her own child somehow. But instead, I walked by her side carrying her child in my arms. I was only a vehicle of words; I transported meaning between Francine and the world of medicine. I was invisible. I liked the invisibility, the slipping away inside the comfort of this foreign language where I could hide in the mother tongue of the woman who had raised me.

Chapter 5 – Francine

Syracuse, New York, 1998

The two women drove home from the hospital in silence. Francine invited Elbe into the house. She thought about the strange stench she could discern as soon she opened the front door and felt embarrassed.

"Tu sens?" She asked Elbe. *Can you smell it?*

"Je ne comprends pas. Je sens quoi?" Elbe did not understand why Francine was asking her about a smell. Francine could not shake the feeling of the house smelling old. Old and *pourri*. Rotten coming from the inside. Was she being polite, Francine wondered. Was she losing her mind?

Elbe looked around the large house which reminded her of an oversized boat, shipwrecked on a beach, no longer serving its purpose in the waters. The house must have been grand at one time in its existence. But that was no longer the case. Elbe did not know why, but she often thought of the world of oceans, even though she had grown up landlocked her entire life.

The women sat in the living room, which was a large, mostly empty room with a large beaten brown corduroy couch and a scratched wooden coffee table.

"Un thé?"

"Oui, merci."

How Francine loved and loathed French. How beautiful it was. No matter how many years she spoke it, she never stopped appreciating its melodious sweetness with its elongated vowels and the glottal stops English lacked. But Francine never once pretended that speaking French was part of her heritage without remembering the brutal history associated with the colonization of the Belgians in her country.

Francine came back carrying a platter with cups, a pot of tea, sugar, milk and a plate of cookies.

Un sucre, merci. Non, pas de lait. "Sugar, no milk." Francine loved sugar in her tea. In fact she loved sugar in nearly everything she swallowed.

Comment avez vous appris le français? Francine couldn't help ask Elbe how she came to learn French.

J'ai été adoptée. Ma mère est française. "I was adopted. My mother is French." Elbe took a quick sip of tea to swallow the moment. She hated discussing her roots, the past, the lineage of ancestors she would never meet.

Je suis indienne. Indienne d'Amérique. In French, like in English, the word *Indian* could refer to someone from India or from the Americas. "I am Indian. Indian from the Americas," she specified to Francine, as if anyone could possibly mistake her for anything else.

Francine noticed how Elbe had spoken of her parents like one speaks of strangers. She had detected the tension in her voice in the way she had referred to being adopted, as if something as normal as raising a child one had not birthed was a big deal. Francine did not understand why Americans needed to render such simple things so complicated. She had not given birth to Devota and Sophie, but now they were her children. In America, everything seemed measured, and counted. Everything was as tight as a knot.

Il faut que j'y aille. "I have to take off," Elbe told Francine while finishing her tea.

Ça va aller," Elbe added. "Everything will be alright." What did those words means exactly? What was alright? Francine no longer knew. She thought about the barrack near the checkpoint where she had lost everything four years earlier. Francine had spent so many moments wishing death on Boy. Now that he was in a hospital, would God know if she had changed her mind? She closed her eyes. Francine had wished for Boy's death since he was born and now that he was sick, she wished no harm would come upon him.

"*Oui, ça va aller,*" she responded to Elbe. Francine reviewed the doctor's words in her mind over and over again. *We need to run more tests.*

Francine thanked Elbe for her services and watched her car drive away in the stillness of a snowy night. Francine knew in that moment that she shared a bond with Elbe she could never define. A bond of shame and danger and love all entwined into their knotted roots and the blood lines of their legacies.

That afternoon, the children came home from school and Francine thought of Boy and his absence from the clamor of their voices at the dinner table. Jean de Dieu worked afternoons and evenings at the local boxes factory and rarely came home before she went to bed. She found comfort in the distance between them, in the way their lives had been pulled apart by the demands of American responsibilities and work.

When night fell and settled, she kissed Angélique and Sylvie goodnight in their room and she thought about how she could almost pretend Boy had never existed.

Francine considered taking the sleeping pills the doctor had prescribed her, but instead she slipped out of bed quietly and sat by the window watching the hard heavy flakes fall outside. For a moment Francine had thought it was rain and she said out loud: "This will be good for the crops," she said outloud, even though she remembered there were no crops to grow here in this land of the Americas.

In the camp, they had tried to grow vegetables. Sometimes they grew, sometimes they didn't. And when they did, the hyenas would come and eat almost everything they had planted.

Francine sat on the couch and thought of Boy lying in his hospital bed; she thought about the barrack near the checkpoint. She thought about Innocent's face, the same face as the man who had come to her that night, except the eyes of her child were filled with sadness. Francine could feel the vastness of the house engulfing her as she tried to conjure some emotion for her child she had just left behind. All she could sense was the hospital's metallic stench still on her—the stench of danger, of death and all of the moments that followed. *Will he live or die? What do I want?* She did not know.

Si tu veux qu'il survive, il survivra. This is what the voice inside her head had told her. "If you want him to live, he will survive." How could she think this when only God decided who lived and died?

Part II

Chapter 6 – Francine

Four Years Earlier

Rwanda, Spring 1994

I remember the time "before" like a dream. I remember the night everything changed. April 6, 1994. Mélanie, my youngest daughter, was turning two the next day and we were going to have a large party with the family. I was baking her a cake. The kitchen smelled sweet with vanilla and butter and the small pieces of chocolate I'd hidden inside the batter to surprise Mélanie when she'd take her first bite. My middle child, Sylvie, who was six and a half, was helping me with the batter. Knowing I would make a cake for her sister, she badgered me all day from the moment she woke up to let her mix the batter. All morning, she tugged at my sleeve, "*Maman*, will you let me help you? Will you let me help you, Maman?" and finally, I had agreed. I agreed to let my daughter make the first and only cake she would ever make. I remember her eyes; she had my eyes—we shared the same look on the world. I liked to say that she and I came from the same place, just 24 years apart. I remember her little hands holding the large wooden spoon as she tried with all of her might to mix the eggs into the flour and butter. I remember her little braids bouncing alongside her head as she struggled with her mission. She was holding the spoon with both hands and making little grunting noises to match her grimaces as she pressed on with all of her courage. She was courageous my little girl. She had the courage of an angel.

My husband, Fidèle came home two minutes after I took out the cake from the oven. I remember because I heard the sound of his footsteps and when I pushed the oven door shut, he was standing there smiling.

"It smells good in here," he said in Kinyarwanda. We hugged. I was happy to see him. Maybe I knew we wouldn't be together much longer. Maybe I could feel it already. My mother-in-law, Maman Jeanine often talked about the world of spirits and how she could talk to them.

"Never spit on the ground, especially not in front of your enemy! They will take your spit and cast a spell on you," she would warn me. I remember laughing. I laughed because I was afraid, I laughed because I did not understand what she meant. Fidèle was always quiet when she spoke of such things. For a long time I thought that his silence was a sign of his respect for his mother. For a long time I thought he was like me, that he didn't believe in that *nonsense*, as I called it then. But now that I look back, I think Fidèle and Maman Jeannine both knew about a piece of what was to come. The spirits must have warned them I think. And this is why my husband was silent.

Sometimes I get stuck on the smallest moments. I get stuck thinking of words I would have liked to have said to them. I think about strange things. Mélanie's shoes, the sandals she wore on the last day. I try to ask myself whether giving her better shoes would have changed anything. I think of our canary's strange and frantic chirp when we left the house. I think of Sylvie and the way she cried when I sent her to bed before the cake was out of the oven. I think about her face and the way she looked at me before she turned her back on me in the kitchen. I think of her little upper lip quivering, of the way she whimpered when I kissed her good night, of the way I never gave in to her fancy. I curse myself sometimes. I curse myself wanting to change the smallest gesture. Take back the smallest word. I curse myself and then I remember how foolish it is of me when I am already cursed.

The cake was already out of the oven when the phone rang. A beautiful cake, *à l'américaine*, an American cake, the way

Eloise at the hospital had taught me to make. Eloise was Belgian, a good doctor with a strong hand for difficult cases. She was not squeamish, nor was she afraid of anything. Eloise had traveled to America and she showed me how to make Mélanie's cake with *pépites de chocolat*, the chocolate chips I tossed in the batter like they were tiny diamonds in a sea of gold.

Fidèle answered the phone. I heard something shift in the way he breathed. He stopped moving and for a moment everything was still and then I heard him under his breath: "God help us. God help us all." I felt a strange chill. The way he said this. The way he spoke those words.

"That was my brother Philippe. He called to say that President Habyarimana's plane has crashed. He was killed just hours ago." We both rushed to the radio and turned it on.

"Classical music everywhere we turn, even on *Radio Television Libre des Milles Collines.*" I fumbled for the dial. My hands were shaking. I looked at Fidèle for answers but he looked as shocked as I felt.

We both stood prostrate by the radio, in the living room of our house waiting for the music to stop. A voice came on speaking of the plane crash. And then the orders began to come: "You must stay in your homes. Everyone stay in your homes and wait for further orders."

"Whether this is an assassination of the president or not, with him gone, the Hutu militia will take over power. We're not safe," Fidèle had a look of fear and urgency I'd never seen before.

"Where would we go?" I asked him. "I think we should stay put and see how things unfold. Let's at least sleep on it."

"I am telling you Francine, we don't have time! Every Tutsi man, woman and child will be hunted down and killed if the Hutu militia take over the government. And with my own work as a member of the Social Democratic Party, we are prime targets." Fidèle's voice was strained.

"But where should we…"

We heard an explosion in the distance. The house shook, or maybe I imagined it shook when I heard the loud, raucous rumble break through the eerie silence of the night. I looked at the clock in the kitchen. It was ten o'clock. The phone rang again and it was our neighbors the Kagirangas who wanted to know if they could bring their kids to our house for protection. They said that they would be safer with us because we were a lot less prominent than they were with their job in the ministry of foreign affairs. Fidèle and I agreed. We didn't know who was in the most danger, but we figured there might be more safety in numbers.

At about eleven, our neighbors brought their three little girls to the house. Elise, the youngest one, Mélanie's age was asleep in her father's arms when we opened to the door. The two older children Sylvain and Philippe, who were six and eight stood next to their father, like little soldiers rubbing their eyes from sleep.

"We will be back later once we figure out a plan," the neighbors whispered before leaving again.

We put the three children to bed and sat in the living room trying to figure out a plan. The radio was still on, it played intermittent classical music followed by orders. The voice kept repeating: "You must stay in your homes, there is a curfew in the city. Stay in your homes." I looked at Fidèle, I saw the danger in his eyes.

"Let's try to get some sleep. We'll need our wits about us when we head out in the early morning."

I slept fitfully and woke every other hour until the first light of dawn bathed the nightstand by our bed. Fidèle and I sprung out of bed, rushing to the radio to hear they had begun reading a list of names of the people who were ordered to be killed by the militia. Clearly, the government as we knew it had toppled and every Tutsi on this land was in danger. We needed to move fast.

I woke the neighbors' children first and called their parents.

"We have to move fast. Come and get the children. We are leaving in half an hour. You should do the same."

I then woke my girls, starting with four-year-old Angélique, even though she was usually the one to sleep the longest.

"Maman, where are we going?" she asked, having seen our suitcases on the floor.

"Are we going on vacation?"

We had traveled to Tanzania the year before and she still remembered playing in the hotel swimming pool with her sisters fondly.

"No, sweetheart. Let's go wake your brothers." I woke the boys next. Michel and Christian shared a room together. In those days, I treated them like tough little soldiers because they were among the oldest. But in reality, they were so young. My boys were so young. Christian was only five years old and my oldest child, Michel was eight. Now that I have had time to think about all of those years past, I realize how tough I was on them because they were boys.

"Get dressed, we are going on a trip," I told them, letting them do it on their own while I went to wake my youngest last. Mélanie was the baby, she was the one who really needed to be spared from everything. I wanted my baby to be spared.

"Where is the cake Maman? Where is the cake?" Sylvie wouldn't stop asking questions. It was as if her mind had been holding that single thought in place from the night before.

She tugged at my sleeve. I knelt down by her side and held her firmly.

"Listen to me Sylvie, we are going on a serious trip now and you need to be good." I saw my own fear reflected in her eyes. I could see myself in her and she in me. We were held by each other's fear. She began to cry, rubbing her eyes with one hand and holding the corner of her nightgown for comfort, with the other. I pulled her into my arms and tried to reassure her.

"Is Calimero coming with us?" That was our canary. I remember my mind registering the odd fact that we had named our yellow canary after the well-known cartoon of the lone black chicken who wore its half shell still on its head, in a family of yellow birds.

"We can't take the bird, sweetheart. Calimero needs to stay home. Don't worry, everything will be OK," I said. "Everything will be OK." My daughter sensed that I was lying to her. I was lying to us all.

Fidèle was making phone calls while we still had a line. I heard him in the background talking to the people we knew, while I took care of the children. Our neighbors, Jean and Marie-Antoinette came by and picked up their children and left. I wondered if I would ever see them again.

Our rambunctious boy, Christian, came running into the room holding up his toy soldier.

"Can I take this toy with me, Maman?" He asked. Although Christian was our middle child, not old enough to distinguish himself from the others with maturity and wisdom; not young enough to require the constant pull of a mother's heart, he did not get swallowed by the needs of the younger children, simply because he demanded to be seen and heard and all times. Instead, this burden fell on my four-year-old, Angélique, whose brooding nature reminded us of those summer skies when everything turns heavy and dark right before rainfall. Most of the time, I didn't know what Angélique was thinking or feeling. It wasn't until later, when she and I were thrown together in the unraveling of our world that I got to understand the mystery of her.

"No, Christian, we can't take any toys with us. We're going on a trip where objects can't help us."

"My toy soldier can help us," he told me before putting it down on the bed disappointed.

When Fidèle got off the phone, his movements were sharp and abrupt reminding me that my husband was scared and there were dangers ahead.

"That was Laurent calling from the party. He said that most of the members of the current government have been killed already. We have to leave the house at once! They will come for us. They will come for me."

A voice came on the radio. "Fight the *inyenzi*, pound them. Stand up. Keep away from lies and rumors. If they pound you with heavy artillery, bombs, go into bunkers. Take spears, clubs, guns, swords, stones, everything, and sharpen them. Hack the Tutsi enemies—those cockroaches, those rivals of democracy—show that you can defend yourselves, support your soldiers."

The radio broadcasts referred to us, the Tutsis, as *inyenzi* or *cockroaches*. I couldn't believe this call to arms and open hatred of our people was being broadcast on the radio.

Fidèle and I began to move quickly. Sylvie began to cry, mumbling something about the cake. I gently took her by the hand into the kitchen and showed her the cake that still needed to be frosted on the counter.

"You see, there it is. The cake is beautiful, you were a great helper." Now that she could see the product of her creation, Sylvie stopped crying.

"Are you going to write Mélanie's name on it?" She asked still rubbing her eyes, now red from her fit of tears. I held both her shoulders firmly and looked her into the eyes.

"Listen Sylvie, you are my oldest girl. You're going to have to be brave now. There is trouble in the city and we need to leave the house right away so we can be safe. We need to leave the cake behind us." Something changed in Sylvie's eyes, the little baby crying about a cake vanished and for the first time, I saw the wisdom in my oldest daughter.

"Do you understand what I am saying to you?" She nodded and I knew that she would be strong. Fidèle had woken

Mélanie; he was holding her in his arms. I can still see my sleeping angel resting her little head on her father's shoulders while sucking her thumb. I still hold this image in my mind. Sometimes I wake up in the middle of the night screaming because their faces, their scent are vanishing from my memory. The smell of Mélanie's neck, Fidèle's laugh, Sylvie's stomping feet and the way her knees dimple when she pounds the ground with her little feet in anger. Christian's smile, revealing the gap in his two front teeth, Michel's eyes, the seriousness in them, the old man's gaze in his eight-year-old body. I scream sometimes because it's all slipping away from me like water droplets slipping through my fingers.

Michel and Christian came into the hallway carrying a small suitcase Fidèle had put together. He handed me a bag to carry.

"Here are our papers, some money and a change of clothes. We don't need anything else. Let's go to Eloise and Pierre's house. We'll be safer there." I took Angélique by the hand, slipped the strap of the bag across my shoulders and offered my other hand to Sylvie. My heart sank as I heard Calimero's strange frantic chirping before I closed the door behind me. *I am sorry bird. This is not the way things were supposed to be for any of us.*

When we stepped into the streets, a strange wave of quiet came over us. For a few seconds, we heard nothing and I felt like we'd just been put under a strange spell where the world had suddenly been robbed of sound. The gunshots from before had vanished and we moved quickly into the early morning streets. Fidèle kept alternating between a jog and a walk ahead of us. I watched Mélanie's head bouncing up and down in her father's arms as the boys ran behind him keeping up the pace. At first, I tried to keep up with them but Angélique was whimpering next to me.

"What's the matter?" I asked her while trying to entice her to keep up the pace by pulling on her hand.

"My foot hurts." I picked her up and carried her in one hand as I held Sylvie in the other—she was my brave daughter this one, running like a little soldier next to me. We passed the gates of several homes. Most of them were closed except for one house; a neighbor we did not know. The gate was wide open and in the distance I saw the shape of two bodies lying down in the garden, a small pool of blood surrounding them. I held Angélique closer to me and pulled Sylvie urging her to pick up the pace. Fidèle was gaining some distance now. Soon, he and the boys would become tiny specks on the horizon.

Eloise and Pierre's house was down from the home with the opened gate and the dead bodies. Suddenly, I saw two soldiers wearing khaki military clothes each carrying a machete in their hands. Others were dressed as civilians. They began running towards Fidèle while I slithered along the wall of a compound. We were still in our neighborhood, but the properties here were more expensive, larger, and occupied mostly by European nationals like Pierre and Eloise.

I put Angélique down on the ground and motioned to both the girls to hush. They looked at me with the seriousness of ancient souls and they stayed quiet by my side waiting for further instructions. The men had disappeared and I couldn't see where they had gone. I moved slowly along the walls of the compounds until I found an opened gate. Sylvie, Angélique and I entered the yard and hid behind large bamboo plants outside of the house of a British man I had met once at a cocktail party. He worked at the embassy. We crouched and stayed there in silence. I could hear my heart beating madly in my chest. Angélique clearly wanted to cry so I squeezed her hand and shook my head "no." She seemed to understand. We heard some gunshots in the distance and the sounds of a dog barking incessantly. Where was Fidèle? Had he made it to Eloise's house? We crouched through the moments of silence that followed and when the firing began again, I got up and took the girls back out on the streets. I felt safer hearing the sounds ahead because I could pinpoint the location of the danger. The men had disappeared as had Fidèle and the children.

I arrived at Eloise's house where I heard nothing. The gate was open and the dog Max, a large German shepherd greeted me nervously by sniffing me and making circles around me as we made our way to the door. Fidèle must have left the gate open for us, I thought. I pounded on the door and Eloise opened it abruptly. She was a short and plump Belgian woman with healthy red cheeks and short brown hair she wore *en bataille*, wild and messy.

"Quick come in. Fidèle and the boys are already here." I ran inside and heard Eloise calling out for Max the dog before shutting the door again.

"The dog won't come in, he's frantically trying to protect us I think. Pierre is on the phone with the embassy. We still have a line. Thank God! We've tried calling many people who seem to have lost their lines."

Eloise's usual calm and pleasant demeanor I knew so well from working in the hospital with her as a nurse had vanished. Her sure hand and her fearless nature had been replaced by the franticness that had infected every single person in the city of Kigali.

Angélique, who had been holding her tears for so long, finally began to cry. Sylvie followed suit.

"Here, I'll take them downstairs into the basement with Fidèle and the boys." Eloise took my crying girls by the hand. I stood in the middle of the lobby of this beautiful, cool expatriate house. I felt safe here in this haven of European protection. Nothing could happen to us here.

I heard Pierre's voice and the sound of the phone being hung up. I waited for Pierre to come to me unable to move. If I could stand here forever, everything would be OK. Something in Pierre's eyes unfastened the paralysis that had begun to set in. Something in the paleness of his blue eyes told me that this house was not a place of rest. I looked at the lines forming on his forehead when he began speaking to me. I had never noticed the presence of his wrinkles before.

"The embassy said that ten Belgian soldiers have just been murdered by the Hutu-lead paramilitary group, the Interahamwe. The UN will come and get us soon." I must have nodded. I said nothing. We'd been stripped of conventionalities. There was no room for anything but survival. I could feel the distance in Pierre's voice. Something large and ominous stood between us. I tried to size up this invisible beast in my mind. I tried to weigh it. It was unlike anything I'd seen before, except maybe it reminded me of my college days when my teacher had said to me one day, on the last day of classes: "You will never be a doctor. Cockroaches should never become doctors." This was my teacher whom I'd trusted all of the years that had come before this moment. This was a man who had instructed me. And now his true light had leaked out of him.

Eloise walked in, carrying Mélanie in her arms. She handed her to me.

"She's been asking for her mommy." Eloise seemed almost calm again. It was as if stepping inside her own house had made her feel secure again. Maybe this house had magic powers. I had always liked working with Eloise at the hospital because she was sure of herself. This confidence had translated into certainty and a respect that never required her to carve out a territory for herself. She was the doctor, she was the woman who saved lives, and she didn't need to remind us of who we were simply because she knew so well who she was. With the other doctors—especially the men—we, the nurses, spent so much time being humiliated into submission.

Pierre was rubbing his hands together; and I listened to the sound of his flesh rubbing against itself, like paper being brushed.

"I am not sure you should stay here." Pierre said. "It's not safe for us." He caught himself. "It's not safe for you, for anyone, he corrected." Eloise's composure was slipping again. I was meeting a new Eloise, a new Pierre. They were both crumbling away from the people I had known before.

"What are you saying, Pierre?" She asked with fear in her voice. "The Interahamwe just killed ten Belgian soldiers. They're killing Belgians and they're after Tutsis. It's not safe for any of us." "But why shouldn't they stay?" Eloise added.

Pierre looked around the room like a furtive animal. He was in survival mode and nothing would stop him from doing exactly what he needed to do to stay alive. Nothing, not even his wife.

"I'm just saying, they should go elsewhere."

"Like where?"

Their voices were drifting off into the distance. This was the moment when I began learning about survival. We were all trying to do one thing and one thing only: stay alive. Even if it meant letting go of one another.

I needed to be with my children again. Suddenly I needed to feel them against me, to feel their little bodies in my arms. I needed to see my husband's face and remember the gentleness in his eyes. This is what had made me marry him. I had never told him this before. I never told him about what I had seen in his eyes that had made me say *yes* when he asked me to marry him. In the end, we are all animals trying to survive, and the decisions that we make along the way are nothing but instincts pushing us forward. Pierre and Eloise's voices vanished as I made my way through the quiet house. Large houses afford for silence, allowing voices to be muffled by space.

Mélanie, my sweet daughter, was tugging at my sleeve. She was a barometer for my emotions.

"Papa? Papa?" She was tugging hard now.

"Yes, we're going to see papa right now." I found Fidèle and the boys sitting on the floor at the end of the long hallway that connected the bedrooms. Eloise and Pierre lived alone in a large three-bedroom house. They did not have any children. I had always had a hard time understanding whites who didn't have any children. Healthy and wealthy adults who chose not to have any children. Even now, living in the west, and with the perspective of time, it seems scandalous, like an insult to God.

As soon as she spotted her father, Mélanie began to squirm in my arms like a fish.

"Papa! Papa!" she gleefully screamed as she ran into her father's arms. Fidèle gathered Mélanie in his arms searching my eyes for forgiveness. I saw the guilt. This is what I saw in that moment but we didn't speak of it. Not directly. He simply said: "I had to move quickly with the boys. I was afraid Mélanie would cry."

"Pierre does not want us to stay here. He says that it isn't safe for anyone."

"And where does he want us to go?" Fidèle asked rhetorically.

"The UN is coming to get Eloise and Pierre soon, do you think they will take us with them?" I wanted Fidèle to tell me that everything would be OK. I wanted him to say that we would magically be whisked away from this maddening world by a UN convoy. Fidèle squeezed Mélanie tighter, as if she were a magic genie who held all of the answers.

"Hard to say. Maybe because I work for the party. Maybe, yes. Yes, they will take us, too." And we held on to this thought, letting it sit there holding us all.

"Where are the girls?" I asked suddenly realizing they were not with us.

"They're in the other room playing."

We heard footsteps. Even the way Eloise moved about had seemed to change. Her gate was lighter, quieter, as if she had already left.

"Pierre and I decided that you can stay here. We'll all wait for the UN to come. In the meantime, it's best if you stay here, away from windows. If someone comes to the house, you will leave at once. You can make your way through here and into the kitchen, or if they come the back way, you can leave through the front or from any window."

Night came and my body was tired, but my mind was racing. We put the children all together in one room, the boys and Mélanie on a double bed and Sylvie and Angélique shared a small bed. Fidèle and I slept on the floor in the hallway so we could be ready for anything. We heard gunshots and dogs barking. Max was barking inside the house and then he became quiet again. Pierre and Eloise stayed away from us like we were a terrible disease that could catch. Now, when I look back at that night, I feel for Eloise and Pierre. I see their fear clearly and I cannot hate them for doing nothing less than trying to stay alive.

In the morning, I was struck by the silence around us except for the sound of gunshots nearby. All birds were gone, their songs replaced by the sound of popping bullets. The firing was coming from right outside the house. Then, out of nowhere, we heard screaming. A woman's pain, someone ran. I moved into the bedroom with the children and covered the mouths of the little ones. I motioned to Sylvie to be quiet but she looked terrified. Michel understood this and he rushed over to her and covered her mouth before she was able to start crying. I heard their voices now. For the first time, I heard the voices of the killers outside. Men voices. One man was shouting: "This way, she is not dead. Catch the cockroach now!" The men were angry now. They did not kill everything they wanted to kill. I looked at the bedroom window where the curtain was drawn. They were outside and the only thing protecting us from being seen was the cloth of the curtain. Fidèle was not with us. He must have stayed in the hallway. I wanted to take the children there, but I was afraid to move. I was afraid one of the children would cry out and the *Interahamwe* would be here, inside the house, looking to kill us also.

I didn't know where Eloise and Pierre were or what they were doing, but we were all alone in different parts of the house listening to the carnage outside our windows. I felt entranced by the sound of death. I remember thinking, *if it is happening to them, it's not happening to us.* I felt protected by the misery of others. This was the first moment when the devil first came into my head. That was the moment when he began telling me lies.

I slid under the bed, pulling Mélanie and Sylvie with me. I motioned to Christian and Michel to do the same and take Angélique with them. I knew these beds could not hide us. I felt the roundness of my back sticking out beyond the edge. I was like a child pulling the covers over my head at night so the monster would not get me. We stayed like this, motionless. I had wrapped my arms around my children. First around Mélanie whose small body was shivering against my own and then in front of her, Sylvie's my oldest girl. My courageous girl who remained calm and quiet.

Outside the screams had stopped, but the soldiers were still walking by the house.

I heard one of the killers say: "The others are dead, but the woman still runs. The woman and her child." A strange shudder passed through me, like an electrical current moving in my body. This woman, her child. Me and my children. We were the same. And then what I feared most happened.

"Maybe they have hidden in this house. I'll go see." I heard them pounding on the door and Max began barking incessantly. I held my breath. I did not need to breathe. I needed to live. I strained to listen but could only hear the short little breaths of my daughters, like tiny animals trying to make their way out of a trap. After the silence, I heard the soldiers again. Footsteps beyond this wall. Beyond this place where I was hiding with my children. I heard Eloise's voice now, intermingled with his. Her words would be my guardian or my death. Our lives rested in her hands. If I had known months ago that my life would hang in Eloise's hands, I might have been nicer to her. I might have smiled at her more often, at work. Had we managed to become friends? I waited. They were right outside the door now.

"I am telling you that no one but my husband and I have been here. But feel free to look around." Her voice was tense, wound up like a rubber band about to snap. I knew this, because I knew her quietude. I knew of her peaceful ways. This man, this killer who cut through flesh with his machete could not discern the variations in a woman's voice. He was numb to the subtleties of humanity. Eloise and the soldier stopped in front of the room. I heard the door open and squeak a little. It didn't open all the way. I knew this from the way the duration of the squeak and the silence that followed.

"I believe you, Madame. I believe you." He passed the door. His voice faded with the distance of his footsteps.

"If you see anyone that looks like a Tutsi, keep them away from you. Keep them away." I strained to listen again. And then I heard Eloise. Her voice was firm and determined.

"I will. Don't worry, I will."

When the silence returned to the house again, I felt my body shudder. I began to shake and then I heard myself crying softly in a whimper. My daughters began to cry too only their cries were loud and unrestrained and the fear came back again. I wanted to keep myself strong. If we were to survive, I would have to be strong. How easy it was to lie to myself when our lives hung in the balance between the world of the living and that of the dead. I invented lies to keep us moving forward. On that day, curled up in a ball with my children against me, I wrongly believed that strength could save us. I wrongly believed that it could save us all.

Christian was bravely trying to entertain Angélique, who had slipped far away into a distant place inside of her. He was playing with her braids, singing her a little song that I had been singing to each of them since they were born. "*Alouette, gentille alouette, alouette, je te plumerai.*"Pierre stormed into the bedroom where I had gathered the children around me. Fidèle came right behind him.

"You have to leave. You all have to leave. They were in our house looking for you. I cannot risk our lives for yours. I can't." When he said this, he held his head in both his hands like he was trying to erase these thoughts from his mind. Fidèle looked at me. The children were looking at me. Their eyes were searching for an answer, but there was no answer to be found. Eloise pushed Pierre out of the way and faced him. I had never seen her like this. There was fury in her eyes. Fury and shame all mixed into one.

"They are not going anywhere. No one is going anywhere. We are all waiting for the UN to come and to take us all out of this hellhole. You hear me?" I watched Eloise as she discovered her husband for the first time. That day, in the face of death, Eloise realized she had married a stranger. Pierre was silent. He was fighting with his own demons. I watched him pacing now in a tight circle. The children were looking at us, trying to understand. Mélanie began to cry. Her tears were strange and unfamiliar like she'd found a way to tap into this collective frenzy. This was something we were all discovering about ourselves. This was a small moment of discovery.

"Do you realize that they could come back again and kill us all for harboring them? Kill us all, in this house! Do you realize this?"

"And do you realize that if we kick them out now, they will all die out there. They'll all get murdered one by one. Do you realize that! You scare me Pierre. Your callousness scares me more than what is happening out there!" And with this Eloise stormed out of the room and Pierre was left alone with us. We were silent. There were no words. I would like to be able to say today that I would have behaved differently, had I been Pierre. But I am not sure. How can we say with certainty what we are capable of doing in order to save our skin? His eyes fell on me. He did not look at the children. He did not look at Mélanie, who was still crying, or Christian, who had stopped playing with Angélique's hair. He did not look at Sylvie, who was huddled against me like a child younger than her age. He did not look at Michel, who was holding his father's hand. He looked straight at me and in his eyes I saw humility—the humility of one man's will to survive.

"You can stay." He almost whispered before closing the door behind him.

When Pierre left the room, something returned to each of us, a sense of unity and the memory of the time before that moment. The time when we were a family with lives, and dreams and hopes. I heard Fidèle breathe a sigh of relief.

We should have sung Mélanie her birthday song. We should have stopped right there, in that moment of waiting and sung our baby girl her second birthday song. But we didn't. We were prisoners of our own terror.

The children were hungry. I went to find Eloise to see about some food. I became a beacon, a messenger traveling to the other side of the house where Eloise and Pierre were containing their own imprisonment. I found them both in the living room, severed from each other, each isolated in their own hell. Pierre was lying expressionless on the couch while tossing a small ball up in the air over and over again. Eloise was sitting in an armchair, reaching over to pet Max, who was lying down at her feet. I stood in the doorway waiting to be noticed. Max noticed me first and let out a single low rumble bark that sounded more like a cough. It was simply his way to tell his people that I was standing there.

"The children are hungry. Is there any way I can go into the kitchen and try to find something to give them?"

"I'll come with you." Eloise said getting up. Max followed her. We made our way into kitchen leaving Pierre to his thoughts and his isolation.

"It's nothing against you. He's just afraid, that's all." She didn't look at me when she said this. We arrived into the large kitchen with the latest European-style gadgets. A large silver stove, a brand new refrigerator, beautiful shiny pots and pans hanging from large silver hooks.

"The domestic hasn't returned since it all started, so the place is a mess." I was weighing everything around me, trying to discover the key to this woman's character, a woman who held our lives in her hands. I could see how she had spoken of the "domestic," her name was Marie. Even I knew this and yet Eloise had detached herself already, preparing herself for the departure. Did she really think we would all come with them? Did I?

I watched as Eloise moved around awkwardly in her kitchen. She placed a pan on the stove and opened the fridge uncertain of her next move.

"I don't know where anything is in this kitchen. I never cook, so…do you want eggs? I can make eggs. We have bread also and cheese. Terrible cheese, but it is cheese."

She laughed. It was strange hearing laughter again. I watched her as she cracked the eggs one by one in a large porcelain bowl. I watched her hands sure and certain the way I'd watched them with patients. I felt safer in the presence of this woman who had saved so many lives. Malaria, typhoid, pneumonia, dysentery. She had combated them all and won most of these battles. Maybe she would win this one.

The next day at dawn, we heard footsteps again. Max began to bark madly and I roused the children quickly and slid under the bed with them once again. It had become a habit. The idea of hiding more than actual escape. Eloise came into the bedroom.

"Francine, Fidèle, hurry, it is the UN. We must all leave now." We came out from our hiding places and ran down the hall. Pierre was carrying bags already. A UN soldier took Max by the leash and lead him into a white Jeep right outside the door. Another UN soldier turned to us. He turned to me and grabbed me by the arm as I walked by him getting ready to climb into the jeep.

"We cannot take you with us," he said in a neutral tone. My heart skipped. Pierre looked at me furtively and kept moving. He climbed into the jeep and held out his hand to Eloise, who stopped dead in her tracks.

"What do you mean you cannot take them? But she worked at the hospital with me. They're our friends, our colleagues. Fidèle here worked for the government."

The UN soldier pulled Eloise up into the convoy.

"We have strict orders; we are not allowed to take anyone but foreign nationals. Do you have a European passport?" The man asked me knowing the answer to his question. And in my silence, he added, "Then there is nothing I can do. Nothing."

Eloise's face was static with shock. Her mouth was gaping. She wanted to say something, but everything was moving so quickly. The last UN soldier climbed into the convoy. Pierre was looking down at his feet. The white truck began to drive away. We all stood; Fidèle and I, each with a child in hand and Michel in front of us, watching the convoy of white faces driving away. In the distance, I heard Max barking. I watched the dust rising from the road until silence fell around us.

Chapter 7 – Francine

After Eloise and Pierre left, Fidèle and I took the children into the kitchen and ate a large meal. We ate not because we were hungry but because we needed our strength for the journey ahead. I try to remember where Mélanie sat. Was she sitting in my lap? I do not remember touching her then. I see Fidèle eating quickly. I remember Michel saying he wasn't hungry and Angélique strangely withdrawn still, eating in silence next to Sylvie. I don't remember Christian. I don't remember his voice, if he ate. What he might have said. Memory is a trickster, a friend of the devil. Always trying to trick the heart into feeling something that doesn't exist.

We left Eloise and Pierre's house and headed to the Sainte Famille church across town where we hoped we would be safe. Outside the air smelled of spring. The bougainvillea were in bloom, making my head swim with memories of all the springs we had spent together, Fidèle and I. But now, we were standing outside in the deserted streets of Kigali, our lives dangling. Fidèle and I decided to split up. We had spent a lot of time deliberating this decision before we left the house and we had finally settled on dividing our chances of survival in two rather than being caught together and killed. He took Mélanie and Michel with him and I took Angélique, Sylvie and Christian. Fidèle insisted we take our bags with us. I told him to leave them behind. What good would our belongings do us if we could not run to spare our lives? But he held on to them like an amulet that would save us somehow. There are two things I remember in great detail from that morning. The first one is Angélique's silence, the way she skidded off into a hole somewhere inside herself. It had started with the killings right outside the house when we were hiding under the bed. With each moment that passed, I realize now that this is the moment when she started to fall behind. It is strange to think that life's greatest moments can be narrowed down to a handful of seconds. It gives me chills now to think that each of our lives hangs by a single thread that can snap at any moment.

I also remember the color of Mélanie's dress: gold, like the sun, like the heart of the Pyrethrum daisies that grow everywhere after the rainy season. The night before everything changed, I had laid out her birthday dress next to the bed; a beautiful gold dress with a bright red ribbon that wraps around the waist. Sylvain, Fidèle's oldest brother, and his wife, Hélène, had bought the dress in Brussels, where they had traveled a few months earlier. As we left the house, it was these small pieces of memory that remained. When I look back on those days, I am left with shards of memory, pieces of buried images like torn-up pieces of a larger image.

I held the girls one on each hand and walked behind Fidèle who was carrying Mélanie in one hand and the bags in the other. My heart pounded in the back of my throat, in the back of my head, like my body had suddenly been turned upside down. Michel walked between us all like a tiny chick protected by his parents. Fidèle and I always wanted to be a sanctuary for our children, we wanted to protect them from the rumble of the world.

Angélique walked diligently next to me while Sylvie whimpered and pulled my hand. I shook her arm like a strange dangling fruit ready to part from the tree.

"Shush!" I said to her in a loud whisper.

"But shoe hurts me, Maman!" Sylvie continued to whine. The next moment, is a moment that I will regret forever. I shook her violently and turned to her abruptly, forcing Angélique to turn as well. I stared Sylvie, my six-year-old daughter in the eye and said: "Do you want to die? Is that what you want?"

My child looked at me with terror in her eyes. For the first time in my life, I had caused more fear in one of my own children than the killers running after us outside. I remember Sylvie staring at me wildly. How afraid she looked. My own child was afraid of me. She shook her small head with all of the determination her small body could muster and she whispered back to me: "No, Maman, I don't want to die. I don't."

"Good." I managed to answer and picked up the pace to catch up to the fainting color of Mélanie's dress ahead of us. In the few short seconds I was menacing my daughter with death, Fidèle and the kids had managed to slip away from us. I wondered how long Fidèle would be able to last without dropping to the ground. I remember wondering how far we would get before we got caught.

That's when I saw them. The killers came out of nowhere. Appeared like ghosts in the quiet streets with the remnants of the violence from the night before. The streets were lined with flowers, bougainvillea that likes to grow in the shade of the tall walls that border expensive houses. I remember the red dust of the road. The copper-colored dust from the mountains and later still, the deep stains of dark blood drying in the sun after each killing.

Two men holding machetes in their hands pulled out of an opened gate; their bodies slinking like predators. They stood a hundred feet away from me and halfway between me and Fidèle and the children. I could see that Fidèle had not seen them, his back was turned as he walked away briskly with Michel by his side. Had the men seen my family? I did not know. I flung my body to the ground and pushed the girls down with me. Christian was walking ahead unknowing of what had happened. I called to him, in a loud whisper, in a forced hushed voice but he kept on walking. My boy kept on walking towards death. I wanted to warn them, I wanted to call out to my son, to my husband and the children but if I made a sound, they would hear me. They saw Fidèle first. I saw them from a distance, the way their bodies quickly snapped in a new direction, brandishing their machetes already soiled with blood, in the air. I inched away from the road towards the side of a wall and hid behind a small bush. I watched in silence as the killers approached my husband. Suddenly Fidèle turned before they got to him and he began to run. He dropped the large bag to the ground and held Mélanie so tightly she cried. Seeing his father running, Christian began to panic. He looked back to find me gone. I inched up from the bush and waived to him and he came running back to me. In the distance, I watched the gold of Mélanie's dress vanish as Fidèle ran off into a side street.

I heard screams in the distance. I convinced myself that I had never heard these voices before. I convinced myself that this was not the voice of my child. That these were not the cries of my husband.

We hid all day at the heart of a bamboo bush in the garden of an abandoned house where I heard the yelps of a wounded dog and waited for night to come. The animal's cries were incessant like an abandoned child's, or the cries of an animal caught in a trap. I remember thinking as I waited for night to fall with my children by my side that we humans are nothing more than animals waiting to die. I huddled with the children around me, pushing their small bodies in the thickest bend of the bush as to better hide them. If I was discovered, maybe they could live. Maybe they would be spared. I heard gunshots and voices in the distance. I asked myself if I should keep moving through the city, but the voices had begun speaking to me. *Stay,* they whispered. I know now that the moment I saw the color of Mélanie's dress vanish and heard their screams in the distance was the moment when the voices began speaking to me.

At dusk, the wounded dog grew quiet and I stopped wishing someone would come and shoot him. *Sit in the dark with your children and wait for death,* the voices said to me. I would have listened but the children began tugging at me.

"Maman, Maman, I am hungry." Sylvie was pulling at my dress with her little hand. Angélique roused herself from a strange sleep that resembled paralysis. She gasped and looked around and then remembered where she was and slid back down on the ground like a forgotten doll.

"I am hungry Maman," repeated Sylvie.

"Me too!" said Christian.

I heard voices rumbling in the distance like a strange quiet storm brewing from the West.

"Hush!" I whispered to the children. "We must be quiet now." I could feel the killers magnetically approaching, like a curse I was unable to shake. The children became restless. I covered Sylvie and Christian's mouths. I knew that Angélique would be quiet. I heard a man's voice: "Let me hit him with a *masu.*"

And then another man replied, "Leave him, he is already dead. There are many others to kill."

I heard the muffled sound of footsteps on the moist April earth, and then they were gone again. I pulled the children out from behind the bush and motioned to them to be silent. We made our way around the garden where we had spent our entire day hiding. In the dark, I stumbled on something that felt like a bag of dirt and then I heard a moaning voice. I crouched to see what it was and I saw the body of a man, covered in blood. I searched for something I would recognize in his face, but I was relieved that I had never seen him before. The man moaned as he writhed in pain. Angélique began to scream; a strident blood-curdling scream and her voice scared me more than the presence of the body we had just stumbled upon. I lunged and grabbed her covering her screaming mouth. With both hands, I picked her up and began to run in search of another hiding place. Christian and Sylvie followed me.

I saw that I had reached the *rond-point of* the Place de la Constitution, the roundabout at the heart of Kigali. We were near Sainte Famille, the church where I spent my entire childhood. We used to pray there every Sunday with my grandmother, Maman Josée, and her sister, Marie—who were both a cross between a nun and a voodoo priestess who spoke to God and the spirits. When I was nine years old, one day, on our way to church, I asked her about the difference between the world of the living and the world of the dead, and she said to me: "Child, there is no difference between God and the spirit world. There is no difference between the dead and the living. There is just *this* holding us apart." And when she said *this,* she held onto my arm and shook it like an inanimate object she had just encountered.

I guess I've been speaking to God for as long as I can remember and for a long time, I thought he spoke to me too. Only now I know better.

That night, I prayed earnestly. I prayed like I never had before.

Dear God, I whispered. *What shall I do?* And the answer was pure and simple: *go to the house of the Lord and seek refuge.* This is what I did.

At the bend where Avenue de la Révolution meets the round about of Place de la Constitution, I met a roadblock. Two or three cars were parked, and the Interahamwe militia were stopping people one at a time. I held my breath. If I wanted to find my way to redemption and protection in the church, I would have to go through the valley of death. There was no way to avoid contact with the men now. It was too late to turn back, I would have to speak with them. When I think of this moment, I think of Boy's face, the same face as the man who stopped me at that night. I remember his shirt, yellow, not the gold of Mélanie's dress or the color of the sun, but the hue of pale urine. I remember the void in his eyes and the smell of bad whisky on his breath.

I walked up to the group of men questioning people and I saw bottles of whisky by their side. They were laughing, and nearby I saw the body of a woman with her limbs severed all the way to the white of the bone. I looked away. The man pushed me aside

"Sit over there!" He barked. All three children were holding onto me now. The man was holding a bottle of whisky. I could see the dirt in his fingernails from where I was standing.

That's when I saw Fidèle sitting there, his body slumped against the wall of the small shack they were using as a checkpoint. He looked like a rag doll. His head was covered in blood like he'd been bludgeoned but his eyes were staring off into space while his hand held his other arm in the semblance of comfort. He didn't see me at first. He sat there still like he was trying to hold onto something that had already vanished. Next to him was our boy Michel, who was facing the wall, looking away from us. Our boy was alive.

The man with the yellow shirt pulled at my dress, tearing it at the shoulder. Fidèle looked up and saw me. He twitched like he'd seen a ghost. And then, propping himself against the wall, he stood up. His body barely held him up, but his spirit had been conjured. I wanted to shout and go to him, but I was afraid of the man with the yellow shirt who had shoved the children away from me like flies. Sylvie, Christian, and Angélique were huddled a couple of feet away, watching me for direction. And that's when they saw their father and brother.

"Papa! Papa!" Christian yelled. Sylvie ran to Fidèle and wrapped her little arms around his legs. The man looked up and away from my torn dress now that he realized we knew Fidèle. He pulled out his revolver. Fidèle was trying to move towards me, as he held on to his children wrapped around him like a tree. He looked at me like maybe he was trying to say something and the man with the yellow shirt shot him in the chest at close range like a dog. He shot him like the dogs they had begun shooting in the city because they were eating all the corpses. I did nothing. I did not move. Michel ran over to me and grabbed a hold of my hand.

Fidèle looked at me. His eyes looked in my direction, but he was already gone, his body had not fallen yet, but he was already with the spirits. The expression in his eyes told me that Mélanie was gone too. His blood flowed out of him like a river. The children fell down with him. They fell down with their father and they began to scream and cry. I wanted them to be quiet. I wanted to yell: "Quiet!" and silence them so they would be spared.

The man stepped over my husband and began pulling at me again.

I pushed Michel away towards his siblings and his dead father as the man continued pulling at my dress. I wanted to help him remove it. I wanted to help him focus on me so he would forget about my children. So he would forget about my crying children in the corner of the room with their dead father. My body became a distant shell inside of which I tried to hide. The way a child buries his head under the blankets in the dark night.

I am mad now. I am mad. I am a mad woman.

I thought of my children in the corner of the room and I thought about God. This was the first time I felt his presence since this whole thing had started and suddenly the madness left me, just like that. Like a ghost pushed out of a room.

"Shhh!" the voice inside me said. "Shhh! Be gone! Go, mad woman, go devilish woman. Be gone!" And then she was. And I was left standing there at the checkpoint with the man with the yellow shirt pushing me against the wall and my children huddled over the body of my dead husband.

More people came by at the checkpoint. Men. Tutsi men like my husband, like me. They tried not to look at Fidèle and our children crying over him. They tried not to look but I know they saw him. I witnessed shame as they averted their eyes away from the body of my dead husband, away from me. They knew what would happen to me now. I knew also. Another man took care of the two Tutsi men. He let them go. Why I do not know. God seemed to have a funny way of taking care of business. Some people lived, some people died and there was no reason for it. The killers walked away. The man with the yellow shirt pulled me towards him and he laughed. I was talking to God now and praying that he would not do this in front of my children. I was praying that my children would stay alive.

I smelled the liquor on the man's breath. The liquor and this sour smell of rotten meat. His teeth were rotting. He held me by the arm and motioned me to walk. He walked behind me shoving me with the barrel of the gun that had just killed my husband. The man pulled me towards a little house that used to be an *épicerie*, a corner store. We walked inside and it was dark. I saw the shelves, previously used to store food, now empty. One shelf was knocked down on its side. The walls were dirty in some places. Blood trailing down, like someone had tried to paint with it and then had changed their mind.

The mad woman came back to me now. Only now she was not leaving. She walked right inside of my brain like she had been living there all her life and she laughed like a witch. In that instant, she became a part of me. And there was no asking her to leave.

That's when I saw the opened case of whisky with just three bottles left inside. The cardboard was dirty, with smeared blue letters on the side that read: *Produit d'Ecosse*—Product of Scotland. *They must have stolen it from the embassy or one of the Belgian houses.* The Belgians, the French, the Americans—all of the white people were gone. The UN carried them, one by one, away to safety in white trucks, jeeps with big black crosses painted on them.

Yellow Shirt pulled me down while he was still standing and opened his pants. I saw the blood on his hands and smelled the acrid smell of his sex and the stains of death on him. I thought of the devil. The mad woman and I we were quiet now. When I tasted the salt of his penis on my tongue, we grew quiet, she and I, and I prayed. I prayed.

Our Father who art in heaven, hallowed by thy name, thy kingdom come… as it is in heaven. I heard a gunshot outside and then a woman's scream. I wondered if it was me screaming. The man came. He pushed me off him, zipped up his pants and was gone. I stayed in the dark for a long time. I thought about my children, but I could not move. I could have run. I should have run. But I didn't. The mad woman inside me said, *stay and wait. Like a rat in a tunnel.* And I did. I heard more screaming outside. I heard the sound of chopping, like wood being cut and a strange blunt sound and then laughter. The men laughed; the mirth of drunkenness. I heard Yellow Shirt return. He slammed the door open. It smashed against the wall and he was still holding a bloody machete in his hand. I saw the madness in his eyes. His yellow shirt was now speckled with fresh blood and his eyes were rabid like a dog gone mad. I had once seen a rabid dog in the village once, how he would slink around the village, looking down and sideways, looking for trouble. You could never shoo that dog away; the disease had gotten hold of him and nothing scared him anymore. We had to find and shoot him. This man, he reminded me of the animal.

Yellow Shirt pushed me down again, only I fell on my back, and heard a snap followed by a crack. I felt a dull pain in my hand. I had broken my little finger. The pain vanished as if I wasn't even there anymore. He was on top of me, pushing his way into me. His foul breath blowing on me. Pushing me into the cement. I looked away; I turned my head away. Tried not to look into his eyes. Tried not to see the rage, the emptiness, the devil. The mad woman was laughing again like a witch. *This is not my body. This is not my body. This is not my body.* When he was done. He moved away and went outside to kill again.

I ran outside to find the children. All around me the darkness fell oppressively like a blanket in the middle of the summer. I needed light. I needed to see my way, to find my children, to recognize the killers, to bury my husband. I wanted to bury my husband. But there would be no time for this.

Men were laughing in the shadows, the kind of laughter that always accompanies drunkenness, the laughter of alcohol gone bad in the heart. I could still smell Yellow Shirt on me, his whisky smell, his sour rotting smell. His blood and semen smell. The blood on his hands, his semen oozing out of me like piss in a latrine.

In the light of the car's headlights, I could clearly see the faces of people making their way past the checkpoint into the night. Scared faces, hungry, tired faces, frozen faces, stone faces. What did I resemble? I inched my way back to the barrack where I had left my children. I had left my children with killers. The mad woman pushed her way in the forefront of my mind again and began to wail—the mourning wail, the wail of widows. I couldn't hear the men laughing outside anymore.

I found each of my babies hunched in a circle, untouched. Anqélique sat her back against the wall, her legs stretched in front of her like a brand new doll from the store. But her face was not the face of a doll's. Her eyes were strange, mad-like, not the eyes of a four-year-old girl, but those of an elder. Christian, Michel, and Sylvie were holding each other, their tiny shoulders sheltering each other from the passing of men, from the darkness of the devil, all around us. I quickly knelt by their side, pulling Angélique from her frozen position. Fidèle's body was still a couple of feet away, lying in his own blood, his body stiff and strange. His right leg twisted bizarrely at the knee. He was not sleeping. This was not my sleeping husband.

The mad woman spoke inside of me, *this is your dead husband. Watch him now because you will never see him again.* I felt as though someone had gotten a hold of my heart and was holding it in their fist, squeezing it as tight as they could. For a moment, the pain startled me because I had forgotten I could feel.

Sylvie's body was covered in blood, but she was moving. I wanted to scream, but I stayed silent. The men should not see us. Christian grabbed hold of my hand patting his sister's body in search of the wounds inflicted and said, quietly: "Maman, this is not her blood. This is Papa's blood. This is Papa's blood."

I looked at him and for the first time I saw Fidèle in him. I saw my Fidèle's eyes, the curve of his cheeks, the line of his hair, the firmness of his ways. When Christian was born, everyone said that he looked just like me. Maman said to me when she was holding him: "This is just like holding you when you were born. This boy is a mirror of yourself."

For a long time, I only saw myself in him. But now that I sit in hell with my children, watching my husband's blood grow colder with each minute that passes, I see him in my boy.

I took Michel and Angélique by the hand while Christian and Sylvie walked next to us. We made our way to the checkpoint. I searched again in the shadows for the presence of Yellow Shirt but he had vanished. The man in charge was holding a machete in one hand and a beer bottle in the other. I could see the drunkenness had already gotten hold of him. The way his body swayed from side to side as he waved some people past the checkpoint. My eyes were peeled on the blade he was brandishing with each wave, with each distorted laugh he let out like a wild animal.

The mad woman's voice came back to me again in this moment of uncertainty. I wanted her gone. I wanted silence in my head so I could pray and ask the good Lord to help us pass to the other side. I heard myself praying inside my head, *Good Lord, let us cross and be on our way to your house my Lord. Let us come to you and be in the protection of your house of prayer.*

The mad woman quieted my prayers. *You will lose another child. Another child needs to be sacrificed for the rest of you to live. Which one will you choose?* She whispered to me. I wanted to scream and yell at her and tell her to be quiet. I wondered if she heard me because I did not hear from her again for quite some time.

When it was my turn to pass there were two men now deciding who would live and who would die. The eyes of the first man with his machete and beer landed on me. He saw me for the first time. I saw him see me, and the fear coursed through my blood as he swayed back and then forward like a tree in a raging storm.

"Look at the cockroach and her children! Look at her!" I watched the other man and searched for signs of God or the devil in him. But I saw nothing. He looked like a colleague of mine; he looked like Joseph who worked at the hospital with me, only his clothes were tattered and speckled with blood. As the Jackal continued to eye me, laughing, the other man looked at us calmly, like someone weighing the measures of the world. I kept the children behind me, shielding them from the men. I stopped as far away from the Jackal as possible.

"Come closer!" He barked as he gestured with his beer-holding hand for me to approach him.

"I can't see your face. I like to see the eyes of the Tutsi women because you can see the devil in them." Then he laughed again, throwing his head back. I tried not to look at the machete he was holding. I inched my way closer to him past the other man who eyed me with stillness. The silence that came from him reminded me of my mother's words growing up: "beware of the quiet rabid dog, have no fear of the raging lion." I had never understood her words until that moment standing at this checkpoint.

I wanted to back up again so I could shield the children from the menacing man. But if I moved away, there was no telling was would happen to us. I could still hear the mad woman's voice resonating in my head.

You will lose another child. Which one will you choose? I could not look at him without turning my head to face him. I did not want to defy him in this way and yet I desperately wanted to know if he held a weapon. I could not remember a weapon. I only remember the speckled blood on his checkered shirt and the quietude of his ways. My eyes were on the Jackal now who had suddenly grown quiet. In the silence that followed, I was almost beginning to miss the man's laugh. I could feel pain in my belly from the blows of yellow shirt in my womb. I pushed away the pain. The Jackal looked at me.

"Go on! Pass! Just be gone. I feel nauseous looking at one more cockroach!" He waved me by. But suddenly I felt the arm of the brooding man grabbing hold of me and I heard his voice for the first time: "No! She should die." The way he said this, so quietly, so tranquil and calm, it made me want to scream in terror. But I said nothing.

"Get on your knees and pray for the last time." He said to me again. The Jackal went from looking surprised to laughing hysterically. He was laughing so hard he had to drop his beer bottle to the ground and fold his body over. I got down on my knees and the children began to cry. They were crying behind me and I turned to hold them. I wrapped my arms around them and held them tightly. Maybe they would spare my children. They could kill me but spare my children. I thought about the mad woman's words and I began to gain hope; if I had to choose between one of my children, maybe I could choose myself and spare them all.

"Bring me that girl," the man said pointing to Angélique crouching behind me. He had picked my next child who would die.

"No! Please, not my children."

The mad woman's voice whispered in my ears. *Never show your fear, never tell the devil what you really want. He will now kill the child you fool!* She was right. I looked up again and saw the brooding man holding a machete high above my head. He leaned forward and reached for Angélique behind me. He grabbed my baby who began to screech, like a wounded bird. I heard myself pray out loud.

"Our Father who art in heaven..." Next to me, the Jackal had stopped laughing. He began to heave and wretch and then he threw up on the ground next to me. The brooding man waited patiently for my prayer to end so he could kill my daughter. His arm came down quickly with the silver of the machete reflected in my peripheral vision. He was killing my daughter. I raised my arm and shielded Angélique from the blow. I heard it then, the blunt sound of the blade cutting into my bone and then the pain, sharp and suddenly numb. I felt nothing. The blood began trickling around the wound, trails and trails of blood pooled down and then dripped onto my daughter's face. She was screaming now, screaming so loud, I thought her vocal chords would break. Brooding man was laughing. And then he stopped. He pulled the machete away from my arm, as if it had been a tree trunk he was in the process of cutting down.

Something else was happening around us. I heard some screams, a woman was screaming and then commotion and some people were running behind us. And then I saw him standing there. Yellow Shirt running up to brooding man and the Jackal: "Some cockroaches have run this way and are fighting back with rocks. You have to come." His eyes met mine. He looked at me for a second.

Everything stood still and for a moment, I could have sworn that I saw shame in his eyes. And then I heard him: "Let her go and come with me." Brooding man looked at me for a second. I watched for motion in his machete-holding hand. But it was still. He looked at me for a second and back at Yellow Shirt again and then they were gone.

My arm was bleeding badly. I tore a piece of my dress and wrapped my arm tightly. The checkpoint stayed open for a few minutes. I got hold of my girls and told my boy to run.

"Run as fast as you can! Run!" I yelled. And we ran into the mad streets of Kigali on the first night of my widowhood.

Chapter 8 – Francine

Everything I had known up until that point became useless. It was as if the world had been turned upside down, leaving only a few familiar remnants to remind me that I was still alive and we were still on earth with the living. My children and I ran in the rumbling shadows of the city until we could not run anymore. I was still bleeding from the moment with Yellow Shirt, and the deep cut in my arm. The children were only able to move slowly, but we were moving forward toward the church of my childhood, *Église Sainte Famille*.

I recognized the corner of Avenue de la Paix and Avenue de la République, with its long artery linking the heart of the city to the smaller neighborhoods. Everything I knew had eerily changed, like a dear, old house haunted by ghosts. Angélique began to cry. I noticed that her feet were blistered and raw. Her right foot was bleeding slightly. I went to pick her up but my wounded arm made it impossible for me to carry my child. I put Angélique down on the ground and held her by the arm.

We saw a horse running wildly down Boulevard de la Révolution with madness in its eyes and its ears stretched back. Sylvie began to scream. Christian stood frozen next to her staring at the wild animal flaring its nostrils as it ran past us. We heard its hoofs echoing in the distance. Our lives hung on the edge of every second passing. The world had been turned on its head. The children and I continued on our journey past the roundabout of Place de la Constitution, making our way along the walls of the city where wildflowers grow. The air, which usually smelled sweet and moist with the fragrance of spring, instead hung heavily with the stench of rotten flesh and blood.

We came face-to-face with three bodies piled on top of one another, their limbs entwined, their flesh cut open in wide gaping wounds made from the chopping motion of a machete. The children stopped and stared but said nothing. I pushed them past the bodies and onto the street where a trail of blood had made its way. We passed a family of four: a young woman, probably her mother, and two young children around Sylvie and Angélique's age. They, too, were Tutsis, walking in the opposite direction. It wasn't in the lines in their faces or in the curves in their cheekbones that I recognized their bloodline, but in the fear in their eyes. We eyed each other, each of us on our way to or from death; we eyed each other, wondering which was the path to safety.

The children and I saw packs of dogs making their way around us as we slinked along the edge of the city's walls. I had always liked dogs and never feared them until that day, but these animals had been rendered wild and mad by the scent of blood. We passed the dogs quietly without making eye contact. Being among the living, we were of no interest to them.

We walked in silence until we saw the red-brick church at the bottom of the hill in front of us. There stood the tall, safe haven of my childhood. In the night air, the church appeared gray; as if the killings had somehow washed the church walls of its familiar pink hue. All around, the streets were quiet—eerily quiet—but beyond the walls of the courtyard where we entered, we heard the whispers and voices of countless people packed together in the courtyard. As we moved forward, I began to see their faces, hundreds of fearful and tired faces, bloody faces, long, drawn-out faces, the faces of people who had forgotten they were still living.

I looked at my arm and it was still bleeding badly. I knew I had to tie another strip of cotton tightly above the cut so that circulation would be stopped altogether. I also knew that this would surely result in me losing my arm altogether unless I received medical attention in the next few hours. The children and I were so hungry we could barely move. I kept them nearby and went in search of food. There were many men among the crowds, some of whom resembled the Tutsi tribe of my people and others who were visibly Hutus. Was there any truth in the eugenics propaganda we had all been fed by the Belgians about the definitive physiological differences between the Tutsis and the Hutus? Was it really possible to discern, without a doubt who belonged to which bloodline? I did not know anymore. But these men's broader features and shorter bodies made me wonder who they were and why they were here.

The doors of the church were closed. I stopped and asked a woman who was sitting on the ground alone in the courtyard why the doors were closed.

"This is so people do not escape at night," she said to me without raising her head. I felt a chill and I heard the mad woman inside me snickering. I willed her to be quiet.

In the early morning, right before the doors of the church opened, a miracle happened. I woke up and saw my daughter Mélanie standing there, playing in front of me, like she had never gone away. She was running through the courtyard, chasing a butterfly. In that moment, I knew that God existed. He hadn't left us completely. Mélanie was running. She giggled, letting out this little laugh that slipped out of her like a hiccup. Then, she hopped and skipped away and she was gone. Had I dreamt her up?

Quickly, I made sure the others were sleeping, and I went after her. I hadn't run since the night before when I had to try to save my life in the streets. Now I was running after a ghost.

When I found her again, Mélanie was sitting in the dust looking at the butterfly on the ground. I stopped abruptly by her side and accidentally kicked up some dust in her face; the butterfly flew away. She coughed a little and looked up at me. That's when I knew that something was different. This wasn't my baby girl Mélanie. This little girl chasing a butterfly around the church courtyard wasn't my child.

She squinted, trying to shield herself from the sun. I tried to smile. I tried to give her something more than just a lopsided smile and a dried up heart, but I had nothing else to give her.

"What is your name?" I asked her.

"My name is Sophie." For a moment, my heart sank. I asked her the question no one should ask in these places.

"Where is your family?" For a moment she considered this. She looked at me again, she had shifted slightly in the sand so she could use my own body to shield her from the sun's direct light.

"My maman is over there," she said pointing to the other side of the courtyard, "and my papa is up there." Her small finger pointed toward the sky.

"He's up in heaven with God." Maybe this was a sign. I took it as a sign. First the resemblance with Mélanie and then the butterfly and now the mention of God, out loud, in the mouth of a child. Even that morning, I knew that it was meant to be like this. She and I. We were meant to find each other. For a long time, I thought she was no more than two and a half, a precocious child. But later, she showed me that she was four by holding up her fingers. She took me by the hand to a corner of the courtyard where a woman my age was sleeping with another older child, clearly Sophie's larger version. I stood silently watching the woman and child as they slept.

Sophie called out to her mother "Maman! Maman!" The woman woke in terror. Her eyes landed on me first, scanning me to determine if I had come to harm her. I raised both hands up in the air instinctively, to show her that they were empty, to show her that I had come in peace. Her body relaxed a little; she blinked rapidly as she gathered herself. Sophie nestled against her mother's body, making herself small on her lap, already partially occupied by her other child's head. I sat down next to them, pulling all three children in front of me. The four of us sat on the ground of the church's courtyard.

"You met Sophie. This is Devota." The visibly exhausted woman indicated a visibly sick and weak girl of five who was about the same size as my Angélique.

"I'm Alice," she said pointing to herself tiredly.

"Francine." I simply responded making the same gesture as Alice had, resting my hand on my chest. Secretly, I hoped for friendship with this stranger.

"This is Angélique, Sylvie, and Christian." I introduced the children. Sophie was eyeing Angélique curiously. Children have the uncanny ability to push out everything else around them and to focus on the present moment with absolute abandon. But I remembered where we were and everything else that had happened before and I began digging for information.

"How long have you been here?" I asked Alice.

"We arrived the day before yesterday. But we got locked out of the church. I went into the convent right there yesterday." The nearby building she indicated was much smaller with a small corrugated roof covering a tiny patio area.

"Sister Imaculée fed us, me and the children." She ran her hand over her face slowly like she was trying to wipe away the exhaustion from her body. "We stayed at the convent during the day but then we decided to come back to the church. It was too late to get back inside. They lock the doors at night." Alice looked scared and tired.

"Do you have any food to share with us? I asked her. "My children and I haven't eaten in two days." I saw her hesitate in her instinctive response to help, she was starting to reach into the folds of her clothes but then she held herself back. I looked into her eyes. She had long, drawn out lines of exhaustion on her face.

Finally, she said, "Yes, I have this, if you want." She pulled out a piece of bread from the folds of her clothes.

"Thank you!" I said, taking it without hesitation. These were the most sincere words of thanks I had ever uttered in my life.

The piece of bread was small, but it would help us keep going until the next opportunity for food. I split the piece into morsels and gave one to each of the children taking the smallest for myself. We ate in silence.

Suddenly, the doors of the church opened. We rose quickly as if we were in a hurry to enter the house of the Lord. As we approached the opened gates, I looked inside the church and sensed the fear moving through the hundreds of people huddled against each other in the enormous building as the light poured all around them. The wide open space of this place of worship had been turned into a makeshift camp. I wanted to believe that we would be safe here, but my heart was telling me otherwise. I could feel danger in the eyes of these people who had been here for days; in the trails of all they had already survived. I could smell death in the air, lingering like a stench, even in the corners of the Lord's house.

I watched little Sophie and her family walking ahead of us and I could not stop thinking about my baby Mélanie and husband Fidèle. I couldn't stop seeing Fidèle's face, the way he looked at me right before he got shot. I could feel pain pushing inside me, the way that man had pushed his way into my body the night before. I wanted to wash their sins off of me, wash the blood that had congealed between my legs.

I stepped inside the church with my children. I could barely recognize the house of the Lord where I had once visited to pray with my family as a child. At first I could not discern what had changed in the appearance of the church. The walls of the church were still their distinct pinkish-red brick color. Sainte Famille had been the place where I'd come as a little girl with Maman Hélène and Papa François. I was the youngest of six children and was the mischief of the family. My parents called me "Kalulu, little wild animal" on account of my foolery.

Now, nearly two decades later, as I was entering the same church with my children, running for our lives, I realized that what had changed since the last two decades when I had first set foot in this church was not the color of the walls, nor the hordes of people seeking refuge, but rather a new presence that had never existed here before. I closed my eyes and took a deep breath and when I opened them again I knew that this presence was the devil in the house of the Lord.

Chapter 9 – Francine

As we made our way inside the church, I could see Sophie and her children walking briskly, as if she were trying to win a prize. What could we win in this altered house of the Lord? I kept the children in front of me, at all times. I needed to see them, to know that they still existed, that I could still protect them. This was a holy place. But were we safe?

A man grabbed me. I jumped. I did not want anyone to ever touch me again. He let go of my arm.

"You're lucky you didn't have to pay to get in. Sometimes, they make people pay," he said simply. I could smell death on him. I could smell it everywhere around me. He stood huddled in the corner, his arm wrapped in a soiled bandage watching me as I walked away with the children towards the crowded pews.

There were people everywhere; some were jammed in the pews, or sitting on the concrete floor, while others were standing. Children made their way around crowds of people. Some even played, forgetting for a moment that their lives were teetering on an invisible edge. I searched for a place where we could finally rest. My eyes caught an open spot on the side of the pews, where I sat on the ground with the children. I tugged gently at Alice in front of me indicating to her where I had decided to settle. She followed me. I liked the idea of being hidden from the people entering the church. I didn't know who could—or would—make their way inside during the day.

Searching for food to feed my children became my first fixation. This place of worship would become a place of obsession, a place where I would carry out my life's mission: to save my remaining children, even at the price of my own life.

I overheard a woman and her two children, young adolescents talking around us.

"He has food in the supplies store. I heard there is more food in there than anyone could ever eat."

Nearby, another boy with a swollen eye leaned over and said: "It's been two days since the last distribution of biscuits, so maybe we'll get some tomorrow."

Before I had a chance to ask them a question, a man entered the church and voices rose all around us. At first, I thought that the man making his way to the front of the church by the altar was a militia soldier and I wanted to scream. I grabbed hold of the children and held them tightly in front of me. But the man walked over to the pulpit and began to conduct mass.

"That's Father Wenceslas Munyeshyaka," Alice whispered. "I know him." I looked at the man standing at the pulpit as he held his arms opened wide. He was wearing a bulletproof jacket and when I leaned forward to see him clearly, I saw that he had a pistol attached to his waist.

"Let us pray." I bowed my head in silence and gave myself over to the Lord. I was glad to see that masses were still conducted in the church. Silently, I prayed for all of us here, and for the priest guiding us home. Father Wenceslas' voice rose around us, as people stirred nervously. Some were praying while others simply stood listening to his words.

"This is a day to rejoice." His words filled the church with a trailing echo.

"It is a day to rejoice for we are all still living."

A knot formed in my throat as I watched these people standing around me, seemingly bored or unwilling to pray. Obviously, there was not one pious soul between these walls. How could they stand and watch this man of the cloth and not give themselves over to prayer?

"But we must look into our hearts and see the truth. Those of you who are Tutsis are standing before God for judgment.

You are all accomplices of the Rwandan Patriotic Front army or RPF and are responsible for the violence taking place outside of these walls. You Tutsi traitors need to come forward and make yourselves known, so that this country can be free of cockroaches."

Father Wenceslas' words hit me. I thought of Yellow Shirt and his breath on me. I thought of his blows to my body. I looked around for a sign that maybe I had misheard, but people seemed accustomed to this speech. Some were shifting anxiously; others looked down in shame. I saw a handful of Hutus standing on the sides of the church nodding their heads in agreement. Suddenly I understood why they locked the church doors at night. We were prisoners here. We were held here during the day by the fear of the killings, by the memory of the Interahamwe militia traveling the city with their machetes, and we were held captive at night by the confinement of these gates. I wanted to run, but I knew there was nowhere for me to go. Alice turned around and looked at me. She had tears in her eyes. And for the first time since I had first laid my eyes on her, I realized that she, too, had lost so much already.

Father Wenceslas was a still a young man. In fact, everyone who knew him called him *the young one* because he liked to use that expression to refer to himself in his sermons. He was a healthy man, with a large, well-fed body. I did not recognize the signs of a priest in this man. He had taken up the habit of wearing a stiff flak jacket at all times.

After the sermon, he left and retired to his sitting room adjoining the church. Voices rumbled. People were whispering about what had just happened. We could not speak freely because there were Hutus from Gisozi around us. These were men who had run away from their province to escape the RPF forces that were fighting for the protection of the Tutsis. There were enemies among us in this church. I reached over and tapped the shoulder of the boy with the puffy eye who had whispered earlier about the biscuits. He had a tall forehead that made him look intelligent and two narrow eyes that closed in on the grief around us.

"What did you say about biscuits?" I asked him.

"Father Wenceslas gives us biscuits every two or three days. But no water. You have to pay for water. If you're a woman, you have a better chance to get it." He looked away, as if he had seen something on me that made him wince.

"But there is a lot of food in the supplies store. It's just that Wenceslas won't give any to the Tutsis." He looked up again and stared at my arm. "That looks pretty bad. There is a man who walks around sewing people up. I think he's a doctor. You might want to try to find him soon." The boy was right. My hands had gone numb at the wrist. I knew this meant I would lose the use of my limb completely.

Devota and Sophie began tugging at Alice's sleeve.

"Mama, I'm hungry. I'm hungry, mama." I felt shame move through me as I remembered that I had asked her for food and she had given it to me. I wondered if she now regretted her generosity. I looked around us and could see the different pockets of people around us. There were many wounded among the hundreds of people sitting and lying on the ground. Many were men; some were small children who lay quietly in the torpor of starvation.

I knew that if we were going to survive, I would have to develop a plan, a strategy that would make me indispensable to those who controlled these walls. The children and I stayed close in silence as others around us wept, whispered, cried and waited. I only remember drifting off into sleep, fitful and shallow like the small streams that formed during the rainy season.

The next day, I woke up at dawn and welcomed the arrival of morning. I liked to wake before the opening of the doors because I could prepare for the day ahead. With the beginning of this new day came a sense of the unknown. I never knew what or who would make its way past the doors. As each morning and night stretched, the stench of our bodies grew worse with the increasing places where people had grown sick or children had relieved themselves in corners without anyone seeing them.

Christian was asleep next to me on the ground in the pew. I watched him, my little man. The only man of this family left standing. His face reminded me of his father's. The way his forehead curved like a half moon at the base of his hairline. I watched his breathing body. Watching my remaining children breathe was the only pleasure I had left on this earth. If I could, I would make them invisible from the world. I would contain them in a bubble; I would wrap them in a veil away from the dangers and the hatred that lurked all around us.

Angélique woke up first. She stirred, opened her eyes and sat up quietly next to me on the pew. She didn't speak, didn't smile. She simply looked at me with such sadness, I almost gasped. I should have worried about her then, but I didn't. She was alive and this was a blessing. How could I worry about the way she was living? The way we were all living? This was not a luxury we could have afforded then. Our mission each day was to stay alive. Stay alive and witness another opening of the church doors. But quietly, I knew that I hadn't heard Angélique's voice since the day we hid in Pierre and Eloise's house. Secretly, I knew that my daughter had stopped talking altogether. Planted in the middle of our battle to survive, I could not worry about details like Angélique's silence. My children were breathing and this was all that mattered in that moment.

The doors of the church opened shortly before eight. I know because I wanted to go to the Caritas office behind the church and ask the mother superior for some food but the doors were still closed. Alice had told me that she'd stood outside of the convent doors with Devota and Sophie and received bread the day before we arrived. I told Christian to watch out for his sisters and our friend Alice and her children.

He nodded seriously like a little man, the way his father used to nod when asked to do something around the house. When I saw Fidèle in Christian's face, I looked away quickly. Outside, in the courtyard, more refugees were waiting to enter the church. I tried not to look at the misery around me. I tried not to see the lines of women waiting to enter with their children. Women like me, women like Alice. I did not want to see any more suffering. I thought about how many of us were here already. I thought about how many people could this good house of the Lord contain? Would there come a point when we would have to turn people away?

When I arrived, the mother superior was already outside the Caritas office handing out some food to a line of refugees. I stood in line and waited for my turn. I thought about Abbé Wenceslas and tried to understand how he could keep food to himself when he had enough to feed all of us. I remembered the young boy's eyes when he alluded to women getting water from Wenceslas in exchange for sexual favors.

The mother superior was a serious woman with gentle eyes and a pragmatic spirit. She divided the food in even quantities to be handed out daily and when that portion was gone; she would go back up and return to the confines of her office, no matter how many people were still standing in line. That day, I was among the lucky ones, I was fourth in line and I knew that I would get my turn on this day. I watched the man standing in front of me. His time on this earth had almost run out, and for a moment, I envied him. I envied his life secured behind him, his years trailing behind him in memories that could not be taken away from him. Later, I'd learn that the past was all I had, all I had to carry me forward. I watched the old man inching forward as he leaned on a cane in his right hand, shaking like a leaf. I couldn't take my eyes away from his hair, the color of the sky right before heavy rains. He turned to face me. His eyes looked almost blue, with the clouding around his pupils. He didn't have to speak. We stood in silence, he and I looking into each other's eyes and we both knew that our lives, his and mine, and everyone else's in these church walls had been altered forever.

When my turn came, the mother superior went to scoop rice for me and my children but I had no can or bowl to contain it. She smiled.

"Hold out your hands, tomorrow you will come back with a can," she said to me.

Within days, I had found a routine within the chaos. I always woke the children at dawn, no matter what happened. I didn't want us to be caught by the dangers of the opening doors. In the afternoons, I forced myself to walk around the inside of the church in search of the man with the needle.

I met Jean de Dieu on the third day after I arrived. I spent two nights like the first and on the third day, I knew I needed a man to protect me. He had a good face. That's why I chose him. I say I *chose* even though he saw me first. In my village we always say that even if the man asks the woman to marry him, it is the woman who makes the real choice.

I chose him on account of his eyes. Something in them said he had never killed before. I was making my way around the church, watching people sleeping in the corners, playing cards on overturned boxes, women nursing their babies when I heard him.

"Bonjour," he said, smiling. I hadn't seen a real smile in so long it almost scared me. Reminded me of the smiles on the soldiers' faces when they were drunk, when they laughed after they came back from the killings. Only Jean de Dieu's smile was different. There was no laughter in his eyes, just a quiet peace. Like he was tired and he'd just found a place to rest. I think that's what brought us together. Our need for a place to rest, a quiet human place to put our hearts down.

"Bonjour," I answered simply. He had his eyes on me and I remembered my vow to find a man for protection.

"You need to let me help you with that arm. It looks bad. Let me see." He moved so close to me so quickly, I took two steps back, instinctively."

"I won't hurt you." He said extending his hand toward me. Like a furtive animal in need of human food, I let him approach me again.

"You might lose the arm," he said finally after examining the deep gauge.

"I know. I'm a nurse."

"Well, then you also know that this is infected. Yes?"

I nodded.

"You may not care about yourself, you may not even want to live anymore but if you want to help your children through this, you're going to have to let me help you." I knew he was right.

That night, he came to find me in the middle of the church where I was staying with the children. He had brought his medical kit with him. It was barely that, a few limited supplies he must have stolen or traded somewhere.

"I know, this isn't much, but it helps me get some people through." He lit a lighter and heated a surgical needle. The glow of the flame lit the small space around us and then darkness returned.

"The problem is there is no light around here and I'll have to see if I can sew you up in spite of the infection."

"Here, take this." He said to me handing me a pill. "It's an antibiotic. I'll come back with more. I wish I had something to give you for the pain, but that's something you're going to have to endure."

"I don't care about pain," I told him. I saw the strange gateway of his gaze that had suddenly opened in front of me. I knew he understood.

"I lost my wife," he paused, "and my children also." We said nothing while he unwrapped my arm completely. Even in the darkness I could see the white of the bone exposed by the open wound. Unfazed, Jean de Dieu went on with our conversation.

"Tonight, the moon is almost full. If you come with me to that far corner, the light will help us with the procedure." Noticing my glance towards my sleeping children, he said, "They will be fine. They are sleeping. There is no use in waking them for this." He said again calmly. I was drawn to his even-keeled energy. How tranquil he was in the midst of all the chaos around us. We made our way through the mass of sleeping bodies to the far corner of the church where a small ray of moonlight was filtering through the window above.

"I used to have a family too. Now they're gone." He said looking down at the ground. For a moment I thought he was looking at the wound or my arm but instead he was looking away. That's when I knew that we both carried shame.

"You still have a chance with this arm," he said piercing my skin with the needle. I could feel the sharp pain cutting through me, only a barrier in my chest kept me from crying out.

"The infection is the worse part but I think I can get you more pills for it. I will come back with them tomorrow. The bottom line is, you will have to choose to live." When he said this, Jean de Dieu held my hand in his and I could see the glow of the moon above reflected in the moisture in his eyes. "It all comes down to a choice in the end." I held my breath when he said this. I knew that what he was saying was true. If I didn't choose to live for my children, they would never survive.

The next day, I saw Jean de Dieu sitting on an overturned box, talking to people who answered him in a low voice. I walked up to the group, but their voices stopped as soon as I approached them. Jean de Dieu looked up at me cooly as if we had never spoken before.

"Do you want to help?" He asked inviting me to join their meeting. I had no idea what I wanted except maybe to be a part of a movement that connected us all to survival.

I nodded and sat down on the ground next to them. I learned that the meetings were held daily to identify and post people with skills around the church. That day, I became a part of the cleaning crew. A group of us were assigned to clean out death and sickness in the dark corners of the church. The biggest problems we had, aside from finding a steady source of food, was getting rid of the dead bodies and finding ways to help the wounded. Berthe, a corpulent woman in her fifties was assigned to the medical crew. She had been a nurse at the hospital in Kigali and for a moment, I wondered if she knew Eloise. Where was Eloise now? Drinking tea on a cool, rainy afternoon in Brussels, musing about the horrors in Africa? Where were all of the whites who had left us just days ago?

I thought about Jean de Dieu's face, his features. *What is he? Could he be one of them?* Jean de Dieu was in charge of organizing crews of people to take care of others. When I first saw him, I wondered whether he was a Hutu in the way people moved around him like they were avoiding a wide hole in the road. Everyone listened but most seemed to fear him.

I liked to be around Berthe. I found comfort in the way she moved with grace in her plump body. I imagined that her dimpled hands could save us all from the death we could all smell around us.

"Who is he?" I asked Berthe as we were making our way around the church in search of the wounded.

"A Hutu who protested against the Hutu militia movement. Now they're trying to kill him. The first person who wants him dead is Father Wenceslas." We stopped by a man moaning in the corner, holding his abdomen. His hands were covered in blood. He had been visibly cut by a machete. The fresh, pink hole in his flesh oozed out with blood as he writhed on the ground. Berthe glanced at me briefly and nodded goodbye before leaning down to assist the man.

My job that first day on the crew was to walk around, count and locate the dead. In one hour, I counted 52 people. At first, it was their faces that I noticed: the infant still in his mother's arms as she rocked him crying, the little boy who had hemorrhaged from a machete wound next to his little sister, the grandmother who had not survived the absence of water and the strain of seeing her whole family get slaughtered in front of her. It was their faces and the sadness that floated around these bodies that I first noticed, but quickly the humanity of each one vanished leaving only corpses, masses of decaying flesh that needed to be removed from the church walls for the survival of the living.

That night, Jean de Dieu returned to me with a handful of pills in his hands. He seemed softer and kinder than the man I had seen earlier with the others.

"These should carry you for a few days. I will try to find more."

"Thank you," I whispered, as I slipped the pills in my pocket. I understood these were the key to my survival, to my children's protection.

On the seventh day, the church doors opened and I saw the killers again for the first time since the night Fidèle was murdered. They came into the church, a group of them like a pack of wild dogs. Their clothes were stained in blood. I slid inside one of the pews with my children and left Alice sitting nearby on the ground with hers. I thought that if I acted more like a churchgoer than a refugee, I'd have a better chance of surviving.

Everything happened so quickly. I remember seeing Father Wenceslas walking alongside with the militia, talking and smiling seemingly undisturbed by the chaos around him. The men came to the front of the church and began calling out names.

"Alphonse Ngendahimana," they said incessantly. They walked up and down the center of the aisle looking into each pew. "Alphonse Ngendahimana."

I felt safer knowing they were looking for a man. All of the men around me had a look of terror on their faces as they stared at the ground.

"We have killed your wife," one of them said, "and now we will kill you." One of the killers walked by our pew and stopped in front of Alice. I held my breath. I could see her, still crouching on the ground with her children, trying to hide in every way she could. The man stopped and then turned and suddenly his eyes were on me. There is a saying my grandmother used to say: "When you stare at a man's back, you're calling the devil out of his shoes." I'd been staring at him and now his gaze had found mine. I looked down at the ground and waited for the moment to pass. I could still remember his machete dangling by the side of his body. In the front of the church, I heard them again, calling out "Alphonse Ngendahimana." When I looked up again, the killer had continued making his way to the front of the church.

"We will be back for the rest of you. All of you *inyenzi* will die soon. All of you!" And they were gone again.

Later that afternoon, whispers traveled through the church about the death of two women who had been killed in a house nearby. Later, when I made my way to the Caritas office for food, I saw their bodies, thrown out on the street, like old sacks of rice. That night, I heard the howling of wild dogs fighting for the dead of the city, and I knew the killers would return.

Chapter 10 – Francine

Every week, Father Wenceslas walked the length of the pews, his flak jacket tightly secured around his chest, as he selected girls to make his own. When he got to my pew, just inches away from me, he nodded in my direction and one of his men who always walked with him around the church, pulled me from the pew.

"Get in line!" he barked, as I stood in line with a series of other young women and girls. Jean de Dieu who happened to be nearby when this happened went up to Father Wenceslas and began speaking to him in a hushed tone. I could not discern what the men were saying to each other, but I knew that Father Wenceslas was not pleased with what Jean de Dieu was saying. When the two men were done talking, Father Wenceslas barked a new order.

"Let her go!"

And just like that, Father Wenceslas' guard pulled me out of the line and shoved me back into my pew next to my children. I don't know how Jean de Dieu managed to convince Father Wenceslas from sparing me but I knew I would have to pay for this temporary reprieve later.

We spent the morning collectively waiting for fate to turn on its head. Everyone in the church knew the killers were coming back. By noon, the sun was searing and I stepped out into the courtyard to look at the sky. I could begin to smell the stench of the dead women's bodies left to rot on the streets from yesterday's killings. I saw their corpses drying out in the sun, and I thought about my own flesh and my own bones and what fragile vessels we all were.

Alice began to crack on the fatal day of the killers' return to the church. I watched her as she sat with the children in the darkest corner of the church. She was holding Devota and

Sophie in her arms and rocking them back and forth. The children looked like oversized infants in her arms. Alice, like all of us was shrinking every day; we were all getting a little smaller with each moment. I knelt by her side and tried to comfort her but she ignored me. She was whispering a song to her children while rocking them.

"Alice? Listen to me! You can't give up! This is not the time to give up." When I try to think back on that day, all I remember is Alice's kindness when she gave me the bread on the morning I arrived from the streets of Kigali with the children.

Everything happened quickly that morning. I try to remember every detail. Sylvie, Christian and Angélique were sitting in the corner of the church with Alice and her children when I returned from the courtyard. I try to remember Sylvie but every time I try to bring forth her little face, she slips into the darkness of that day. Sylvie was my oldest daughter. She fell in the cracks between her siblings. Older than Mélanie, Angélique, and Christian younger than Michel, she was never noticed. I know this now. I know this in my heart, and no matter how I try, I can never undo the past.

They walked into the church when the sun was still high in the sky. I remember the sound of our collective fear when they walked in. A low hush, a whisper of swallowed terror as we each tried to find strength to face what we already knew. I saw him among them. He was standing there in the middle of a group of men. It was him I noticed first. His eyes. The way he scanned the room like a predator. The way he let his machete dangle at the edge of his fingers. When I saw him in the distance, I quickly closed my eyes and prayed that Yellow Shirt's eyes would not find mine. And in that moment of communion with the Lord, I prayed our lives would be spared.

"Everybody stand!" The oldest among them ordered from the front of the church. Alice remained knotted in her corner holding onto her children. I grabbed hold of my own and whispered to Alice to stand.

"Get up! You must get up Alice!" I tried to grab hold of her hand but she was holding on tightly to Sophie on the ground. Devota looked up. I could see that she wanted to get up; she could sense the danger around her but she did not want to abandon her mother and sister. Hundreds of people around me were pulling themselves off the ground. The old, the sick, the ailing, all were pulled up from the ground of this holy house.

Wenceslas stood among them. He did not speak. He just scanned the breadth of his congregation, admiring his flock. Among the pack of men gathered at the front of the church, I noticed a boy, he couldn't have been older than twelve. He was still a child, but in his eyes, I saw something raw and ancient, something wild and dark gnawing away at him. Just as I watched him, he brandished his machete up in the air triumphantly and smiled. In the hatred in his eyes, I saw pleasure. The oldest pulled out a list from his pocket and began reading names out loud.

"Viateur Ruzindana, Antoine Kabaragasa, Olivier Bazimaziki, José Bikindi, Jean-Aimé Gatabazi, Victor Higaniro, Frédéric Kanzayire, Emmanuel Karugarama, Augustin Gafaranga, Albert Mutaga, Albert Bugingo, Diogene Sekalimbwa"…the list went on and on. No one moved. Not one person stepped forward. But the man with the list continued to read the names out loud as his friends walked around every corner of the church. This roll call was part of the torture the killers had organized for us. They knew that no one would step forward to be killed, but most of them knew the faces of the people they were calling. They knew their faces, they knew their names and they were going to pull them out of the crowd to kill them. This strategy was a way to show the living, the people who would be spared that one day they would be next.

Alice began to shake next to me. I could see her body rattling like an old tooth, getting ready to fall. I wanted to calm her down. I wanted to keep her quiet but I was afraid to move because I did not want to be seen. The militia soldiers liked to travel at random through the church. No corner was spared from being covered by roaming eyes. I knew that they would come our way at some point—it was only a matter of time. If we were to survive, Alice would have to be quiet. The young boy of twelve was harassing a man at the front of the church. He was gesturing with his machete to step out of the pews but the man was arguing with him.

"I am not Olivier Bazimaziki. My name is Jean. My name is Jean."

The boy was getting angry now. I could see that he was getting ready to snap and I closed my eyes and began to pray in silence. Next to me, I heard Alice whimpering in the corner. They had come for a man the day before and now she was convinced that they had come for her instead. In the silence of my prayer, I asked the good Lord to give Alice courage and the strength to be quiet.

While I prayed, the killers had lined up a handful of men they had pulled at random from the crowds at the front of the church. The man who had argued with the militia boy was among them. When I closed my eyes again, they were all taken away to the courtyard.

Our Father who art in heaven, hallowed be thy name... ten shots sounded outside. Alice began to cry. Two men pulled away from a group at the front and made their way in her direction. Michel and Sylvie were hiding behind me. Angélique stood by my side quietly staring off into space. I held her hand as it rested loosely in mine. When I looked up at the men approaching, I saw that one of them was Yellow Shirt. I looked down at the ground. I wondered where Jean de Dieu was. I wanted him to come out magically and save me. I wanted someone to save me.

"What is your name?" I did not know who they were addressing. I could smell them, alcohol and the sharp metallic smell of blood. I looked up and saw his eyes on me for the first time since that night. He briefly glanced at me and looked down at Alice and repeated his question: "What is your name?" Her whimpering had stopped, but the children were now both crying. My children were quiet. I could feel them behind me, pressing their little bodies against mine. I could feel Angélique's hand in mine.

"Marie. My name is Marie Kayiranga."

This seemed to satisfy Yellow Shirt because now his eyes returned to me; he studied my face for a long time. I remembered the way he had torn into me; the way he had shot Fidèle at close range, like a dog.

"And yours? What's yours?" I looked down at the ground because I could not bear his gaze. When I looked up to answer, I knew that he did not recognize me.

"Josée Mukamana." I took the name of my neighbor I'd heard on the radio as one of the dead on the first night we had fled.

Yellow Shirt did not like weakness. He did not like people who loved. He had shot Fidèle when the children had run to him. Remembering this, I let go of Angélique's hand next to mine. Caught in the memory, I let go of her hand and I knew that I had made a mistake. I knew that this simple gesture would break my daughter. This man, Yellow Shirt, the same man who had taken the life of my husband, the same man who'd killed something off in my womb, would then take the last remaining semblance of safety from my daughter that day. I knew in that instant that Angélique had just lost a piece of herself. I felt her standing there next to me, vanishing. I thought of the words of my mother when she told me that there were two things she could always predict. One was the first sign of rain, and the second was the fields that would never yield life again. My mother could always feel when a field was dead; they were like "holes" she said making a circle with her fingers. This is how my daughter Angélique felt that morning standing next to me, like a field that would never produce life ever again.

The killers rattled off a second roll call. They pulled more men out of the crowd at random and tied them to each other by their shirts.

"This will keep them in a straight line," one of the militia announced. The others laughed. The boy with the bloody machete brandished his weapon in the air again.

"Oh yeah? *This* is what I use to keep them in a straight line!" More laughter.

The boy was their mascot; they were proud of him. Wenceslas laughed with the militia but he never spoke a word. He followed them like a hungry dog on a crowded street, and, when they stopped and pulled men out, he simply watched and said nothing. In the crowd, I saw Joseph, the young man from the cleaning crew. I tried to stare at Joseph for as long as I could. I tried to press his face into my memory forever. Someone should remember the dead, I thought. Someone should remember us. And before I had a chance to pray for him, he was taken outside with the others and shot. Today, when I think of Joseph, it isn't his face I remember but his laugh. The way he laughed at Jean de Dieu when he said that whoever didn't finish his assigned work by the end of the day would have to beat him at poker that night to get away from having a heavier workload. I remember his laugh, and I remember his dignity when he was taken away to be killed.

The call lasted until four o'clock that afternoon. We stood in the hot church watching our men get carried outside to be killed. They left as quickly as they came, and when they did, I heard the cries of wailing women released into the afternoon air like songs of the damned.

The men stayed long enough next to us to see that they had won. They did not need to kill us to show us that they were the strong and we were the weak.

When they left, I looked down at Angélique and saw that she was crying in silence. I took her in my arms and held her closely, but her body was stiff.

That night, Jean de Dieu came to me. I saw that something had changed in the way he looked at me. There was something new in his eyes, something fearless and loose, and for a moment, I wondered if he was the same man I had met a few days before.

"Come with me outside. You need to see this." I left the children with Alice and told her I would return shortly. Outside the sun was still hot and fierce and when I looked away from the sky again, I saw them there, piled up like rocks in a quarry. The bodies of 120 boys and men were tossed one on top of the other slowly rotting in the heat. I felt my body curl onto itself; my stomach turned and I leaned forward and vomited bile and saliva.

"We need to bury them. Tonight, I will go to Wenceslas in his office and speak to him about permission to bury the bodies. Something twisted inside of me when he said this. The confidence with which he said: "I will go to Wenceslas." Like they were dogs from the same pack. Jean de Dieu did not notice my eyes on him, the way I was dissecting him.

"Tonight, we will have a meeting at the back of the church and we will talk about burying the bodies." As I listened to his voice, I wondered if the man I had chosen as my protector was not one of the killers.

Chapter 11 – Francine

The mind can be easily tricked into believing what it wants. I wanted Jean de Dieu to be a man of protection and quickly, I forgot the strangeness in his eyes and the camaraderie he seemed to share with Wenceslas.

The first night after the killings, Jean de Dieu and I began to sleep near each other. We said nothing about the killings, nothing about his absence during the roll call. And I tried to forget what I saw in his eyes when he showed me the bodies in the courtyard. We helped each other around the church. He was in charge of the dead, I was in charge of the living. We worked for hours in silence. For two days, Jean de Dieu buried bodies around the church with the help of six men. By nightfall, I would come to meet him in the courtyard before the closing of the doors to see the pile of bodies that still needed to be buried. No matter how hard Jean de Dieu and the men were working, the dead never seemed to diminish.

I almost liked working with Jean de Dieu like this, with his shadow by my side. The children were calmer now that I had a man around to protect us. Alice still sat in the corners of the church, unwilling to move for hours on end. Every night, I'd bring her a little cup full of rice for her and the children, forcing her to hold on.

For days, I was afraid Jean de Dieu would force me to be his "wife," that he would force himself on me. But his presence made me believe the killers would stay away from me now. The only physical contact I shared with Jean de Dieu was his touch when he cleaned out my wound and changed my makeshift bandage using the clothes of the dead boiled in the dispensary. My arm was healing slowly. The deep gouge was closing on itself like a knot in the trunk of a tree.

I didn't see Father Wenceslas for three days, and on the third day, after the killings, he came to the front of the church and led mass. I'd begun hating these moments of worship. I'd close my eyes and pray silently in my head, hoping the dark forces around us could not see me. In his homily, Father Wenceslas told us to "pray that the Lord would forgive the *inyenzi* for bringing so much misery onto themselves."

After mass, I was getting ready to go to the Caritas office when I saw Wenceslas pulling Jean de Dieu aside by the front of the church. The two looked in the direction of the church doors and Wenceslas pointed to the courtyard and the two men shook hands and then they were gone. I wanted to talk to someone, I needed a voice other than madness to reason my way out. I knew that Alice had slipped away into a place darker than my own and with her absence I had lost a friend altogether. Who were my allies? I looked at the children beside me. They were ghosts, silent and still, beings of light that hovered around me in this hell. I needed to find the plump woman Berthe. Suddenly, Sylvie tugged at my sleeve.

"Maman, Maman, Christian is gone." I looked around and saw that my little boy was no longer there. The children had always stayed by my side since we'd arrived in the church. This place was like a city, a crazy market place with confining ramparts forcing all of us to recoil on our own weakening humanity. Where was my boy? I ran outside into the courtyard where the sun was beginning to shift into a trailing afternoon light. The air was cooler now, but the stench of the dead floated around us like a thickening balm. There were people everywhere, some, newly arrived, were being detained right beyond the gates of the church as militia asked for money. I saw Jean de Dieu and Wenceslas standing together. I needed to find my boy before nightfall. This was the single thought that pushed me into motion. I heard their voices. Jean de Dieu did not see me. I slid behind a group of people who were making their way towards the church entrance.

I heard them: "Tomorrow, the journalists and UNAMIR will be there. We cannot, in all good conscience, let these bodies rot in the sun."

Wenceslas threw his head back and began laughing grotesquely like a strange circus clown. Jean de Dieu looked at him, I thought I saw fear in his eyes but then he smiled and he shook Wenceslas' hands.

"So, we have a deal?" Wencelas said holding on to Jean de Dieu's hand as he was about to pull it away.

"Deal." I heard Jean de Dieu respond before he walked away behind the church, leaving Wenceslas alone to admire the breadth of his work in the dozens of bodies left to bury.

I ran away quickly before Wenceslas could see me. I had to find my boy before nightfall, before the closing of the doors. Where could he have gone? The courtyard filled with bodies and people waiting to enter. I knew that I couldn't cross the gate past the courtyard to the street without risking loss of re-entry into the church. Would Christian have left the church walls? What if someone had taken him? Why would anyone take him when there were too many mouths to feed, too many lives to save? A stranger's child had no value to a survivor.

When I began looking, I saw that there were hundreds of children who were my boy's age. Hundreds of boys like my own, roaming the church alone, squatting in corners, sleeping against the back of a relative, huddled in the arms of their mother. But no matter where I looked, I could not find my son.

As I was about to leave the courtyard to re-enter the church, I saw Jean de Dieu making his way from the pile of bodies with a wheelbarrow full of entwined limbs, feet on top of feet, hands knotted around unrecognizable faces, puffy and swollen, purple in places where the flesh had already peeled away from the bone. I watched him wheel these corpses away as others carried more bodies behind the church. I stood watching this strange procession of death, when I heard one man say to another: "They will never find them there. No one will find the bodies in the garage."

When I returned inside the church, I noticed that everything had dimmed already in the dwindling afternoon light. It was then that I began to believe in miracles. I saw them sitting there; Christian and Michel were talking to their sisters. Before I had a chance to hug and kiss him, I found myself grabbing him violently by the arm.

"Where were you?" Christian jumped; his body recoiled as he watched me fearfully. Seeing the fear in his eyes, I released him.

"I thought you were dead." I whispered to myself. "I thought you were dead, like the others." I began to cry wrapping my arms wide around my children. I cried for a long time until I fell asleep. When I woke, the church doors were closed and we were confined again to the darkness of night and the wails of the ailing.

That night, Jean de Dieu did not sleep by my side. The next morning, I saw Berthe sitting at the front of the church with two other people I did not know. Wenceslas pointed to them giving them orders to carry a task. I still wanted to talk to Berthe about my fears with Jean de Dieu.

That afternoon, journalists came as Wenceslas had predicted. They wanted to write about the living conditions in the church. Wenceslas had selected three people to talk to the press to tell them how safe we were now that we were staying in the house of the Lord. Berthe was among the ones selected to fabricate this reality. I heard her talking to them almost in a whisper and for a moment, I wondered if they knew that this woman was lying to save her life. Father Wenceslas was sitting with them the whole time. He nodded and smiled and even placed his hand on Berthe's shoulders as she began to cry. When the journalists asked her why she was crying, I heard Berthe saying: "Sorry. It hasn't been easy. It hasn't been easy since the beginning of the killings." And when she said this,

Wenceslas and the journalist both seemed satisfied with the answer and the interview ended.

I didn't see Jean de Dieu for two days after that. I did not know which I feared most: his absence from our sleeping area at night or the truth I was seeking.

On the third day, Jean de Dieu returned. When I tried to talk to him, he simply remained quiet and stared off in front of him in silence. When night fell, I heard a woman screaming in the distance and then people gasping in response. Someone had just gotten killed in the darkness and fear spread around the church like brush fire. I searched for Jean de Dieu's hand in the dark. When I found it, he pushed me away and recoiled in the other direction.

"What is that sound?" I asked. Outside beyond the church walls, I heard a series of pops that sounded like fireworks on a wedding night.

"Jean de Dieu, what is happening outside of the church?"

He did not answer. More pops resounded outside. Clearly the militia were shooting outside and someone had gotten hit. I held the children close to me. I could feel Angélique besides me, Sylvie, Christian and Michel. I pressed my body against theirs and lay down flat on the ground. I heard one of the children whimpering beneath me as another shot resounded in the darkness.

"Jean de Dieu? Are you there?" I could not feel him nearby. I heard people rising. If people panicked, there would be a stampede. There were no lights in the church at night, and I had learned to make my way in the dark around the mass of sleeping bodies. People began to move and usual reference points vanished. If I moved quickly, I knew that I could reach the church wall to my right within seconds. Hundreds of people were moving. Some were running, others were trying to get up. I knew that if I stayed on the ground, the children and I would be crushed.

"Sylvie and Christian! Hold on to me." I yelled in the midst of the commotion around us. I stood and grabbed hold of Angélique and my youngest boy. I could only hold two children and I'd chosen Angélique and Michel without thinking twice about my choice. Later, I realized I was trying to make up for that day in the church when I let go of Angélique's hand in the face of Yellow Shirt's menace. With the chaos around me and the absence of light, I had no way of knowing whether or not Sylvie and her brother had managed to hold on to me.

"Sylvie are you there? Christian?"

"Yes, maman. Yes maman." I heard their pitiful voices reply among the rumble of voices around us.

"Keep holding on and walk behind me," I told them. The mass of bodies around me pressed its way into us. My plan was to remain as close to the wall of the church as possible so that I could remain away from the panic of the masses. But suddenly as I was pushing my way through the crowd, I realized that I could not feel Christian next to me anymore.

"Christian, are you there? Christian where are you?" I began to scream now. I could barely hear myself screaming among the screams of others and the sound of gunshots outside. The four of us reached the wall.

"Get down on the ground." I said to Angélique, Sylvie and Michel. "I need to find your brother."

I let go of the children's hands and I heard Sylvie crying out: "Maman, don't go! Don't go Maman!"

"Just stay down. I'll be right back." I disappeared into the mass of writhing bodies. I tripped on the limbs of someone lying on the ground. People were trampling the body trying to make their way across.

I heard someone screaming: "Stay away from the church walls, they are shooting at us." I had not thought of the walls being a dangerous place to be. I suddenly felt trapped between the will to find Christian in the crowd and the thought that I had to move my other children from the proximity of the walls. That's when I heard the mad woman in my head again. I hadn't heard her since that night at the checkpoint with the children when she told me that I would lose another child.

Look at you running like a rabbit in a field, she whispered.

I heard the laughter in her voice in the way she said the word *rabbit*.

You are the hunted. And soon, you will need to do the hunting.

I tried to push her voice out of my head as I made my way around the people screaming around me. I heard a man yelling.

"Everyone get down! Get down everybody!" A woman began to wail.

"My baby! My baby! They shot my baby!" I tried to train my eyes to see beyond the shadows. But no matter how hard I tried I could only discern shapes and shadows moving quickly. I was becoming disoriented. I had been turned around several times in the chaos of people pushing their way around me and I was uncertain of the location of the wall. Where had I left my children? I knew that even if I wanted to return to them, I would have to wait for light to return.

Where was Jean de Dieu now? I'd lost him shortly after he'd pushed my hand away from his. Why had he grown so quiet? Where had he been for two nights before this one? These were answers that seemed unimportant in the face of this moment.

You see the way, now. You can see your way through the darkness of the human heart. Soon, you will become one of them. And when the mad woman said this, she laughed.

Once you kill, it is easy to kill again. She continued.

A hand suddenly grabbed hold of mine and pulled me.

"This way." I heard Jean de Dieu's voice in the darkness. I found myself letting go, letting my body be pulled like a magnet slowly peeling away from its union with gravity. Everything I knew was slowly fading away. And as I made my way through the darkness with this stranger, I knew that the path to survival resembled nothing I had ever seen before.

We made our way into a small room. I heard Jean de Dieu fumbling for a key and then a door opened and I saw a faint trail of light inside as we entered. Jean de Dieu quickly closed and locked the door behind us as if we were being chased by a monster. I pressed my back against the door to catch my breath. As I looked around, I saw the room was lit by a candle. I could discern the shapes of people's bodies in the distance. There were dozens of faces all around us. I was afraid to see who was among us in this secret room. Who else had access to safety when the others were getting killed outside? My heart squeezed madly. I needed to leave this room and go to my children. I tried to leave but the door was locked.

"I need to find my children. Let me out! I need to find my children!" I was pounding on the door now. I heard her laughing inside me.

You think you can save your children by running with the devil? And when she said this, I felt a hand taking hold of my shoulder.

"There is nothing you can do for your children, right now. Just sit down and rest for a while." I looked at the hand resting on my shoulder, the strange slender fingers, I'd never seen up close before. I wanted to scream, to let out a scream louder than the screams of the women who were crying for their dead children right outside this room. But when I went to scream, I saw the menace in Father Wenceslas' eyes and I felt the tightening of his fingers on the lines of my shoulders.

I slid along the door's surface and began to cry quietly in the low rumble of a weep I'd learned to master since childhood. I needed to become invisible; if only I could disappear then I could leave this room and be with my children. I cried for as long as my eyes were able to produce tears. And when I stopped, I noticed that the people around me had forgotten I existed. My eyes had grown accustomed to the absence of light and I could see the faces of the men and women sitting on chairs, leaning against the walls as clearly as I would have in daytime. The mad woman had grown quiet inside me now. I think even she didn't know what she was going to find among these walls. I saw Jean de Dieu talking to a man I had never seen before. They were whispering in the corner of the room while others were playing cards or sleeping. The gunshots had stopped outside and people were no longer screaming beyond the door. I thought about asking for a way out again, but I knew that the only way out was from within. If I was to survive, I needed to connect with the people in this room. I recognized some of the faces. What was the common bond between them? What linked us all in our confinement of safety? My heart almost stopped when I saw Berthe slumped over, alone in the corner of the room. Her eyes were open, she did not appear to be sleeping, but her body was still, as if she were trying to make herself as small as I felt. Why was she here?

"Berthe, are you OK?" I said placing my hand on her shoulder. She jumped as if I had startled her.

"Hmm? Yes, yes, I'm fine."

I scanned the room. Were all of these people Hutu? I remembered the lessons I'd learned in childhood about recognizing the races. Hutus were stout and short. Tutsis were tall and slender; but even I had been fooled into not knowing the origins of my own father. Jean de Dieu noticed that I was no longer crying and he came by my side.

"You feel better now?" his voice was calm and confident, unlike his cool and distant way a few hours ago. I looked up and saw that Father Wenceslas was playing cards with the man who had been by his side during the roll call in the church nearly a week ago. I wanted to blurt out *who are these people?* But I knew that strategy was the only way to win this game.

"I feel better. Yes." I answered trying to control my voice.

"Good," he said, placing his hand on my shoulder. I noticed Wenceslas pausing in his game of cards to look at us from a distance. Berthe was looking at me now. I wanted to speak with her but I didn't know who were my allies. We

exchanged glances in the dimly lit room and for a second, I
noticed sadness in her eyes. The room was discernible now. I
could see every single person clearly outlined, as if each person
were held in some deep contrast to the others. The man sitting
a few feet away from Berthe was the man who'd also been
questioned by the journalists. The two men standing next to
the table where Wenceslas was playing cards were among those
who had taken the bodies to the garage behind the church
along with Jean de Dieu. We were all players in this game of
evil. What were the rules?

At dawn, I felt someone shaking me abruptly. When I
opened my eyes, I realized that I had fallen asleep on the floor
where I'd been standing before. Jean de Dieu was kneeling by
my side.

"Francine, wake up! Wake up Francine. It's time to go!" My
heart began to race. I could feel it in my throat as I thought of
the children.

A new current ran through the church: a collective wail rose
from various corners of the holy house that I'd never heard
before. I quickly made my way around the groups sitting and
standing inside and around the pews. I noticed dozens of
people tending to the wounded, mourning the dead. Knowing
that I needed to start with what I knew, I ran back to the wall
where I had left the children. Clustered like frightened dolls,
Angélique, Sylvie and Michel were still in the same place where
I'd left them, holding on to each other.

"Maman!" Michel yelled as he saw me running towards
them. Even Angélique who had been silent for days now
seemed relieved to see me.

"Maman, where were you?" she asked. I could hear an
incriminating tone in my daughter's voice. I looked at my
children and didn't know what to say.

"I was taken somewhere." I heard myself answer. "I could
not return. Have you seen your brother?" The children shook
their heads no. I knew they were hungry and I needed to get

them some food, but first I needed to find my boy. I drew a plan in my head. First, I would have start with the farthest corner of the church and circle my way in a spiral until I'd made my way all the way around back to the center.

At first, I saw nothing. My mind was blank. I could not absorb any of the images I was seeing as I made my way through the devastated church. Slowly, life around me came into focus. Dozens of women were wailing around the church, carrying dead or wounded children. I saw a young boy cradling an old woman in his arms. He struggled under the weight of his grandmother's body as he cried quietly. Everywhere I looked there was a wounded or dead body, some were alone; others were tended to by their relatives. My heart began to sink. I could feel that something was terribly wrong.

"Christian!" I knew screaming was useless. My voice was drowned by the mothers already mourning their own. I recognized none of the faces I saw as I made my way around the spiral of the church. That's when I heard her again.

Go to the heart, and you will find him. I'd never heard the mad woman speak to me as an ally. She had always been an enemy, a buffoon laughing at my misery. But now, she was trying to help me. I ran to the center of the church, only feet away from the place where I had lost Christian the night before. That's when I saw him. I recognized the blue of his shirt, like the blur of a river's waters gorged by the rainy season. I felt my heart stop, for a second, for a minute, for eternity. I saw his hand, curled up on itself, like he was trying to hold on to a treasure in his tiny palm. I moved, I think I moved, but I could not feel my limbs as I made my way to him. Hundreds of people were writhing and walking around us. Everyone was searching for a piece of themselves, a severed piece of their spirit soaring high above us watching our human misery. Christian's body was still. My boy wasn't moving and when I touched him, I felt the coolness of the night still wrapped around him, like an eerie blanket.

"Christian!" I grabbed hold of my boy; I grabbed hold of the stillness in his limbs and rocked him like I'd seen mothers rocking their babies in stillness.

Nothing prepares a mother for the death of her children. Nothing that has ever been written, nothing that has ever been said can carry a woman during that moment.

I carried Christian back to my other children. Somehow, it made sense to bring them all together. We needed to be joined again one last time. Michel ran to me as I carried Christian back and placed him on the ground. In that moment, when Michel understood that he would never hear his brother's voice again, he remained very quiet and very still. The girls did not scream or cry or say a word. They simply stood stoically, like little statues. But when I placed Christian down in the corner of the church, where I had wanted him to be all along, Sylvie burst into tears, letting the damn of her grief finally break. Angélique simply looked at Christian and placed her hand gently on his small body. Christian seemed so small now that he was gone. My heart burst remembering the shock and the fear in his eyes the day before when I shook him and yelled at him about disappearing earlier. Now he was gone for good.

We gathered the bodies out in the courtyard and counted them for burial: 39. I did not want to bury my son in this land of evil, but I prayed that we would bury him quickly, and not let him rot in the sun like the bodies I'd seen only days ago.

In the afternoon, Jean de Dieu appeared again with two of the men I'd seen the night before in our hideaway. I watched him digging and opening up the earth with the bluntness of each blow of the shovel. He said nothing to me when he saw Christian's body among the others. He simply looked at me with the same kind of matter-of-fact simplicity as Wenceslas the night before when he told me I could do nothing for my children. He had been right. In the end, this man of the cloth, this man of darkness had spoken the truth.

By dusk, 23 bodies had found the earth, leaving the others waiting for morning. Among them was my boy, Christian.

Berthe came to find me right at the closing of the doors. I had not seen her since the night before, when she seemed to vanish. Her eyes were as sad as they had been the night before.

"Francine. You must come with me. I have something to show you." Our days in the church had stripped us of the formalities of human interaction. "Hellos and goodbyes" were luxuries of the living, luxuries of humanity that had no place here. I followed Berthe to the northern corner of the church where many of the wounded had been placed for easier care. I wanted to ask her about the night before. I wanted to tell her that I knew she had been a prisoner of privilege, just like me. But I knew that neither of us would say a word, as we were gagged by our shame of having survived.

"They've been calling for you since I found them." Berthe said pointing to Devota and Sophie sitting closely together on the ground. Instantly, I knew what this meant. I knew that Alice was dead.

"Sophie, Devota." I said kneeling by their side. I had no words for them. I had lost language now that Christian was gone. They wrapped their small arms around my neck and held on tightly, as if without my hold, they would drift away into raging waters. I held them in silence. And when I turned around, I saw that Berthe was gone. In one moment, I had lost a child and gained two others. The world was spinning out of orbit. This was all a grand comedy, a joke of sorts and I was its object.

In the morning, we continued the burial of the others. Wenceslas never came to conduct mass, and for this I was grateful. Instead, we conducted makeshift burials with collective prayers that rose above the stench of the bodies. We each prayed for the dead. We prayed for each other and ourselves. We prayed, not for protection, but for dignity, for swift blows, a quick death, a decent burial, and the ability to erase all that we knew.

Two weeks went by without any killings inside the church walls.

On the fifteenth day after burying my son, I woke up with heaviness in my breasts and nausea tugging at my stomach. I thought of Yellow Shirt and his stink. In the darkness of the church, before the doors were opened, I stood quickly to find a place to vomit. Now I understood how easy it was for people to soil the church. I understood how children could relieve themselves in corners, how the sick could bleed anywhere, how pregnant women like myself could vomit in dark corners.

I had been pregnant five times in my life and recognizing the signs of life in my body was something I knew without fail. I could feel the weight of my breasts, the openness of all of my senses, the heaviness in my limbs. That morning, only hours before the opening of the doors, I knew I was carrying life inside of me.

The smell of the church I had previously accepted was now making me sick. Mornings were the worse, the time before the opening of the doors when the air was thick with its rancid smell of sweat and feces, the smell of tears and fear.

**

I met a new arrival named Rose on the fifteenth day. The moment they opened the doors, I saw her. I was struck by her beauty, by the chiseled lines of her cheeks, by the path of her jaw, the almond of her eyes. Beauty was rare among these walls. I knew she was new in the way she scanned the church. Her drawn face riddled with fear and exhaustion. Something in the way she moved made me want to help her. Maybe it was because Alice had gone and I had lost a friend, maybe it was because I saw myself in the way Rose shielded her two young boys, with her arms as she entered the church. I could feel her anguish as she tried to protect her children with her body.

"Do you need food?" I asked her. She nodded in gratitude. I took her to the Caritas office where we stood in line to receive a ration of food.

"I come from St. Paul's church," she said. "The militia raided the church two days ago and killed 60 people in one night."

Without knowing the details, I knew her story by heart. I was well-versed in the sounds of machete against bone. I was an expert in recognizing the reek of fear in the air. I knew about the inclination to abandon hope and the push to protect our remaining children. As we stood in line, I saw that Rose's clothing was torn in places and that she had been spattered with blood. I averted my eyes.

"The Tutsi army, the RPF came to rescue people from being massacred at St. Paul's church. I was hiding outside with a group of others when they came. People inside were so scared they wouldn't trust the RPF who was trying to help them and they never opened the door to safety. I ran with the others when I had the chance and came here."

I wanted to tell Rose that this place wasn't much safer. That I had lost my son. I wanted to tell her that Wenceslas would be the most dangerous one of them all, that her beauty would not serve her here. But I said nothing.

"The army took us to Sainte Famille. They said it would be safer for us here."

Rose seemed to understand my silence and she held her children closer as we made our way through the food line. Killing a survivor's hope, her drive to wake, to feed herself, to pray, is worse than killing her body. I could not find the courage to warn Rose about this place she was calling a sanctuary.

At night, I had dreams of Yellow Shirt, the same man who had taken the life of my husband, the same man whose child I was carrying in my womb. In my dream, he was standing in the half-light of the checkpoint, wearing nothing but a machete in his hands. The blade dangled on the edge of his fingers, casting shadows against the roughness of the cement floor. I was watching him in the corner of the checkpoint. I was alone. The children had been taken away. I knew this, in the weight of their absence. In the way my longing for them took up space at the center of my chest. I was not afraid to see him. I was not afraid to be seen, for I had lost everything and the blood in my body was the only thing left to spill. The shifting light made shadows dance around us. Was it the moon or the half-glow of a lantern? I did not know. I heard the rustling in the distance. Wind, brushing up against the desolate grass on the edge of the city. Red soil rose and flew like magic dust. I could smell him. The stench of his breath, whisky and something coarser, the transformation of flesh against earth, the return of the body to its source. Decay. I could smell him now. His face eaten by shadows, I persisted in my discernment. My eyes slid along the surface of his body, like a hand on the slimy flesh of a tilapia. His skin was flaccid. I knew this because I had touched it. I remembered the touch of my fingers on his flesh. In the dream, I remembered this. The lines forming along the angles of his body where the flesh meets the bone. It was cold and wet around us. I could smell the rains past the stench of his flesh. April rains are violent, and soon the red of the earth would surely rise and we would all be swallowed.

Chapter 12 – Francine

Rose's beauty gave her the dignity and the hope for survival we had all already lost somehow. I'd lost that hope on the day my husband died. I'd lost it on the day Mélanie disappeared in the distance, leaving only a blurred image of her tiny body in my memory. I'd lost it on the night I held Christian's lifeless body in my arms and rocked him in stillness. But Rose believed. And it was her faith that kept me by her side.

I was not the only one who saw Rose's beauty. Everyone could see it, everyone including Father Wenceslas. On the third day after she arrived, Rose and I were dozing with the children in the afternoon when I woke up abruptly sensing danger by our side. I looked up and saw him standing there. His flak jacket tightly securing his heart. He stood at our feet staring at us in silence. I knew what he wanted in the moment he arrived. I knew it in the way he held his body like a predator trying to avoid scaring his prey. I knew it in the way of his silence. I sat up and Rose opened her eyes when she felt me move next to her.

"Hello Father Wenceslas," she said rubbing her eyes. Wenceslas smiled, eerily and walked away again. I imagined his impatience in wanting to collect the prize of Rose's intact innocence.

I felt sick. I did not know if it was the nausea of the pregnancy or the fear, but I just had enough time to lunge forward away from Rose and the children and vomit on the dirty cement floor of the church.

That night, Wenceslas conducted mass. I knew that his need to hide behind the shield of the Lord only meant more trouble was on the way. I scanned the church in search of Jean de Dieu. I wanted to know where he stood during mass; I'd lied to myself believing that knowing his whereabouts would tell me something about his character.

"My brothers and my sisters." Rose sat up out of respect for the holy words spoken. I wanted to warn her, I wanted to tell her about the presence of evil among the walls of this false house of the Lord, but I did not want to kill the faith she still visibly carried within. Also, I secretly knew that I depended on Rose's hope for my own survival.

"Let us pray together my brothers and sisters." Wenceslas closed his eyes. Rose began to pray solemnly with him.

"Let us pray for all of those who died needlessly last night. Let us pray for the souls of the traitors, for the soul of the cockroaches who tried to raid St. Paul's church last night, causing people to die."

Rose looked at me in disbelief. I could see her trying to make sense of what she was hearing. She looked at me with a look of terror. I remained quiet. Rose had been at St. Paul's. She'd seen the militia raid the church, time and time again, the way we'd been raided here. She had hid outside with her children when the RFP Tutsi army tried to rescue people inside the church. The truth had just been rewritten by Wenceslas.

"As you know, many of you will be evacuated from the church by the UN forces UNAMIR. They have told me they will come and gather the men and women of honest worth. *Honest worth*, my brothers and sisters. Who among you can say in all sincerity that you bear that name? I know and many of you know that there are many traitors among us. There are many cockroaches among the living trying to pry away the life force from the rest of us. We cannot let this happen. This is why I ask for your help. I ask that you look not only inside your own heart, but inside the heart of your neighbor to see who among us deserves to live. Who among us deserves to bear the label of *honest worth*. Let us pray my brothers and sisters. Let us pray to find the courage to find the traitors among us."

We sat in silence as people pretended to pray. And in the silence of the church offset by coughs, cries and shifting bodies, I saw that Rose's eyes were filling with tears.

"I ask that you put your name on one of two lists. There is the list of those who would like to go to the Tutsi RPF zone, the zone controlled by *inyenzis*—the cockroaches of this nation. And those of you who are upstanding citizens and are willing to be evacuated to the Hutu military-controlled zone in the west. I have volunteers who will come around and take your names to put it on the list of your choice." When he said *volunteers*, I searched again for any sign that Jean de Dieu might be nearby but saw none.

"Let us pray my brothers and sisters. Let us pray that we can bring out the evil among us and cleanse the walls of this church."

That afternoon, Wenceslas asked people who could write to raise their hands. I hid in the corner with Rose and the children and tried to make myself as invisible as I could. The three men who raised their hands came by and asked everyone in the church which list we wanted to be placed on. I knew this to be a trap. No matter what we did, Wenceslas would select the names he wanted for evacuation and place them on the list of his choice. If we chose the Tutsi-controlled RPF zone, we would pay the price of being openly against the militia. If we chose the government-controlled zone, we would be killed upon arrival. I watched as the men made their way around the church. I pulled Rose by the sleeve.

"Get up!" I told her. "We must get to the back of the church to talk before they get to us."

People nearby heard me and wanted to know what I had to say. A man with his head bandaged looked at me inquiringly. I ignored him and pulled Rose with me and the children to the back of the church.

"This is a trap." I finally said when we found a small open space among the wounded in the back. I knew that if people overheard us here, they would be too weak to do anything about it. "But you have a chance to make it." I said to Rose.

"What do you mean?" I knew this was happening too fast for her and I had no time to soften the blow.

"He wants you, and this will save your life." Rose looked at me incredulously. I could see her brain, her body, and finally her spirit process the information slowly. The poison of my words slowly sank in like lead landing at the bottom of a pristine lake.

"There are rooms nearby where he takes the girls he chooses. If you agree to be one of them, you can survive. Your children can survive."

"But what does this have to do with the list?" The men were making their way towards the back with their pen and paper. We did not have much time left before they'd reach us and we'd have to announce our choice. I only had seconds to explain the strategy of survival to Rose before it was too late.

"Don't you see? If you put your name on the RPF zone list you will be killed by the militia when they come back again. The UN may not arrive for days."

"Yes, but if I get evacuated to the government zone, I will be killed. We would all be killed there."

I looked at Rose, I looked at her eyes, the way they had managed to change in such a short span of time. I scanned her face for a sign of the hope that I'd sough out in her earlier but I could not see it anywhere.

"If you give yourself to him, it doesn't matter where you put your name, you will be saved." Finally the words had sunk in and I watched Rose as we both waited for the news to settle.

"What about you?" she finally asked me when she had made up her mind.

"I have other ways." When I said this, I did not know which one I hoped more: to be right in my assertion or to be wrong and free of my dependency on Jean de Dieu.

A man with a long thin scar on his nose came to us. "Which one will it be?" He asked us, his hand shaking from all of the writing.

"Government." We both answered.

"But you are both Tutsis. No?" the man asked us his hand suspended in the air like a shaking leaf in the wind.

"Government," I repeated with determination. As I watched the man write down all of our names on the government side, I prayed that I had not just given Rose, her children and mine a death sentence. As for me, I had already been condemned.

Chapter 13 – Francine

That night, Rose and I found a place to sleep with our precious offsprings huddled between us. I fell into a strange sleep with my mind alert and my body still. I thought I could hear the night sounds of the church. I thought I knew all that happened around me. But I woke at dawn to find Rose gone and Jean de Dieu in her place. He was sleeping when I opened my eyes. I wanted to scream. I wanted to call out Rose's name in the darkness. But I knew I would scare the children and only draw attention to the place where I knew Rose had gone.

That morning, like clockwork, the doors of the church opened and the militia walked in searching for bodies. Some people had prayed all night for the UN to arrive and save them. I knew that the presence of the killers in the church had saved my life. If the UN had arrived on that morning to carry out everyone's choices, Rose, the children and I would have all been sent to our death in the government zone, as we had requested. Now, I needed to see if my strategy of survival had worked. I had not planned on having Rose be absent when the killers would come.

The air was electric. When the militia came in, a current moved through the thousands of us scattered around the church. Hundreds of whispers and gasps, hundreds of prayers filled the air at once creating a strong unrecognizable sigh. Jean de Dieu took me by the hand and began pulling me away from the children. I could not leave them alone here in the presence of killers. Rose's children were still young, tiny boys of three and four. I thought their innocence and purity could almost make them invisible in the madness of this place, like two lost angels in the middle of a battleground. José was the youngest; his hands were the size of Christian's hands just a couple of years earlier. And when I thought this, I realized that Christian would never grow again. My memory of the size of his hands would remain static, even if I lived to be one hundred.

"Come!" Jean de Dieu said, pulling me again. This time he was waiting for me to respond. Maybe he knew that I would go hysterical if he insisted, and a scene in the presence of the militia, was a death sentence even for a man like Jean de Dieu.

"You'll be safer on the other side," he said.

"What about them?" I pleaded looking at the children again. Angélique was as still as a spring breeze right before the rains. I caught Devota's eyes on me, her incriminating gaze. She was the inquisition, and in that moment of hesitation, I knew that I had just been judged by God's greatest witness. Her eyes were saying everything my conscience felt inside: *Will you leave us to die? Will you leave us to save your own skin?*

I turned to see that Jean de Dieu had gone. Why did he want to save me when there was nothing between us to save? Why had our paths crossed like this? Thierry, the older of Rose's two children began to cry. He did not know that crying could cost him his life. Angélique, Devota, Sophie, Michel and Sylvie all turned to him as if they all understood his tears had no place in this house of madness. Mad woman was in my head again, laughing at the pity of our situation. For the first time, I ignored her and tended to Thierry's tears.

"Don't cry sweetheart. Don't cry. We will all be OK."

"I want my mommy," he whimpered in between tears. And before I had a chance to comfort him, the mad woman said loudly in my head, *so does the priest!* She let out a wild laugh that resonated in my head, louder than the voice of the killers.

"Quiet! Everyone quiet!" One of the militia boys yelled. I tried to think of the way his body was pumping blood in that moment. I tried to think about the push of his muscles against the rage of his voice. In his madness, he was trying to quiet 2,500 terrified souls who were facing death.

"We know that some of you are trying to get away to the RPF. We know you're trying to help the enemy and we will not have this!"

He brandished his gun up in the air and the other militia boys behind him roared. From the outside, this was a strange sight, this handful of young men, on the cusp of manhood, each conjuring madness in a singular way. But no one was watching us from the outside. There were no witnesses to this lunacy.

The boy was wearing a Primus beer T-shirt, tattered and torn in places. Another man moved up to the front to address us, and I noticed how strange it was that he was wearing tall leather boots. Only the Europeans wore *those* boots—Belgian soldiers to be exact. Now, when I think back on the death of the ten Belgian paratroopers who had been killed days earlier, I realize this boy must have been among the killers. In the distance, I thought I saw specks of red on the black of the leather. Here were the hungry boys of Rwanda. They were the empty-belly boys, the sit-on-an-overturned-case-of-beer boys, the spit-in-your-face boys, the end-of-the-rope boys existing without a place to stand. These boys were now the men of our nation, their overturned manhood gone wrong without a place to land. But today, these boys had been given a mission; they had a purpose. Kill *the other* and fill the void.

Wenceslas came out of nowhere, a ghost that suddenly materialized with the conjuring of evil. The boy with the boots began to wave a piece of paper in the air. I hadn't noticed the origins of the paper. Had Wenceslas given it him? I knew that in his hand, this killer held the list that would decide if we lived or died.

"I have a list here," he said waving it in the air. "That tells me there are many traitors among you. This list tells me who among you are the inyenzi we must kill like cockroaches invading a kitchen." The others laughed. I searched among them for the presence of the Primus beer shirt boy, but he was nowhere to be seen. Thierry was quiet now. Sophie, who couldn't have been much older than him was holding him as he looked around the church with eyes as round as saucers. Even the children understood we were waiting for our sentence to be pronounced.

"I will read the names of the people who signed up to go with the RPF. As I read your names, come forward."

I had been right. This had all been a trap and at the heart of the ambush was Wenceslas. He had collected our names and given the lists to the killers. Anyone who had opted for the RPF zone (which was most of the Tutsis) had just been condemned to die. People began to scream, women mostly and the cries of children followed. The speckled-boot killer began reading the names out loud, but the cries of the damned were quickly drowning out his voice. Shots were fired.

"Quiet!" People grew silent instantly. The militia boy continued to read the names out loud. Most names were that of boys and men. A thin line of them began to form on the side as they made their up to the front after being called. I wanted to understand why these boys came forward. Couldn't they hide and pretend they didn't exist? Why were they giving themselves in to this death sentence? Maybe this was the power of naming. From birth, we are named; we are summoned to respond to a calling that connect us to the world. Our name is the thread that holds us together, that keeps us from slipping away into the void of nothingness. So that even now, this call—this need to respond to the thread of identity, to the line that assures us of our existence—is stronger than our fear of death. Even in death, we wanted to be called. We wanted to be pulled out from the mass of the crowd, from the void of nonexistence.

I knew this instant would be with me forever. I knew that it would define me, like the handful of moments that define all of us. We are all called, pronounced by a handful of seconds, minutes in our lives that recur eternally. This is the refrain of the broken song, the only rhythm we know, the only cadence that pushes us to dance to the half tunes life has brought us. This was one of those moments. Waiting to be called or not to be called. Waiting for my remaining children to be saved or killed. I waited for this man whose feet were encased in a dead white man's leather to determine my fate. Watching these boys weighing out their youth in how they could conjure death. This moment would become my name, the sound to which I would always respond, no matter what the circumstance.

The line of boys formed like a curling worm, the solitary kind that eats away entrails in silence and calls out hunger when there is nothing else to consume. I watched to see if I recognized their faces. I wanted to make sure I knew none of them. Maybe if they remained unrecognizable, I wouldn't have to share anything with them. Maybe then I could be spared. I caught myself wishing Jean de Dieu would be called. As absurd as this thought really was, it began to fill me, entrap me like the strange thickness of cement and the way it fills every crack in the earth. I knew the likelihood of Jean de Dieu being called was almost as logical as Wenceslas himself being pulled up from the ranks of priest—of God's assistant—to the denounced criminal that he was. But I wanted to make this happen. I began to pray, a solemn prayer. For the first time since I had set foot in the church, I called for the angel of death himself. *May his wings grace the shoulders of the man with whom I have shared so many nights.* This is what I prayed for, this is what I wished. And for the first time since the killers had walked into the church, this prayer quieted the mad woman inside me.

I sensed movement on my right. I opened my eyes again and saw a man my age pull away from a group and walk up to the front of the church. As this man had been suddenly dislodged from the living, I realized how fear had kept me from the others. I had hardly looked around at the hundreds of others around me until that moment. I looked at the man as he walked up to the front. I caught a glimpse of his hands, the way he held them cupped by his sides, as if he were still expecting to use them for a long, long time. I looked at the way he held his head high, looking ahead as though something still waited for him in the future. I held on to the sight of his back, the speck of his red shirt, the creases of the fabric as he moved away. I needed to hold on to this man, to my recollection of him. I needed to engrave every detail of his face, of his body imprinting in my memory. He reached the front and became part of the line with the others. It became difficult for me to see him. Others were blocking the view. I panicked; I needed to remember every detail around me. I was the witness who would live; I was the one who would now have the burden of carrying the memory of these people across to the other side. The other side of what? I did not know. I began to look around me for the first time.

A group of three people were sitting next to each other; the oldest of the three was a woman with strangeness in her eyes. It took me a while to figure out what was wrong with her, and for a moment I thought that maybe she was blind. Her gaze was blank; she looked in front of her without holding on to anything. Her body was lifeless and yet I knew that she was still alive. She must have been no more than 40, although it was hard to tell from the weariness in her body. Two young men, barely out of boyhood were holding on to her, each with a hand placed on her thigh like they were trying to anchor her to the ground. I needed to carry this woman with me to the grave, to carry her memory with me through however many years I had left on this earth. And when I looked again, I saw that her eyes were dead. She had lost her spirit somewhere in the battle of this city. And now her body was waiting to let go. Her sons knew this; they knew they needed to hold on to her if they did not want her to drift away completely.

A child was whimpering a few feet away, and for a second, I thought that maybe the sound came from one of my own. But when I looked again, I saw that it was coming from a young girl my Mélanie's age. She wasn't crying so much as she was whimpering. A strange low, constant cough-like cry I knew would become this child's permanent refrain, even long after she had silenced it.

In my newly gained awareness, I realized that I had been avoiding the children. I caught myself standing a foot or so away from them. I was not holding them. I was not touching or comforting them. I could suddenly see them. Their singularity: Sylvie with her mass of hair that hadn't been brushed since we'd left the house more than a month earlier; Angélique in her quiet enclosure; Michel in the contrast of his wisdom with his size; Devota and Sophie, whose mother I had known only briefly. And now José and Thierry, too young to fend for themselves, too green to understand that their innocence had been crushed the moment they had entered this church. I couldn't touch them. I couldn't see myself holding them. My hands were cursed. My touch only brought on the rancidness of all that was once living. I had witnessed the rotting of a mango once. I had watched the fruit go from its green and firm state to a pulpous mass that gave off a pungent smell of sweetness and something else that called out the earth. I remember the way my mother had been annoyed by our carelessness. How could we have allowed the fruit to go so quickly? How could we not have been more vigilant in our witnessing of time? Now it was too late. The decay had set in and we had not been there to stop it. My hands knew of decay. My hands spoke of the touch that brought on instant death. If I held these children close, the way I had held Fidèle, Mélanie, and Christian, they would surely die. I needed to keep my distance. Keep my distance and watch the faces of the hundreds of strangers who would die around me. I needed to remember them all from a distance. I was the embalmer; I could preserve anything forever, as long as it was already dead.

Sixty-seven in all. This is how many men they gathered in one serpentine line. Wenceslas had gone shortly after they had all gathered. As simply as they entered the church, the militia walked out, escorting the men out with them. They were encircled carefully surrounded by the militia who made an effort to keep them in line. Was this not a gesture of humanity? These men exerted their energy to keep the prisoners in one line. They exerted their bodies to keep the mass of killings going. At dawn these boys woke with the same pang of hunger as we all did. Their hearts were the same organs of blood, pumping oxygen to their brains, to their limbs. They defecated as we all did. They slept and swallowed, spat and pissed; they sweat and bled. We were all the same animals. And seeing these eight militiamen pushing the men by the tip of their machete into the light of the courtyard, I asked myself, *what made us any different?*

Night fell, and Jean de Dieu returned, like a strange nocturnal creature to his nest. I saw him for the first time that night, when he returned after all 67 men were killed. Why had I never seen the scar on his nose before? A tiny gouge, a nick in the flesh almost at the tip of his nose. The mark was old; it had been made years earlier. Why had I never seen the breadth of his forehead? The way it opened up like a half moon at the top of his head. He had thick eyebrows, bushy and full like his hair. His mustache covered his upper lip, giving it a false notion of thinness, as if he were a man who would be prone to sipping instead of slurping soup. His ears were pushed back on his head, bringing his half-moon forehead to the forefront, giving him an air of inherent intelligence. He had two faint circles under his eyes, and for a moment, I tried to remember if this was new or if he had always looked a little tired. What could this man have exhausted himself doing? Had he buried more dead? Had he held a weapon recently? Had he simply used the power of his mind to select names on a list? I wanted this man to rest, I wanted him to sleep, to stay still and never move again.

"You should have come with me. You could have died by staying here," Jean de Dieu said to me as if he could hear my thoughts. I caught Angélique looking at him. In that moment, he had ensured the children would never trust him. He was a man who could leave them out alone to die.

"Do you understand I could not leave the children alone?" I asked rhetorically.

"I know what you're thinking," he said scratching the top of his head. He was turning his back to the children now. "You think I'm one of them. You think that maybe I am one of the killers." And when he said this, he looked at me with a look of uncertainty, as if even he were unsure of his own identity.

"If I were a killer, if I were even *one of them*, I would not be here. I would be out on the streets. I would be free. I am a Hutu after all."

Was he actually telling me that he was a Hutu or was he alluding to my suspicions? I did not know. I said nothing.

"Tomorrow, the UN will probably come and take people away. But the people who will be taken will not be the people you think. It is not the people from the lists that were formed days ago." I knew all that already. Jean de Dieu was not saying anything I didn't already know. "Your friend Rose will be among them, if she wants to leave."

"And the children?"

"The children will be saved also."

In the silence between us, we both knew that we could not talk about my own salvation since I had turned down Wenceslas early on. In this moment also, I knew that the only reason I was still alive was because Jean de Dieu had bargained with Wenceslas. No woman turned down Wenceslas and lived to tell about it.

The children were hungry. I hadn't fed them since the day before. I hadn't eaten either, but hunger had stopped affecting me even though I was carrying a child inside me.

"Come with me to the Caritas office." I said to Jean de Dieu. I wanted to be alone with him, without the children. I needed to understand who this man was. Why did he try to help me? What did he want?

We made our way past the bodies entwined on the church floor. Outside, the sun was bright, unaware that this place was hell and that nothing or no one in this city deserved a ray of light. But nature was both forgiving and cruel and shedding light on this church was its way of showing us our own vacuity.

"Why are you not married?" I asked Jean de Dieu.

"I was married but she died."

Suddenly I felt myself caught in some kind of storm, a rush of air and I needed to catch up to if I was going to stay in one piece.

"They all died," he added.

"Who?" I asked.

"My children and my wife." And when he said this, he pinched his index finger between his other index and thumb.

"What happened?"

"She was a Tutsi and—"

"You collect them?" This last part just slipped out of me, the way Boy would later slip out of my body.

"Collect what?"

"Dead Tutsi wives."

"You're not dead," he said, this time looking straight at me.

"Right. And I'm not your wife either."

We were in the line for food now. There were fewer of us now. I didn't know if it was because more people had died or if people were simply afraid to leave the church. Whatever the case, the line was thinner. This was a blessing. I had stopped believing or praying for blessings for myself, but I needed them for the children.

When we got almost to the top of the line, Jean de Dieu grabbed me by the arm. "Let me get something straight here. I'm not a killer and I'm not going to waste my time trying to prove it to you. Either you trust me, or you don't. But given your situation, I'd say you don't have much of a choice." His fingers were digging into my flesh. Our faces were only inches from one another. Aside from our bodies laying side by side at night, this was the closest we'd ever been.

"This is where you're wrong." I could have spit, splattering his face as I said this. "We always have a choice. I can choose to get shot, right here, right now if I want. At least I'd know that I died with a clean conscience. Can you say that? Can you say that if you died right now, you'd have a clean conscience?"

"God gave us life to preserve it, and I do what I can to stay alive."

"God gave us life to live it in all good conscience, and sometimes it means dying with dignity." I pulled my arm away and moved to the top of the line where I received food for the children and for myself.

"For your information, she died almost three years ago, visiting her family. We lived in Kigali, but her family was from Bugesera where the killings took place in 1992. Her car was ambushed at night with the children and they were all killed. I have been alone ever since."

I pictured this faceless wife riding with her children in the dark. Like me, she had probably tried to protect her children, but in the end, she had died on some country road, her children slaughtered along side her.

"Who died first?"

"What?" Jean de Dieu did not understand the question. He was a man. How could he understand the importance of what I was asking?

"Did she have to watch her children get killed? Or did she die first?"

Jean de Dieu stopped walking now. We were standing in the courtyard right at the spot where he had buried the bodies over the last few weeks. The earth was still freshly overturned, and for a second I thought he was looking at this. But he was thinking about something he had never considered before. He waited, his head leaning towards the ground like an oversized fruit dangling at the edge of a weakening branch. And when he looked up at me again, I saw sadness in his eyes.

"This, I do not know."

When we returned, Rose was sitting among the children in the church. She did not look at me. At first, I thought that she had not seen me walk up with Jean de Dieu but then I realized that she was avoiding my eyes. I handed the food to the children and then I gave her my rice. She shook her head. I pushed it to her a second time, this time she looked up at me and when she shook her head no again, I saw that shame had forced its way into her body, past the dried-up tears on her face, past the fear of getting killed. Shame had eaten away at every inch of her body. Jean and José were hanging all over her, pressing their tiny bodies against her own. Rose was still, sitting like the trunk of a tree that been recently been severed from its roots.

The next day, the UN trucks came as scheduled. Wenceslas handed the list of names to the UN soldier in charge of calling the names to be saved. Little did they know that the men that had been scheduled to climb into their white truck on that day had been killed two days earlier. The lists had been reshuffled. The names that were read had nothing to do with choice or with luck. Wenceslas had carefully compiled the list himself. There were many girls and women on that list. Girls whose bodies he had savored. This man of the cloth had become an expert at plucking young girls before their time. He knew of the perfect timing of a girl's season, the moment when she would not taint him with her menstrual blood. He knew of the perfect predatory cycle of his touch on young flesh.

Rose was called with the others. Her body shuddered when they called her name and she pulled away from her clinging children, instinctively, like a spring rebounding after being coiled too long. But then she caught herself and realized they had only called her name and not theirs. The confusion lay in many of the children having different last names from their parents. UNAMIR did not seem to understand this and read the names in alphabetical order separating children from their parents. At first, Rose waited hoping that this was the case. They had just read the *B* for Bayingana and she would wait patiently for them to read the *R* – for Rukamba. They read José and Thierry Mukarubibiza. Then, the *R* passed and she was still standing by our side. Jean de Dieu began to stir. He felt responsible somehow.

"Rose, you must get on the truck. This is your only chance." The fragile trust Jean de Dieu and I had managed to create since he had told me about his wife and children in the courtyard suddenly vanished in this moment. How could he suggest she get on the truck without her children? This was a recurring theme. Seeing my consternation, Jean de Dieu added.

"The children can join you later. They can stay with us and we'll make sure they get to you safely." This was a lie. How could we ensure their safety when we could barely ensure our own? Rose did not move. Wenceslas was standing at the front of the line waiting for UNAMIR to finish reading the names. They never paused or waited for people to come, when a person did not come, they simply added one more person at the end from a secondary list. If Rose did not hurry, she would lose her place.

"Take the children. I am going to get you on the truck with them."

Jean de Dieu grabbed hold of Rose as she pulled her sons with her to the front of the line. I watched as Jean de Dieu pushed people out of the way to make his way with Rose and the children to where Wenceslas was standing. UNAMIR continued to read the names while Jean de Dieu began to argue with Wenceslas. I could see him gesticulating and pointing to the children and the line and then to the list in the UN personnel's hand. Wenceslas was shaking his head. I knew, I had learned in the past few weeks that appealing to Wenceslas' emotions or logic was a pointless endeavor. Appealing to his pride was the only way. As if Jean de Dieu heard me, he began addressing the UNAMIR soldier who had finished reading the names on the list. Jean de Dieu had just shifted the axis of power from Wenceslas to UNAMIR, keeping Wenceslas out of the loop. The priest could not stand being left out of the equation. As if the idea had been his own, Wenceslas grabbed hold of Rose's children and placed them in the line himself. Rose followed closely behind while the UN nodded and called out the end of the evacuation.

"That's it for today!" He called raising his hand in the same way the killers had brandished their machetes in the same spot days earlier. One convoy of death, one convoy of life. It all depended on the day.

I watched as Rose climbed onto the truck with her children in tow. I wanted to see her face one more time. I wanted to be able to hold her with my gaze, to tell her that she was getting out for all of us. But she never looked back. Now I know that Rose had lost the ability to look into another human being's eyes on the day Wenceslas had called her to his chambers.

Everything changed on that day. Jean de Dieu and I and the children were left alone in our reclusive existence. We lived inside a cocoon of our own making, along with thousands of people who lived and breathed beside us. But we were alone. We existed alone inside a pallid shell that had been cracked so often it was a miracle it still existed at all. But miracles were not a part of this world. And we knew that the only thing that could save us from everything else was time itself. We would never be chosen for evacuation. Wenceslas needed Jean de Dieu to help him bridge the cockroaches that we were with those in power. He needed Jean de Dieu and he knew that he could not touch me as a result. We dangled, he and I. We dangled on the edge of our sheltered world. Our privilege contaminated us and kept us from the others. These all-seeing eyes I had gained when the last group of men were called for execution had suddenly vanished. I had climbed into the darkness of my own severed existence. The children knew that I was drifting and this knowledge made them needier, more desirous to hold on. At night, they held on to me tightly. Five sets of hands pulling at me in the darkness, pulling me to the center of the earth. The children kept me grounded against my will.

The other child was still growing in my body. I had not yet told Jean de Dieu. I would not tell him. Nor would I tell the children. This is what I did. I existed in the silence of this gestation until my body would betray me and silence would no longer be my ally.

One more evacuation took place two days after Rose and the children left and then nothing. I had stopped waiting for something to happen long ago. For days, Jean de Dieu was busy working with Wenceslas, keeping the place as orderly as possible. I had begun understanding Jean de Dieu. He was riding the fence between the world of the powerful and that of the oppressed because staying on the other side of the weak meant vanishing in fear. I wanted my children to live. And on days when I could manage to imagine us outside of these walls, I even wished life for the baby growing inside me.

On July 4th, three weeks after the last evacuation, the RPF came to the church and took us to the refugee camp of Kabuga.

"It's over," the RPF soldiers said. "It's all over."

I don't remember marching out of the church with a sense of freedom and relief. In fact, I don't remember walking out of the church at all. But I do remember Wenceslas' eyes when he realized that his sense of control had just ended. He looked at me on that morning, right after the RPF arrived and I saw the hatred in his eyes, the hatred he felt for everything he had not been able to destroy.

Chapter 14 – Francine

We stayed in the camp of Kabuga long enough to know that our misery had not ended with our departure from the church. Memory is not a faithful servant. I only remember patches of light and long drawn out waves of darkness. The ride to Kabuga from Kigali was endless. The children cried incessantly early on, in the trip and then later, when hours turned into more than a day, their cries stopped. I must have slept most of the ride because I am only left with the shards, sound bites, and blurred-out images on the way there. Night fell, and when I opened my eyes the truck was rocking back and forth. Sylvie's head rested against my stiff body; she was sleeping. It was still raining outside. I remember the sound of the rain on the large oversized leaves of the banana plantations. I heard the sound of a woman crying and men laughing. Or was it in my dreams? Jean de Dieu pressed his body against mine on the other side of Sylvie and Michel. Angélique, who was in need of containment, slept between us. Devota slept by our feet. We were all heaving, together in the storm of the country's madness. Our bodies rocked and plunged into the abyss of potholes along with the rest of our cargo. Inside me, Boy was already growing. I carried the enemy inside my body.

We arrived in Kabuga at night. It was a small town, a peapod of a village really in comparison to the capital to Kigali. But its size had been replaced with oversized chaos—a dose of madness so large, the tiny town was quickly swallowed by a wave of doom, giving it an air of grandiosity. Kabuga was not really a camp but a monster of a village with humanity turned on its head, a looting ground where we were called to continue fending for ourselves as we had inside the church. Hundreds and thousands of wounded lay everywhere. Some people were fortunate to stay with locals while others slept outside.

God has a funny way of making his power known. The house where we slept was nothing like the houses in Kigali. There were four walls with *terre battue* or bare dirt as the floor, without electricity or water. I remember wanting to wash, wanting to rid myself of the stench of the church. I remember hunger and the children's eyes on me. Their neediness, their desire to be saved. They demanded I save them when I couldn't even save myself.

I remember the eyes of Marie Josée, the woman of the house. Marie Josée and her eyes on me like a stigmata on a sinner. She had lost her husband but lived with all of her children. Six in all. The oldest of the boys Sylvain, who was 18, limped around carrying water, sweeping the house, cutting wood for the fire. Marie Josée's children were older than mine.

"How far along are you?" Marie Josée said to me placing her hand on the mound of my hidden belly. Even though she was beyond her childrearing years, Marie Josée was the first one to know about the child growing inside me.

"There is nothing more sacred than the gift of life," she added.

"I think I am four months along," I told her averting my eyes.

I was relieved Marie Josée had freed me from having to tell Jean de Dieu directly about the child growing inside me.

"You are pregnant?" Jean de Dieu shot a glance of surprise in my direction.

I wanted to tell Marie Josée about the provenance of the child. I wanted her to know that she should not be kind to the child, that she should not regard it as a creature of God. But her comment about the sacredness of all life told me this would be futile. Marie Josée was obviously a pious woman who believed that God had a plan in everything he did, even if it was murdering a woman's husband along with two of her children.

Like us, Kabuga was a powder keg waiting to explode. The RPF controlled the town, but at night, militia would make their way inside and terrify us. There were so many wounded, we had to lay bodies on the ground at the center of town under a large tent to rest. Later, after they died, we simply carried them a few feet and buried them almost in the spot where they had fallen. There was not enough food to feed all of us and Jean de Dieu would sometimes go roaming in the village and dig for potatoes. When he was lucky, he would come back with enough for each of us to have a bite or two.

Marie Josée was making chai as we sat on empty overturned cases of beer.

"Drunk militia boys drove their trucks into the camp last night," Marie Josée told us, her eyes gleaming with tears.

A convoy carrying militia had driven into the town while people were sleeping.

"Is that what all that noise was about?" I asked.

"Yes, they ran down tents and drove over the bodies of sick men, women and children who were sleeping inside."

"How many dead?" I asked, unable to conjure any emotion.

"Two dozen people, maybe more."

"That's a bold move for these militia boys to drive their truck right into an RPF territory" I added.

"Those boys have lost their fear of death. Death is only a veil to them. It isn't real. Death is just the canvas of magicians."

I wasn't sure what Marie Josée meant by *the canvas of magicians* but I knew enough to understand that these boys who had killed the wounded in their tents last night were as dead inside as I felt.

"Didn't the RPF fight back?" I asked.

"They shot at the trucks, but the bullets only grazed them. This was a joy ride for them. Something to distract their minds from the void."

I looked at the face of the man I had chosen as my companion. I wanted a sign that we were all absolved of the sins of sharing kinship with the killers. We were all human and I wished it were otherwise. But Jean de Dieu sat still. A remarkable stillness that had inhabited us both since we'd arrived in Kabuga. We'd found nothing but the emptiness of our fragile shelled cocoon since leaving the church. Jean de Dieu and I existed together in this place we'd made our own. The children were outside of it, outside of our veiled world. How can I explain my own connection to Jean de Dieu in this quiet place of exclusion? How do I draw upon the silence and find words to describe our own dreamlike state?

Jean de Dieu sat in Marie Josée's kitchen and said nothing. I watched her tiny frame sitting on the only wooden chair in the kitchen, next to the fire where Sylvain had placed wood for tea. She was no typical Tutsi. Where was the tall frame of her ancestors? Where were her long and slender limbs? In her lineage, the ancestors had forgotten to give her the mark that would make her recognizable to our clan beyond any doubt.

"We Tutsis need to find a way to get revenge. We need to find a way to rid the earth of all Hutus." Marie Josée's words opened a gateway inside of my own dormant rage. Jean de Dieu shifted in his chair. I sat in the stillness I now knew so well. Something broke loose inside me and I found myself on automatic pilot as I listened to Marie Josée's words speaking a sentiment I'd carried inside me since the killing had begun.

"If I had a blade in my hand, I would slice open the throat of every Hutu I found." Marie Josée added taking a sip of her tea.

"Every Hutu?" I asked her. "Even if he were sitting here with you at this table?" I let the words slip out of me like I had just tossed a lit torch at my own house. Marie Josée stood up abruptly and took a step back as if she had been scalded by the embers of a fire.

"Are you saying there is a Hutu sitting here at my table?"

Jean de Dieu shifted nervously in his chair, shooting me a glance of panic. I'd never seen this man I'd spent so many weeks observing, express so much fear in the face of uncertainty.

"Francine, what are you doing?" Jean de Dieu asked after having regained his composure.

"Well, isn't that what I saw this morning in the leather pouch containing our passports?" I felt myself bolstered by the presence of Marie Josée. As if her words of hatred for the Hutu had suddenly breathed life and words into my desire to confront Jean de Dieu about what I had suspected since the day I had met him.

"Francine, you don't understand what you saw," Jean de Dieu said as calmly as if he were greeting me good morning.

"What is going on here? Are you a Hutu? If you're a Hutu, you have to leave my home at once!" Marie Josée was screaming in the direction of Jean de Dieu who was still sitting on the empty overturned case of beer. Things were unraveling so fast. I wanted to be able to confront Jean de Dieu before Marie Josée's rage took over completely.

"I know what I saw. How many different ways are there to understand the four-letter word HUTU written on your ID card?" I blasted Jean de Dieu.

"Get out of my house!" Marie Josée screamed lunging across the table to grab hold of Jean de Dieu with her bare hands. She knocked over my cup of chai, barely missing him by a hair. Instead, the hot liquid scalded me, landing on my thigh. I felt no pain as I thought of the memory of the softness of the worn leather pouch containing Jean de Dieu's ID card. It was strange to think how worn and soft leather becomes after years of contact with the human hand. Alerted by the screams of his mother, Sylvain came marching in holding a pistol in hand.

"He is an impostor." Marie Josée screamed again. "There is a Hutu in our house!" She pointed her index at Jean de Dieu like the stereotype of an accusing fury. This reminded me of the stories I'd read regarding World War II in Europe, when people pointed to the Jews as they marched to their death.

Everything loosened inside me; I could feel a letting go, a severance, a watershed. It was like knowing what I had always feared made everything around me finally lighter. Knowledge is power. I felt free.

Sylvain brandished his gun in our direction. The memory of the moment when Fidèle had been shot in front of me and the children suddenly engulfed me.

"Please don't shoot him," I yelled. He is the father of my children." I heard myself crying and remembered Fidèle was dead and this man next to me had never fathered a single one of my babies.

"She told you to get out," Sylvain said gesturing towards the exit pointing his gun in Jean de Dieu's direction. We scrambled to gather the children and our belongings before landing outside in the heart of Kabuga just in time for nightfall.

We never spoke about his identity or mine again. We never said the words *Hutu* or *Tutsi,* the words that saved or killed people. That night we slept outside on the moist earth after the rains and waited for the sun to rise.

The next morning, we made our way to a refugee camp in Goma near the border in the Congo. Travel was dangerous and the roadside trenches were the graves of most travelers, but we we'd heard that some people, especially mixed Hutu/Tutsi couples were sometimes selected to go abroad. We traveled to the camp without too much trouble. The night we arrived, it rained. I took turns carrying Sylvie then Michel until they became too heavy. Sylvie and the others all cried, except for

Angélique whose little face full of dirt remained stoic. The children were all so very hungry.

When we reached the border with Congo, a woman walking with a cane who couldn't have been older than thirty stopped us. "Those camps are worse than Kigali where the killers were running free." I never forgot her words and when we arrived I knew that she was right.

They say a woman's emotions are not her own when she carries life inside her. The camp is where the crying began. I would cry all night and when the light would rise outside I was still crying. I'd move around the camp and go about my day forgetting the tears in my eyes trailing alonside my cheeks. Jean de Dieu would lie very still next to me and wait for the crying to stop. There was the time when he put his hand on my head and I screamed out and pushed him away or the time when Angélique must have touched me by accident and I pushed her away so hard that she fell. She didn't cry, but she looked scared; like she knew there was a demon inside me. When she touched me I heard my own cries and wondered who it was. There were also the moments when the children's voices brought me back to myself with the fear in their eyes and their need for love. These were the moments when I would hold them and rock them as I had when they were babies. I didn't know my children much anymore. A mother's touch brings back memories of the others. Sometimes I felt bad for being a mother to the living, when all I wanted was to hold the dead. There were days when I was angry that they were here and the others were not. And other days still—and I don't like to think this—when I even resented my remaining children for being alive. I often wished I'd died that day. But dying was not as easy as I thought. The Lord had given me another chance and He asked me to care for my children. He had even asked me to care for the baby inside me.

The first night at the camp, I didn't sleep. I could hear the others sleeping. I could see their shadows at night, their bodies on the ground and it made me think of nights in the church. Ghosts come out at night and that first night at the camp was a night for revenants to visit. Sometimes I think spirits are laughing and saying, *look at her now, all alone with that Hutu, those sickly children and this baby growing inside her.* I think that human suffering is laughable when you watch it from heaven.

The camp was full of killers. A woman like myself, especially a Tutsi was just waiting to be slaughtered. People were sometimes killed in their sleep; I knew that I needed to become Jean de Dieu's wife if I was to survive. On our tenth day in the camp, Jean de Dieu placed his hand on my belly and said: "It is time for us to be married."

The next day, we gathered the children and washed each one in preparation of the ceremony. I washed my hair and made my body clean. I could not be cleansed of my sins but the cleansing of my body made me feel closer to God. Jeau de Dieu called Father Juvénal, the priest of the camp to carry out the ceremony. We stood in the open field of the camp near the white barrack tents used for intake. The children stood around awkwardly looking in our direction, waiting for the ceremony to start. People milled about, some gathered to watch our wedding, even though they were strangers. While others carried on and went about their business around us, as if this occurrence was the most banal thing in the world. Father Juvénal opened an old worn bible and read Matthew 19:4-6 solemnly to us:

"At the beginning the Creator 'made them male and female,' and said, 'For this reason a man will leave his father and mother and be united to his wife, and the two will become one flesh. So they are no longer two, but one. What therefore God has joined together, let man not separate."

I thought of my marriage to Fidèle. I remembered the day when we had been married at Saint Paul's church where Rose had escaped death with her children. How could God unite a man and a woman, as he had done for me and Fidèle, only to have him taken away from us? Was there really such a thing as a *sacred* union? I knew that this marriage meant nothing more than a ticket for me to have better protection in this new camp where we lived. Father Juvénal's words floated flatly around the hustle and bustle of the camp around us.

"We are gathered here today to honor the union of this man Jean de Dieu Lucien Nkunda and Francine Marie Fernande Shingiro. Dear Lord, we ask that you bless the union of Jean de Dieu and Francine, as they are children of your flock, dear Lord. We ask that you forgive their sins and wash their hands of the crimes they may have committed in your name dear Lord. We ask that you watch upon this couple Lord and their children from another union, as you will watch over their unborn children born under this union. We thank you dear Lord for your mercy and for your forgiveness. Amen."

Wash their hands of the crimes they may have committed in your name dear Lord. Those were the words Father Juvénal had spoken to us. Did he know something I didn't?

When the ceremony was done, Jean de Dieu embraced me, placing his lips on mine. I realized this was the first time I had ever kissed this man who had just become my husband.

That night, we spent our first night together as man and wife. It was easy at first to be Jean de Dieu's wife. Boy was getting ready to be born and he knew that I couldn't give him anything with my body. And he asked for nothing. I didn't talk about Boy. Never mentioned him. But he was excited at first, I think. I remember after that first night together, he put his hand on my belly. "I hope it is a boy."

I hoped for the same. Boys don't get raped.

I thought about telling him that I had no desire for him, that sharing my flesh with him would only come out of desperation, out of a way out of wanting for myself and my remaining children. But I said nothing.

The past came to haunt me when the voices came. They came mostly at night when I would scream and wake everyone around us. But I was not the only one overcome with ghosts in the dark. The camp became alive when the sun set. Many of us made sounds we couldn't control. In the bunks near us, I heard the same woman screaming the same phrase in her sleep, over and over again: *"Pas ici, pas ici."* Not here, not here, like she was trying to shoo away some beast. Keep it at bay.

When I began crying out that night, I knew that the others would not say a thing. They knew my voice, as I knew theirs. But Jean de Dieu was not ready for this. He sat up on the cot and shook me violently.

"Wake up, Francine! Wake up!" The touch of his hands on my shoulders and his shaking of my body would cause me to scream even louder. I couldn't remember who he was or where I was and I thought he had come to get me and the baby. I looked for the baby everywhere. I looked for my Mélanie, but she was gone.

I remembered this was all a dream and the others were gone.

At first Jean de Dieu was kind. He was kind that first night. "It's OK. It's OK," he whispered in my ear, as he tried to hold me but I pushed him away. When the voices came, I didn't like to be touched by anyone, especially not by the hands of a man; even if he was my husband now. At first Jean de Dieu didn't seem to mind me pushing him away.

"Are you OK?" He would ask sweetly.

"Yes," I would tell him so he would leave me alone. I lied and we returned to darkness. I didn't sleep, but I waited until I could hear his breathing changing next to me. And I felt quiet again. I tried talking to the ghosts. I tried to reason with them. But I think they were angry at me for trying to start a new life with a new husband. After the marriage, they came to visit me more often until the day Boy came. One day, the baby just came.

The rains came before Boy came out. Full heavy rains with big drops. I listened to drops whipping the earth. Dust pushed into itself and grew quiet. I closed my eyes and smelled the earth. Sweet and strong like manioc. The air smelled like rain, heavy like the clouds were going to open. And I was crouching in the hills with the boy readying to come. I call him "Boy," but the women in the camp named him: Innocent Philippe Xavier. Innocent to remind me that he is a child of God. I was in the back of the camp, all the way on the other side from our living quarters where we keep the wood and carry the water. That's when the pain came. Cut me up, like metal. Like the machete, only it was inside me now.

"Don't carry that, it's not good for the baby," The women in the camp would say each time they saw me doing heavy labor. But I had stopped thinking a baby was growing inside me long before he was born. And when he came, I called no one. No one came to me. It was getting dark around me; I crouched in the bend in the road where it curves like a woman's breast. I smelled the rain before it came. Pungent and the smell of my own blood. Like metal, woman's blood and Boy's blood too.

Boy just slipped out of me like a tilapia when he was born. He came out of me in silence and then he cried. His voice scared me. Reminded me he was a child and not the devil I thought I'd been carrying all this time. But when I saw him, I knew he wasn't evil. He was just a baby. He came quickly. He was my sixth child; I knew how to bring them out. But with him, it was different. God brought him out on account of him being different.

Boy's head was small and round. I held him in my arms and smelled the earth on him, and, long after I'd washed him, I still smelled blood on him. I felt no pain after the birth. Not like the others. The empty feeling took the pain away, now that my belly was empty. When I held Boy, his body was small and narrow. Not like my other children. Not like my ancestors. I wanted to bring him to the place where we relieve ourselves and drop him in the hole. But I made a deal with God. Never break a deal with God. The fate is worse than death. I didn't look at him when he was born. I washed him but didn't see him. I fed him but didn't see him. I held him and felt how small he was. Small and round like a ball and I knew he came from the outside.

I didn't want to hold him. He reminded me of Mélanie's tiny body in my arms, my last baby before Boy. I just wanted to be alone. I couldn't stand the sound of his baby voice screeching all the time, asking me for something I didn't want to give.

Jean de Dieu was happy about him being a boy. "I knew it would be a boy," he said when he was born and took him in his arms, like he was the proud father.

Jean de Dieu began loving the boy. I try to remember this now, and it seems like a lifetime ago. But in the beginning, Jean de Dieu began loving the boy. He would wake me up at night when the child would cry and he would tap me. The child's cries themselves rarely woke me but Jean de Dieu would gently nudge me and I would slip the child onto my chest and let him suckle me. If I lay there and closed my eyes I could almost imagine it was the little one. I could almost imagine that she was still with me and that I was feeding her. This fantasy sometimes brought me joy.

Jean de Dieu looked out for the child. I carried him on my back during the day and then, in the afternoons, Jean de Dieu would walk around with Boy in his arms and carry him proudly. I liked the relief of being left without the child. I could get more work done around the camp and care for Angélique, Sophie, Devota, and Michel while Sylvie helped me around the camp.

When Boy would cry for food, Jean de Dieu would bring him back to me. He would bring back the crying hungry child to me so that I could feed him. I could see the bond forming between them, like a chain forming quietly without my noticing it. Even the child found comfort in his eyes; it was like he was beginning to know Jean de Dieu. He was beginning to know his touch. And when he cried and Jean de Dieu carried him, he would often grow quiet. The bond between them began to confuse me. I would look at them, the two of them when Jean de Dieu was not looking and I would begin to see the resemblance between them. I could see Jean de Dieu in the boy's face. Or the boy's face in Jean de Dieu and the fear came out of nowhere.

After Boy was born, the ghosts came to see me during the day as well. It was as if they knew that things were changing around me and they were becoming uneasy.

One day, as we were standing outside while the children were inside, Jean de Dieu announced: "Soon, we will have children of our own," he smiled again. That same smile he had on his face when I first met him in the church.

I thought of his hands on my body. I thought of hands and feet and limbs everywhere and the voices in the church. I thought of the smell of their bodies. Their breaths against mine. And the darkness. I thought of the cold of their blood on me. And the way they made their way inside me. I began feeling the nausea again. The way it had come to me on the day I was raped. That's when the words slipped out of me. The words slipped out like pebbles falling out of my pocket.

"They raped me and the child grew inside me." He was silent, and for a moment I didn't know if he had heard me the first time. I didn't look at him when I said this. I didn't look at him at all. I heard voices again all around, and I asked myself if they were voices from the present or voices from the past. Boy began to cry. He cried this fierce little cry that sometimes turned his cheeks darker; and it seemed he knew we were talking about him. The silence scared me more than anything, so I turned to look at Jean de Dieu, but he wasn't looking at me, but at Boy. Jean de Dieu was looking at the baby and for a second I got scared he would hurt him.

I picked up the child in my arms and I gave him my breast. I let him feed to quiet him, to make the place grow silent again so I could try to find my way around this. I tried to find the words: "It happened at a checkpoint in Kigali." Once I'd started the story, I couldn't stop and I didn't care if he was listening to me or not. I didn't care, but I couldn't stop the words that were just coming out of me like puss, like an infection, like a disease, a monster that had been unleashed.

"One of them was young; I tried not to look at him. He was holding a bottle of Primus beer in his hands. And he was drinking it. He was drinking it and laughing. This strange laugh, excited laugh like he couldn't control it. Like he was caught in a fit of laughter. The other two were older. Maybe 20. One of them punched him in the arm.

"Shut up. Just shut up. You're going to ruin this," he said. *Ruin this.*

In one instant, my memories flooded back and I was on the ground; one of them standing over me. He kicked me in the side. A pile of bones. Something snapped, this little sound of branches snapping inside me. I felt a sharp pain in my ribs. I knew that he had broken my bones. I said nothing. I just lay there. They tore off my clothes. They tore off my clothes and the young one was laughing again. He was done drinking his beer, and he pushed the older one out of the way.

"Let me stick this inside her, he said holding the bottle up. It was broken. I would die in that place with these men while my children were alone. I thought about the children and I closed my eyes. *Dear God, who art in heaven.* I heard God laughing at me. I thought of the others he had allowed to die. I wanted to scream. How could I think that God would save me when he didn't save the others? What made me so special?

"I'm first." One of them said. He tore his body into mine. Nothingness engulfed me. I felt so much pain, I felt nothing. I kept my eyes closed. He was quiet. When he was done, he got off me. I knew the young one was going to be next. He was just a boy; something of an animal in him too. He landed on me, and spit on me. He punched me in the face. I opened my eyes, involuntarily. I wanted to die. *God, don't save me, let me go fast.* God was not with me that day.

"When I am done with you, I am going to take you to the mass grave with the others and I will kill you. I will cut you up," the boy said as he ripped into me.

With each word, he pressed harder and faster, grunting like an animal. I tried to see the others but I couldn't. I didn't know if they were there. I closed my eyes. Then he was done.

He kicked me in the face. My mouth bled. He took the broken Primus beer bottle and brought it close to my face lashing me with it. I heard myself screaming.

One of them kicked him out of the way.

"This one is not going to make it," he said seeing all of the blood I had lost. His eyes filled with disgust as if he'd come upon a slaughtered animal rotting in the sun. I heard the sound of cars, an engine, and then footsteps. The men were gone.

I stayed there for a minute and didn't move. I thought about running. I thought about trying to escape, but I didn't want to move. I remembered the children all alone at the barrack in the checkpoint, and I knew that my reason to live had only to do with wanting to save my children. I needed to save them. I pulled myself off the ground and made my way back to the barrack. The men were gone.

Jean de Dieu was looking at me. His eyes bore into me. I tried hard to remind myself where I was, who he was and why he was looking at me. Boy had stopped crying. Jean de Dieu said nothing that day. He said nothing the next day. But he never touched Boy again. Never held him in his arms, never looked at him again.

Everything changed with Jean de Dieu after I told him where Boy came from. It was like he was a different man looking at me with new eyes. I don't know when the fear really began. Maybe that's when I began being afraid of him. I feared his hands at night, on my body. Everything blurred in my mind, the way it always does at night. It was hard to remember whose hands I feared the most.

Safety was not something we could conjure. It did not have walls, doors, or even locks. Safety was not an armed RPF soldier who could guard us at night. Safety was not silence in a time of killing. Safety was something we had created for ourselves, a made-up world of kid's imaginings. A world of paper castles and matchstick figures who could walk away, unscathed, from the wreckage of our country. I brought Jean de Dieu with me into my made-up world of the safety I thought he would offer me. He had no knowledge of his presence in my paper mâché cell. He knew nothing of the mutability of the walls in which I placed us all, me at the center and him holding the children in his arms. How could he have known that I had created everything in my mind that held us together? How could he have stopped my imaginings? In this place of perfect stillness, there was no desire. I wanted nothing to do with his body or mine. Limbs remained untouched, body parts unshared. Mucous and semen, saliva and sweat remained unshared in this world where I existed with Jean de Dieu. Sometimes the child pulled me out of this reverie, tugging at my nipple, demanding the viscous quality of my milk. He would pull me tightly out of my dream, drawing on the demands of the body, his and mine. My breasts would produce milk at the sound of his cries, or the sound of the dogs barking outside. Each minute sound, their pitch tugged wildly at my organs. Jean de Dieu's desire also pounded on the roof of my world each night with a violence that woke me. He would come to me at night, pushing his body against mine. I tried telling him about the pain in my belly but he shrugged. He just shrugged leaving me contained in the world of my own making. In the morning we both liked to pretend that nothing had happened. We both had different reasons. Male pride drove his pretense while mine was held by my fragile balance in the shell of my life.

In the days that followed Jean de Dieu's first attempts at claiming his rights as my husband, he began telling me about his rounds in the camp at night.

"I like the camp at night," he said to me when we sat down to drink some tea and have some rice. "I like it because I can hear the people's true voices, their cries. I can see their real faces. No one's pretending at night. Night is when all the demons come out."

I was looking at his face when he said *demons* and I realized in that moment that my fear of Jean de Dieu had nothing to do with his origins or mine. My fear was held by the push of the frailty of our lives, mine and the children's, Jean de Dieu's and the killers', each of us facing the crimes of our own humanity.

Part III

Chapter 15 – Francine

Syracuse, New York, 1998

Francine spent so much time thinking about the way God decided who would live and who would die. She thought about the countless people in her own life who had been chosen to die. Only God decided. Francine tried not to think about the others, the ones that had transitioned unjustly. Was there such a thing as *justice?* Francine did not know. She closed her eyes and tried to forget their faces. And even so, even if she could push their cries away, sometimes the spirits called her in the form of dreams. These reveries were more than just the imaginings of Francine's brains during sleep; these were visitations, incrimations of the dead—what she called *spirit calls*—begging Francine for answers that she did not possess. Francine disliked these visits, which would leave her feeling a vast emptiness.

The phone rang. Francine picked up the receiver.

A man's voice sounded on the other end. Her heart was racing. Why did she answer the phone if she could not speak the language? It was an old habit. The voice was male with little affect. The caller spoke in rapid-fire English.

"Mrs. Mwanzimba? May I speak to Mrs. Mwanzimba please?"

"Yes," Francine responded matter-of-factly. Answering like this in English was a mistake since it only invited the person on the other end to speak even faster.

Francine interrupted the stream of words that poured into the phone. "No English, no English." She hung up and called Elbe.

"I think the hospital called with Innocent's results but I couldn't talk to them."

"No worries. I'll call you back as soon as they tell me what they have to say."

Francine was beginning to like Elbe, how efficient she was. How distant.

Francine closed her eyes and took a deep breath. She wanted to understand what God wanted from her. What did he want her to do with Boy? Why was he sick? She wanted to understand why God had sent Innocent to her in the first place. Why the pregnancy, under those unspeakable circumstances…why take away her other children while bringing her new ones? She became frightened. Maybe this was the devil's work. What if God had left her for good? Francine knew she had a strange relationship with the Lord. She wished she could let go of Him but somehow she held on to a faint thread of hope that kept her imploring.

She got down on her knees and began to pray. *Notre père qui êtes aux cieux. Que Votre nom soit sanctifié.* She prayed for God to return to her heart. She prayed for protection for them all, even for Innocent who was still in the hospital. She prayed for her ability to forgive herself for not having been able to save her children. When the doorbell rang, she was still praying.

Francine peered through the peephole to see who it was. She saw Elbe's face impassive and comforting, somehow. She opened the door.

"I called you back but you didn't pick up so I thought I'd just come over directly. We have to go pick up Innocent at the hospital. He is going to be OK!" Elbe was now beaming with the great news. "The doctor said that this type of viral infection can be treated with mostly rest and absolutely no stress. As long as he rests, he should be fine."

Francine's heart lept for her son, for the first time ever. This surge of emotion surprised her, for even when he had taken his first breath, she had felt nothing more than the rush of adrenaline that came with physical pain.

Francine entered Elbe's car and sat quietly in the passenger seat watching the houses moving on by as they drove quietly back from the hospital. The roads were still white but it had stopped snowing. Francine liked Elbe's silence and how she knew enough not to force her way inside the dark corner of Francine's head. She wanted to sit with this newfound feeling of love she now felt for Innocent. Her prayers had been answered and yet, she was afraid that this love which had just seemingly appeared in her heart would somehow be taken away just as easily as it had been given. *He giveth and he taketh away.*

Elbe pulled the car over in front of a store.

"I'll be right back," she said running inside Abdo's Grocery.

Sometimes Francine caught a glimpse of herself as if she were observing her own life from the outside. She could see her own reflection sitting in this car, in this small city, in a country that was not her own. She thought about the quality of light in this new country and how sad and gray everything was around her making her feel like God had left this place long ago. Yet the love she had felt just moments ago when Elbe had told her that Innocent would be fine told her otherwise. Francine looked at the bit of snow that had accumulated overnight on the ground. Before coming here, she had never expereinced snow. Of course, she'd seen pictures, strange and beautiful but nothing that even came close to the stark reality of this new life in cold country. How many times had she tried to visualize this snowy landscape when she was still in the camps in Africa? She would close her eyes and imagine herself in a large field with snow everywhere. Now, she didn't have to imagine it, the cold was all around her, a deep cold that settled in her bones.

Elbe returned with a triumphant look on her face, holding a pint of ice cream in her hands.

"This is not exactly an ice cream cone, but I promised Innocent he would get ice cream. Ice cream he will get!" Francine was moved by Elbe's kindness towards this child she herself was learning to love for the first time.

When they arrived at the hospital, Francine saw him before he noticed her. How small her boy seemed in that hospital bed, with a tube coming out of his arm. The doctors had put him in

Pediatrics, on the third floor. The room was crowded with two other beds occupied by another sick child with IVs and oxygen and all kinds of bandages around his head. There was also another boy Innocent's age who seemed to be sleeping deeply. Francine walked in while Elbe waited on the other side of the glass window, in the hallway.

Innocent's face lit up upon seeing his mother.

"Bonjour Innocent," Francine said to her son a bit more formally than she had hoped. She knew she would need to unlearn the distance that had settled between them as a matter of habit for the last four years since her son's birth. In many ways, Francine felt as if she were meeting her own child for the very first time. Francine conjured the love she felt for her departed daughter Mélanie, the love she felt for her son Christian and her husband Fidèle. She could feel it hovering above them in this sanitized room, in this strange country, governed by an unfamiliar season and she leaned down and embraced Innocent. Francine could not remember the time when she had touched her boy in this way. A touch beyond necessity. She buried her nose in the crux of his neck and for the first time since they had vanished, she smelled the others on him. Innocent smelled like her other babies, like the baby boy that he was, a cross between caramel and freshly-washed cotton.

On rentre à la maison? "Shall we go home?" She asked her son.

He nodded and smiled.

Beyond the glass, Elbe was beaming as she brandished the pint of ice cream in her hand. Innocent's face lit up and pushed the covers off him with excitement.

In spite of the distance between them, Francine could see that Elbe was crying.

Chapter 16 – Elbe

I walked in the door of my apartment and felt myself vanishing quickly until I became narrow, a thread so thin, a filament that passed through the world unnoticed. This feeling of strangeness was the same I felt when I would sometimes say my own name over and over again until its syllables lost all meaning. When I looked at my face in the mirror, I erased myself trying to find meaning in my own genetic pool. No one around had ever looked like me—except in ninth grade, when a boy came to our school from Peru and all of a sudden, everyone asked me if we were siblings. I didn't see the resemblance, but everyone around me did. It was the black hair they said. *Hair so black, it's hard to believe you wash it sometimes*. Peru. The Indians of the Americas. We became relatives of strangeness.

I sat down on the couch and examined my life. I knew that I had no friends. This was not something I liked to admit, but it was a fact. I wanted nothing. I remembered given up on the false comfort of acquaintances back at the end of high school. When I entered college, I pared down, seeking only that which I knew. And since I knew so little about myself, I sought almost nothing from other people.

I'd asked my mother about the circumstances of my birth, and she told me all that she knew which was very little. My biological mother was young. A full-blooded Lakota, she lived on the Pine Ridge reservation in South Dakota. And in the place where my father's name should have appeared on my birth certificate, it said *unknown*.

I spent years imagining him in countless forms. In the week after my mother told me those few facts about my birth for the first time, I imagined my father as a pirate, a traveling man who sailed the seas. He'd met my mother in a secret port. I knew nothing of South Dakota in those days of my childhood when I first learned that I was adopted. I did not realize that South Dakota is landlocked and imagined my father to be a man of the seas; his long dark beard covering the paleness of his face. The first father I imagined was white, a Southern-looking pirate from Spain or Portugal. For a long time, this is the only way I was able to imagine the world, a place *discovered* by a white man from the European continent.

For the first time in my life, I thought about how continents are not discovered but conquered. I thought about the existence of my twin sister, another one of me, waiting for me somewhere on the other side of the world.

**

When the phone rang, I felt as I always do when the outside world tries to pierce through my cocoon: anxious.

Over the years, I'd learned to force myself to answer the phone.

"*Bonjour*, Elbe?" a man's voice was on the other end. He spoke French with an accent and I barely recognized the pronunciation of my name. *Elbé* with an accent at the end.

"*Oui?*"

"*Bonjour, c'est Jean de Dieu ici à l'appareil.*" It was Francine's husband.

"*Oui, bonjour!*" I tried to sound cheerful, civil. Through the years, I had forced myself to be more civilized, to sound more human than I felt. Jean de Dieu was talking on the other end. Something about a dinner invitation to thank me for all the kindness. I accepted even though I didn't know what he was referring to exactly. I had accepted this volunteer thing as a filler. Like everything else in my life, it was a reprieve from the hole I felt inside at all times.

Francine opened the door, smiling broadly showing the white of her teeth. I walked in. Her home smelled delicious, a mix of onions, garlic, and something else: meat of some kind, roasted, or fried. Francine moved towards me, unexpectedly and for a second I was thrown off balance by her gesture. She took me in her arms and kissed me twice on each cheek. My body bounced and swayed trying to follow her cue awkwardly. She laughed. I laughed with her. Innocent came bounding from around the corner and ran to me wrapping his tiny arms around the breadth of my legs. "Ice cream lady! Ice cream lady!" he yelled before scurrying away.

I felt oddly tall and large in this house filled with family.

Jean de Dieu came from the living room and greeted me shaking my hand.

"Bienvenue chez nous!" He welcomed me into their home.

I sat in the living room; we exchanged smiles. Francine disappeared into the kitchen. I tried to remove myself from the immediacy of this moment. I thought about the strange trajectory I'd made so far. A constellation of planets had pulled me into their orbit, and now I didn't know where to turn. I was sitting in this unfamiliar home and my usual cues of the white world I knew by heart had been discarded.

An elderly woman came into the room and Jean de Dieu got up to help her make her way into the room. Her hands were resembled crystallized wood grasping her cane like a claw. She inched her way across the floor, paused halfway, looked up at me and smiled, a toothless grin. She looked a century old. Instinctively, I felt the urge to stand, to show her the respect she deserved for having been on this earth so long. How could anyone live that long? I remained standing. I wanted to go to her but I was an outsider. I had nothing to offer. I smiled. Jean de Dieu helped her make her way safely across the floor, next to me on the couch. When she finally sat, she let out a deep breath and turned to me again with her smile. Her eyes were smiling more than her mouth and I felt instant warmth pouring out of this stranger. Something released inside me, as if a wedged piece of grief deep inside me had suddenly been freed. I wished this woman could hold me, cradle me like a baby. I felt tears welling up inside me, but I had mastered the art of pushing back emotion, and the tears returned in their place forming a tight ball at the base of my throat.

"This is Maman Elaine, my grandmother," said Jean de Dieu. Francine had told me about Maman Elaine and how, a few months after the genocide, they found out she was alive and initiated the immigration visa process as soon as they had settled in Syracuse. Maman Elaine took my hand in hers. It was as soft as I expected it to be, soft like silken paper or parchment, smooth and warm. I held onto her tightly. Her grip was firm. We sat like this quietly. She smiling, me holding back the tears. I didn't know what to say, I wanted to talk about the usual, the weather, work, the kids, the house in order to anchor me through the grief dislodging itself inside of me but I could not muster the strength to pretend anymore. Innocent sat next to me on his chair, too big for him, feet dangling, giggling as he looked up at me, smiling.

The house was pulling me inside it. A part of me wanted out of this unraveling. If I could slip out and away from this family's entanglements, I could remain intact. I looked outside. The moon hung low and full in the sky. It was full and pregnant with its young hanging low, read to be birthed. Francine came back in for a moment, four girls came in with her. She was in a hurry, wanted to make contact. Francine pointed to each one in turn and said their names. "Sophie," she said placing her open palm on the top of an eight-year-old. "Devota," Francine said again pointing to a smaller version of the first child. "And these are Angélique and Sylvie." The last two girls were maybe six and eight years old, respectively—a perfect replica of Francine's fine chiseled features. Then came the boy Michel whose tootless smiles brought me out of the density of the flood of my emotions.

"Ça va? Veux-tu quelque chose à boire?" Something to drink? I accepted soda. She came back running into the kitchen. Jean de Dieu was sitting across from me and Angélique, Sophie, and Sylvie were now sitting with us too.

There was so much I wanted to know about Francine and her family, so much I wanted to say.

Il fait très froid. "It's very cold outside," I said unable to unravel the undercurrents between us.

Oui, nous n'avons pas l'habitude. "Yes, we are not used to it," Jean de Dieu responded.

I tried to imagine Africa. I was afraid to even bring up their place of origin. I knew they were exiled. Did they want to talk about the place from which they fled?

L'humidite, la chaleur… Jean de Dieu told me about the heat and the humidity of the Congo. We remained with the topic of climates and fluctuating temperatures.

Il va neiger bientôt. "It will snow soon." I told them. They smiled. I told the girls that I could take them sledding. I made the gesture to describe it because I had forgotten the word in French. They giggled, having no idea what I was talking about.

We were each holding the world we knew in our minds on our open palm so we could share it with each other. Their world was unfamiliar: vast, moist, and warm, with large insects and the persecution of people. What about my world? How could it be reduced to a handful of images? Adopted. White hands holding me as a baby. The snowy mountains of Vermont.

At the volunteer organization, they warned us about asking too many questions about the clients' former lives. I could still remember the director of the refugee relocation program telling me: "Many have lost loved ones in atrocious ways. We must not pry."

The house was large, but old and run-down. The worn, wooden floor was warped and stained in some places. The walls needed a new coat of paint. The windowpanes were thick and the woodwork around them was warped and swollen with moisture from past seasons. I imagined the sub-zero winter ahead and the cold drafts they would feel in this house. When dinner was ready, we got into a small dining room and squeezed at a table made for three or four people. There were eleven of us. Maman Elaine was placed at the head of the table with Jean de Dieu at the other end. Francine sat on the side, she said that she'd need to get up often and didn't mind it. I sat next to her. The three younger girls were sent to eat into the living room. Sylvie, the oldest came out of the kitchen with Francine. She said hello to me timidly and helped her mother serve dinner. I felt like I should be helping them, but I didn't know what might be perceived as offensive or courteous. Was it better that I sat there not offering my help or that I offered it? I sat still waiting for the commotion to settle.

The food quieted and grounded us all into a common goal. We passed around the dishes; everyone was served. Jean de Dieu, then Maman Elaine, then me and the children. Francine served herself last. She offered me another piece of meat. I accepted. Her sleeve was pulled up halfway on her forearm. I noticed a huge scar, a carved out piece of flesh was missing. I almost gasped when I saw it. I said nothing. She noticed my eyes on her, on her arm, but she looked away, furtively, almost fearfully, like a small animal almost caught in a trap.

"The food is delicious," I said my heart racing. *What kind of wound was that?* I had never seen anything like it. The crater made it seem like her flesh had somehow closed on itself trying to make up for the void left behind as best it could. Another few millimeters and the bone would have been exposed. The skin was dark and knotted in some places, where the flesh had tried to close in on itself. I wanted to touch her scar. She pulled her sleeve back down.

"Does anyone want any more potatoes?" asked Francine pretending I had never laid eyes on her arm.

For dessert, we shared the cheesecake I brought. A sliver for everyone. One tiny piece for each person. I turned down a piece saying that I was not hungry. We stayed seated at the table for at least two hours. Everything took place at the table. We drank coffee after the meal. The plates were cleared.

"You've never had a single snowfall in Rwanda?" I asked trying to find order in the mundane.

"No, never. Sometimes it gets cool at night, especially up in the hills, but we never get any snow."

We talked about everything that could be contained. The closest we came to speaking of the darkness was the moment Jean de Dieu told me he was an engineer back in Africa.

"I worked for a large government contract firm in Kigali until *everything went bad.*" Silence returned.

"They said it might snow all day tomorrow. All day and all night." Francine grasped the opportunity to tell us about the more temperate climates of Rwanda.

"That's why we're called *The Land of a Thousand Hills*. There are so many summits, you can always look at the world from above," Maman Elaine chimmed in, as if she were already speaking from beyond the grave.

The evening ended. I kissed everyone on the cheek four times, including Maman Elaine. I told them that next time they would come to my house, even though I didn't know how I could possibly fit ten people in my home.

I wanted to hold on to this moment of familial levity for as long as possible. When I slammed my car door and drove away, I waited until I was at least two blocks away to pull over. I held my face in my hands and began to wail. I cried like a baby, loud and strange cries that poured out of me. Wiping away the tears, I continued driving and wailing; the blur of the moon's face was ahead, full and round, a blue orb in my hazy vision.

Part IV

Chapter 17 – Home

The phone rang in Elbe's apartment, waking her from the dead. *The problem with taking medication to stabilize your mood is that it keeps you anchored to the ground*, she thought.

"Road trip!" Joey blared on the other end. "Get your shit packed, we're going to South Dakota to find your peeps and mine."

"And yours? I thought this was supposed to be about me." Elbe nervously played with her hair.

"When is something not about me, darling?"

They both laughed.

"I want to go see my mother and since I have that little dribble of Lakota blood in my veins, I thought we'd make it a pilgrimage to our homelands. What say you?"

"I say, I'm in."

**

The following week, Elbe and Joey drove to Francine's house on their way out of town.

"Keep the car running," Elbe told Joey as she ran to the front door. She was embarrassed by how eager she was to leave town and everything else behind, even Francine. Elbe rang the doorbell and waited. She could feel the pounding in her chest from the few steps she had run from the car to the door. Elbe looked back at Joey waiting in the car, as if she wanted to ground her way out of the squalor of this town.

Francine opened the door.

"*Bonjour, Francine*," Elbe said trying to convey warmth.

Francine seemed relieved to see her and invited her to come in.

"*Je ne peux pas entrer*," Elbe told Francine she could not come in, explaining that she was on her way out of town. She had pointed to Joey's car still running, as evidence of her freedom.

"*Comment va Innocent?*" Elbe asked about Francine's boy, and as if the child sensed he was being discussed, he peeked his head behind Francine. He was wearing footy pajamas and smiled at Elbe as soon as he realized it was her.

"*Rentre tout de suite, il fait froid!*" Francine snapped, the way any mother would snap at her child to spare him from catching his death. The little boy vanished.

"Everything is OK now," she said to Elbe, thank you for everything." *Tout va bien. Merci pour tout.*

Elbe took Francine's hands into hers. They were warm, *full of life,* she thought. The two women looked at each other. They knew in that moment that their paths which had converged in sadness was now coming to an end. Would they ever see each other again? The uncertainty of this answer did not evoke sadness but possibility for both of them.

"*À bientôt Francine,*" Elbe said, as one blurts a formulaic phrase that has lost all meaning.

"*Au revoir,*" replied Francine, before kissing Elbe on both cheeks.

Francine shut the door of her home with a smile.

**

Elbe and Joey drove for two nights and two days, arriving in Decatur County, Southern Iowa. This region was not only the poorest county in the state of Iowa, but also one of the poorest in the nation.

"Welcome to my hometown of Le Roy!" Joey yelled in some kind of Midwestern drawl that sounded forced and borrowed. His loud voice seemed out of place in the end-of-night darkness engulfing their car. "This is the smallest city in America. No joke! Guess how many people lived here when I did?"

Elbe noticed the sinuous line of the road ahead of her. A black trail of light in darkness. "By the looks of it, zero."

Joey made a loud, obnoxious buzzer sound indicating Elbe's answer was incorrect. "Wrong! 13 fucking people. You heard me right, lucky 13, and I was one of them."

Joey stopped the car and admired the vastness of a flat horizon at the edge of corn fields.

"Joey, what the hell are we doing here?" Elbe was annoyed. Somehow this whole road trip which was supposed to have been about finding a piece of herself had now turned into the Joey show.

"But wait, do you know how many nonwhites lived in Le Roy when I was growing up? 6 percent. That's right, 6 percent of 13. I know you're a historian, but do you know how much 6 percent of 13 equals? Tataaaah! Less than one," he said pointing at himself.

Elbe ignored Joey's clankering voice and thought about what had taken them on this trip. She knew that something had led them here. Something other than herself, other than Joey's sense of space and time. Something outside of themselves.

"Seriously, Joey. What's the plan? Because I want to be in South Dakota by tomorrow so I can actually meet my twin sister."

"Okay, okay. You want serious? Here's serious. My mom lives here, somewhere down that path. And I haven't seen her since she left me when I was five and I went into foster care. I want her to see me, as Joey, as me."

Elbe thought about Joey as a girl. She thought about the cosmic error that had assigned him the wrong body at birth. Michele must have always known that she was Joey, that *she* was a *he*.

"Dude, can we just sit here quietly for a moment and not speak?"

"Dude?! Okay, white girl."

Elbe felt that same strange fluttering she had felt the night she had gone to Francine's house for dinner, a fluttering in her solar plexus where she liked to keep her index finger. This was something she liked to do. She drew the silence to her like a cape and got out of the car before Joey even moved. The sun was rising on the eastern horizon. The air outside was cool, crisp. It was fall and for the first time; she felt the changing of seasons. Elbe saw a small path open up ahead, dissarayed and sinuous, the way paths can appear to be in the country where there is no money.

Joey joined her and they watched the flat of the endless Midwestern horizon light from the inside.

"Follow me," Joey said taking her hand.

In the strangeness of darkness, they moved together. She clasping her heart like an ailing widow and Joey moving slowly, ever so slowly, as if he had suddenly lost his battle with gravity. Immense, the fading darkness around them drew them into a place that united them instantly, like two sudden orbs connected in the places of connection. *This was the circle of change*, Elbe thought. She wanted to stop Joey in his tracks and tell him that uncovering the past unravels the world. She wanted to grab him even, and speak of her gratitude for his presence on this journey with her, but she said nothing. There was no turning back now. Even Elbe knew the momentum they had unraveled could not be stopped, or even slowed. They continued to walk in silence until they came to a bend in the road. The curve was slight, the bending of an elbow.

"Here," Joey said, pointing to the first trailer in a string. Night had given way to morning. The light was pale and gray, barely holding them.

A dog began to bark madly while pulling at its chain. The animal lunged forward pulling towards them like a ball dangling at the edge of an elastic band. When they came to the periphery where the dog could almost touch them, Elbe stopped and looked at Joey for direction.

"That dog won't bite you," Joey said smugly.

"Um…how the hell do you know that?"

"Don't know, just a feeling I guess. But look at how it's observing us now. It's not even trying to get to us anymore." Joey was right. Now that they were close, closer than they had ever stood to the dog, the animal became calm and lay down.

The dog's body was shaggy and grey in places where dirt and mud were caked on an otherwise tan and beige fur.

"Fuck it, I'm going for it!" Joey moved past the invisible line that separated him from the dog and entered into the animal's span of space that lead him to the trailer door. The dog sniffed Joey slowly, carefully, and then leapt on him while wagging its tail.

"See, I told you," Joey said before pounding on the door. Once. Then a pause. And then again. Elbe closed her eyes and moved towards the animal as if she were approaching the edge of a cliff. When she opened her eyes again, she saw that the dog had barely acknowledged her. It was fascinated by Joey instead. No one was answering the door. But when Joey looked up, he saw that someone was looking at them through the parted curtain of the trailer.

"Someone's here." There's someone in there," Joey said pointing to the window. "Hello?" Joey began pounding on the door, this time with more insistence.

A voice, faint and feminine trailed from behind the thickness of the peeling door.

"Who is it?"

Joey paused and waited. He knew that if he said who he was, they might never meet the woman who lived inside. "You've won a prize. I'm here to get you to claim your prize."

Elbe looked at Joey in shock and then burst out laughing. She knew that the laughter had more to do with the tension of this moment and the fear coursing through her rather than hilarity. Something shifted inside the trailer, rustling, and then the door cracked open.

"What do you want?" A frail woman peered from behind the partially opened door.

Elbe tried to find Joey's face in hers. She tried to find a trace of genetics that connected them to each other but she couldn't see even the faintest of resemblance. The woman had deeply set, tired and sad, washed-out pale blue eyes, as if time had tried to push them into her face, like strange marbles that needed to be dislodged.

Joey stood very still staring at the woman who had brought him life. He said nothing for what seemed like a long time. It was difficult to say whether she recognized her own child. If she did she said nothing. Elbe almost spoke, afraid the woman would slam the door in their faces but she too stood there waiting. The moment hung like this until the woman asked again.

"What the hell do you want?"

"You've won a prize. Sweepstakes." Joey hesitated. Elbe knew that he was searching for the next words.

"A lifetime supply of coffee."

The woman's face brightened briefly and then crumpled in an expression of mistrust. "How do you know I drink coffee?"

"Who doesn't drink coffee ma'am?" Joey smiled. The woman smiled with him and she pulled the door open.

"What do I have to do?" She had a scar on her face. A line in the shape of a half crescent moon across her forehead.

Elbe noticed the scar; Joey saw it too. He eyed the line on the woman's face pushing him off balance, into some kind of shaky constellation of memories that began to whirl in his head.

"You don't have to do much of anything," he finally answered. Joey looked to Elbe for direction. She shot him a look of confusion.

"Well, you do have to answer a few questions, a questionnaire really. Once that's done, we'll deliver the coffee." Joey added.

"Yeah?" she asked again unsure of the situation.

"Yes, we can deliver it later today, if you'd like."

"Wanna come in? I'd offer you some coffee but I got none." She snorted a strange kind of laugh. "Hey does this coffee come with a coffeemaker? Cause I don't got one."

Joey hesitated for a moment and then said, "Yes, of course. It comes with a nice and new coffeemaker."

Elbe was now shrugging looking at Joey, as if to say, *are you nuts*?

"My name's Jennie, with '*I E*' at the end. Well you know that, if you're from the sweepstakes and all. You know my name, I guess."

"Yes, Ms. Stevens, we know your name. My name is Joey and this here is my assistant Elbe."

Elbe shot a look of visible annoyance in Joey's direction.

Jennie pulled up her stained yellow housedress as she climbed the two small steps back into the trailer. Her legs were swollen in places exposing varicose veins.

"Sure. We'll come in," Joey said as he stepped into the trailer with Elbe in tow.

"I never won a prize before," she said, sitting down on an old mustard-colored armchair. "You can sit right there, if you want," she said pointing to two chairs covered in animal hair and unopened mail. "Just move that stuff out of the way. You can put it on the floor."

Elbe and Joey moved the piles of old mail and sat down next to each other.

"So what questions do you got for me?"

It was hard to determine her age. Her face was worn in the way alcohol and poverty gnaws at the body. Elbe knew Jennie could not have been older than 45, given the fact that she had had Joey when she was only 14. The three of them sat like this in the fetid smell of the dark trailer. Elbe scanned the room for clues, something that would give her an understanding of how this person was the woman who had given life to her friend

Joey. Elbe searched through the darkness of the room; the two shades that covered the two small windows were drawn. Outside, Elbe remembered the sun was shining. She looked at the pile of dirty dishes in the sink, the opened cat food can on the counter, the piles of unopened mail on the floor, and the crowded room. The formica table between them, the peeling linoleum on the floor, the plastic flowers covered in dust.

Jennie held her hands clasped on her lap. Her nails were short and chewed, with pieces of skin red and raw in places.

"Well, let's see." Joey said clearing his throat. "First of all, what is your favorite TV show?" Jennie hesitated.

"Is this some kind of quiz or somethin'?"

"There are no wrong answers Jennie. So you don't got to worry here."

Elbe noticed how Joey had adapted his way of speaking for Jennie. She was shocked. She had never heard him *speak down* before. Jennie thought for a moment, she unfolded her hands and scratched her head.

"That ain't easy, but if I got to pick one, then I have to say *Everybody Loves Raymond.*

Joey began writing the answer in a notebook, giving this process an air of legitimacy Elbe found disturbing. She knew it was the same notebook where he'd been jotting things down like the address of the nearest fast food joint where they had eaten the day before. Elbe did not know however that it was also the place where he'd begun writing thoughts and feelings down in a makeshift journal.

Everybody Loves Raymond. OK. What is your favorite food in the whole wide world?"

"Well, that's easy. Macaroni and cheese. Kraft, from the box. It tastes good and it's easy to make. There ain't nothing better than that macaroni and cheese."

Joey scribbled again in the notebook.

An orange cat crawled out from under the couch and peered at the trio. They glanced in the cat's direction as if the animal's presence was suddenly bringing light to what they were doing.

"That's Mimi. Short for Michele."

Joey made a strange sound with his throat like he'd suddenly swallowed a bug. Elbe looked at him. His hands were shaking. He tried to clear his throat. He began to cough. Elbe knew that it was a fake cough, the kind that Joey sometimes used to cover up overwhelming emotion.

"You OK?" Jennie asked. "Want some water or somethin'? There is a cup up there, you can grab some water from the sink if you want."

"I'm OK." He scribbled down something in the notebook, his hands still shaking.

"You writin' down the freakin' cat's name?" Jennie asked giggling. She seemed youthful in this moment. "Come here, Mimi. Come look at the coffee people." She laughed again. The cat who had settled with its body half out and half under the couch ignored her.

"What is your greatest accomplishment?" Joey shot a glance in Jennie's direction when he asked this. Sensing unnamable but palpable tension, Jennie asked, "What does that got to do with coffee?"

Elbe jumped in. "Well, it has nothing to do with coffee but we have to ask these questions, all ten of them because the company we work for won't give the coffee away unless we bring back a filled questionnaire."

"Well, I ain't done much of anything. Been here most of my life. My kids maybe. Having my kids, I guess."

"Kids? You had more than one?" Joey asked clearing his throat again. Elbe was trying to think of a way to alter the direction of the questions but she knew that no matter what she did, Joey would not stop now.

"Three kids I got. Three girls. Pretty as buttons. All three of them. I guess you wouldn't know that looking at me, huh?" she grinned humbly.

"Where are they now?" Joey asked aggressively. He was tapping the pen on the corner of the notebook. Jennie did not notice Joey's hostility. The mention of the girls had opened up an invisible gateway. Jennie tried to smooth her knotted and unkempt hair. She kept smoothing the hair pulling on its ends expecting longer strands.

"They had to go away. They had to go away, that's all." Jennie repeated as if she were trying to make sense of her own words.

"What is your favorite color?" Elbe jumped in.

"Michele had those brown eyes. The speckled brown with gold in 'em. You know. I loved looking into her little eyes."

Joey sat motionless pen in hand, dangling in the air. Drinking Jennie's every word. Joey could not stop looking at the scar on Jennie's face in the shape of a half-crescent moon. His eyes remained on these lines, in the way they curved with both tips pointing to opposite sides of her face.

"Little Mary had those pale blue eyes. The kind that make you think of a pool of cool water, you know?" Jennie looked away in the distance, as if alone in the room.

"What is your greatest regret?"

Jennie sat very still as if waiting for an answer to come to her. Joey was plunged into the past. He could see Jennie's scar, the way it had formed with time. Pink and thin on the edges. Deeper at the center. It is dusk. They live in a house. The house is large and blurred on the edges. It does not have a shape the way houses do. It is not whole or structured. Joey is standing at the center. He is holding a knife. He, her father. The father of the girl he once was. He is holding a knife and Jennie is crying. Her mother is crying. The woman who birthed her is crying. She is crying over and over again. The same words coming out of her mouth. "Stab me, fucking stab me. I want you to stab me." The words are falling out of her strangely and disappearing in darkness. And she, the little girl is crouching in the corner of the room. They do not see her.

They do not see themselves. The man is bunching his fists, the way his fingers are grasping the knife tightly. His knuckles are white. Jennie's face is white. The moon is out and it is white. She is standing so close to him her breath is on his face. The knife is by his side. She does not look at it. She knows its presence. The little girl is waiting. She is waiting for them to do it. She wants it done so that she does not have to wait anymore.

"They had to go," Jennie says her feet planted on the linoleum of the trailer. "The girls had to go." When she says this, Jennie looks at Joey as if for the first time. "You remind me of my Michele. It's funny how much you look like her."

"I think we're done with the questions." Elbe breaks in again. She wants to find a magic wand, something that will peel Joey away from Jennie, away from the stench of the past between them.

"No, we're not. We have more questions." Joey snaps. "I look like her? Yeah?" Joey barks strangely.

Elbe was afraid of him, of the unwound spring in him. She was afraid of the force inhabiting him.

"I was five when you left me, Jennie. I was five."

Jennie shook her head uncontrollably as if she were trying to shake a swarm of bees from the sides of her face.

"I was five, and I didn't have to go away. You did." Joey's face was flushed with rage now.

Jennie was still shaking her head.

"Do you remember me now, Jennie? Remember my eyes? The speckled brown with gold in them?"

"But…" she hesitated, looked to Elbe for an answer, for escape. Elbe was still. She was looking at Jennie then at Joey, back and forth as if she were watching a tennis match.

"I didn't have a son. I had three girls."

"I am a boy now. But you made me a girl. I was born a girl."

Jennie's body slumped a little, fell on its side; her hands were crooked claws on her lap. She had become a fallen tree in a storm. Her own weight betrayed her. Gravity was her enemy. She wanted to rise from the chair and leave the trailer, but she could not move. She wanted to ask them to leave but she could not speak. Instead, she looked from Joey to Elbe and back to Joey again in horror.

"There is no coffee then?" she finally asked.

"No, Jennie, there is no fucking coffee. And there is no fantasy of your children having to go away. You left me. You fucking left me and when you were done leaving me apparently you left the others.

"So, I have two sisters huh Jennie? Where are they now? Do you even fucking know where they are now?" Elbe looked at Jennie and felt a pang of pain in her chest seeing how fragile she looked. She had gone from being brittle to becoming a bag of bones on a chair.

Jennie's eyes watered and then scanned the room furtively like an animal searching for a place to hide. Elbe searched for Mimi the cat, but she was nowhere to be found. Jennie's body was shaking. She had unfolded her clawed fingers and was now grasping the sides of the chair furiously.

"They had to go." Jennie repeated as if trying to convince herself. Joey wasn't listening. Elbe knew he was on an unalterable path.

"I remember, you left at night. The lights were flashing when you went away." Joey's voice seemed almost calm now.

"They came to get me," Jennie whispered to herself.

"Who came to get you? Joey asked.

"The doctors, they came to get me."

The whites of Jennie's eyes were the color of a pale sunset. Jennie was no longer holding on to the sides of the chairs.

"I didn't want to go. And when I came back, the girls were gone. They were gone. They had to go away." She began to scream. Her voice rising in a strident pitch. Elbe motioned for the door. "We should go," Elbe whispered.

But her words were lost in the raging of Jennie's screams. Elbe was sitting still at the table. She was watching Jennie screaming across from her as one watches a car crash. The woman who had brought Joey into the world was no longer aware of his presence or Elbe's. She was crying and shaking and contorting her body in the chair.

Elbe walked over to Joey slowly and placed her hand on his shoulders. She leaned gently to his ear. "Joey, we really should go." A few seconds went by as Joey sat still continuously staring at his mother. Elbe waited. Joey stood up slowly. Then, imperceptibly, he began to pull away slowly from the table, keeping his eyes on Jennie. Outside on his chain, the dog was barking again. His booming voice echoed in the distance, almost beckoning them to come outside. The world was calling them back to the places they knew. At once Jennie turned and saw them both, as if for the first time.

"Who are you and what are you doing in my house?"

Elbe and Joey had their backs turned to Jennie. Elbe pulled the door open. A cold late autumn wind whipped them both in the face.

Jennie ran to the door. When she reached Joey, she grabbed him by the arm and pulled him towards her. "I did not leave you. They took me away."

For a moment everything stood still. As if untethered, the dog stared at them in anticipation of freedom. Elbe thought it strange that the wind had magically died down. Joey faced Jennie and her smeared make-up, eyes bulging out of their sockets. Joey stared at every line on her face as if trying to decipher a secret code. For a momentk Joey saw the lines that spoke of her broken life, of the love she had never had, of the children she had lost. Right below the mouth, a groove pulled her bottom lip towards the ground in a state of permanent grief. Both eyes were sunken and around them, a deep circle had formed. Joey thought furtively about the ways we carry the past around with us. He thought about the way Jennie's life had drawn a map of itself, etched in her skin. Each groove was a memory that wouldn't fade.

Elbe was now outside. The mangy dog had begun barking again. The wind was blowing. Joey knew their moment had ended. He turned his back on her. In the growing distance, he heard her crying faintly. When they were both in the dog's circle of contact, the animal jumped on them and licked their hands respectively. *Don't go*, he seemed to be saying, trying to lick them as fast as he could while they were still within reach. What hung beyond this moment? The wind began raging again. Jennie's cries could not be heard.

**

For a long time, they rode in silence. Elbe drove and Joey sat quietly watching the road go by. All American highways looked the same after a while. The scarcity of trees and nature made it impossible to discern what region they were in. Joey counted each exit they passed and sounded out the names of the towns in his head. *Elkhart, Weston, Elyria.* If he could ground himself in reality, Joey thought he would survive.

Elbe broke the silence knowing this was something Joey could not do for once.

"Have you ever seen *Seven Guitars* by August Wilson?" she asked, staring straight out at the darkening road. Joey shook his head in silence. She turned on the headlights.

"There is a scene where this old loon, Hedley, is hanging out with his two friends Floyd and Canewell. They're all sitting around shooting the shit and Hedley starts nailing a string to a two-by-four saying he's building a guitar. Both musicians, Canewell and Floyd make fun of him telling him he's crazy for thinking that he can make music out of a single string. They're on his case but Hedley hushes them. '*Watch!*' he says 'Listen to this,' and he starts plucking the shit out of this string."

Elbe looks over as Joey intently stares out at the road ahead in darkness. She continues.

"So while he's playing his one-string guitar, Hedley tells them a story about his grandfather and how he, too, played a one-string guitar back in the day because it allowed him to hear his mother praying. And suddenly Floyd and Canewell get it. They're sitting there, listening to this strange sound coming from this single string and they begin to think about their mothers who are now gone. My favorite part in the play is when Floyd says, 'If I could hear my mother pray, I'd pray with her.' Floyd's like, 'I'd give anything to hear my mother's voice again, just one more time.' That's when the guys figure it out, you know?"

"What do they figure out?" Joey asks looking at Elbe as she's driving.

"They realize that their mothers, their ancestors are all there, all around them and anytime they want to hear them, all they have to do is play the one-string guitar."

"Huh." Joey adds staring at the dark road

"You don't get it, do you?"

"Not really, no." Joey shrugs.

"Never mind." Elbe felt a surge of loneliness at the back of her throat. Ahead, the road had become a single passage of light pierced by headlights. Elbe drove in silence. Moments later, in the faint glow of the headlights of their car, Elbe saw that Joey was crying in silence.

**

By midnight, they pulled into a motel in the town of Adrian somewhere near Toledo. Joey had hardly spoken since they'd left his mother's place and Elbe had grown accustomed to the silence between them. She felt a strange comfort in their ability to stay in each other's presence without the necessity for words. Elbe unlocked the door of the dingy mustard-colored room they got for $49.99. The place was stuck in some kind of time warp from the 1950s with velvety gold and maroon wallpaper. Joey marched straight into the bathroom and closed the door. Elbe sat down on the bed and turned on the television. A flood advisory in a town a few miles away came on the news.

"We might not make it all the way to Des Moines without getting caught in that storm."

Joey's voice fused back from the bathroom. "Yeah? We'll be alright." Elbe was relieved to hear Joey's voice again. Although she had found comfort in the silence between them, she had begun worrying about him. The door opened. Joey came out of the bathroom wearing boxer shorts. Elbe noticed the lines of Joey's body and for the first time, she laid eyes on him as if she had never seen him before. She got lost in the way his boxer shorts hung low on his body, exposing the line of his perfectly flat stomach. She stared at Joey's exposed chest. The two scars under the line where breasts had once existed. Elbe could not take her eyes away from Joey's body as he babbled about the inclement weather. To Elbe, Joey had always been a boy but now, seeing seeing his body like this, the faint traces of femaleness had taken her by surprise. Joey's maleness was not something Elbe could reduce down to elements like genitals or the absence of breasts. Joey was a boy beyond all of that.

"I don't give a shit if we get caught in that fucking storm. It will make for a nice joyride." Joey said before shutting the bathroom door. Elbe lay down on the bed and closed her eyes.

**

The next day, Elbe offered to drive while Joey, completely unphased by the events of the previous day, had returned to telling wild, cavalier stories about his life.

"So I'm dating this girl named Lotus, right and all she wants to know about me is if I'm black." Joey relaxed back into himself again.

Elbe drove keeping her eyes on the slick turns after the brief rainfall.

"*What are you,*' she asks me—when I'm still inside her! I push her off me laughing and she keeps on gnawing at me like one of those fucking chihuahua puppies. '*So are you black?*' she asks, all whiny and shit. I'm like, 'do I look black to you?' And she goes, 'that's the thing, you look black, but you don't act it.' Can you believe this shit? And then—wait, it gets better—she says, in her girly voice, 'OMG, that's what throws me off! I mean, yeah, you're light-skinned and all that, but it's your hair that gives it away.' Can you believe that shit?

Elbe laughed, rolled down the window. "You like it that way, Joey, don't give me that bullshit about being a victim of the ladies."

"I can't help it. I'm a sucker for good pussy. You know what gets me every single fucking time? It's that whimpering they do during sex, like a tiny wounded animal. The first time I heard it, I was about eleven, sharing a room with two foster brothers, tiny boys of two and three. My foster mother Lisa was in her room next to ours and I heard her crying like she was wounded. I sat up in bed, real still and waited for the sound to come back. And when it did I got up out of bed and inched my way quietly to the door. Inside the keyhole, I saw a tiny sliver of my foster mother buried deeply under a man's body, moving above her to the rhythm of her cries. It made me scared and excited both. I turned to see if the others were sleeping, and when I saw they were, I returned to my bed and beat off for the first time. I wanted to have whatever it was that man had to make a woman sound like that."

"Dude, TMI!"

"Oh shut up, you fucking love my stories." Secretly, Elbe did like the intimacy she shared with Joey, how open he was with her about his past, his life and experiences. She knew she couldn't give him what he gave her, but she also knew he didn't need it as much as she did. Joey was on a roll. He was talking about his childhood and nothing could stop him now. Soon, they would come upon a series of small towns where motels became scarcer. Elbe made the mental decision to keep driving through the night.

"I didn't stay long in that foster home." Joey continued. Not long after that day, the same guy who'd made Lisa cry, showed me his dick when I was in the bathroom brushing my teeth one day. He came right in, didn't say a word. Closed the door and pulled down his pants. I just stared at him and then without thinking, I kicked him in the balls. He just folded over like a cartoon character and made this strange muffled grunt and that was that. The next day I was with Social Services again and I was sent to my sixth foster home."

Elbe thought about how relieved she felt that the focus of the conversation was not on her. She was glad she didn't have to think about what they were about to do in Pine Ridge. She thought about the fact that she would meet her family in less than 12 hours. She closed in on Joey's words and gathered them around her like a safety blanket.

"So I come home one day, and Lotus is sitting outside of my apartment on the doorsteps all crumpled. 'I waited for you,' she says to me, all girly-like. I'm thinking, shit, I'm in trouble. So I put the key in the door and she follows me inside and I can smell her. God, a woman's smell gets me every time. She wears this perfume, the fragrance of summer flowers. Some shit like that. Makes me want to be inside her all over again. That's the problem with me. I don't think straight. Think with my dick most of the time. It's like one moment I know this woman ain't for me and the next I'm fucking her. I don't care what they say, but a woman with nice legs in a short dress can turn the world upside down."

Elbe laughed. Joey's obsession with his maleness was worse than any cis guy she had ever known.

"So, we get upstairs and I look at her and for the first time I notice she'd been crying. 'What's wrong baby?' I ask her. See, that was my dick talking again. I hate to admit it. But it's true. And she looks at me with those puppy eyes, her mascara all over the place, with a fresh coat of lipstick. And she says, 'I just don't know where this is going.' Red flag! Red flag! Nothing good can come out of a woman saying some vague shit like that. I'm trying to think on my feet. There is a fragile place in the presence of women when you can get sucked into their vortex. And before you know it, two hours have gone by and you're tired as shit and you still have not gotten laid. You know what I mean?" Joey doesn't wait for Elbe to answer. "So I'm trying to think on my feet, I'm trying to be quick here. But she's looking all fragile and small like she needs my help and I'm thinking, *you're done buddy. Game over. She's got you now.*

So I'm like, 'What do you mean baby?' I ask her as I'm walking over the fridge This is a tactic that works sometimes. With some women. Gets 'em confused. Diverts the attention away from the drama and then sometimes they get sucked into the action of me spilling something on the carpet or breaking a glass or something and that puts us back on track, you know? So, I pull out two cool beers from the fridge. I open them. Grab one glass from the cupboards. She ignores me. I can see her on the couch now. Her little sundress is pulled up to her thighs. I can almost see her panties. She's pouting. Her lips are all droopy like and she's crossing her arms, underneath her breasts, propping them up so they look even bigger. And I can feel the weakness in me pulling at me again. And I'm thinking: "*Damn! I love that mole on the top of her titty.* The way it curves real smooth like a fruit, like an orange, like a fucking melon. And that tiny dark brown dot on the mound of the curve is winking at me at now, you know? So she sees me approaching and she looks away, like a kid. Like a stereotype of someone being pissed. I put the beers down on the table. I take her glass, her favorite glass, the fancy one, with the nice slender body and I pour her the beer. No foam, just the way she likes it. She's not looking at me. Her arms are still crossed. I try not to look at her tits anymore. What good can come of this in this moment, right? But I can't help it. I hand her the glass, and I try to kiss her neck. She takes the beer. 'Get out of my face,' she says to me and pushes me away. She takes a sip of beer like she's realizing what she's doing, she puts the glass down firmly on the table and says, 'Why you give me beer, when you know I'm hungry!' You just can't win, you know?"

Elbe laughed.

"That girl drives me crazy. She's high maintenance. So high sometimes I can't even see her up there. She's so far gone.

"Finally I say to my girl, 'Why you need to pull at me like that? Why you gnawin' on my leg all the damn time? You know I'm black, so what's the problem?' *'Are you?'* she says. And I go, 'you know I got the world in my veins baby.' She's all up in my shit, you know. She asks me about my father and my mother. She's all like, 'cut the shit Joey! Your father black?' 'Yeah. So? It's not like I knew the man.' 'And what about your mother?' She's got her arms still folded on her chest. She's mad as hell and I know I'm not going to get away with this without spilling a little blood. So there I go talking about my white mama and the foster homes. So now she starts asking me about my mother, my real mother, and why I was taken away from her. And I'm thinking *damn, I hate talking about this shit. What does it have to do with what we're doing now? That was like 20 years ago.* And guess who won that battle? Her titties, that's what. It's like I'm sitting there watching her unfold her arms, slowly. Her breasts bounce a little and then settle under the pull of gravity. I can still see the little mole. It's not winking at me anymore. I don't feel the perk of her tits pulling at me. Even that's gone. Now I'm the one pouting. I catch myself for a second, sitting like a pacha, like I'm some kind of angry king. I feel her hand slip onto my thigh. Her hands are small, real feminine with long red nails. Shiny red nails that she digs into my back when I make her cry out."

"Okay, that's enough!" Elbe yelled pounding her hand on the dashboard.

"Well, I mean, I can't help it if she likes it hard. And you know what kills me? When she whispers in my ear, 'I'm sorry baby. I didn't mean to make you mad.' When she says *mad*, I think *sad* and I know I've won the battle.

"You're a pig, you know that Joey?" Elbe laughed.

"That smeared lipstick on my collar and the mole on her titty can make me forget about all the bullshit and all the drama. Worth it every fucking time."

Elbe felt like she'd been standing in Joey's bedroom hovering above his bed, illicitly watching him do it with his girl. She said nothing about the voyeuristic shame she secretly enjoyed, like a pervert masturbating in a dark public room.

"You know what, Joey? You're psycho. You and all those girls. You need to give yourself a little space from the ladies otherwise you're not going to make it."

"You're telling me. You know I can't walk away from the pussy though. You know?"

"Oh God, here we go again, the pussy, the pussy, the pussy. That's all you care about Joey. Can't you ever think of something else?"

"Not really. No." They both laugh.

"How's that crazy place where you work going?"

Elbe wanted to change the subject. The discomfort was beginning to outweigh the pleasure of his stories. Joey barely took a breath before launching on the next tale.

"You should see the kids I deal with at work. Those girls have taught me more about myself than anyone else I know."

Elbe listened to Joey talk about his job as a counselor for abused girls.

"The school smells like chlorine, you know? I like to call it a school but it ain't no school. More like a residential facility for troubled girls. It's really nothing more than a jail for wounded girls, sometimes a jail, sometimes a laboratory, depending on the staff and who's trying to work out what shit with the girls."

Elbe tried to keep her eyes steady on the shadowy lines. The road was slick after a brief rainfall.

"So on my first day in this joint. I get there, right? And the breakfast shift is still going on. The staff leaves me there with this pack of girls. I don't have a fucking clue as to what I'm doing. I'm like, *what can go wrong here? I'm strong, I'm intelligent. I know what I'm doing.* The school looks like a series of small houses from the outside. And for the most part, they're just that: houses containing girls with shattered hearts. Some have had exploded ribs, crushed skulls, broken jaws, cracked knee caps, splintered wrists, punched out faces, ripped toe nails…"

"OK, OK, I catch your drift." Elbe interrupted.

Joey ignores Elbe's comment and continues. "Pulled out hair, violated bodies. All this done by their loving parents, by the people who brought them into the world. So I'm walking in the main hallway that leads to the community room. It's fucking pitch black in there and out of the corner of my eye, I see this eight or nine-year-old girl lying on a mat, rolling on her side like a beach ball blowing in the wind. She looks at me, right and laughs this inane cackle and keeps rolling as I pass her. I'm thinking *what the fuck?!* Turns out, she's been put in 'mild' time out. A place of containment where she can get a hold of herself, away from the group, without having to be isolated completely, into *the chair.*"

"The chair? What the hell is that?" Elbe asked.

"Yeah, We don't call it solitary confinement but *the chair.* It's a padded room with neon lights, small, narrow and rectangular, an empty room without a chair where the girls are forced to sit for hours. Fucked up, right?"

Elbe nodded.

"So, I'm assigned to my first group of girls—Group Blue— a mild group, so I can get my feet wet without too many snags. Eight girls ranging in age from 7 to 18. They stare at me. Lucy, this fat chick in her forties wearing a Winnie-the-Pooh sweatshirt, introduces me. 'This is Joey, everyone. Say *hello.*' So, in unison, like a dragged out chorus of *The Waking Dead*, I hear 'Helllllo Joooeeeeyy.' So, this chick Lucy hands me a sheet of paper with their names and ages on it. She points to each one, like dolls in a window and names them. *This is Sandra, Jen, Kathy, Minnie, Shawn, April, Julie and Mary.* I'm like, seriously? Then this girl Sandra—a tiny little blond thing, couldn't be older than seven—stares at me blankly and returns to her coloring activity. I'm thinking, I got this. That's when I see this girl Carly with her leg in a cast, like a fucking tree trunk, from her hip all the way to her toes. She eyes me like I'm prey. Minnie, Shawn, and the others ignore me. I'm thinking, alright, no biggie. Mary, a chubby little girl with curly red hair and a stained T-shirt that read, *Girls rock*, is all giggling and staring at me. I'm like, OK.

Elbe jumps in. "Can I just say I have NO idea how you even do this job? OK. Go on."

"Yeah, well, I don't know how I do it either. OK, So the girl, Carly, the one with the leg in a cast, says to me, 'Can I go to the bathroom?' She's raising her hand like we're in a classroom. So I'm thinking, it's a simple question. I stop, I hesitate for like a second and then I ask, 'Where's the bathroom?'

'Right there.' They all answer pointing to a door a few yards away, all excited, like they're getting ready to start a house fire. 'Sure.' I tell Carly, feeling confident. She gets up, picks up her crutches and hobbles over, disappearing into the bathroom. Sandra, the youngest, giggles under her breath. I don't think anything of it. They're just little girls, right? Minnie and Kathy, who are teaching each other how to play *Shoots and Ladders*, look up from their game and join in the giggles with Sandra. OK, so now I'm kinda nervous. Something's up: it's like this secret language is moving through the group and I'm the outsider. But I ignore the signal. My inflated ego gets in the way and I choose to act like everything's under control. Big fucking mistake!"

"Oh God!" Elbe laughed nervously.

"Yeah. So, the two oldest girls in the group, April and Shawn, are playing a game of cards on the floor and I decide to join them. 'Can I play with you?' I ask them.

'Sure,' April the 18-year-old, answers innocently. It's fucking sad to think of this girl being 18 and being trapped in this place, all doped up on psychotropic drugs, playing stupid card games with these girls when she should be thinking about dating and smoking cigarettes and making out, you know?"

"Yeah. That's horrible."

"So then Shawn, this beautiful 16-year-old-girl—"

"Joey!"

"No, it's not like that. I don't mean, like, hot. She's just beautiful. She almost seems *normal* you know? Her body doesn't show any sign that something tragically wrong ever having happened to her. She's wearing her chestnut hair in a neat ponytail. Her eyes give nothing. No sadness, no trauma, no sudden burst of life either. She's wearing these tight jeans and a snug baby pink Hello-Kitty-T-shirt. You know what I mean?" Joey asked Elbe.

"OK. Yeah, I thought you were going to tell me this girl was hot."

"Elbe! I'm not *that* fucked up!" They both laughed.

"So, as soon as I sit down to play with them, Shawn gets all giddy which is weird because you have to remember these girls are real doped up. I mean we're talking drugs that pound you into the ground you know? Many of them are drooling, dozing off, they slur their words, but this girl Shawn perks up and sits straight up like she's in a yoga position. And she goes, 'let's start a fresh game.' Then she yanks the cards from April. Well, they go at it. 'Hey, bitch, watch it, you scratched me.' So, I try to keep the peace.

'OK. Let's not call each other names.' They calm down. Now we're playing and then all of a sudden, I realize that Carly has been in the bathroom for a fucking long time. I try to figure out how long it's been. I look at my watch. April notices me and she goes: 'She's not coming out of there alive.'

'What do you mean, she's not coming out of there alive?' I'm thinking, *what the holy fuck is going on here?* And April goes, 'She's trying to kill herself again.'

"Oh my God, you're kidding!" Elbe jumped in.

"Yeah. So I shoot out of my chair. The girls all look up, from their games and when they see the fear in my eyes and the terror in my body, they feed on it and start giggling. Minnie and Sandra are cracking up, hard. They both start singing in this fucked up singsong voice.

'She's gonna die! She's gonna die!' "I run to the bathroom door and I begin to pound the shit out of it. I'm yelling. 'Carly, open the door! Open the fucking door!' Then, wait it gets better. Lucy the staffer who introduced me to the group, walks by and she's like, 'Joey? What's going on here?' So I tell her that Carly's in the bathroom and that she's been in there forever and she freaks. She's like. 'Oh Jesus! You let her in the bathroom? What were you thinking!?' She alerts everyone. This guy Mark and this woman Rose run out with a look of terror in their eyes. They run past me and outside of the building. The girls in my group are now all laughing, watching from a distance. Each one of them has this strange look of excitement in their eyes like they're watching their own house burning and they're enjoying it. I run out there with the others. In the back of my mind, I'm thinking *uh, you're leaving the others alone?* But what could I do, right? When I get there, everyone is gathered around the side of the building. I stop dead in my tracks and feel this huge rush when I realize what everyone is looking at. You're not going to believe this, but Carly's teetering on the edge of the roof—two floors above our heads."

"You're shitting me?!" Elbe laughed.

"No, I am totally serious. Mark is standing right below her. He's like, 'Carly, turn around and go back through the window. Step back from the edge.'"

"Holy crap!" Elbe added.

"I know! So, Carly's cast is resting in the gutter of the roof, dangling like some fucking prosthetic limb. And I realize that she's looking down at the ground trying to find the courage to jump. So I tell myself, *quick, think fast*. So I'm like, 'Carly, what the fuck? Get back in there now!' Mark and Lucy and all the others look at me in shock. They're pissed. They start yelling at me.

'What do you think you're doing? You're going to make her jump, if you speak to her that way.' But I'm not listening to them. My eyes are totally focused on Carly who's now looking at me. So, I keep giving her shit. 'I'm serious. This is bullshit. Step away from the roof and get back in there. This shit ain't cool. This is my first day of work and look at what you're doing.' So, she starts to wobble along the edge, dragging her fucking pogo stick of a leg back towards the window. Everyone just starts to *oooh* and *aahh* and freak all around us. And I hear the guy Mark say, 'Holy shit, she's gonna jump.' And he's trying to talk to her, all wimpy and shit. 'Carly, can you hear me?' But I'm thinking *this is no time to be a pussy*. So I tell her, 'Step the fuck away from the goddamned roof Carly!'

Elbe laughed.

"I'm yelling now. She looks at me again and pulls away from the edge like she's suddenly realized where she is. She fucking crawls back in through the window and gets her sorry ass back in the bathroom. I run back inside and I get her to open the door. This little bitch just opens that fucking door and hobbles out like nothing happened. 'Don't ever pull that shit again. You hear me?' I yell at her. She barely nods. They wrote me up, my very first day and I was written up for letting a girl go to the bathroom unattended."

"Holy shit Joey! Your job is so stressful. I thought teaching history to regular kids was hard but you've got me beat!"

"I know. I have no idea how long I'll be able to pull this off but it works for now."

Elbe and Joey were approaching the last rest area before Sioux City.

"Hey, I gotta pull in here and take a leak, OK?"

Elbe felt a strange kind of bond with Joey, a familiarity that felt like a tug pulling her closer to him. *This must be friendship,* she thought.

"Yeah, and let's get some food too. I'm starving. You know how much I love good ol' junk food."

"Umm, yes, the delicacies of Roy Rogers. Yum!"

Elbe pulled into a nondescript rest area. She thought about how they could have been anywhere in America. The parking lot was barely one third full. It was two hours from dusk. They parked next to a monster Suburban SUV.

"You wonder why anyone would need to drive one of those. I mean, short of the apocalypse, or having to live out of your car, why would anyone need such a thing?" Joey asked.

"Americans need their protection from the world." They both laughed. Elbe knew exactly the type of political comments Joey enjoyed. They walked into the neon-lit building. The muted browns meant to appease, made Elbe feel anxious. They ran to the bathroom and ordered their meals. Chicken nuggets and fries for Joey and a vanilla shake for Elbe.

"I don't know how you can eat that shit at this hour." Elbe told Joey.

"How can you not eat when you're in this Saran-Wrapped world of plastic? It makes me wanna eat my way through life. I understand obesity." Elbe laughed.

"OK, kiddo. We've avoided this topic long enough." Joey finally said looking at Elbe seriously. You realize what we're about to do, right?" Elbe's heart began to race.

"What do you envision when we get there? Tell me what you see."

"You mean, the scene that I keep playing in my mind over and over again?" Elbe let out a slight nervous chuckle.

"'Exactly. What you keep replaying in your mind's eye?"

"I keep seeing me. Her face. Mine. Staring back at me."

"Wait, you've lost me already."

"My twin," Elbe whispered, still playing with the tip of her straw. Speaking those words brought a wave of nausea. She could suddenly feel the gulps of vanilla shake she had ingested come back into her throat. She forced a swallow.

"I just keep seeing her face; it's my face, except it's not me. I think that for as long as I remember I've dreamed of having a sister. Someone who would be like me. Someone who could understand me, you know?" Elbe felt her throat closing again.

"What about your parents? What do you see there?"

Elbe did not know what she saw. Every time she imagined the people who had brought her into the world, she drew a blank. All she could see was Marie's face, her nervous smile, the way she pursed her lips when she was about to cry. Her father's hands, his absentminded gaze. Their voices blended strangely together in her head.

"I don't know." She finally answered. "I have no idea."

Elbe felt a sadness. A strange pang in her chest. She knew what it was. She had never named it but it had always been there. A void. This strange pit in the place of her heart. This is where she had always felt it, the pain of missing. The wanting to be held, to be soothed, to be rocked. To be filled and drawn in. She thought of Leon. She wondered what he was doing in this exact moment.

"It's cool. No worries. What will be, will be." Joey wanted to make Elbe feel better, but he knew that nothing he could do in this moment would take away the anxiety she was feeling.

Elbe wanted to be able to make room for the face of her *real* parents. She wanted to be able to conjure the faces of people who looked just like her, or even people vaguely related but she couldn't. All she could see what her own face staring back at her and this feeling that in her own features, she could finally find an ally. Another one of her who would suddenly understand everything she had endured all of these years.

Over in the next table, Elbe watched a rotund family of four sit down with their meals. She watched their large round bodies finding each other in their resemblance and the way they each echoed each other visually. Mama's hips were a mirror image of her daughter's smaller, still well-squared and wide pelvis. Their asses were equally flat. The children bickered.

"You didn't take enough ketchup. I told you to get more ketchup. How am I supposed to eat these fries without any ketchup?" Freckled boy's face could be found in the line of his father's jaw, in the short roundness of their pug noses.

"Just eat your damn fries, will ya?" the mother snapped right before taking a huge bite out of her oversized burger. Overhearing them, Joey jumped in.

"Poor kid might starve to death. Should we intervene? Should we send Child Protective Services over?"

"I think we might need to." Elbe tried to joke to fight off the sadness devouring her. She did not know how she would survive this moment. The emptiness of this place, the longing she felt, the terrible pang of all the hope she had built up through the years. Twenty-eight years of sadness had built up and now it was all about to end. *Or was it?* She did not know. Elbe knew that it was the not-knowing that threatened to kill her. Thinking of herself as all alone on this earth had been strangely comforting. Having this sudden possibility of meeting others who shared the same DNA with her terrified her more than the pain itself. Hope was a burden Elbe could not afford.

When Joey and Elbe left the rest area, they drove in silence again. This time, Joey was doing the driving. Elbe counted the exits along the way. Twelve. Twenty-eight construction signs.

Four white cars. Two trucks. Two lanes, one single line of hope ahead.

Part V

Chapter 18 – Edgar Owl Feather

Pine Ridge, South Dakota, 1973

I remember the red of her dress bleeding through the dark South Dakota night.

The memories tumble, everything falls together in my mind, out of sequence. I remember her hands on the day we first met. The lines in her open palms—she had the hands of a woman who'd worked all her life, rough hands with calluses at the base of her fingers, hardened skin. Skin nobody could mess with. Felicia had been working a long time by the time I met her. Working the land with her mama Marie and her old man Larry. Working the kitchen in the little shack she shared with her family on the eastern end of the res. We call that part of the res *the dead zone* – the place where nothing grows. She'd been working all her life: she was only seventeen.

The first time I held her hand was at that dance at the Calico Community Center. We still had dances then. This was before that crook-son-of-a-bitch Washington came into power and his goons and their guns forced us to stay home. Felicia, she was quiet. "Don't like dancin'" she said to me when I came up to her, all macho-like. She looked down at the ground real shy, but not weak. Not like those girls that make you think of wilting flowers. No, Felicia she was a willow, always bending in the wind, rarely breaking.

Felicia was smiling at the ground and I couldn't hear if she was talking to me cause of the music, so I grabbed her hand all, gentle and pulled her to me. That's when she looked up at me fiercely with sparks of rage in her eyes. Felicia, she didn't like to be forced to do nothing she didn't want to do. And it wasn't me or nobody else who was going to change that for her. But then our eyes met. Our eyes locked and something changed in the way she looked at me; I felt her arm relax and her hand giving in to mine; her fingers loosened. We didn't speak on account of the music playing. I remember the feel of her hands, like the feel of butcher paper, kind of soft and rough at the same time. I wanted her to wrap herself around me and hold me there for a long time.

We danced like goofballs. I'm not a dancer. Never have been. In fact, this was my first dance, truth be told. But I wasn't all bad either. I can't remember the song that was playing. Sometimes, I try to remember it. I sit on my bed and stare at the ceiling and try and try to remember the rhythm of the music in that moment. I try to bring back the exact words but I can't. The more I try to catch it the more I begin to forget.

Silence fell after that first song and this strange moment followed and hung in the air like a rotting piece of meat, dangling at the end of a rope in the sun. All the boys and me, we all eyed it like hawks, we just stood there in the silence, wanting. We were all hungry and vulnerable, and most of us broken somehow.

Felicia walked off the floor, grabbed her coat, and left the hall, knowing I would follow her. Came right up behind her without a coat or nothin' and followed her out to the edges of the building where a few straggly trees were waiting for summer to return. Spring on the res can bring violent cold fronts, which means it was cold as fuck, but all I can remember is watching Felicia and thinking that I'd been asleep for most of my life.

It was early spring, the time when the magpie hides in its nest waiting for sweetness to return. Maybe the moon was full that night. Maybe it was full and awkward, rich and vulnerable like we were. I don't know. But I remember Felicia's face; she had a few freckles, a trail of them—a distant constellation that made me think the white man had a hand in everything, even in this beautiful full-blooded Indian woman I wanted to know.

As full-blooded as any of us can ever be anyway. I tried not to look at her freckles. For once, I wanted to forget the white man had ever stepped on this land. How could I forget him? All I can do right now is see him in the way we held ourselves under that puny tree. In the way Felicia covered herself with her worn-out open coat, folding her arms on her chest because she hated her "used-up dress" she later told me. Her dress was the color of blood, blood or a tired sunset, with a fading pattern of aging cotton. I remember wishing I'd worn better shoes. Shoes without a hole in the front. Shoes with an attitude. The shoes of a warrior. But Felicia she didn't care about my shoes.

"You work?" She asked me looking at the ground, trying to loosen a chunk of frozen dirt under her foot. I hadn't worked in two years. Not since the factory had closed down the road.

"Nah." I answered coyly like I was trying to sound proud. "I'm a free man, I don't need to work." I answered.

"Free men have the financial independence to travel the world and work anywhere they want. You ain't free."

When she said that, she looked up at me with that fire in her eyes again and I could see her looking through me like she was talking to someone else. Felicia's hair was long and smooth. I could smell her from where I stood: pine and something sweeter, wild berries in late summer. I wanted to move closer, but she was still talking and I could hear the anger in her voice rising and falling like the motions of a flag in the wind.

"My brother, Mika, he left the res a few years ago so he could get work."

I was listening to her now. There was no stopping her.

"Mika stayed around here for three years like the rest of us after he'd learned to be a carpenter from the Bureau of Indian Affairs training office. But there were no houses to build. He came back last month all fucked up and broken."

I felt a strange piece of shame loosening in my chest as I heard her talking about her brother like that. She wouldn't stop talking and I just stood there listening, letting the fire run its course.

"Mika came back with this white girl and their baby and all he talks about now is how much money he used to make. I tell him: "Why you back here then?" And one night when he was all drunk, he said to me: 'I came back cause there ain't no place for an Indian like me out there.'"

I didn't know what to tell Felicia. I wanted to be strong and to be whole and to come back with something clever to say but I had nothing. Truth is, I couldn't imagine leaving this land, even if staying only meant spitting on the ground behind the out houses with my friends like Crazy Jimmy. This land was all we had. All that had been taken away from us. Since that crook Washington had been elected chairman of our people—the Oglala Indians on the Pine Ridge Reservation—everything had gone haywire. Everybody knew that crook wasn't really legally chosen by our people, that he was nothing more than a puppet through and through. He had this crazy private militia we called *goons* cause it stood for *Guardians of the Oglala Nation*. I don't know what they think they were guarding, except their own best interests, running around beating and killing people like they were shooting kittens out of a bag. The truth is, I already knew all that, but I'd never thought I could do anything to change it before that moment with Felicia.

I blurted something out that I only began believing in later. "I think we should stay here and make something of this res." Not sure if I was just sayin' those words to be all hero-like for Felicia or whether I already believed them, deep down. But when I heard myself say it, I knew it was true. That was the moment when I began making it happen. Felicia looked up from the ground again. Her ankles were a deep copper color on account of the cold. She watched me like a hawk, like I had something she wanted. Maybe this is how I began to believe that staying was the solution. That was the moment I began to follow whatever I saw in Felicia's eyes.

"Staying and building is the only path to our people's survival." That's what she said. That was the night I first saw myself waiting to be born.

On the days when the roads were clear enough, I'd ride my bike to the eastern side of the res to see Felicia. She was always working outside, even in winter doing chores. I'd leave late mornings and I'd ride my old rickety bicycle that I'd left to rot and rust outside for the last two years. But after that first night at the dance, I fixed the bicycle in half a day's work. The bicycle wasn't anything special, but I loved it because I had fixed it and now it carried me around the res. Secretly, I felt powerful knowing that I could put my hands to work and mend the broken.

Felicia was a hard-working woman. She wasn't a girl no more. This I knew from looking at her. I knew this when I watched her chopping wood behind the house. I knew it when I saw her carrying her three-year-old sister on her hip and a bucket of water in her other hand. I knew it when she looked at me that first day when I first pulled up with my bike.

"When are you going to do something worthwhile with your time?" She asked me.

I'd never consciously thought about having a mission until I'd met Felicia. I'd never even thought about my life as something that needed planning or fixing or direction. I knew somehow that I'd always stay on the res. This I knew. But it wasn't a political statement. Not at first. Not then. I remember watching all the boys my age leave the res one by one. Most never came back. Some did and when they did, they were changed—filled with a strange need they couldn't meet on the land. That's when they usually started drinking. Those boys reminded me of a story I'd heard from a guy named Kohana who'd left the res and visited a zoo one day. Kohana said the zoo was the saddest place he'd ever seen. Sadder than anything he'd ever imagined, except for the res. He told me about the strange and beautiful animals that'd been removed from their homes and placed in cages for the white folks to see. And it made me think of the people who'd left and come back. These boys were turning, round and round on the res with nothing to do and nothing to build. Wound-up boys in the prime of their lives without any place to be strong. That's what it meant to be broken.

When I met Felicia, I realized I was one of those broken boys circling the res round and round. I was never drawn to alcohol. This was a blessing and a curse. I'd envied those boys who could sit, drunk for hours and spit out their rage. I didn't know what I thought, or felt about anything. I felt empty and I had no way of ever filling up the well.

Sometimes it's hard to remember if things changed on the res because I met Felicia or if they'd been different before but I never saw them. Whatever it was, I could see it all clearly now.

Felicia borrowed her brother's old beat-up car one night so we could go and see the res. She said she wanted to show me the *sacred places* of our land, and I remember wondering what she meant or what she wanted to do with me. But I was happy I'd be alone with her in a car for one night.

We drove in the dark along Porcupine trail. The road was full of potholes and I could see tiny snowflakes throwing themselves at us in the reflection of our headlights. Felicia was driving.

"He wouldn't want you driving it," she said to me when I offered to take the wheel. I felt strange being driven by a woman on the land I'd known my whole life.

"You need to really get to know the res if you're going to be a part of it." She said.

I watched her silently and tried to figure out what she meant. We drove to Wounded Knee and Felicia stopped the car and left the lights shining onto the massacre site. I'd been there a thousand times I thought. I'd been there as a child. I'd played in the muddy land with my friends, trying to kill time. I'd sat at the back of the cemetery a million times, and shaded myself from the burning sun. But Felicia insisted we'd never been there before.

"Not really, not like this," she said.

"The cavalry soldiers came from all sides on horseback. It was a cold day like this one, December 29, 1890," she told me. "They were caught by surprise. Women carried their babies, they had no idea the soldiers were coming. The white folks began to shoot and they didn't stop until nearly 300 of our people were lying on this soil, dead. Most of them were little children and their mommas."

A strange silence came over the car now that the engine was off and our voices muted. Felicia took hold of my hand and held it tightly, letting me feel the presence of the spirits around us. It was like they rose out of the ground and surrounded us. They held us there. I saw them for the first time. I saw the women and the children running in front of us, right past the line of our headlights; they were running and screaming and the soldiers were shooting behind them on horsebacks. I saw a young woman Felicia's age run with her child in her arms, as she was shot in the back. She fell in the curve of the land, right where the hill begins to form and her child fell next to her crying and screaming for comfort. The soldier picked up the child and took it with him. Felicia was crying now. I heard her cry softly next to me and we sat still in the dark for a long time until we couldn't sit no more. I turned off the headlights and wrapped my arms around her in the darkness holding the massacre site.

Felicia's body was warm against mine. Warm and soft like fresh tilled earth on a late spring afternoon. I felt my body hunger for hers, both separate from, and entwined in the violence of our memories. My muscles tightened and I held her closer. We slid in the back of her brother's car. Felicia was still crying when I kissed her. I caught a drop on the tip of my tongue and I thought of the ocean in our landlocked nation. We were held inside our desire for each other.

Felicia opened her shirt. She offered herself to me and I wanted to cry. I could still feel the spirits among us. Not watching, but holding us like a canopy under the sky, rocking us gently into each other. Her breasts were firm and soft like fruit wrapped in silk. Softer than anything I had ever imagined. I'd never touched breasts before. Never held a woman.

That day, I learned that Felicia liked to talk about the spirit world. She liked to close her eyes and tell me the stories she'd heard from her grandmother. Stories passed down through the generations all the way from Felicia's great grandfather, a great medicine man who'd lived through the first Wounded Knee massacre—all the way down through the rabbit hole of time.

As I listened, I let my fingers fumble in search of her face and touch the rapid eye movement of her eyelids, as she talked and dreamt. That night, Felicia told me about the evil spirit Inyan, and his son, Gnaski, on the same night she told me about Raymond Yellow Thunder's murder.

"Raymond Yellow Thunder was an old ranch hand living in Gordon, Nebraska the day he decided to have a few too many beers at the American Legion bar. Two white brothers got a hold of him and forced him to take his clothes off. They beat him in front of everyone and threw him in the trunk of their car and drove around Gordon for hours. A kid found Raymond Yellow Thunder's body a week later in the bed of a pickup truck on a used car lot."

Everyone knew about the murder that'd taken place a few weeks earlier. I'd heard about all of the pain in our land. I'd known about it, the way I knew about the poverty on the res, the way I knew the color of my skin or the texture of my own hair. But Felicia, she had the gift of bringing light to old ways and making them shine all over again.

"See, in our ancient ways, we know about the devil. His name is Gnaski. And while Tate, the wind, was busy breathing life into the first people of the universe, demon Gnaski was running around the world creating diseases, poisonous plants and the ways of darkness. That murder is the work of Gnaski." Felicia told me about the ancient stories of our people.

"Gnaski and his father Inyan were there on the night Yellow Thunder was murdered."

Felicia spoke to me in a murmur and the images of her stories pushed into my imagination like bruises on an infant's skin.

"He didn't cry," she whispered. "Raymond Yellow Thunder didn't cry when they threw him in the American Legion Hall. Some say he was already dead when his naked body landed on the rough cement floor, but others say that he was still breathing."

I listened to Felicia with a knot in my throat, a ball of tears that I later swallowed when she told me about the way he died.

"No one in the hall showed any sign of compassion."

She later told me that compassion was the spirit named Woope, a beautiful daughter created by Skan, the great spirit of action.

"No one raised a hand against the two men who'd just tossed the body of a naked man in the hall. Some people laughed, women giggled under their breath. No one moved."

I placed my hand on Felicia's heart, right on the curve of her breast and guided my way by the beat of her pulse.

"After they'd tossed him in the American Legion Hall, they dragged him by the legs and threw him in the back of their trunk where they left him to die." Felicia's pulse quickened like a whip, like the sound of a twig breaking.

I could feel myself waking somehow. It reminded me of the waters of our rivers thawing in the spring. Transformation is always slow, deliberate and slow. Felicia turned to me. She had opened her eyes again. I knew this somehow because I felt her eyes on me in the darkness. She wanted an answer. She wanted everything from me in that moment: she wanted to see if I could love her, if I could love myself and my people, if I could love Raymond—this man I'd never met. But I had nothing to give her. I had been silenced, long ago, and now she wanted me to speak.

I wanted to find words to offer Felicia. The way we make offerings to the spirit world. I thought of the trickster, Iktomi, the spider, and the way he'd been deceived by Gnaski, the devil son of Inyan. Iktomi had once been Ksa, pure wisdom. But now he was reduced to being a trickster. How do we know the difference between folly and wisdom?

I felt my sex harden against the fabric of my pants. I knew Felicia wanted me to speak, but I had nothing but silence and desire as I listened to her story of death. I placed her hand on my sex. I wanted to remind her that we were alive, that our bodies were breathing. We were living. Felicia's fingers rested there briefly and then twitched and moved away quickly as if she had burned herself on me.

"Do you even care about your people? Do you even fucking care?!"

I became flooded with shame; she was forcing my mouth open and filling me with mud. And in that moment, I thought of my mother, of the way she had looked at me as a child when she found out that I that had soiled myself while playing. Strange how I could remember that moment crisply, like an imprinted leaf on the melting spring ice. Every detail of that day was intact: my desire to relieve myself, wanting to play and knowing that the pleasure of play weighed more than the embarrassment of wetting myself. This had been a choice on my part. But how could I explain this to my mother in my three-year-old language? Felicia's voice startled me.

"It could have been you. It could have been me!"

Felicia got dressed in the dark. My sex had fallen.

On the way home, we drove quietly. Felicia did not offer for me to drive and I did not ask. The roads were deserted at this time of night. Now I remember the moon. It was full and round, its glow guiding us home.

Chapter 19 – Owl

Summer is strange in our corner of the world. Everything turns soft and white and you can hear the meadowlark in the highest branches. Wild violets blossomed. And on the day I had a shitting contest with Crazy Jimmy behind Gerber's Barber Shop, I remember thinking that these flowers had never existed before that summer. I'd never seen them before. In the middle of the broken down cars on the side of the road, cars that had been there for as long as I could remember, wild prairie roses grew out of the ground. That was the first hot day of the summer after I met Felicia. It was so hot, we felt like we'd died and gone straight to hell. It was the kind of day when we'd play behind Miss Ellie's shack, spitting on the ground with nothing to do. Crazy Jimmy was my buddy back in those days before he became all busted and dangerous. Jimmy liked to be the best at everything.

"I betcha I can take the biggest crap in this whole wide world," he said in what sounded more like a threat than a promise.

"Yeah, right. Like you're the king of shit all of a sudden," I laughed.

I squatted first; Jimmy liked it that way so he could see what he was up against and then he went. He took watch to make sure no one was coming while I took a big dump. Nobody was out there on account of the heat. And then it was his turn. Jimmy took one look at my crap.

"Oh, that's nothing, watch this." He squatted and took the largest crap I'd even seen. It was a monster dump, huge and steamy and firm and that day I knew Jimmy was crazier than fuck.

We sat around spitting on the ground until Jimmy thought up a plan where we'd try to break into the jail and free up some prisoners.

"My cousin Marty is locked up in there. Let's go get 'im," he said. And just like that, he was off running in the heat in the direction of the jail.

Now, nobody ever tried to get *into* a jail, people were always trying to get *out*, but not Jimmy. He wanted in.

Jimmy was proud of knowing an inmate inside the jail. I think it made him feel alive like something was finally happening around him. Like life was worth living. After we took a shit behind Gerber's we walked and ran to the other side of town. We walked and kicked some cans around.

"Let's get the fuck outta here and go to Billy Malls Hall," Jimmy said. Jimmy always had a plan and he liked to keep things rolling.

When we got to the hall, we saw that it was closed. We spent the rest of the afternoon squatting again in the dirt, only this time we weren't shitting but drawing circles on the ground.

"This is where we'll get in." He said drawing an X on the ground with a broken branch.

"We? I ain't going in there," I said.

"Oh Jesus, Owl, you're such a fucking pussy. Aren't you tired of being a pussy all the time?" He looked at me with such hatred, I remember feeling scared.

I stayed quiet for a long time and secretly swore I'd make Jimmy believe that I would follow his plan. After what seemed like hours of planning. Jimmy and I ran to the jail right when the sun was getting low in the sky. It took forever to get dark in the summer and I was plenty hungry by then but I said nothing. We ran like weasels, like field rats in the shade until we got to the main jail. The building was surrounded by a big wall, a huge, unscalable, massive mountain of concrete. The wall was old and chipped and fucked up in places and Jimmy said he could use those imperfections to get to the other side.

All of a sudden, I saw a beam of light, scanning the premises. We'd wait for the projectors to be pointing in the other direction for Jimmy to start climbing.

"Give me a hand, will ya?" he said, telling me to interlace my fingers so he could climb. Something told me that we were safe from getting caught. How many people were trying to get into the jail? The guards would be watching for people trying to get out.

Jimmy thrust his body up into the air, bracing himself up against the wall. I heard him gasp and then he winced as I looked up to see that he had scratched his face on the way up. He was standing there with one foot in my hand, and the other in a tiny crevasse, trying to reach up and place his fingers in an opening in the wall. The hole was too far up and I could feel his body dangling and moving unsteadily in my hands that were beginning to hurt. I said nothing. I knew enough to say nothing and bear the pain in silence.

"Push me up, for fuck's sake. Push me up!" He said groaning. I was trying to shove Jimmy's foot higher but I couldn't. Something about the laws of physics and the weight of his body too low in my hands made it impossible for me to move him. Suddenly, I felt Jimmy's body sway off to the right and then his weight was out of my hands. That's when I heard it. The *snap* of something brittle as his body hit the ground.

Jimmy grunted involuntarily and then he was up like nothing had happened. We walked back to town. His arm hung real strange by his side.

"Hey, Jimmy, I think you're arm is broken, man."

"Shut the fuck up, you idiot!" Jimmy never said nothing to nobody about his arm and he just let it heal on its own, all broken and twisted and strange.

But that summer, the summer after I met Felicia, we were men. We weren't boys no more. That day we tried to break into the jail was the last time Jimmy and I hung out together.

In the spring of the following year, Jimmy began running around with a pack of broken boys, a wild bunch who drank every afternoon and every night until their visions blurred and their speeches slurred and they couldn't hold back no more. There was something I envied in the way those boys drank themselves to death, in the way they chased their own tails until they couldn't run no more. Those were the days before I met Felicia when I envied destruction because I didn't know I could envy life instead.

I heard about the looting of the Wounded Knee Museum. I'd been roaming the res most of the day to help my mother fix the door of our shed the day it happened. That night, I was so doggone tired, I lay real low and didn't hear about what happened until the next day when my mother heard the story from the owners of the trading post. Hard to say if the details are all true on account of who told us the story in the first place. Some say there were hundred of kids that broke into the museum that night, while others say it was only a few dozen. I know Crazy Jimmy was among them because the night after it happened, he came back with a busted hand, all bandaged up and he told anyone willing to hear it that he'd cut himself punching his hand through the window of the museum to break in. Most people say they don't understand why Indians would destroy the artifacts of their own history. Folks—mostly folks who live off the res—like to say they don't understand why anyone would do such a thing. Why would anyone get drunk and smash the windows with rocks? Why would anyone steal beadwork from the dead, whose bodies were looted after they were murdered like rabbits? Why would anyone break down the doors with clubs and urinate on the walls of the museum honoring their dead?

Some 200 boys formed a stoned fence and marched right into the museum after having blasted the windows with rocks and the doors with clubs. They went right in and tore up photographs of the massacre, urinated on artifacts and stole some sacred objects. The clothing of those who'd died was left untouched, un-mangled. It was as if touching their clothes brought them too close to the spirits of those who'd come before them. Most people don't understand why those boys vandalized that museum or pissed on their ancestor's graves. But I know of those breaking points when the soul cracks and everything changes.

I can imagine Jimmy there that night. I can see him kicking in the doors and breaking some chairs. I can hear him howling to the moon like a caged animal. I can see him laughing even after he must have cut or scratched or injured himself in the violence of his rage.

The next day, the elders said they couldn't understand how anyone could do such a thing. How anyone could ravage through their own history. But I understood. I'd seen the hatred in Jimmy's eyes when I looked at his busted arm that summer before the looting. I'd seen it in the way he looked at me, my full-blooded face, my strong features. I'd seen it when he called me *faggot* touching my hair with disgust like he was touching a piece of himself that made him wanna hurl. I knew that hatred is swallowed and passed on, like a virus. I knew that pissing on your history meant swallowing hatred and throwing it back at the world.

**

Everything changed after that season. Winter returned and the earth waited for harvest. That following spring, the story of Raymond Yellow Thunder's murder grew and spread like weeds through the res. People began getting together and talking about doing something *in the name of justice*. To be honest, I wasn't thinking about Yellow Thunder. Not at first. I just wondered what Felicia would think of me if I didn't take part in the action.

We got together, a group of us, at night in my cousin's house. We called him "Brave," but his full name was Brave

Bull. He lived in a small house. It was really a shack, but I didn't really come to know this until many years later when I first left the res to go off to jail. I'm getting ahead of myself here, talking about another kind of confinement. Here we were sittin' in Brave's house with Young Bear and Billy Joe. Before that time, we'd all sat around waiting for seasons to change, with nothing to live for. And then we met Grey Stone. He came out of nowhere. It was like one day, he'd just taken form. I remember him that night sittin' in Brave's house, on that rickety stool. The one Young Bear later broke over Billy Joe's head 'cause they were chasin' after the same girl. But that night, we were all tight, a brotherhood, feeling the pride we'd been missing all this time.

"I want to show you something," Grey told us.

We piled up in his Cougar glad to be going somewhere even if it meant staying in the same four corners we all knew. I was in the back with Brave and Young Bear while Billy Joe sat in the front next to Grey as he drove. The sun hadn't set yet. It was low in the sky the color of strange fruits we'd never eaten.

We were driving when we saw these three little kids playing in the cold, they must have been five or six at the most and they were pulling each other on this rickety red cart. One kid had no coat. The other had a torn boot. I remember because when we saw them, Grey Stone slowed way down and said to us: "Look at these kids. These are our kids. Soon, they'll be our men, playing in the void."

The *void*. Grey Stone liked to talk in strange ways. I wasn't the only one thinking that either.

"Jesus man! What the fuck are you talking about?!" Billy Joe laughed from the front seat. And just then we saw this sign on the side of the road that said: "~~Only~~ Jesus can forgive your sins." Someone had scratched out the word "only" like they were trying to tell us something.

We kept on driving. Grey Stone didn't talk. Billy Joe was off in his own world making wise cracks, taking sips from his beer.

And me and Brave, we were real quiet sittin' in the back watching everything. I know Brave was getting it like me. I know he could see everything in a new light 'cause he stayed real quiet for the whole night except when we made the loop back to the entrance of the res and drove by the sign that read: *World Famous Indian Village—SEE how they live.*

Brave, let out this strange muffled sound, real low, like someone had hit him in the gut. I was the only one who heard it and I looked 'im in the eye, and I knew that nothing was going to be the same for any of us that spring.

That night, Grey Stone took us to The Crazy Horse Café after we'd driven around in silence absorbing what we'd seen. We drove down the main road in the Pine Ridge Village right at sundown. I had no money for a drink, none of us did, but Grey walked right up to the bar, talked to Toothless Harry, and got us drinks. I watched Grey Stone talk to Toothless for a while and then he came back with drinks. To this day, I'm still not sure if Grey got us the drinks for free or if he paid for them.

The café was one square room with a small bar and a few tables; the room was filled with smoke and men—mostly us boys. Sometimes Helen or Sue would come in there and talk up a good talk about everything that's wrong in this world. But that night, it was just us boys and a few old men. We sat down with our beers, and I thought of Felicia working at home, taking care of the house, of her parents and her baby sister. What was I doing here?

"Some folks met in Omaha to talk about getting justice for Raymond Yellow Thunder. They took a vote and passed a resolution to drive down to Gordon and talk to the authorities about investigating the murder." Grey scanned our faces waiting for us to respond. It was Brave who jumped in first.

"Why the fuck for? You know no Fed ever gave a shit about a dead Indian."

"If we don't try, we're never gonna get a thing," Grey responded. I couldn't get myself to say a word. I watched Young Bear who hadn't spoken since we'd left Brave Bull's house. He listened quietly to Grey's every word.

Billy jumped in. "The only way to get justice is with the barrel of a gun. That's…"

"Killing throws off the balance of our land," interrupted Grey.

Young Bear listened quietly the whole time and for some reason, I watched him watch Grey. Something about Young Bear's intensity got me thinking about how still I was. So still, I thought about that moment right before a storm, the perfect moment of quiet when the sky turns green and heavy and hailstones the size of hen eggs fall from the sky. Grey always wore a small hat, the color of crushed leaves and muddied ground. He said that the famous guerrilla leader Che Guevara, who led the Cuban revolution wore the same hat when he freed his people from oppression. Something about that moment made me think of these storms. Brave Bull began talking a mile a minute and said we should organize here in Pine Ridge.

"Why don't we have our own meetings?" he asked. I watched Grey holding his head square, never cocked, never like an animal at slaughter as he listened to the excitement in their voices. I liked Grey Stone's silence. I liked my own; it had the kind of weight of something you could cover yourself up with—like a blanket, something making me feel proud again.

It all started happening quickly after that. That spring—that April to be precise—Washington took office. This fat bastard liked to wear his hair in a tight crew cut, military style with his belly pulling tightly at his clean cotton shirts. Washington always wore dark shades: I later learned to never trust a man who hides behind glasses.

Spring was here for an instant and the grass turned red again in the black hills. A million and one blades of red grass breathe as one while nothing stays the same. I live in the windy land of tall, uprooted grass, if left unburnt, will turn from red to silver by the middle of summer. Silver grass that puffs up and rises like a snake coiling around the poverty of our res.

That spring, I saw Felicia as much as I could. We met in hidden places, away from the world. This was not because we were ashamed of our love, but because we wanted to protect it. We met around Felicia's schedule. I was a roaming boy of the res and planned my days around hers. Felicia saw me when she was not taking care of her grandmother, when she was not watching her sister or caring for her parents' home. We rarely had a place to meet; we had no money, and privacy was a luxury we couldn't afford.

Felicia would borrow her brother's car and we'd drive around the res. I had no place to take her. No place decent. I lived in a tiny barrack: a small four-cornered room made of planks that let in the light on bright sunny mornings in the places where the large wood stove meets the walls of my home. I grew up in darkness because light required money and windowpanes and everything that my parents could not afford.

My father built the shack when I was born. He said he didn't want to live in government housing so he bought the material for the shack and built it with the help of his friends when my mother was expecting me. My father was a man of his word. He was a quiet man who spoke only in times of necessity. Necessity on the res was like a monster turned on its head, so that after a while, we didn't need nothing.

My father had a large armchair he brought back from some rescue mission one day. The church was giving away old furniture to people on the res and my father came home with a monster chair. He placed it in front of the stove and spent his life looking at the glow of the fire. In the spring, he'd leave the shack to cut wood, and in the summer, he spent most of the nights with his friends roaming bars and cafes outside of the res. My father's regular bar was The Blue Wolf, owned by a white woman named Minnie. She'd made a fortune selling booze to Indians right outside the res since alcohol was illegal there.

I was an only child, not because my parents didn't want other children, but because my baby sister, Winona, died before I was born. I often wished I had another sibling. Mostly because I wanted someone who could help me with the work I had to do around our home growing up. When I turned ten, my father said, "Now you're strong enough to go down to the well." *The well*, which we shared with four other families living within a quarter-mile-radius was a place I hated.

Every morning after breakfast when the sky was still coal black, I would empty the large slop bucket outside in the outdoor john. The worst were those days in the winter when it was too cold to go outside in the middle of the night and we used the bucket for more than just peeing. After emptying the slop bucket, I'd march down with an empty pail and carry water back from the well. The truth is, I was terrified of walking outside in the dark to get water. Every time I had to go, I'd rush and spill half of it on the way home. Most mornings, I'd have to go back for a second run. I never told anyone how scared I was. Never told a soul. For a long time, I didn't know why, but my father wanted nothing to do with the well. Then one morning, while I was outside, just on the other side of the thin wooden panel separating my home from the cold, I heard my parents talking about Winona and how she had died.

"Why do you make Owl go down to the well when he's still a boy?" my mother asked my father, who remained silent.

"Why did you make Winona go to the well when she was still a child? You knew she wasn't strong enough," my mother relented.

"Do you want me to say that I killed our daughter? Is that what you want me to say?" my father burst.

"She was too young to go to the well, and you know it," my mother cried.

"The rope broke and she fell in. There was nothing any of us could have done."

That was the first time I ever considered the possibility of accidents unraveling lives and being unable to do a damn thing to stop it from happening. I never mentioned hearing that conversation between my father and mother, but I never forgot it.

For a long time, the shack was all I knew—the darkness, the smoky winter evenings when the wind would kick the smoke back into our home. We slept on piled up mattresses along both sides of the room. My parents slept on one side and I slept on the other. This is how I lived with my parents.

**

Felicia drove me to Hawk Eye, this place near Wounded Knee where the earth meets the sky. Remembering that night reminds me of our prairie fires when the smoky air travels fast while every blade of grass burns to the ground until it reaches a river and the wind goes down with the sun.

We pulled the car up right by a quiet piece of road and we sat still, looking at each other. Felicia took my hand in hers and she told me about the hunts. She was almost whispering as she explained to me how the women made the paint for the men's horses.

"They'd make a fire," she whispered. "They'd make a fire with stones in the pit and they'd mix buffalo fat with the sacred colors." I came back to myself on those nights when Felicia talked to me about our ways. I came back to myself as she told me about the colors that came from the earth.

"Blue earth called *thó* came from Minnesota when our people were still free. And the white earth or *makhá ská,* was found on the plains." Her voice was clear on those nights. A clear voice that breathed me back to life. She told me of *makhá gí,* or brown earth that the women mixed with the fat. The sacred colors: red, yellow, white and black were painted on the men's horses to tell the spirits that it was a sacred animal, a messenger of thunder. It was spring and I wanted to be a messenger of thunder. But I had no horse and I barely knew who I was.

Felicia pressed her lips against my ear as she whispered the stories of the early hunts in darkness. Prairie fires are quick and unpredictable with flames jutting out ahead, burning everything to the ground on its way. This is what happened that night.

"*Makhá gí,*" she whispered, "the brown of the earth; this is how the men honored their horses. This was still a time of honor."

I took Felicia's hand in mine. Her hand was small and soft, firm with nervous fingers that could turn into claws if protection was needed. But that night, she turned to softness. She placed her hand in mine, open palm facing the sky and she offered me her neck. I thought of the way the men circle their way around the buffalo using the animal's strength to turn it against itself. I kissed her softly on the nape of her neck as she continued to whisper.

"*Makhá ská.*" The white of the moon was absent that night; I closed my eyes and listened to her breath quicken like the wind carrying the prairie fires for miles.

I sometimes circle around the memory of that night for hours, for days making myself drunk with it. Felicia's voice trails off into the distance, like a dying echo until I can't remember her no more. Then suddenly, like a storm returning from itself, I am flooded with desire from that night, with Felicia's scent, with the lines of her body, the curves of imaginary hills that only exist in distant places.

Felicia cried when I kissed her. She didn't make a sound. I know she cried because her tears fell along the line of her jaw like a river that could arrest a fire.

When she offered herself to me, I remember thinking about the way hunters become one with their horses.

"Messenger of thunder," she had whispered. "You are my messenger." She gasped when I first kissed her breast. A small gasp, like an animal surprised to find itself cornered. When the hunters roamed the prairies freely for days, time became as flat as the land with only moments of change with the moon, and the shifting sun in the sky. How can I still visit this place of desire now that I have lost everything? When I close my eyes, I hear her breath quicken against my cheek, shallow, like the silver fox in winter.

I entered her in darkness, and when I did, her body folded onto itself, onto me like a young sapling bending in the wind. I held her there, without moving, without making a sound. My desire for her threatened to take hold of my mind for good; I remembered the story of a medicine man who'd been trained in the ways of the sun dance. Breaking the body allows it to be whole again, this was the path to manhood. I did not move inside Felicia for what seemed like the end of time. We held each other, she with her legs wrapped around my waist, her chest fallen against mine, her breath buried inside the moisture of my neck. Her words hidden, fallen words that waited to return under the ground of our desire. I wanted to look at her; I didn't know if I could. I didn't know if I had the strength to hold her with my desire and with my eyes at the same time. This I did not know. The way of the sun dancer is to look for his own strength, to search past the strength of the body, past its weakness for the spirit to rise.

Felicia began to move on top of me, slowly at first, so slowly I thought we were sitting still on a shifting ground, and then quicker, with more force. We traveled together along the line of our desire. We moved along the path of the wind, like the prairie fire. At times, she jumped ahead of the flame. At others, it was me who traveled quicker than the fire. We followed the trail of our scent until we came upon a river.

"*Wakan*," she whispered. "*Wakan*."

Later, I asked her what the word *wakan* meant.

"*Wakan*," she whispered again and when she looked at me, I knew that she had said the word, "sacred".

Chapter 20 – Owl

When I think of my childhood, I think of myself in the four-cornered world of the one-room cabin my father built so we could live in peace. "Live in peace," he had said.

The summer after my father got his job at Wright McGill making fish hooks, we added a wood floor to our cabin. Up until then, it had been dirt, and when it rained, the ground became muddied when we came home with our wet shoes and filthy boots.

My father was a full-blood who didn't speak a word of Lakota. Most full bloods his age spoke a combination of English and Lakota but not my father. One day, I asked him why he didn't know the language of our ancestors and he told me that he'd been sent to the Holy Rosary Mission School in Pine Ridge, where they punished children for speaking anything but English. This was the school where the children were forced to be as white as white could be.

"If you didn't act white, you were beaten." My father said.

I never met my father's parents. My grandmother died of diabetes when I was two and my grandfather died before I was born. I never knew how and where or what happened to him. Whenever I'd ask my father about him, he'd say: "What is past is past," and he'd grow quiet and sit in his oversized armchair by the stove and stare off into space.

My father was a happier man before the war. As happy as a man can be after tragedy hits. Sometimes, he'd take me fishing into small creeks on the res. We'd spend an afternoon sittin' by the side of the creek waiting for the fish to bite. Some days, they'd bite and when they did, we'd come home to my mother feeling all proud, feeling like men who could provide.

When the fish didn't bite, my father would make up crazy stories about how a fish so huge had jumped out of the creek and almost knocked me out before my father had to release him to the waters. My father was a storyteller. He liked to tell tales of monster fish and traveling spirits who lived in the waters and the land and the trees.

One day, my father told me about the spirit of the north who consumed people. He described him as an enormous monster, a glutton who spent his time eating people as they tried to travel across the land in the winter months. In the end, the only thing that could kill the monster who spit out all of the people he'd eaten throughout the history of the land when he died, was fire.

Whenever my father had a bit of free time, he'd take me somewhere. We'd get in his truck and drive around the seven districts of the reservation: White Clay and Medicine Root, Porcupine and Eagle Nest. We'd drive to Pass Creek and LaCreek and Wounded Knee. My father never spoke of the shame of our history. He never liked to talk about the past. No matter how hard I'd try to ask him, he'd always come back with the same answer: "What's past is past," and that was that. It wasn't until I met Felicia that I really found out about our people's story. I had to wait to be a man to find out about my past.

When I was 12 years old, my father left for Vietnam. I remember the day my father was drafted like it was yesterday. The mailman came to the door. We never got any mail. Never got a thing worth reading. My father took the letter in his hand and opened it. We all knew what it said before he had read a word of it. He read it real slow, to himself and then he said, "I'll be leaving early next week." The next day, he quit his job at the fish hooks factory.

When my father left for the war, my mother got a job at the BIA (Bureau of Indian Affairs) office in the village. She hadn't worked before then, not in an outside job anyway. My mother worked her whole life making our meals, keeping our cabin clean, sewing our clothes, and planting vegetables on the small plot of land around our home. In early fall, she'd go to work in nearby Nebraska and pick beets or potatoes when it came time to harvest them. But when my dad left, she had to get a full-time job. Jobs were real hard to come by, but my mother had two things going for her: good looks and good luck for heartless things. She'd told me once how she was unlucky in *matters of the heart* but lucky in everything else. I always wanted to ask her if that meant marrying my father was part of the bad luck, but I never dared.

My mother was a mixed-blood with light hair the color of wheat. She wasn't one of those mixed-bloods where you couldn't see the Indian in her no more. She was clearly one of us, but you could see the traces of her French bloodline trailing back from the time when they they came to pillage our land and kill our people.

For a while, when my father was gone in Nam, my mother and I got into a rhythm of life together that was easy. I'd go off to school and she'd go off to work and after a while we never mentioned my father. It wasn't that we didn't care about him being gone; it was that his absence was all that we had left of him and we couldn't carry it around no more. So we said nothing.

Before he left my father worked at Wright-McGill making fish hooks. He'd leave every morning at dawn and come home when the sun was getting ready to set. He used to say that putting food on the table for his family was the best feeling in the world. *The best feeling in the world*

My father and I used to laugh a lot. I liked to play the trickster, play jokes on everyone. One time, I told him it was snowing outside when it wasn't. We didn't have windows and he got all dressed up wearing his wool pants and long johns and everything else only to find out it wasn't even that cold outside. That night, he said he'd spent the day sweating like a hog.

"My son made me sweat today," he told his coworkers. Everyone laughed. I was never that funny, but I could always laugh with my father. In school, I remember the kids that could make everyone laugh. It wasn't me. I wasn't one of those kids. I was always trying too hard, thinking too much about what was and what wasn't funny. Later I realized that the funniest people don't think about it, they're just funny. I was never one of those people.

Every time I think of my father, I think of him in those years *before* Nam. I try not to think of him in those years after he came back.

My father came back from the war four years before I met Felicia. After he came back, he spoke in his sleep and cried out at the enemy. When my mother and I would wake him, he'd look at us with empty eyes, with his arm raised like he was holding a gun and he was getting ready to shoot. This was the beginning of the end for my father. People say that around here a lot, *the beginning of the end*. But when I think of this now, when I think of the ways my father died, when I think of the time I spent with Felicia, I know that nothing really ends. Nothing starts and nothing ends because we are of the earth.

Sometimes, my father would sit in the sweat lodge praying.

"I can hear them women crying," he'd say when he changed his clothes after the lodge. Those times of prayer were the only times when he would ever speak openly about the spirit world and what he saw and heard, not counting the times when he was drunk.

"They're hurt," he'd say. "Hurt real bad." I knew he didn't like to talk about the spirits.

One night he came home drunk from The Blue Wolf. My mother and I were already asleep in our beds, when the door banged open. I didn't move; I'd lived through my father's drunken returns a million times and I knew there was nothing for me there. I pretended I was sleeping. I heard my mother, her wounded animal voice, like a fox in a trap.

"You'll wake him, Bill. You'll wake your son."

"Maybe he should wake up. Maybe it's time he knew there are ghosts on this land." Then something changed in his voice. Something strange happened and I realized that my father was crying. I almost sat up; I wanted to see his face in this moment. But I knew that if I moved, I would be pulled into his fury.

"I heard 'em Mary. I heard 'em crying in the bushes."

My mother shuffled over to him. She'd learned not to touch him in these moments when his body and spirit were not in the same place. My father's body lay drunk on our floor and my mother was consoling him. She was whispering words I could not hear. He continued to cry out as if he were alone in the room.

"Little children crying, little children crying for help and I did nothing. I did nothing." My father was sobbing now. He was downright sobbing. I sat up slowly in bed and I looked in the darkness. I had learned to see inside the heart of darkness since birth.

I saw him sitting on the ground with his muddied boots still on his feet, his legs spread open like a broken doll trying to sit upright. I searched for his eyes; I searched for the sign of tears in his eyes. I wanted to see a sign of what I had heard. My father could cry.

My mother was crouching next to him, keeping her distance, but close enough to touch him. He was looking at the ground, his face lost in a place neither me, nor my mother could see.

"Crying women and children." From the distance of my bed, I saw the strange gleam of his tears in the silver light spilling into the cracked lodge where we lived. The moon was full outside, its light leaking onto my father's tears.

Suddenly, his face jerked as if he had been called back to this place. He looked at me like an arrow being shot by faith. I saw the fear in his eyes turn to shame. For the first time, my father had seen me and what he saw was a crying man, a broken, fearful man being watched by his son, his body fallen on the muddied ground of his homemade shack.

My father never spoke to me again.

Chapter 21 – Owl

I spent all of those summer weeks with Felicia, the year Washington was elected as tribal chairman. When I say *elected,* I don't mean democratically chosen by the people of the res. That's not what happened. Washington was a puppet leader placed in power by the white-led government. Even though he was an Indian just like us, everyone said he was an apple. Truth be told, Washington didn't give a shit about us people of the res. Didn't give a damn about our safety or anything that had to do with justice. The only thing Washington wanted was power. But I have to wonder how powerful can you be when your ass is bought and you can't make a move without having the white man breathing down your neck. To talk about Washington is to talk about hate amongst brothers. I remember the night Felicia and I almost died together. Sometimes I can't help but wish we had lost our lives that night.

When fall came, colors changed and the air became crisp and our bodies quickened in the cooling air. By then, people had grown restless on the res. Washington wasn't playing by the rules. Instead of holding regular quarterly tribal council meetings, the way it had always been done, he'd just skip out on them altogether. Felicia was the first one to speak out against the injustice. Truth be told, it's the women that started getting organized.

Washington skipped the October meeting and called it in November instead. Grey Stone later told me that the chairman is required to call the Council into session under the Tribal Constitution. But Washington didn't care. All he wanted was to make money off of the res.

The night everything changed, Billy Joe came running into The Crazy Horse Café where me and the boys were sittin' having a beer.

"Craziest shit just happened. I just been to a meeting at Billy Mills Hall."

"What were you doin' there man?" Grey Stone asked Billy Joe.

"I was just comin' out of work when I found out about the meeting for tribal employees, so I figured, *why the hell not.* Sat my ass down and listened to the elders say something about AIM comin' to the res to celebrate their takeover in DC last week."

Truth be told, I didn't know much about my own history and who was what and what had taken place on my own land. I think that Grey knew how ignorant I was. How ignorant most of us were. *Brainwashed* is what he'd called us. "Not our fault," he said, "if we were taught to fear our own people." Grey liked to explain things to us in words we could understand.

"See, we Indians were never intended to survive the settlement of Europeans in the Western Hemisphere. They'd counted on all of us all being dead by now. But it didn't turn out that way, now did it?" Grey raised his glass and laughed. "Cheers, assholes, cheers!"

Billy Joe told us, "everybody got spooked at the meeting. They kept saying *you can't let AIM take over the res. You can't let them hold a victory dance.* And people got to votin' and they said that dances couldn't be held at Billy Mills Hall no more."

"People like to talk shit about AIM. They like to say the devil this, the devil that. AIM doesn't just stand for the American Indian Movement, it stands for the restoration of the treaties that were violated by the United States government. It stands for giving our Indian leaders a place to address Congress. It stands for the restoration of 100 million acres of land having been taken away from Native Nations by the United States. And most of all, it stands for the integrity of our people and our freedom on this land we call Turtle Island."

I'd heard about the takeover of the headquarters of the Bureau of Indian Affairs offices in DC a week earlier. Everyone had heard about it. It was not the first time our people had tried to occupy land that had always been ours. In 1969, people from several tribes had occupied Alcatraz for 19 months to reclaim federal land in the name of Native Nations. But this was the first time most of us were ready for change. Our leaders who had organized the Trail of Broken Treaties and marched on Washington occupying the Bureau of Indian Affairs headquarters presented a 20-point solution paper to President Nixon. Did we really think that Nixon would listen to our demands? Did we really believe that change would come? All I know is that I was ready to join my brothers to reclaim ourselves.

Grey Stone grew real quiet. I didn't know what to think. Broken Arrow who had been listening to Grey telling us about our own history, didn't seem to give a shit about our revolution. He just held his beer like we weren't in the middle of a land where war was about to break. Sometimes, I try to think and see if I knew that my whole life was about to shift. All I knew, I think, is that I was a boy, a boy so green, so young and foolish I didn't even know I should have run to Felicia that night. I should have run to her and held her forever instead of everything that followed.

Grey Stone let silence return to our table and took a sip of his beer and then he told us: "We have to take this into our own hands." When he said we, I remember feeling a lump in my throat, like I was trying to swallow a small egg. I thought about Felicia on the other side of the res. I thought about how much I wanted to hold her in that moment. Something about Billy Joe's words and the way Grey Stone was speaking to us made me want to hold everything that was precious to me. All I had was Felicia. She was all I had.

On the way back, I asked Grey Stone to drop me off at Felicia's. I knew she'd be sleeping and I knew I had no plan to get home that night, but I didn't care. I needed to see her. They drove away leaving me standing in the moonlit night. It was getting cold already. Late November and the night sky had changed. I'd taught myself all of the stars, the map of the sky, and when I looked up I saw that summer was gone. I stood in silence waiting for a plan to come to me when I saw that she was standing outside in her nightclothes, holding her arms across her chest like she was trying to grab hold of herself.

"What are you doing here? Are you crazy!" She was shivering. "If my father sees you here, he'll kill you!" She was whisper-yelling, and all I wanted to do was laugh.

"I just wanted to see you. I wanted to see you so I came." Was all I said and I saw her body relax and her face open into a smile.

"I'll get some clothes, I'll be right back." And she was gone again. I thought about what Grey Stone had said to us that night.

We need to take this into our own hands. What did he mean? What did I have to offer to my own people? I didn't know. When Felicia came back, she was wearing oversized boots and a large coat and she was dangling keys in her hands. Now I was the one who was whisper-yelling.

"Are you crazy! Your father's car! We can't take your father's car. He'll kill us!" I'd only met her father once and he'd given me the once-over look and just nodded hello. I knew then that he'd never like me. What did I have to offer his daughter? Who could blame him for not liking me?

"Shhh," she whispered taking me by the hand to her father's car.

"It's too cold to sit outside." We slid into the vinyl seats of the pick up truck and looked at the sky. I told Felicia about what Grey Stone had told us, and she said nothing for a long time. Later when I held her so close I could smell every inch of her skin, she said: "He's right. It's up to us to do something about this." That's when I knew that I didn't have a choice. I had already been chosen to act.

Felicia said we should go for a drive. She shot up and *bam*, we were off pushing her father's truck slowly down the road so we could start it away from the house.

Our love was bound by the motion of cars. We drove in silence for much of the trip until we saw the lights of the village ahead. Felicia took the wheel.

"It's best the fate of this truck rests in my hands, don't you think?" Felicia laughed. I agreed. I'd never once driven Felicia anywhere and in the winter months that followed, I'd become obsessed with owning my own wheels so I could drive her around the res.

We pulled over on the outskirts of town by the side of Oak Road. I'd learned to love the smell of vinyl, along with Felicia's sweet softness and the way she always held me with her eyes. She leaned forward as if she was about to kiss me and just when I was about to close my eyes, she whispered in my ear: "I have something to tell you, but first I want to teach you a song." I pulled away lightly to look at her and a truck drove by us slowly kicking up some dust from the road. Felicia looked in the direction of the road waiting for silence to return and then she leaned forward again in the same way she had done before.

"This is the spirit invitation song our people sing during the cleansing *inipi* ceremony. We don't usually sing this outside of the sweat lodge, but I want us both to sing it so that we can both be prepared for what I am about to tell you."

I had no idea what Felicia was about to share with me but I trusted her guidance. Her voice began to rise in the cool night air around us.

"*Tunkasila Wanmayanguye.* Repeat after me." She told me. "*Tunkasila Wanmayanguye.*"

I repeated the words and followed the melody.

"It means *grandfather, come and see me.*"

With each word we sang in unison, I could feel my heart fill with pride. We sang that verse three times, each time varying the rhythm of the cadence, making it clumsy at first for me to follow Felicia's voice.

"*Ikce wicasa tacannunpe. Wan yuha hoyelo.*" Felicia continued to sing and teach me the ways of our people.

"This means, *I send a voice with the people's pipe.* It is calling all of us common folks to send our voice to call the spirits to join and purify us. And in the last verse, *Mitaye ob waniktelo heyaya. Hoyewayelo*, we are saying, *so I may live with my relatives.* This is a song of unity, calling the spirits to join us."

We sang the song a second time without any interruptions.
"Tunkasila
Wanmayanguyelo
Ikce wicasa tacannunpe
Wan yuha hoyelo
Mitaye ob waniktelo heyaya
Hoyewayelo"

Grandfather come and see me
I send a voice with the people's pipe,
So I may live with my relatives."

"Thank you," I told Felicia leaning over to kiss her lips gently. Thank you for guiding me home."

"You don't have to thank me for showing you what already belongs to you. What belongs to all of us Lakotas. The *inipi* ceremony is one of the seven rites practiced since the beginning of time. It helps us transform from our old selves to our new selves. What I am about to tell you will change us both forever. And we will be called to move in a new way. Do you understand?"

"I understand that nothing will be the same again from this moment forward."

"Good," she said pleased to see I understood her.

"I'm pregnant," she added. My heart stopped only to be jump-started again by the touch of her hand on mine and the feel of her belly under our fingers.

"Here," she said. "Feel." And I remember the tiny roundness of her belly, small inflated hardness unlike softness of fat, or the airy bounce of a belly full of gas. I could feel the firmness of Felicia's skin under the small mound of her flesh and this is where life was growing in the tiny pod body of my wife. Even though we had never wed in front of our community, that night, Felicia became my wife under the Orion sky of autumn. That night, my spirit married hers.

We drove slowly on the way back. Slower than usual. It was as if Felicia's choice to speak of the life she was carrying made everything else around us appear more dangerous and fragile. The roads were deserted for the most part, and when we crossed another car coming in the other direction, Felicia turned down her beam lights. I remember thinking that kindness to strangers on the road is a strange kind of brotherhood that moved me.

When the lights of the car behind us shone in the reflection of the rearview mirror, Felicia was in the middle of telling me about how she'd found out two weeks earlier but she wanted to wait before telling me. The lights behind us became so bright Felicia had to shield her eyes so she could see the road. She rolled down the window and gestured for them to pass us but before we knew it, the car was pressing up against ours and honking madly.

"What the…!" Felicia was cursing now. She kept gesturing outside the rolled-down window for the car to pass us. "Go! Go! You bastard." But the car began to bump us. First lightly and then harder each time, our car would jerk forward. I searched for a seat belt but there was none and I held on tightly to the car door and the dashboard bracing for the worse. I thought about the life growing inside Felicia.

"Speed up!" I yelled.

"I can't go any faster. The car won't go any faster, not on this road." Suddenly they passed us on the left but instead of moving past us completely, they stayed by our side threatening to hit us again. Two men I'd never seen before were in the car, the driver looked Indian, mixed blood I think, but the other was white with a trace of red hair, reddish blond in the moonlit night. He was laughing, his face all twisted up with a wild look in his eyes. The driver grimaced and then bumped us sideways pushing us closer and closer to the ditch.

"That bastard's gonna run us off the road!" I yelled. I could feel the car picking up speed. Felicia was trying to outrun them. But each time she moved past them, they caught up to us. The banging was pretty crazy now. They were hitting us sideways every few seconds; each hit harder than the first. I wished I had a gun in the car in that moment. I'd never owned a weapon before and definitely not a gun, but in that moment I knew that I had more than myself to protect. I had Felicia and the life inside her.

She slammed on the breaks and my body went lunging forward; I banged my head against the dashboard. The other car kept on whizzing forward and they disappeared in the dark as we screeched to a halt and spun in a circle a few times before landing in the ditch.

All I wanted was for Felicia to be OK. But my head was pounding and I couldn't see out of my left eye where I'd hit the dashboard. Felicia was slumped over the wheel. She wasn't moving.

Chapter 22 – Owl

I wanted to scream out Felicia's name to bring her back to me but found no sound. I couldn't move. Outside, I heard crickets and imagined them all around us. The car rested almost fully on its side, leaning towards the passenger side but it was still upright where a boulder had stopped it from rolling.

Felicia's head was pressed against the dashboard; her body folded in half like a rag doll. She looked broken, as if someone had tried to fold her and succeeded. The road was quiet now. There were rarely any cars so late at night. I moved my hand slowly on the surface of Felicia's back and neck like a dowser searching for a sign of water. I could feel her energy still vibrating. Felicia's body was almost still but she was moving. I didn't want to budge or even touch her after that. Knowing she was still alive had made her all the more fragile.

I thought about something I'd seen on TV once about not moving victims from an accident sight and now I wondered if I'd ever be able to touch Felicia again.

Something in me wanted to flee the scene. To run as far away as I could and pretend that Felicia wasn't lying unconscious in this car in the ditch. I tried to open my car door but it was stuck. It was all banged up and wasn't budging. I heard Felicia moaning. I turned to her as she sat up slowly. She had a small gash on the side of her forehead. She was bleeding.

"Where are we?" She asked touching her head. Hearing her voice, made me come back to myself all at once. The desire to run disappeared and I was back again with Felicia alive by my side.

"Don't move."

"Your hand is bleeding," she said still rubbing her head slowly. I held out my hand and saw nothing.

"The other one," she said trying to crack a smile. I saw that she was right. My left hand was badly scratched. Now that I knew about the hand, I could suddenly feel the achy pain of my scratched fingers and bruised knuckles.

"We have to get out of here," I said still trying to open the car door.

"Maybe you should stay here while I get us some help." I wasn't sure what I was saying. I pictured Felicia all alone in this beat-up car at night and I knew that I shouldn't leave her alone.

"I ain't staying here by myself. Are you crazy?" She yelled echoing my thoughts. I opened the window and slipped out of the car. The ground felt firmer and harder than I had expected. I could suddenly feel every inch of my body responding to gravity.

I ached all over but seeing Felicia still inside the car, made me push the pain out of my mind and motion for her to slide onto the passenger seat. As she struggled to move where I had sat, I could see that her forehead was bleeding more than ever. The blood was trickling onto the car seat as she leaned forward.

"Push on your forehead to stop the bleeding. Push on it."

"I can't, I only have two hands Owl, and I need to get out of this damn car!" I'd never heard Felicia use my name in annoyance before. I'd never seen her in danger, her body in crisis. The bleeding really scared me, but I knew to stay calm.

Felicia struggled her way out of the car. I handed her one of my socks I'd taken off and told her to push hard on the wound. We made our way back to the road and limped along in silence. Now that I knew I would be a father, the whole world seemed different. I could smell danger all around me.

An hour went by before a car drove by and stopped to pick us up. I took one good look inside the truck and saw the man had a good face. He was about the age my father would have been now. Lines of laugher and hard work marked his worn face. His hair was greased up real good like he hadn't seen a shower in a while. He took one look at me and said: "Hey aren't you John's son Edgar Owl Feather?

"Sure am."

"Your dad and I worked together for ten years at McWright. A good man your father. Hop in."

Felicia got in the car and I slid along side of her.

"You don't look so good little lady. What are you two doin' here this time of night?"

"Two men drove us off the door. Our car is in a ditch about four miles back." I explained.

"Yep, and it's too bad I didn't get killed 'cause my father sure is gonna kill me now." Felicia was still pressing my dirty sock against her forehead. The bleeding seemed to have slowed.

"Two men drove you off the road, you said? Sounds like goon activity."

"What do you mean?"

"A couple of months ago, Dick Washington brought in some US Marshals and parked them on the Bureau of Indian Affairs office building roof. They got rifles and when they're not aiming their guns at us, they're terrorizing people in town. Don't bother reporting it; Dicky's men will put you in jail for being attacked. Ain't that something?"

Felicia and I sat in silence grateful to have a ride to the hospital.

"Did ya hear about the Bad Heart murder over in Buffalo Gap?"

Felicia and I both shook our heads no.

"I'm down on my way to a meeting in town. An Indian boy, about 20 or so; Wesley Bad Heart was his name. He was beaten to death with a 2x4 studded with nails by a white guy in a bar just for asking for a drink."

Chills ran up my spine. "When did this happen?" I asked.

"Happened just last night. I tell you this mess ain't gonna stop here. Some of us are gettin' goddamn sick and tired of our people gettin' killed for being Indian." He ran his hand over his face, like he was trying to wipe the anger from his skin.

"I'ma drop you off at the hospital in Pine Ridge. You better get that forehead of yours checked. Looks like it's bleeding pretty bad."

We walked into the hospital that smelled like chlorine. Hobbled in was more like it. Felicia was holding on to me. A nurse, white as all nurses in the Pine Ridge hospital were, looked us up and down when we approached the registration desk and said sharply: "Can I help you?"

"My wife…my girlfriend here is hurt real bad. We were in a car crash just now."

I'd let the word "wife" slip out for no reason. It wasn't like I was thinking we were married. Wasn't thinking it so much as feeling it.

The nurse looked down at her registry like we weren't there at all. But she addressed us anyway.

"Just fill this out." She pushed a piece of paper in front of me without looking at us. I'd seen the hatred in her eyes when we'd first walked in. She must have been no older than 28 years old. Married. I'd noticed the ring on her finger. She was the proper type. The type of white woman who should have lived in a large city away from us Indians but for some reason just kept on sticking around for more torture. Hers and ours.

After an hour's wait, we finally got to see the doctor.

"You can wait outside in the waiting room," the doctor said when I tried to join them.

"But she's my…"

He interrupted me looking down at his chart. "It says here that she's single." And he walked away. Felicia looked back with an air of a sad smile as if to say, *Don't worry, I'll be back.*

I sat down in the waiting room, full of patients waiting for care. There were two other Indians in there. The first one was a guy my age with a bleeding hand, he was holding it wrapped in a handkerchief. The other person was an old woman whose hands were shaking uncontrollably. She tried to hide them under her shawl but even then I could see the motion of her hands under the fabric. She must have been a few years older than my mother.

I thought of my own mother and wondered if she'd realized I'd gone. Would she have woken up in the middle of the night and seen that I was missing? I knew she would. Now that my father was gone; I was all she had to worry about.

I went to the payphone and called Grey to see if he could pick us up. I was torn about waking him up but I knew Felicia and I shouldn't try to hitch now. I heard his voice, clear as day on the other end.

"You're not sleeping?" I asked him almost forgetting the reason I'd called.

"Owl! What's up buddy?"

"I got in an accident with my girl Felicia. We sure could use a ride back to the res from the hospital."

Felicia came back what seemed like an hour later with two stitches on the side of her head, her arm in a cast and a sprained ankle.

"Shouldn't you get checked?" she asked me when she came out.

"I'm fine," I told her.

Grey's Cougar pulled up in the circle. I opened the back door for Felicia and sat shotgun next to Grey. He didn't even look at us and started driving before my door was barely closed.

"Something just went down. One of our boys was murdered again. A meeting's about to start. You're coming with me," Grey said as soon as we got in his car. I'd never stood up to gray before, but this time I needed to protect Felicia. She needed to go home.

"Grey. We're real hurt. Here. Can …"

"Oh shit! You both look bad!" He said finally looking at my face.

"We were driven off the road by some crazy guys in a truck. You should have seen it."

"Goon activity, no doubt."

"Some guy on the road was nice enough to give us a ride to the hospital," I told Grey.

"You were lucky that's for damn sure! You go home and I'll go to this meeting. I'm gonna fight this right."

**

When we got back, the moment of truth when I'd have to face Felicia's father and tell him we'd totaled his car, and his daughter was hurt came to hit me head on.

The house was as dark and as quiet as houses are in the middle of the night. Felicia limped to the front door, took a key from under a plant and opened the door.

"Shhh," she said. "Don't tell anyone about the key."

Felicia was smiling. I didn't understand how she could still find the strength to make a joke at a time like this. The house was dark and still smelled like home cooking of beef soup and the sweetness of Indian fry bread.

We made our way through the kitchen in darkness. Felicia knew the house and she moved easily in spite of her injuries but I couldn't see a damn thing. She was ahead of me and I could barely see her hobble.

"This way." I heard her whisper. I tried moving my hand along the wall's surface like the blind getting to know a face. I felt a strange shape along the tips of my fingers, and before I could realize that I was pushing my hand along a shelf, I heard the sound of a dish crashing to the ground. No sound had ever seemed so loud, so startling in my life.

"Oh shit!" Felicia giggled nervously.

The lights came on in the other room. I heard a door opening and closing and then a body filled the doorframe.

"Hi daddy," Felicia said sounding like a little girl.

The light came on in the kitchen. Felicia's father was a large man with a healthy belly hidden by a white work shirt. I noticed he had it on backwards and thought about him fumbling for his clothes when he must have heard us. He took one look at me, one look at his wounded daughter and he grabbed hold of her. His arms were long and broad like the limbs of an old maple.

"Baby, what happened to you?" and then dropping his voice: "You! Don't move!" I could see that he was shielding Felicia from me.

"Daddy. I can explain." Felicia's mother peered in the doorway.

"Daughter! Are you hurt?" Her mother said grabbing her by the arm. It was a cross between a punishing and nurturing gesture.

"No, mother. I'm fine."

"Get in here! Felicia! Do not dishonor us like this! Have you no shame?" The woman who had given her birth grabbed her daughter and pulled her into the other room.

I heard the women's voices fade. They were gone. I was alone with the man who had raised the woman I loved.

"We were in a car accident, Sir. That's how we got hurt. People drove us off the…"

"Were you driving?"

"No, sir. Felicia was driving."

"You let women drive you around, boy?"

"Well, sir. It was your car." I saw that his hands became fists. He made his way towards me and for a second, I was certain he would hit me. I didn't move. There was nothing I could do. If I fought back, I'd lose my honor forever. His body came right up. I closed my eyes heard him push by to the front door where he searched for his missing car.

"Where is it?" he was yelling now. "Where is my car?"

"In the ditch, sir. It's in the ditch."

We spent an hour talking until dawn. The four us at the kitchen table. Her father made me promise I would pay him back for the destroyed car. I had no idea how I would do that but I gave the man my word.

At the first sign of light, they sent me on my way. I walked the eight miles back to my mother's place until my legs couldn't hold me no more and I dropped onto my cot to sleep.

**

The week that followed the accident, I became bound by Felicia's family. It was as if the crash had pushed me through and into her family. The next day, I came back to Felicia's house and she took me to see her grandmother Ihanblapi who'd told her about the ways of the elders. We walked up the hill behind the house to a grove of apple trees surrounding a small house. I could see colorful leaves blowing in the wind, and when I came closer, I saw that they were pieces of cloth wrapped around the tip of the tree's branches.

"Tobacco ties," Felicia said to me as she saw me observing the branches." They're sacred offerings."

We entered the small house that smelled of sweet grass. A woman the size of a child sat up slowly from her chair. Her hair, whiter than snow was pulled into long braids. She came to meet us at the door as we waited patiently for her to reach us. Grandmother Ihanblapi radiated with sweetness and love. I felt like I'd known her my whole life. The three of us stood in the frame of the woman's house.

"*Winunh'cala*," she said pointing to herself. "Old woman." And she smiled a toothless grin. She then placed her hand on my chest and held it there: "Koškalaka. You young man."

We walked in and sat on wooden stools in the center of the house. Grandma Ihanblapi placed her hands on Felicia's belly and said: "Wacanheja." She smiled again and this time I saw that she was missing all of the teeth on her bottom gum.

"Children," smiled Felicia. My heart was racing. I looked at Felicia who knowingly smiled.

"Numpa. Two babies."

"We're having twins?" I asked not believing my own words.

"How does she know? You're not even showing!" I said looking at Felicia.

"She can feel these things." The old woman handed me a cup and told me to drink. I took a sip nervously.

"World begin with two babies," she said.

I turned to Felicia looking for an explanation.

"There is a myth about the world ending in a flood. As the world was getting swallowed, an eagle saved a woman from the waters and made her his wife. They had twins who became the renewed people of the Indian race."

I looked around the woman's house. It was small but neat. There were pieces of polished wood resting on a wooden table. A pile of rocks surrounded a porcelain bowl containing an animal's jaw. She placed her hand on my chest and said: "You cut from people." When she said this, she made a gesture with her hands that showed a hatchet cutting down a tree.

"You cut," she repeated again making the hatchet gesture with her gnarly hand. "You find people again," she said pushing my body towards Felicia's. "And you become *hocokatoya*."

When she said *hocokatoya* she made the sign of a full circle with her hands.

"You need to reconnect with Indians again," Felicia translated for her grandmother.

I felt a sense of peace in this house. A deep sense of peace I'd never felt before. The house reminded me of a place I'd always known, but I could not remember visiting.

"You have wowakan wowašake but careful of wowahtani."

"She says that you have sacred powers but you must watch out for evil."

"You take vision."

"She wants you to go on a vision quest." Felicia translated.

Grandma handed me something. I opened up my hand and saw that she had given me a stone carved in the shape of a wolf. I'd never had a spiritual practice before that day. Been cut off from my culture for so long, I knew enough to respect the old ways but not enough to know what grandma was talking about.

"Šungmahetu. When you ready. He find you."

I had no idea what she was saying, but I said nothing. I saw that we were sitting in a circle now, a perfect closed circle. I did not remember moving, but our line of chairs had magically turned into a circle. I drank the rest of the tea. We sat quietly absorbing the peace of the house. Later, as she walked us to the door grandma said: "Important I tell you, cincala waziyata."

"What does that mean?" I asked turning to Felicia. But I saw that she was as puzzled as I was.

"I am not sure what she means exactly. *The baby is in the place of the pines* is the literal translation which I think means *the baby lives in the north*. I am not sure."

"One day he understand. One day he understand." Ihanblapi told us.

Chapter 23 – Owl

All hell broke loose on the res, after the murder of Wesley Bad Heart who was stabbed to death by a white Air Force veteran named Darld Schmitz in Buffalo Gap, South Dakota, a month earlier.

Grey Stone traveled to Custer, South Dakota with a man I later came to know as Jerome Bean. I didn't know Jerome very well but I'd seen him around with Grey. He had a large forehead, wide open like the plains at the belly of the Black Hills. He wore his hair in braids that thinned out at the ends, so thin they looked like woven black thread pointing to the ground. I could feel there was much to know about this man.

When they came back from Custer to clean up the mess of the Bad Heart murder, they were in bad shape. I don't mean just physically but they were torn up and angry about the crazy shit that went down over there. The boys and me, we went to The Crazy Horse for a beer so we could get the story from Grey. When we sat down, I noticed something new in Grey's eyes. A look that said something had broken loose inside him.

"I'd called the Rapid City Journal and asked them to put the meeting we had called at the courthouse in the paper, so we could get other Indians to show up and support us. Trouble is, some feds called up the paper pretending to be one of us and said the meeting was cancelled. This is the kind of shit they pull so people won't show up. 200 still showed."

Even Grey's voice had changed; it was lower somehow, trailing out like a broken piece of music.

"We went to the courthouse, it was snowing like crazy. Sarah Bad Heart, Wesley's mother was there. That woman was shaking. They'd killed her son, you know?" Grey wasn't looking at us when he spoke; it was like he was retelling the story to himself.

"We get there and they let us Jerome, Don and me through but they stop the others." I notice Grey's hand shaking as he puts his palms out flat on the table, pushing hard as if he was trying to find meaning in the wood.

"I'm thinking, this ain't right. They told us they'd meet with us. They said they'd meet with the Indian community to address Wesley's murder. So Jerome's yelling at the cops to let 'em through and I go to get Sarah Bad Heart 'cause you know it ain't right to leave that woman standing out there in a blizzard when we're talking about the murder of her son. And all of a sudden an officer blows his whistle and about 90 cops run in there, like fucking termites in a tree trunk. They start grabbing Sarah and me and hitting her with an ice stick. I'm yelling and some asshole throws some fucking tear gas in the room. I'm thinking, *shit we've got to get out of he*re. So I grab a billy club from one of the cops and I break a window. The cops just grabbed my ass and threw me in jail."

The place was silent now, silent and still like the whole place was listening. I heard the sound of glasses clanking on the other side of the café.

"Sarah's in jail. The mother of that boy is in jail while her son's killer is out free."

Grey's story filled me with rage. It wasn't anger; it wasn't something I could control. It was like a wild fire that could burn down the entire prairie.

Turns out, the cops didn't keep Grey in jail long. Just enough to humiliate him, to kick his face into the ground. I knew that night that I couldn't sit around no more and do nothing.

**

After that, I saw Grey almost everyday. He'd usually come and pick me up from my parent's place, swing by Felicia's house and we'd drive right up to the Billy Mills Hall. People had finally had it with the corruption in the government on the res and Dicky Washington's impeachment was scheduled for 10 a.m. on the morning of February 22nd. We hooked up with a caravan of cars and pulled into the hall's parking lot raring to have the man step down. Our boys had drums, and brought a peace pipe and we had singers ready to sing a song of victory. But when we got in, they said that they weren't going to let us in and just filter the news out through some television. They said it was a private meeting. Hundreds of us started yelling and talking all at once and after a while, they figured they'd better let us in so they did.

Like any ol' court, the room was divided into two sides, Dicky Washington's side and the rest of us. We all sat away from Dicky, all 600 of us packed like sardines. While only a handful of people filled up Dicky's side. They were getting underway and then they postponed the meeting again until the afternoon and they played this movie for us called, *Anarchy, USA*. This was this crazy old movie about blacks burning and looting cities. I guess they were trying to brainwash us into thinking that nothing good can come out of rioting. I watched the movie and thought that when you got nothing to lose, anarchy is the only road to change.

Felicia and I sat together the whole time. I hadn't let go of her hand since that night of the accident. In that moment, I imagined the madness of losing my wife. Things were coming back to me from the crash. Strange thoughts that'd been erased started filtering back. Thoughts like: *If she dies, I'll die too*. Thoughts of suicide, thoughts of vengeance. Thoughts of wanting to go for *payback*. I'd also been thinking about goons a lot. Thinking about them being Indian, just like me, just like Felicia. I could see them at the court now with their crew cuts and their dead eyes, standing there by the door, guarding us. Guarding their own brothers and sisters.

I wanted to understand how our people could lose their way and turn against Indians. How did this happen? And then I remembered how easy it was to lose your way growing up on the res.

The goon is a boy turned on his head with nothing to do. The goon is the boozer at the corner. He's the boy playing in the village dump. He's the kid counting cigarette butts on the ground. He's my brother and your son. He's the one no one remembers until it's too late. He's your broken and forgotten boy. Using native against native is as old as time itself. Not the time of the prairies and the mountains. Not the time of the rivers and the fields. It's not the time of the spotted eagle. This is the time of the *crucifix throwers*, this is the time of the carriage builders and the sacred fire throwers, the time of the white man who came to live on our land like it'd just been discovered. We were here when there was no time. Our people were here when there was only lightning coming out of the west and mornings coming out of the east. We were here before all the spring times where the whitetail deer returned to feast on young violets at the first sign of spring. We were here before any of the seasons, before the white of summer, and the elk grazing on the earth Grandfather had created. We were here before the last trail of winter ever started and the buffalo roamed in search of better pastures. We were here before the swallows and the darkness of fall and the dance of the blacktail deer at the foot of the hills.

Our time dips into the rivers where the waters run mad with the thawing of glaciers. Our time flows with the course of the wind in the path of the pipe's smoke, before there was a pipe. In the moment when the eagle and the last woman on earth conceived their babies together on the highest peak. Our time comes and dances around the return of rains after long seasons of drought. Our time is the fall of the lightning and the crack of the thunder on young vulnerable shoots.

The goon is a boy of wandering spirit. A boy whose *šicun* has already left his body even before death comes. When spirit leaves the body before its time, it drifts to the far corners of the world in search of a place to rest.

Seeing these goons in the courtroom made me think of crazy Jimmy when we were growing up. We were kids still and we were playing by the side of the road racing chickens. The thing about chickens (and this is what made it fun for me) is that they don't listen. They just run all over the place like crazy little fuckers. Jimmy had a chicken that was *his* and I had *mine* and we'd place bets on whose chicken would make it to the finish line first. The key was to stay behind your chicken the whole time and yell like crazy so it'd keep running in a straight line. But chickens never ran in a straight line. The last race I ever did with Jimmy, my chicken crossed the finish line first and I was jumping up and down cheering when all of a sudden, I saw Jimmy pick this huge fucking rock. It was more like a boulder and he held it up above his head and smashed it down on his own chicken. It was the craziest thing I'd ever seen. The chicken just exploded and lay there all body, a pulp of flesh and bloodied feathers. I stood there in shock just staring at Jimmy when I heard him say: "This shit game is for dirty Indians and I ain't doing it no more." And he ran off.

That day, I didn't understand what had run through Jimmy's head. It would take me until that day in court to understand the poison of the government on young Indian minds. We'd been left in the prime of our youth in the poorest, most deprived piece of land in the whole nation with nothing to learn and nothing to do. We were left there to rot. But youth doesn't rot, unguided youth goes mad, it turns on itself like a scorpion biting its own body. Like a mad wolf trying to kill its young. Crazy Jimmy and the goons and all of our brothers had been lured off the res to big cities, only to find there was no place for them out there except a chance to go mad. For some, the madness happened in a 40-ouncer; for others, it was in cheap whisky or weed; for others still, it was in pulling a gun on another Indian under the white man's orders. It was easy to go mad in the poorest corner of this country. Staying sane was the challenge.

In the afternoon, we took a vote on whether or not Washington should be impeached and everyone voted *yes*. The next day, we came back for the actual trial. The problem was we needed a judge to act in Washington's place. Dicky yelled out, "What's the matter, nobody want this hot seat of mine?" Washington was accused of stealing money from federal funds meant for programs on the res and using them for his own use. He was accused of not being for his people. They brought in a referee, some bought-out, brainwashed puppet. Every time a witness came in to testify against Washington, the referee would cut them off after three minutes and go on to someone else. It was clear the whole thing was rigged. After this charade went on for about an hour, Dicky Washington was voted back into office with a 4–0 vote based on *the lack of sufficient evidence*.

As soon as the verdict was pronounced, all hell broke loose and someone yelled out: "I'm taking this to Federal Court." Everyone started hollering and yelling and all the people on our side stormed out. Felicia and I took one look at each other and we ran out of there.

Caravans of cars drove off to the Calico Community Center six miles north of Pine Ridge to have a meeting. We wanted to talk it over to see what we needed to do. Felicia and I rode with Grey, Jerome, Juan, and Lea. When we got out of the car, I looked up and saw that there were dozens of marshals up on the roof pointing their guns at us. They were waiting for an excuse to shoot us down.

Inside, Grey and Jerome Bean said we should figure a way to stay calm. Others jumped in and yelled obscenities about Washington and his goons. The whole time, we were being watched. Four or five goons came in while we were talking. They were drunk as skunks and banged the door wide open when they came in.

Taking one look at them, Lea Fight Wolf yelled, "Get the hell out of here."

The goons zigzagged around the place for a few minutes and saw how many we were and they left.

"Listen, I don't know about you guys, but I'm sick of sitting around and doing nothing about this. Us women are going to go to Wounded Knee and stay there until we find a solution." Lea told the entire room.

Voices rose around us like waves. I heard someone say, "That's a good idea!"

Then I heard Felicia's voice in the crowd: "Let's go back to the place where our ancestors were killed!" She had her arm raised up in the air to mark her words, our pride carrying us right to the pages of our history.

Chapter 24 – Owl

A caravan of 54 of our cars meandered down to Wounded Knee—the land where our ancestors had been murdered one hundred years earlier. Felicia and I drove up with Grey and the others, packed right into his Cougar, all eight of us. Grey had a police radio scanner in his car so we could hear the marshalls on the BIA radio reporting on our progression from the Calico Community Center to Wounded Knee. With each mile, we heard the voices announce over the radio: *they're coming down the road, they've passed the jail, they're driving east, they're not stopping!* You're damn straight we weren't stopping. Nothing was going to stop us now. Today, as I look back on what took us to Wounded Knee, it's hard to pinpoint the exact straw that broke our backs. Maybe it was the Wesley Bad Heart murder and how his mother had been beaten and jailed because she had come to Custer to seek justice for her son. Maybe it was having Washington voted back in for another round of corruption. Maybe it was the feeling that our time was running out for good and if we didn't move now, we would all be wiped out for good. It's hard to say but all I know is that we weren't turning back.

It was real late by the time we got there. I saw a long line of cars lined up bumper to bumper all the way to the Sacred Heart Church. We all piled up into the church like we were home. Some people had carried drums with them and began to play. We moved the pews out of the way and tried to make ourselves comfortable. It was cold but mild for an end-of-winter night in South Dakota.

Felicia and I huddled in a corner and decided we'd try to sleep. We were both exhausted from all of the excitement of the previous days. I wore a thin wool jacket that let in the wind while Felicia had worn her overturned sheep's coat; we huddled together to stay warm. The moment that followed is permanently engraved in my memory. I pulled Felicia towards me that night; looked into her eyes and made a promise to her I would not be able to keep.

"No matter what happens here, I will always protect you."

I remember the look of trust in her eyes. The way her body pushed into mine as if she were saying, *I know you will always protect me.* I wanted to be strong for Felicia but truth is I was scared that night. Scared the goons would come and shoot us; scared I wouldn't be able to protect Felicia. I knew Dicky Washington wanted one thing and one thing only: an excuse to shoot us all down. I remember thinking something bad was going to happen, something real bad. It was like I could feel the future unfolding in my body. But I pushed those thoughts out of my mind and watched Felicia as she fell asleep in my arms.

It was cold in the church. Felicia pressed her warm body against mine pushing her head into the curve of my chest like a wounded duckling. I don't know why I thought of her as a wounded bird. Thought of us both that way. Like we were trapped in some clearing waiting for hunters to get us.

That night, there was more than just fear in that church. I could feel the energy of the others rising like some kind of strange storm. Grey Stone was full of something I couldn't name at first. It was like the rage from before had given into a new life force.

Later, I realized that the energy that coursed through Grey's veins that night was pride. Pride in the land we were reclaiming, pride in the unity of our people, pride in our strength and our courage. Pride. That's what we been missing all this time since our people had fallen.

The next day I woke up real early when the light was just beginning to filter into the church. Many people were still sleeping. Some were gone. Felicia's head rested on my lap, her body folded in the fetal position. It was cold, real cold and when I coughed, I saw my breath in the cool morning air. I moved slowly pulling my legs from under Felicia, leaving her with my small bag propped under her head as a pillow. She didn't wake.

The bad feeling I had from before hadn't left, nothing had changed but this time I ignored it. I wanted to talk to the guys. They'd know what we should do next.

When my fear hit the mix, everything got garbled again and I thought for the first time that staying maybe meant dying. Were we all going to die in this place? I thought of Felicia and the babies inside her and the fear grew. But something had shifted for me in the middle of the night. The fear was still there but a new feeling had planted itself at the center of my chest—*hope*, like a strange young tree taking root. I could feel it tugging at me.

Outside the light had brightened from a pale rose to a muted blue, a young light promising everything a new day can offer. Grey Stone sat outside the church with a group of guys. They had made a fire and were sitting around it talking. When I walked up I saw Grey Stone with a stick in hand marking the ground with large strokes.

"They'll try to enter here, here and here," he said, each time marking the ground with an X. "And it's up to us to guard our posts and make sure no one enters."

I sat down on the ground by the fire making myself small. Grey Stone looked up and nodded at me in acknowledgement and went on talking. Broken had fought in Nam, he'd fought for the government and now he was fighting against it.

"We'll need ammunitions, and food and other supplies," Grey said.

"What if we just go out, get the stuff we need and we bring it back here?" Broken Arrow was looking at Grey Stone waiting for an answer.

"We can't. It's too risky. If we try to leave now, we'll weaken the camp and they'll come in and take over. We can't let that happen."

"I know how to break out of here and back with supplies." Broken insisted.

Everyone grew quiet. I could hear a rooster crooning in the distance. I warmed my hands over the fire waiting for someone to speak.

"There's a trading post down a couple of minutes from here. We should talk to the owners and see if they'll agree to give us supplies."

Jim Catches Crow spoke out: "Give us supplies? Yeah, right. Those white bastards ain't never gonna give us shit. I say we just break in and just take what we need."

I silently agreed with Jim but didn't want to say nothing. I was watching not knowing what would happen next. And I wasn't about to speak out and make myself known.

I'd heard Grey say to us before that our *war* on the res was not to fight the white man but to fight his evil ways. It had never been a war of races for Grey but a war of principles. For others whose suffering had run its course, the war had turned into a blood war.

"We'll ask them, and then if they won't give us the stuff, we'll do as you say." Grey said. But Sammy wouldn't have it.

"This is bullshit man! That trading post hasn't been about our people. It's been owned by those white folks making money off our suffering. Have you been in there? You been in there Grey?" Grey nodded like he understood.

"There's pictures of our bloated people killed in the Wounded Knee massacre a hundred years ago They're charging fucking money to tourists so they can see that shit! Pictures of fucking soldiers grinning over the bodies of our women and children. And you want us to ask them to give us supplies?"

"I just want us to give off respect, even if we're not getting it in return. You know everything comes back in the end," Grey said. But Sammy he couldn't hear a word.

"That ain't right. It ain't Grey, and you know it." He walked off shrugging his shoulders.

Broken Arrow, Billy Joe, and I just looked at each other. I'd never looked at Billy Joe up close till that morning. His hair was parted in the middle and his two black braids pulled tight on either side of his face, I realized that he was as scared as I was.

I walked back to the church and found Felicia still sleeping. I caressed her head gently. She looked like an angel sleeping with the morning light streaming down on her face from the church window. She opened her eyes and smiled like she was both surprised and happy to see me.

That morning, we held a meeting in the church. No one was really in charge, we all were. We pulled our heads together only I stayed silent and watched it all spin around me. By the time everyone had woken up and gathered in the church, I saw that there were many of us there that morning. Some people had gotten word of our gathering and had come during the night. There must have been almost two hundred people piled up in that church that morning.

Everyone took turns talking about what was on his or her mind. Some people were getting ready to leave to get their things from home. Grey tried to discourage them saying it wasn't safe but they wouldn't listen. Others said they'd come back later with some of their things. Later we found out that those who left had all been arrested and held in jail for no reason.

"I think it's time to stay on our land and reclaim our nation," Felicia yelled out. Everyone cheered.

"Reclaim our nation, that's what I came here to do. What about you?" She yelled like she was trying to reach every last person in this large church. I heard some voices *yeahing* and *uh-*

huhing. People were on her side. Many people were thinking like her. That time again, I stayed silent and prayed that we would all be all right.

I kept thinking about the babies that night. I remember wishing real hard that Felicia and I would leave this place and move to a small house on the plains and raise our children quietly. This is what I wanted. As the others kept on talking about getting the *revolution* on the way, I thought about the games I'd play with my little boys. Little boys is what I wanted and nothing else mattered. But Grey Stone he had other things in mind for us.

After the meeting, he pulled me aside and he said: "Why don't you go with Jim Catches Crow to the trading post and see if you can get the people to let us take some supplies."

Felicia overheard him and said she'd come with us. And before we knew it, the three of us were on a mission of our own.

When we got there the store was dark; they'd kept it closed out of fear. Jim walked around the building looking for a way in but everything was locked. I kept thinking about what Grey Stone had said to us about asking the owners for some supplies and I knew that asking instead of taking was not something we were going to do. Felicia was looking into the windows.

"There's everything we need in there. Food, canned goods, powdered milk. I even see some rifles in there, and blankets too," Jim said as if we were kids all over again and we'd just found the biggest loot of our lives.

I heard a loud bang and the sound of broken glass when Jim came around from the inside of the store. He opened the door for us.

"I got us in. Let's carry some stuff back to the church," Jim said walking around the broken glass.

I liked Grey's idea of asking the owners for permission to use their supplies but deep down, I knew that asking for someone to give you a key to their safe was as naive as thinking that we were going to get our land back without a fight.

Jim and I took three .30-30 rifles each, hunting rifles and a box of ammo. Felicia gathered some blankets and a large bag of rice. She could barely walk with all of the weight she was carrying. I offered for us to switch our loads but she refused. I found myself worrying about her all over again but I kept it under wraps.

It was getting warmer by the time we got back to the church. Didn't need to wear no gloves or nothing. People were milling about all over the place turning the land into a camp.

We knew the Feds would show up sooner or later. It was only a matter of time. We gathered the handful of whites living in the few houses nearby and put them in the church. Father Johnson didn't like us taking over his church but he stayed pretty calm when we told him he had nothing to worry about.

One of the people we gathered was a guy who looked like a field mouse only he was a representative for the government. He was more of a rat than a mouse. His face was small, and his nose pointy like a trumpet. He wore glasses that kept on falling on his nose. Each time he looked at one of us, he kept pushing his glasses up as if he were trying to see us better.

"Can you please let me go?" he asked Grey.

"We'll let you go as soon as we're done making our demands. Sit tight." Grey told him, and he did.

The other people we had gathered were people who lived in the village. Grey Stone said that we needed to make sure that we keep these people safe.

"Nothing will happen to them except maybe get shot by their own people when they show up."

Jane and Jeffrey, the owners of the trading post were there standing around with the others. They looked out of place, like we all did, I suppose. Jane was younger than Jeffrey. She was maybe in her late sixties with gray hair pulled back in a bun. The lines on her face told me that she had been a kind woman who'd suffered losses. Faces always carry the pain on the lines they carve out through time. I wanted to ask her how she could feel good about making money off people who were already poor. I wanted to ask her how a woman who looked kind and sad could exploit the suffering of others. But I asked none of those things. Instead, I found myself walking over to her standing there with her husband and apologizing for breaking into her store. I walked right up to her real slow and she looked at me. Jeffrey, her husband was too busy observing the people milling about the church busying themselves with the creation of a camp. But Jane looked straight at me and smiled. Maybe she'd seen the apology on my face before I even spoke 'cause when I said the words, *I'm sorry for your store*, she just nodded and let out a real sad smile then looked away. I wanted to tell her that we were all prisoners in this place. That she was a prisoner too but we weren't the captors. I wanted to tell her how everything was crazy now that we had started the machinery of reclaiming our country. I wanted to tell her about Felicia and the babies on the way and how scared I was to lose everything I had to regain when I couldn't even remember having any of it in the first place. But I said none of those things. All I said was, *I'm sorry.* And then I was gone.

The Schmidt family were among the people who'd been summoned. They were the youngest in the group of whites, along with Father Marlin. The little Schmidt girl couldn't have been more than 12 years old. A real smart girl who seemed scared, just like the rest of us. There was an old, frail man, so vulnerable he looked like he was going to keel over any second now. I began to worry about him too. Next to him were two old guys one of them real fragile-lookin', with his white hair and his shaky hands that sometimes swept a loose strand of hair.

"I think it's best if you sit down," I told him. Took him by the arm and showed him to the pews. He looked at me real calm and just went along with me. Didn't look scared or nothing. When he sat down, he cleared his voice.

"I need my medication otherwise, I'm as good as dead," he said. His voice was as shaky as his hands. For a second, I thought I could smell him. Old moth balls and some kind of shaving cream. A strange mix of clean and old.

"What medication is that?" I asked him.

"It's for my heart. Keeps it nice and steady." I memorized the name of the medication and its dosage and I returned to the others. Looking at him so vulnerable on the edge of the pew waiting for something to happen made my heart ache. He reminded me of my own grandfather. The way he'd be now, old and fragile.

The camp got ready to gather for a meeting. I pulled Grey aside and told him about the old man and his medicine.

"I'll take care of it as soon as I can. I'll make sure the old man gets what he needs," Grey told me.

Quickly, everyone around began transforming every inch of the land into a community. Grey, Jim, Jerome and I took over the back of the Wounded Knee museum, a sturdy log building attached to the trading post and transformed it into the security headquarters. Grey found a large, bright orange paper and pinned it up on the wall so we could draw a map of the whole camp. He drew a large X by places like the Cluster Housing Project, which we turned into a roadblock called The Last Stand. Right across there was the Hawk Eye bunker and across from that on the Big Foot Trail was the Little Big Horn bunker. In addition to these, there were four other bunkers and roadblocks on the other side of the trading post. The guys and I stood and pointed to the different posts calling out names of those who would man the roadblocks and dig trenches. We handed the guns to the men by the map. Felicia had gone with other women to hand out blankets to the elderly and families with children.

It was funny how we had all naturally become leaders. There were no orders to be given or rules to be followed. We just went with the rule of brotherhood. Everyone did what they knew best. I became part of a roaming team with Jim and three other guys. We used citizens band radios to communicate with each other. Our job was to make sure no one tried to infiltrate from the outside.

I had a .30-30 hunting rifle from the trading post store. Jim carried a .22 shotgun and along with the others. Billy Joe had an M16—the only automatic weapon of the whole siege — which later got us in trouble when a puny man with wired-rimmed glasses showed us his journalist card and came in the perimeter to talk to us. It was funny, 'cause this boy looked like he couldn't have been a day older than 16. He was not threatening nobody so Grey yelled to the roadblock crew: "Let 'im in!" Little man came in with the excitement of a trapped mouse in a maze. He took pictures and took notes every time we spoke. When night fell, we fed him dinner, not much of a meal really—a warmed-up can of pork beans is what we had, and Billy Joe posed for a picture with his M16 cocked against his chest. We never expected that journalist to run the picture of Billy Joe with his M-16 into a headline that read: "Indians Armed with Automatic Weapons."

They just bled that story to death and made us all to be crazy Indian terrorists armed to the teeth, when in reality we didn't have much of anything and we hadn't come to hurt or kill nobody, only to reclaim our land.

After roaming duty, I began digging the Denby Bunker, right next to Lil' California, an area we'd named that way cause it was nice and easy to defend. Billy Joe and I dug for two hours and didn't see time go by. By the time I started digging, my fingers were just about ready to fall off, but a little while later, my blood started flowing again and I'd never felt more alive than I did holding that shovel in my hand. With each dig, I was building my pride. Pride in my people, pride in my history. We were still here. Indians were still here. They couldn't just get rid of us with a turn of a page in the history of this country. We were warriors, our people had been warriors and I was beginning to understand for the first time that power had nothing to do with how many people you killed but with how well you knew and loved yourself and your own people.

It was no coincidence that the first thing white folks did to control the Indians was to put 'em in boarding schools away from the traditional ways and forbid 'em from speaking their language. But we were reclaiming all that now. We were becoming who we really were.

After I finished my bunker duty, I went to visit Felicia at the clinic, the only house nearby with running water and heat. Felicia decided to run the clinic with Jerome Bean and Lea Fights Wolf. They were *tough broads*. That's how they liked to call themselves.

The clinic was set up in the small two-bedroom house across from the trading post. It wasn't far from the security building and whenever I could, I'd go visit her.

I walked into the clinic and saw the slogan on the wall: "Bleeding always stops if you press on it hard enough." It was written in Felicia's oversized handwriting. I recognized it from the note she'd written me once to tell me she loved me. Felicia walked me around the clinic showing me around.

"You're going to save the world?" I asked her smiling.

"I'm going to save some lives." She was proud and I didn't want to take the pride away from her, even if I was only kidding.

"Cough syrup, a few band aids, aspirin. Not much of a hospital. But it's better than nothing." She'd found her calling and I mine. Overnight, we'd turned into warriors on the run. We were at the top of our game. In love and driven to save the world. But later I had to ask myself: *How can you save the world when you can't even save yourself?*

**

Later in the day, we held a meeting in the trading post with a hundred of us, all crowded in there. It was log cabin-style place with cement floors. Some of the guys gathered some wooden Pepsi crates, stacked them upside down and sat down on them. Some people were standing all around the sides of the room. I remember feeling like we were coming home to family, to our brotherhood. There were all kinds of people here. Old and young, women and children, elders. Holy men and healers and young girls. We were all here, waiting to reclaim our land. A couple guys—not more than two, really—carried a rifle between their legs, the butt resting on the cold cement ground, barrel pointing straight up. Some of the guys wore all kinds of hats: a white cowboy hat, felt and leather hats. Most of the men wore their hair long with eagle feathers in them and those who didn't would soon let it grow out. I looked around the room and saw men my age who'd suddenly been transformed from drunks and misfits into warriors. We all had a reason to live now.

Adam Delmario, a small man built like a tank walked right up to the front of the meeting hall and began addressing the audience.

"As most of you know, I'm the communications guy for AIM—I'm the spokesperson for AIM and for our people with the outside world, namely the press. I contacted the press about our situation here. I figured if we get them involved, it'll be harder for the government to kill us all without having to be held accountable."

Jim Catches Crow jumped in: "Having witnesses to crimes never stopped them in the past. Look at the Wounded Knee massacre. People knew about it, nobody cared."

A roar, like a brush fire rose from the audience. Adam pointed his chin forward like he was getting ready to talk. He'd shaved his beard into a tiny goatee giving him an air of wisdom.

"Look there are no guarantees that we won't all be killed once again. But it's worth a try." Two days later, Adam's house was firebombed by Dicky's goons and his wife badly hurt. We would all have to pay a high price for being there; we'd all need to give up the one thing we thought we couldn't live without. And I was no different.

People took turns talking. White Crow Dog raised his hand and then spoke: "It's about time we reclaimed our land. Never was their land to begin with, and now we've got a chance to get it back. I say we go for it!" White Crow Dog looked just like a white man. In fact, if nobody told you he was an Indian, you wouldn't know it. He wore a cowboy hat and kept a long black beard. Strange-looking Indian for sure. But just cause his blood had been diluted didn't mean he wasn't one of us. This was what brotherhood was all about: a band of brothers, no matter how much Indian blood we all had running through our veins we were all brothers. People clapped and cheered after he spoke.

A man I'd never seen before—a boy, really—spoke out: "They've been building on our land for as long as our people can remember. Back in Michigan, they flooded our ancestral graves and built a parking lot right where we buried our elders. When is this going to stop?"

Turns out the man was a Chippewa from Michigan. He'd been visiting relatives in Pine Ridge when the whole thing started and now he was banding with us. All Indians were brothers and nothing could separate us. When I saw him again a couple of weeks later. He'd started growing his hair out and wearing a red bandana around his forehead. Red like the color of blood, red like the north, like winter, the buffalo, and the magpie. Red like renewal.

Lea Fights Wolf joined in: "Our women have been getting raped in the back of police cars for years now. I'm tired of giving these pigs the rights to our lives."

It was hard to tell how old Lea was. Everyone's age had been washed out by suffering and the hardship of our lives on the res. Someone who might look 40 was probably only 30. Lea had a weathered face, like most the people in the church, except for us young ones who could still hide our pain in the smoothness of our youth.

Sam James, a stout and short woman built like the toughest shrubs on the res— the kind that could withstand winters and storms, droughts and floods—joined in on the comments: "I don't care if it means dying. Our people have died before us and they're watching us now. Waiting for us to do what's right. And if I need to die to give this land back to our children. I say bring it on!"

Everyone knew that Sam James was a tough woman. She took no shit from nobody. She liked to argue for the sake of arguing. This time though, she wasn't trying to pick a fight; she just wanted people to think.

"Think for yourself," she'd say. "This is the best gift God ever gave us humans." Sam James was only a few years older than me and Felicia but she seemed as old as the earth itself. She had round beady eyes and a broad nose to offset her face, so nobody could say she was pretty.

More people clapped and cheered. Inside me, the huge ball of fear from before began to loosen. I could feel myself filling the room, expanding into who I really was.

Felicia stood on the other side of the room with some of the women. She didn't look fragile; she was full of life smiling and clapping, standing there with her legs parted like the roots of an old tree pushing into the ground.

Later when Felicia joined me from across the room, she pointed out six older men who were there at the meeting.

"See those men," she whispered to me brushing her lips against my ear.

"They're the medicine men," she added, pointing to the men I later came to know as John Fools Crow, Jim Red Cloud, Martin Wounded, Evan Catches, Jason Wounds Enemy and Seymour Little Dog.

In the meeting, Felicia told me about the men and how they'd gathered before the meeting to strengthen spirit powers to prepare for the fight ahead. "They've smoked the peace pipe together and their visions are clear," Felicia whispered.

After we'd taken turns listening to everyone's comments, Juan Baronnette helped out in the writing of the demands. Some people wrote down what they wanted, others just spoke, like Grandma "Any Kind of Dance" Wacilowan. She couldn't see no more and it wasn't clear if she could write. It took a while for us all to get down what we had to say and it took even more time to have us cut down everyone's demands and comments into a one-page document we could hand the authorities. After a long meeting our demands came down to one main point: *The United States of America will have to wipe out old people, women, children, and men by shooting and attacking us or they negotiate our demands.*

We were tired of being ruled by a corrupt leader like Washington. We were tired of having our treaties violated. We were tired of our land being soiled with the blood of our people. We'd chosen to take over Wounded Knee because a hundred years earlier our people had been brutally murdered on this land. 300 women and children shot down without a fair chance for battle. We wanted our land back. We wanted to be able to elect our own leaders, and not a stand-in puppet like Washington. And most of all, we wanted to be respected and seen for the first time in American history.

Juan—who was in the Oglala Sioux Civil Rights Organization—and the others signed the document. We sent mouse guy, still huddled in the corner, out of the camp so he could hand our demands to the authorities.

After the meeting, everyone quickly took their position wherever they were posted: on the roadblocks, in the clinic, in the security building or in the church. Some of the men started digging trenches and making bunkers. Others made trips back and forth between the trading post to see if they could find anything else they needed. Truth is, by nightfall, the store was pretty much cleaned out of anything worthwhile, except for food.

I helped the others gather cinder blocks and lined them up around the perimeter we'd outlined that afternoon in the security building. Cinder blocks made great barriers because if stacked well, we could lie behind them and place our guns through the openings to shoot. When I thought I couldn't move no more, I grabbed a shovel and went back to digging more trenches.

Night came full on, and the shooting began. I guess nothing gets you ready for the line of fire. I suspect the Feds wanted to scare us into giving up the siege. I suspect they were hoping we'd surrender and give up our fight. But our people were not going to give up the pride we had finally found again. Even though I knew we were dealing with the Feds, I didn't expect it to go down like that. Didn't think nobody would shoot even though I'd spent most of the day preparing for that moment. See, the Feds or the pigs, that's how we called them—were well armed, much better than the rest of us. They had tanks, and automatic weapons. We knew we were outnumbered. We didn't have good weapons and if we were going to win this, we'd have to outsmart them with our knowledge and passion of the land, and our unity with each other.

I couldn't see shit except for a sliver of moon. I was sitting around in the security building finally trying to rest for a minute with Jerome and Sammy when the fire started.

"Holy shit!" I yelled out when the firing started.

"Yeah, little buddy. That's what happens in warfare. You can actually get shot!" Sammy laughed while cocking his gun.

M60 shots whizzed by us. We could hear the 7.62 NATO rounds crackling in the night air. Grey jumped up and grabbed his hunting rifle and began to take aim at something moving in the distance. At first I didn't know what he was shooting at. I remember thinking: *We ain't got a chance in hell with the kind of weapons they have.* But I didn't say nothing. I just thought it, got up and grabbed my rifle too. I ran to my post at Lil' California. That was the plan. Run to your post and guard. Billy Joe was already there. All of a sudden, I could see what Grey had been shooting at—a car was driving right up without stopping. We kept on shooting until it drove right up within a mile of the roadblock. The car stopped, did a U-turn and drove away again. Goons no doubt trying to come in.

Billy Joe and I sat down and took a breather. He was unphased by what had just happened.

"In Nam, we used to used to wait around in the bush at night until we smelled them, then we'd blast their ass." Before I had a chance to say something I heard a shot in the distance and then a flurry of 'em came right at us. I could see them crossing the grass in the distance like fireflies traveling faster than the wind. The shots were coming closer, I heard them whizzing by.

"Jesus, man! I don't think I'm cut out for this!"

"What did you think was gonna happen? People shoot at you, that's what happens. You can actually get killed!" It was Billy Joe's turn to laugh at me now. They were really giving me shit. They were right, even though I'd been preparing for this moment for days, the reality of getting shot at was a whole different thing than just plain imagining it.

"Hear that? Ain't no automatic weapon. Those are fucking .30-06 hunting rifles. Billy Joe knew his guns. He'd grown up with guns. Even before the war, his father had owned a collection of them. As a kid, he used to play with them in the back of the shack where they lived until one day his father shot himself in the head. They said it was suicide but Billy Joe told me it was an accident.

"I bet those are white ranchers trying to shoot our asses." Billy Joe was right. Vigilante ranchers had signed up wanting to shoot us directly and take care of the *problem* as they later said.

"Those bastards can't sign up fast enough to get a chance to kill an Indian."

My heart was racing. I wanted to run to Felicia at the clinic, but I knew that once the shooting had started, we had to stay at our posts until things calmed down. I could see the clinic from where we were—the lights were out. I was relieved. With the lights off, it made it harder for the enemy to shoot.

I pictured Felicia all alone with Lou and Lea sittin' in the dark not saying a word. Then, we heard a strange sound, and then we smelled it: the grass around us was on fire.

"Did you see that?" Billy Joe almost yelled.

"I think that was a flare or something," I said almost whispering.

"Yep they just shot a flare at us to set the grass on fire."

The problem with hunting rifles is that they ain't made to shoot so far away. So we sat quiet waiting for them to try to get closer. They did. Suddenly, I saw a shadow in the smoky grass. It was hard to see and truth be told I did wonder if I wasn't hallucinating or nothing 'cause of the sliver of moon, the real dark night and the smoky grass and all. But then I saw it again. I tried a clear shot in that direction and saw whatever it was, retreat in the distance.

"Fuck! I think you got one. You shot 'im good!" Billy Joe was laughing. Billy scared me a little. The way wild animals scare humans. There was something unpredictable about him which made him dangerous to the enemy, to himself, and to us who worked with him. Billy came back from Nam like the rest of them, all crazy, and unwieldy.

"There ain't nothing like the moment you first kill a man," Billy Joe said looking at me with madness in his eyes. The way he talked about the *enemy* was nothing like the ideas I'd heard from Grey, Jerome or Juan about our fight to reclaim our land.

"Killing is not the way, Grey had told us. "Red, black, white, or brown, every single life is precious."

But that's not how Billy Joe thought.

"All you have to do is aim your rifle at the line of fire and take your enemy down," Billy Joe said looking in the cross hair of his rifle. He'd been trained to kill by the American government and now that he'd been wronged, he didn't know how to stop.

Chapter 25 – Owl

By morning, the shots had died down and we all took turns getting some shut eye. When I woke, I went down to the *Crow's Nest* roadblock and saw a fed drive up right up to the barricades with a white cloth for truce, on his car antenna. The boys at The Crow's Nest roadblock made him get out of his car and walk the last 100 yards into the camp.

"I want to talk to the *man in charge*," the Fed said.

"We're all in charge here," Grey told the man with the beady blue eyes and a balding head of red hair.

"We're very concerned about the hostages and we're asking you to free them," he told Grey.

"Can you promise us that your boys won't fire at us no more or try to move in here?" Grey asked the man.

"I can't promise you that we'll never move in or fire at you but I can say that we'll notify you first." I wondered what he meant. I remembered us the night before with ranchers shooting at us and the flare burning the grass. I could see it now, all black and dead. The fire had stopped, but the grass was burnt.

Would the Fed run up to us and say," Hey, we're about to shoot your ass, get ready!" I didn't know.

"Can you promise that you'll release the hostages safe and sound?" The Fed asked again.

"Why don't you come back later this afternoon and we'll see once I've had a chance to talk to the people of the Oglala Nation."

Before the man left, Grey handed him the name of the prescription medicine for one of the hostages, old man Mr. Rivers. I loved that Grey had said, *The Oglala Nation*. That was what we were—a nation, under God.

Later that afternoon, the man came back with the medication for the old man and more information for us. This time, it was Juan Baronnette who met him, instead of Grey.

"Is there any way you could release the hostages today?" The Fed asked again.

Juan gave him a card with the names of some of our people who'd been arrested the night before.

"This is a list of our hostages we'd like released in exchange. Can you do that?" We wanted the release of our people from the jails. This was a tactic the government had used on us a million times. I thought about Jimmy's cousin Marty rotting in jail for no good reason, other than being Indian. How many wrongful arrests had we all endured just to intimidate us? But now we had bargaining power.

The agent just handed him a list of the names of our people who had been arrested, only confirming what we already knew. In return, and as a way to return the insult to the agent, Juan handed the man a list of the hostages. We were determined to get our way and not let them get us down.

"The white man has killed our people before at the last Wounded Knee massacre and we're prepared to die again." Juan's anger rose like a whip with a life of its own.

"Your only hope for change is to surrender. I strongly advise you surrender." The agent barked back. Tension was rising.

"This is our land, we're the landlords and the rent is overdue!" Juan added. The agent must have felt scared shitless cause he said nothing and took off like a lightning bolt in the sky.

In the days that followed, all kinds of people made their way to the camp. Senators McGovern and Abourezk came to see us to find out about the *hostages*. McGovern walked around crooning and shaking people's hands like he was running for president. The Feds and their people had called the press and made a declaration about the unfair situation with our keeping hostages. But they just about took a shit in their pants when one of the *hostages* said to the press, "We're free to go. We're not the hostages, the Indians are."

We had a good laugh over this one. Turns out we'd told people they could leave whenever they wanted but most of them opted to stay. The senators left in a huff and the war really began. Nobody likes to lose face in front of his enemy, and after this, it seemed war was the only way.

**

At night, Felicia, the others, and I sat around the Sacred Heart church to rest. We took turns to keep watch of our posts and when we were off, we sat around talking. I loved listening to people's stories. Our people had so many stories to tell. I'd never been around such a strong need to tell their stories. Grey lit a cigarette. I didn't know he smoked, and I guess he didn't either cause when Jim looked at him real strange, he cocked his head to the side and said: "What are you gonna do? War does that to a man." And he took a deep drag and let the smoke out slow.

"*Umm* it's been a good…ten years since I've had one. Ten years. Feels so good." I could tell from the way he held himself that he was about to tell us a story.

"You know, people keep asking us: *why AIM? Why did AIM get involved?* And you know what? I remind 'em of the old man in Rushville, Nebraska. That was just three years ago, but I remember this story like it was yesterday. An old Indian man was on the streets of Rushville, walking along, minding his own business when the police came right up to him and knocked him over. Every time the old man tried to get up, the sick policemen would hit him with a club and kick him in the ribs. Now, Rushville is a real small town and that poor old man crawled on his hands and knees from one end of Main Street to another. The two Indian women who saw this attack and couldn't do a damn thing to stop it came to see us and told us the story. We listened to it and knew we had to do something for our people."

We'd all known and lived the horrors of our people firsthand, but hearing it from a man like Grey sure made it all the more real.

Gun shots were slowing down and Billy Joe called me over to a game of chess. I'd never played before. He put the game board down on the ground next to me and said: "I learned in Nam. Sitting around waiting to kill more gooks. People always think that in war, you're always running around killing people. That ain't true. There's a whole lotta time spent on our asses, waiting to kill more people." He let out this laugh that made me think he was going to start coughing. Billy got up from the overturned case where he sat and went to the altar where we kept some of our ammo.

"OK, so the .50 caliber shells here are your king and queens. Then we've got our ponds, tons of little ponds. Those are you .22s. And these short and fat suckers here are your fucking towers. Go that? Bro?"

I don't think I learned much about chess. But I did learn about Billy's vision of the world.

"See, the white man likes to lock shit up and fight neighbors for what they already own. Look at their houses. All fenced up, locked up with security and shit. Why they do that? You know why? 'Cause they know they've got enemies everywhere. Their neighbor is their enemy. Their children are their enemies. Their wives are their enemies."

Billy moved a .22 shell forward. I was trying to think about my next move.

"Like the Paiutes in Nevada. My cousin's a Paiute and he told me that when the settlers came through in the beginning, they were lost. Didn't know the land, didn't know where nothing was. And the chief Winnemucca, he'd come around and help them out. He figured out, that's the Indian way. You help your neighbor. The land belongs to everyone. But when spring came, whites were strong again, back on their feet and they'd get drunk and go out and shoot the Paiutes like coyotes. The Indian and the white man, we don't think the same way. Your turn to play asshole."

I moved a .22 caliber ammo forward on the board.

"You bastard, you think you're gonna get me?" I heard Billy Joe laughing. I looked up and saw him making a strange face like he was trying to hold his breath under water. He clutched his chest. Blood came out of his nose and then I saw that he'd been shot.

Chapter 26 – Owl

Billy Joe was our first casualty in the camp. The next day, the government declared a ceasefire and asked that women and children leave immediately. We held a meeting. The Feds said they wanted to negotiate with us and it couldn't be done *at the barrel of a gun.* For once, we agreed. We wanted to remind them that we hadn't been the ones declaring war in the first place.

As I stepped into the trading post building for the meeting, a man tapped me on the shoulder. I turned to see the medicine man Whitetail Deer standing behind me. I'd seen him around at the meetings in the church and the trading post. The skin on his face was wrinkled and loose. He wore a traditional beaded suede jacket, fur tails tied around his braids and beads around his neck. The thick bottle glass look of his glasses gave him a strange air magnifying his eyes as he came closer to me.

"Do you have the wolf stone?" he asked resting his hand on my shoulder. I'd never spoken to him before. He looked at me piercingly through the distortion of his glasses and when my eyes found his, I felt a pang in my chest, like someone had just punched me.

For a second, I tried to understand what he was saying then I remembered the stone Felicia's grandmother had given me. People were pouring past us, leaving the building. Felicia was walking in to find me when she saw I was with Whitetail Deer. She hesitated, stopped, and then turned around to give us privacy.

"Yes," I answered. Fumbling in my pocket for the stone I'd been carrying ever since. I opened my palm and showed it to him as a sign of good faith.

"Good," he said leaving the stone in my hand. "Tomorrow, you will come with me to the sweat lodge at sunrise. I'll see you there." And before I had a chance to say anything he was gone.

The meeting where we talked about the government's ceasefire swallowed me. I didn't have time to think about Whitetail Deer or the wolf stone.

Negotiations were under way, and we told our women and children to leave, if they wanted. A friend of Jerome Bean named Flores was about nine months pregnant. We told her it'd be better if she left but she refused. She sat on an overturned case, her belly as round as a bubble ready to burst, pride written all over her face.

"There is nothing for me out there. My home is with my brothers." She stayed.

In the end, two people left the next day, only to be replaced by a hundred more who came from all over the country. A small plane carrying 400 pounds of food owned by the Chipewas in Michigan landed in the field behind the church. We spend the evening carrying this precious delivery they had brought for us. People all over the country had started to hear about our struggle and they were joining in. We formed lines and carried the hundreds of pounds of eggs, powdered milk, flour, baking soda and rice inside the trading post. People were happy. But some of the warriors and I felt that the government had something else up its sleeve. We felt they were planning a massive attack and they were trying to get our women and children off the land so they could finish us off and not be blamed for killing the innocent.

That night, Felicia and I made ourselves a little nest in the corner of the clinic and tried to sleep behind the medicine cabinet.

"What did he want?" Felicia asked me that night.

"Who?"

"Whitetail Deer. What did he want?"

"He wanted to know if I still had the wolf stone your grandmother gave me. He also told me I need to join him in the sweat lodge first thing tomorrow morning."

She smiled proudly, like she'd suddenly turned into a mama hen.

"You better get some sleep. Your first sweat lodge, you will need the energy."

The next morning, I found Whitetail Deer sitting outside of the lodge cross-legged and praying. Gordon, a guy I'd seen at one of the roadblocks was poking rocks in a roaring fire. He nodded at me in recognition and continued his task. His face was covered in soot from the smoke. He was shirtless and bathed in sweat.

Whitetail Deer opened his eyes."Take out the wolf stone," he said.

I pulled it out of my pocket and held on to it like my life depended on it. When I came closer to the lodge, I saw a handful of guys getting ready for the sweat. I knew a few of them, guys like White Crow Dog, Juan, and Jerry. I wondered what a guy like Jerry could be looking for in a sweat. He just didn't seem like the spiritual type. I removed my clothes and crawled inside with them. Whitetail Deer entered the lodge last.

I remembered building the lodge with the guys a few days earlier. I remembered the pliability of the sixteen willow saplings we'd cut from the far corner of the land on the porcupine side. We had to wait for night to fall to cut them so the marshals wouldn't see us. When I'd heard gunshots in the distance, I'd asked myself: Is this worth dying for? I was just about to find out.

I crouched and crawled on the far side of the lodge, the farthest point from the door. One of the guys had joked with me about being a *fucking weakling* and probably wanting to sit near the door on my first sweat. But now, I had no choice but to brave my fear and sit down inside the lodge.

This sanctuary seemed much smaller than what I remembered. Maybe it was the fact that it was now covered by layers of wool blankets. Outside the air was cool and the warmth felt inviting, at first.

Facing east, the door was still open. I could feel the spring air coming into the lodge and chilling my naked body. The fire tender came to the door and placed four rocks at the center in the very pit I'd dug myself with the guys. Four rocks, as a symbol of the four directions. This is what Felicia had told me.

"Remember the power of the north," she'd said to me.

"Remember the wisdom of the west. Remember the sweetness of the south and most of all, remember the promise of the east." She'd learned this from her grandmother, the same woman who'd given me the wolf rock. I tried to remember what the wise Ihanblapi had said to me as she had placed it in my hand.

"When you're ready, he will find you."

The fire tender came back with two more rocks and placed them in the hearth around the existing four. Two rocks like the world of the sky above and that of mother earth below, like the forces of good and evil. Whitetail Deer tossed something on the rocks. I heard the crisp rustling of burning leaves the smell of sweet grass filled the lodge. The tender came back with one last rock for the spotted eagle, for our Grandfather who had fathered every one of us sitting on the ground in the lodge.

"*Yuȟpa yo*! Close it!" Whitetail Deer requested, his voice resounding in the circular warmth of the lodge. The fire tender came and pulled the heavy layers of blankets shut. Darkness swallowed me and I was plunged into another world.

I held the wolf rock tightly in my closed fist as I felt the heat of the lodge rise around me. *This isn't bad*, I thought. Why had everyone told me about the challenge of the heat in the lodge? Suddenly, I heard the scalding of the water being poured on the rocks. Steam released in the tiny space pushing against my skin, burning me alive. I wanted to scream. I'd just been plunged alive into a cauldron of boiling water. But I said nothing.

"Crawl close to the ground. If the heat gets to be too much." I remembered Felicia's voice advising me. I moved down towards the ground in the fetal position. I could feel the limbs of my neighbors pressing up against me. Whitetail Deer began singing a prayer I'd never heard before. His voice rose and fell like a flag in the wind. I heard him pouring more water onto the rocks.

"Wankatakiya hoyewaye lo
Cannunpa kin yuha hoyewaye lo
Mitakuye ob wani kla ca lecamum we
Eyaya Tunkašila cewakiye lo."

I send a voice upward
With the pipe, I send a voice
I do this so I will live with my relatives
Saying this I pray to Tunkašila

Hau! Everyone repeated after him.

"Ho! Tunkašila!" He was calling to the great Grandfather spirit of the universe to protect us.

Outside, I heard a wolf howling in the distance. I tried to open my eyes wide to see if it made me see any more clearly, but I could not see even the tip of my nose. There were no wolves in these parts of the hills and even if there were, I'd never heard a wolf howl like that in the fullness of morning. I prayed for Billy Joe, I prayed for our brothers and sisters on the land. I prayed for Felicia and our babies.

"Open it!" The fire tender opened the lodge door marking the end of the first round. The cool morning air poured in soothing our burning skin.

"Mitakoyašin," everyone changed in unison. "All of my relations," and I remembered the voice of Felicia's old grandma as she made the motion of a circle pushing me towards Felicia. *"Hocokatoya!"* she'd said to me. "The circle of unity with all Indians."

In the second round of the lodge, I felt more confident. I knew what to expect with the heat and I thought I could handle anything. Little did I know that the heat was the least of my challenges. I closed my eyes because trying to keep them open in the darkness only made me more aware of it. It gave me a feeling of wanting to possess something I couldn't have. I listened to the sound of the steam as Whitetail Deer continued to pour water on the rocks. I felt a circular source of energy form at the center of my chest. I'd never felt anything like it before and I opened my eyes trying to see what I felt inside. I remembered that I was wrapped in darkness. I closed them again and tried to keep my focus within.

"Sunkmahetu, Sunkmahetu," Whitetail deer hummed over and over again.

I did not know what this meant but each time he said it, I felt the circle at the center of my chest become larger, stronger. I lost track of my surroundings. I don't remember whether Whitetail Deer continued to hum the word or whether he stopped but suddenly I had a vision. Eyes still closed, I saw myself in the black hills, crouching in the bushes. It was summer. I was following something, tracking an animal, a wolf. I caught a glimpse of it, its sleek body moving faster than the wind. Bearing no physical limitation, I kept up with the animal, running as fast as I needed. The wolf took me to a cave right at the foot of the hills. The sunny hills of before had been replaced with the dimmer, more somber mouth of a cave. Fear gave way to excitement, as I knew that whatever was going to happen there would change everything. Not just for me, but for everyone around me.

I walked into the cave. The wolf was already inside and I could no longer see him. I smelled and sensed him now that I had other ways of seeing. I ran for a while in darkness finding my way instinctively. My feet were secretly guided by the wolf's energy. I knew every step, every corner of the cave, even though I couldn't see with my eyes. Suddenly I stopped. I waited in the darkness. The same darkness as the lodge's only this cave was cool and dark. I heard the sound of footsteps behind me. I wanted to run.

"Stay," said the wolf without using words.

When I turned around to face the source of the sound, I saw a woman standing there. She had the face of a woman but the body of a calf, a white buffalo calf. I had seen her before. We knew each other, and as if she could read my mind, she smiled. When I looked again, I saw that she was holding a pipe in both hands. She raised both hands above her head.

"*Cannunpa wakan*. Sacred pipe," she said, handing me the pipe. When I held it in my hands, I felt the circle in my chest grow the size of a watermelon. I wanted to scream. I opened my eyes to see that I was still in the lodge and the fire tender had just opened the curtain again.

"Mitakoyašin," everyone whispered. *All my relations.*

In the third round, I returned to the cave again, in the same place I'd been when the previous round had ended. It was as if time had collapsed and I was taken back to the woman and the pipe. I held the pipe in my hands. I heard the White Buffalo Calf Woman make an offering to the seven directions. First she turned to zenith and I was flooded with a blue light. She then turned to the west and the light became dark like that of the lodge. In the north, I saw a red so brilliant it was the color of fresh blood. When she faced east, Calf Woman whispered, "*wakantaka.*"

The entire cave lit up with the brightest golden light I'd ever seen, only to be replaced with the palest light of dawn as the woman turned to the south. Calf Woman made one last turn towards the nadir. I saw spring and the return of green life and when she shifted to the center of the cave, the most beautiful rainbow I had ever seen appeared above us all.

Whitetail Deer opened the lodge again and this time I wanted to scream and say that he should have kept it closed longer. I wanted to return to the cave and find out why the woman had given me the pipe. But instead, I took a sip of the water being passed around and I realized that in the three hours since the first round had begun, I had not had a drop to drink. As I later found out, it was unusual for Whitetail to give his initiates water before the end, but something in the energy of the lodge must have told him that we needed it.

Finally, I returned to the cave in the last round. I knew that she had something to tell me and I was eager to take the message back to Felicia. When I stood in the cave again, I saw that it had opened up to the sky at the base of the woman's head. It was as if her head was a beacon of light that led way to the sky itself.

"You are the path for the people to walk," she said turning into a black calf that ran around the cave. I was still holding the pipe in my hands. I listened to her as she handed me the seven rites.

"These rites must be kept sacred and handed down from generation to generation. Do not let the fire go out, for the flame will be extinguished forever."

She named the rites in turn and as she spoke I knew the nature of each ritual. She spoke slowly in the cool darkness of the cave as I remembered the wisdom of my people.

"*Inikagapi*," she said, speaking of the first rite of the sweat lodge. And I knew that I had already begun walking the sacred path.

"*Hanbleceya*," she said, invoking the vision quest. This is what I was doing here, with the wolf stone still in my hand.

As she named the third ritual, my heart tightened: "*Wanagi tacanku*." Ghost keeping. This was the ritual performed for those who had died so that their spirit would return to their place of origin and for the living to be more mindful of death.

I felt fear course through my body as she pronounced the words *wanagi tacanku*. Who would die? Who would need our community to perform a ghost keeping ceremony?

As she called out the last four rituals, the White Buffalo Calf Woman danced around the cave changing form as quickly as she spoke. The sun dance *Wi wanyang wacipi*, allowed the men in our community to find their own spiritual strength while the making of relatives ceremony, *hunkalowanpi*, was used to create a bond with others that was stronger than kinship. A girl's puberty ritual, *Isnati awicalowan* celebrated our girl's entry into womanhood.

During the mention of the last ritual, I became aware of both worlds where I existed: the fire of the lodge and the coolness of the cave where I had my vision. I knew that no matter what happened during the siege, our people would survive because we carried the history within us.

Tapa wankayeyapi, she whispered one last time before we parted. She had spoken of the most important ritual of all: *the throwing of the ball*. This was the time when we could toss a ball among our people as they ran to catch it. The ball contained our collective wisdom, our knowledge and freedom, the connection with our ancestors. The time had come for all of us to run for the ball, and to catch it, before it disappeared.

Chapter 27 – Owl

That night after the sweat lodge, I came to see Felicia at the clinic. I wanted to hold and smell her and make sure she was okay. She saw the fear and excitement in my eyes.

"Everything will be fine," she said taking me into her arms. I felt a twinge of shame run through my body. It wasn't supposed to be like that. It wasn't supposed to be a woman comforting a man, but here she was telling me what I wanted to hear.

"I had a dream while I was knocked unconscious during the accident." Felicia said.

People didn't have dreams when there were knocked unconscious, but she had and I needed to believe her.

"I dreamt that our children were grown. They were strong and you were laughing with them in a clearing with tall spruce trees planted in a straight line. It was a beautiful summer day. I heard the birds chirping nearby and I remember the breeze, soft and gentle on my skin."

I liked hearing about our children, being all grown and safe. I was holding Felicia's hands in mine when I felt a strange current moving through her. I looked up and I saw that something was wrong.

"The strange thing is, the three of you were standing there laughing and I could see you, but I knew that you could not see me. I wanted to call out to you, but I knew that I was invisible."

Was this a terrible omen about what was to come?

That night, we both slept deeply, each held by the messages spoken by our spirit guides.

**

On the day that followed the cease-fire, our people declared this land of our ancestors to be the *Independent Oglala Nation* or

ION. This was the day of our independence. Whitetail Deer and the other medicine men met for the day in the tipi at the center of the camp while Grey, Jerome, Sammy, Juan, Ellen and the others drew up the declaration of independence that read: "Let it be known this day, March 11, 1973, that the Oglala Sioux people will revive the Treaty of 1868 and that it will be the basis for all negotiations.

Let the declaration be made that we are a sovereign nation by the Treaty of 1868. We intend to send a delegation to the United Nations…In proclaiming the Independent Oglala Nation, the first nation to be called for support and recognition is the Iroquois Six Nation Confederacy. We request that the Confederacy send emissaries to this newly proclaimed nation immediately to receive first-hand all the facts pertaining to this act…"

Nothing or nobody could take our pride away. We thought that nothing could touch us again. We were wrong.

As a result of the ceasefire, we had raised the roadblocks giving access to vigilante ranchers volunteering to shoot our asses. One night, they snuck in the camp at night and lit the trading post building on fire. Luckily, one of the women in the camp was walking by at that moment, and we put the fire out without too much damage. The message was clear. War was not over.

The ceasefire didn't last long. Within a couple of days, the government started shooting at us again. Only two people left the camp and while the roadblocks were open, hundreds more poured in from all over the country to help us. We had Paiutes from Nevada, Pit Rivers from California, Chippewas from Michigan, and Chicanos from New Mexico, Texas, and North Carolina. People came pouring into our nation to tell us about stories of support. 10,000 people all over the country had demonstrated in support of our struggle. We had all lost so much: the Pequots, and Narragansetts, the Mohicans and Cherokees, Black Hawks, Navajos, and Apaches. We'd all been massacred. Now it was our time to cry out for our freedom.

2,000 Chicanos marched in our support in Denver. Stories poured in from the outside like the story of Graciano "Chano" Juaraqui in Denver who was shot to death by cops in an alley and left to bleed to death because he was demonstrating for peace.

**

After the ceasefire, after our brief moment of rest, the war began again this time with a greater vengeance. Dicky Washington hired Indians to do his dirty work. The Feds stayed in the back and the goons were sent on the front lines so they could start shooting at us again. There is nothing worse than having your own people trying to kill you.

Unlike most of the guys on the land, the goon, cropped his hair short, like white soldiers. He liked to booze up first before a good shooting. I always thought of these boys' mothers and how they must be feeling knowing that their boys were out shooting Indians.

At night the sky lit up with flares. Midnight suns we called 'em 'cause they lit up the whole camp with a strange eerie glow. The Feds had every toy in the book. Tracer bullets that lit up on every fifth round, sniping rifles with starlight scopes used in Nam, .50 caliber machine guns and enough M16s to start a firearms store.

I felt for our sorry asses having to wait to shoot every 50 rounds with our .22s and .30-30 hunting rifles. We were a sorry sight for sure and this is how I began to understand the way goons became goons. Grey had told see that back in 1934, the government passed the *Indian Reorganization Act* without the 3/4 consent of Indian males required to pass a vote. They took away our treaty rights and left us Indians to rot in reservations all over the country. The res had nothing for us, and the world had nothing to offer except booze and a game of pretend telling us we had no families back on the res.

When they hired the goon, the government always promised them big sums of money. That kind of game was still happening around us. One night, a guy crossed into the camp from the outside and came to find us at the bunker. He said he wanted to talk to the *man in charge*. Shit, we almost pissed our pants listening to an Indian talk just like a white man.

"What's it about?" I asked him feeling something wasn't right.

"The government paid me to rat on you guys, but I ain't gonna do it."

I called the others from the different posts. Left one man out to man each bunker and we all sat around and listened to this poor bastard with his short hair and shaky hands.

"They told me they'd give me twenty grand if I ratted out Grey Stone and Jerome Beans. At first I told 'em I'd do it. But my buddy Larry told me this was just somethin' they promised without ever delivering. Guess I was right, 'cause in the end, they gave me nothing but a twenty dollar bill."

"Jesus man, you're a fucking rat!" Sammy cussed him out. I just felt sorry for the son of a bitch. I couldn't stop thinking about what would have happened if they'd given him the money they promised him. Would he have ratted us out, like he'd planned? He was a sorry sight. Sorry-sight-of-an-Indian, all droopy eyed and shaky, like a lost puppy in a storm. Nobody trusted him no more and he sure as hell couldn't go back to them. He hung around us for a little while and then he left after a couple of days 'cause nobody had nothing to say to him. Made me think there is a little bit of goon in all of us.

I remembered Billy Joe telling me how in Nam they'd used *gook against gook*, he called it. He said that's how they were able to get most people. If you tap a tree at its center, the core will rot and pretty soon, the whole thing will come tumblin' down.

In the end, I found out that we Oglalas at Wounded Knee were better off than some of the others. Yeah, we'd been robbed of our language, our history, our women, and our children, but many of us still had pieces of ourselves hanging on. Many tribes had been wiped out completely like the Schaticoke in Connecticut, related to the Pequot-Mohican tribes who were raped and murdered in the late 1600s and none of them had anything to remember or recover. They were like ghosts without a ghost keeping ceremony. Wandering souls without a place to go. This was the story of goons. And in the end, we could all go that end if we didn't build the sacred hoop again.

**

Chicanos came to help us. They came from all over the country wanting to be part of *la lucha para todos*, they said. The fight for all. A medic named Carlos came to work in the clinic with Felicia. He was a young guy like myself. Wore his hair long made him look traditional except for these black framed glasses that made him look smarter than me. I guess he was like the rest of us. I guess he wanted a piece of freedom, but the thought of him staying with my girl all alone at night when I was out in the front line made me want to scream. I didn't say nothing. Not at first. Couldn't come down on a brother who was fighting the good fight like the rest of us. Besides, I had no reason to be jealous.

Sometimes Felicia would talk about Carlos. She'd tell me about how he had cured a boil on Grandma Wasiyun's leg or how he was able to help out the two Crow dog's children who were coughing like hell. He was becoming her hero leaving me out in the cold.

I guess I just feared I was losing Felicia. A girl like that is not made for fools like me. Felicia was prettier than I'd ever seen her. It was as if being here on this free land had turned her into a powerful medicine woman. She wore her hair differently now. Braided on either side of her face, and when she walked she married the earth with her feet.

The night when Carlos started his shift, she came to see me at the Lil' California Bunker, she was wearing a long silver ring on her finger in the shape of a buffalo. My heart sank and I thought that Carlos must have given it to her.

"The pregnant girl Flores gave it to me," She brought the ring closer so I could see it clearly and when I looked again, I noticed that the animal only had one leg.

"Does it only have…"

"Yes." She cut me off.

"The one-legged buffalo symbolizes renewal. When the buffalo only has one leg left and it is bald and its back is almost bare the world as we know it will come to an end."

Something ached inside of me when she said this, a feeling that looked like love and loss all mixed together.

"No, this is a good thing. When the world reaches its end, a new world is waiting to appear." Felicia said as if she had read my mind.

When she talked about the new world in the making I pictured her alone with Carlos curing the world of diseases. The world was free again and Indians were free to be Indians all over the world. She'd be traveling with Carlos and they'd have many children.

"What are you thinking about baby?"

"Huh?" She startled me.

"Nothing."

Carlos wasn't a bad guy. Things got a lot better for me when I found out about his past. The night after the firing started again, we turned out all of the lights at the clinic. Sammy was covering for me at *Lil' California*, helping Grey out with the heavy fire the bastards were shooting at us. I'd decided to man the clinic with Carlos, Flores and Felicia, in case anybody got hurt. There was something crazy and good about sitting in the dark in this tiny clinic we'd made our own.

This was our free land. The independent Oglala Nation. I was a free man and a warrior living in ION now, and it was my job to make sure we'd stay that way.

Carlos and Flores had spent the evening cleaning up the clinic as good as they could. Felicia updated the inventory of supplies from the brand new load that came from the Chippewa plane that had landed a couple of days earlier. After a few days on the land, I noticed that Carlos had grown a mustache. He was a strange one this Carlos. His bookworm glasses, his traditional hair and now his Chicano mustache.

Carlos came from Oregon where he worked as a migrant worker. He spoke in a Mexican accent, rolling his Rs and tossing in a few Spanish words when he couldn't find the right ones in English.

"I came when I heard about *la lucha*. I wanted to be a part of this, you know." Carlos was a delicate man. His fingers were slender and long like a woman's. He told us the story of how he'd traveled to Wounded Knee.

"It took me two weeks to arrive here. On the way, we found many people who opened their homes to us. *Puertorriceños, Mexicanos, Dominicanos*. Everybody helped. Gave us food. *Somos la raza unida*." Felicia and I nodded. Outside the bullets were whizzing by. I could hear them like insects buzzing in the air. We were used to this. We were used to being under attack.

"In Montana, the cops stopped us. Searched the car expecting us to be illegals and when one saw that we had papers he said: 'Aren't you tired of being a fucking burden on this country?" They let us go."

"In Cuerna Vaca, in my village in Mexico, I was a doctor, but I had to leave because they wouldn't give me a license to practice medicine." Carlos rolled his eyes in a girlish way and looked in the other direction like a blushing girl. The night after my first jealousy fit about Carlos, I'd started spending time with him. That's when I noticed his girlish ways.

"This is not the only reason why they wouldn't give me a license. They called me *puto*, *carbron*, *pendejo*. All the words that say the same thing."

"You are a *wikte*," said Felicia, excitedly. Carlos and I had no idea what she was talking about.

"A *wikte* is a sacred he/she. A boy/girl person who names the children of the village. We have had *wiktes* among our people since the beginning of time. You are a sacred man Carlos."

Now, I was jealous again. I'd gone from fearing Carlo's manliness to envying his girlishness.

The day before, in the large room of the trading post, Carlos had received his ION citizenship like the many other Chicanos. We were brothers of one land, living under the roots of the same tree. Together we would be buried under this tree.

"When the conquistadors came to our village in 1654, they raped our women and the people of our village and my people were born. We are not indios or Mexicans. We are not whites or mulattos. We are everything. We are the blood of our history. We are Chicanos."

Lou came charging into the clinic holding her bleeding hand.

"Shit, I'm fine but they made me come in here." She looked embarrassed, holding her wounded hand with the other while her blood trickled onto the ground.

"Lou, what happened?" Felicia came running up to her and tried helping her sit down.

"I'm fine. I tell you, I'm fine. I was fucking sitting there in the church when I almost got dusted I guess." Lou sat down on the ground next to Carlos. She took one look at him and said: "What's wrong with you? You look all sad and shit. You guys been talkin' about our history or some'ing?"

We all laughed. It was a private joke among us. We all knew that the only thing that could get us down was the story of how our people had been treated.

Carlos wiped the mist in his eyes; tears that had threatened to come when Lou came in. He examined Lou's hand. Her finger was badly wounded but she'd be fine. The bullet had flown right into the church, bounced off a wall and hit Lou's finger, taking a chunk of it on its way out.

"That sucker almost got me dusted!"

That night was a night we would all remember.

"Those bastards are going to pay for it now!" Lou didn't give a shit if bullets were flying or not, she was going back and finishing what she'd started. Lou went back to her post at the church, one hand wrapped in bandages, the other holding a gun.

We got word from Broken Arrow posted over in *Hawk Eye's Bunker* that Flores' water broke. She sent her sister to run over to the bunker from the cluster housing project on the northwest end of the camp where most of the local families lived.

We asked if she could wait a little before she got some help; at least until the fire let up. We waited for a couple of hours, talking, cleaning and preparing what Felicia and Carlos would need, to help with the baby. Felicia wanted to go out to the project but it was straight clear on the other side of the camp. I said, "No way. You stay here or I go."

In the end, we all waited. At dawn the firing let up a bit and I radioed Broken Arrow and told him we'd be there in about half an hour. The three of us ran out of the clinic like rabbits. The light was pink and soft from the early morning. There was frost on the ground, on the blades of burnt grass. All around us were patches of smoke where the grass was still burning. I hated running out like this with Felicia. I wished she could stay in the clinic. If I had my way, she would have lived in a cocoon the whole time the war was going on. But Felicia was no kind of woman to live contained inside of anything. She was the kind that threw herself out there with danger.

Smoke rose from the ground giving the place an eerie feeling. Everything was quiet now. I could hear the magpie singing in the distance, taunting me. The good thing about smoke is that it gave us cover from the pigs across the way. Sure is hard to shoot rabbits in the fog. But this was no fog and we were no rabbits so we ran as fast as we could. No matter how you sliced it, you had to run straight into the open fields. We had two choices, both involved risk. We could have run along the ditch on Manderson road to try to protect ourselves from possible bullets, but the ditch ended before arriving at the bunker and we'd be exposed the last one hundred feet or so. This was the shortest way, and I think it was the safest but instead we cut across the massacre site where we thought we had a better chance of being hidden the whole way. It was Carlos' idea and this fact gave me a little comfort when I later remembered that night.

"This way!" I heard Carlos say. He was up front, running like the fastest rabbit I'd ever seen. Felicia and I could barely keep up; I kept her between us. I thought if she was ahead of me but behind Carlos it'd give her a better chance of survival.

"Not that way," I yelled. "No! It's too long that way. Too long." I wanted to explain to Carlos that there was no shelter from the bullets in that direction but he didn't want to hear a word. He was too far and too fast for us to stop him. I heard him in the distance saying something about the smoke from the fields and how this would shield us somehow. Maybe he was right. We'd run past security into the open clearing of the massacre site. I hated every second running through the site. I remembered the pictures from the museum and the piles of bodies lying like bags of sand. Some people in the camp had said they'd heard a woman and child wailing. I remembered how my father used to hear them on the nights he was drunk and I prayed I'd never have that burden.

The nearest cover was the Whitetail Deer Bunker ahead of us. I was confident we'd make it there, shielded from the smoke of the fire until we reached the building. The load of supplies I was carrying was beginning to cut into my shoulder. I put the load down and changed sides. Carlos was out of sight. I watched Felicia reached the bunker and hide in one of the bushes. She was resting, waiting for me.

"Where is Carlos?" She asked when I got there.

"I don't know, but we should not waste any time and go on." I told her.

As she was about to step out of the bunker, a series of shots were fired. Felicia and I both gasped at the same time. We thought about Carlos out in the open in the most vulnerable part of the path to Hawk Eye's Bunker. It was at least another half a mile until we reached the other bunker.

"We should go get him." Felicia said visibly alarmed. She was getting ready to run out.

"We can't!" I pulled her back into the ditch. "If you go out there, you'll get killed."

"But Carlos needs us!" she cried.

"What do you want us to do with fucking .22 caliber rifles when they're going at it with rounds of .30 and .50. We're no match for them Felicia. We're no fucking match!"

I'd never spoken to Felicia like this before. I'd never raised my voice to her. I was still holding her tightly by the wrist. She pulled her hand away and when she did I saw the marks of my fingers still imprinted on her skin. We were like rabbits again, only now we were caged, turning against one another, ready to draw blood. We waited in the dark until the shots had calmed down.

We ran past the Catholic church into the open space between the *Hawk Eye Bunker*. The sun was rising now and I hoped that this would discourage the Feds from shooting at us in broad daylight. Their patterns had been to let up by daybreak and take up again by nightfall. I looked into the distance and couldn't see Carlos anywhere. Maybe he'd make it to the bunker already. Felicia and I kept close to each other. I wanted to be by her side in case we got hit. I could see the Little Big Horn Bunker on our right. I kept on running. My arms were beginning to hurt under the weight of the supplies we were carrying for the delivery.

Suddenly out of the corner of my eye, I saw him there. Carlos had been shot. He was lying on his side absolutely still. A thin trail of blood flowed onto the grass around him.

"Carlos! Carlos!" Felicia was crying.

He was still alive, his breathing labored. He'd been shot in the side, like an elk being hunted. I knelt by his side and wiped his sweaty brow. His body was fighting to stay alive.

"They got me," he whispered his voice garbled with pain.

"Shut up man, save your speech for the stories you still have to tell us."

I heard them firing again in the distance. The shots sounded pretty far away. But we were out in the open with no way for protection. *Hawk Eye's Bunker* was still quite a way's away. I could see it in the distance but it was going to be a trek with Carlos' body to carry. I handed the supplies to Felicia, who was already carrying a bag of meds and medical instruments.

"You go! I'll bring him to Flores' house." I said to Felicia. For a moment, she hesitated, like she was thinking about staying with me but then she realized there was nothing she could do and she was on her way. I made a quick prayer for her as she ran ahead and I focused my attention on Carlos.

What if something happened to her? I had a man who was bleeding in my arms and a woman waiting for me to help her bring her baby into the world. I couldn't get lost in *what ifs*.

"OK, man, here's the deal: you're going to have to get up. You think you can do that?" Carlos moaned and groaned as I helped him on his feet. The side of his abdomen was bleeding like crazy.

"Press on it," he said. "Press on it hard." And I remembered what Felicia had written on the wall in the clinic. "Bleeding always stops if you press on it hard enough." He moaned as I pressed on his wound. Carlos wrapped his arm around my shoulders and leaned most of his weight on me. We inched our way to the Hawk Eye's Bunker and arrived when the sun had risen completely.

The Cluster Housing Project was a tricky place to live. It was caught between *The Last Stand* government roadblock on one side and the *Hawk Eye Bunker* on the other. The project had been hit heavily by crossfire. I saw bullet holes all over the walls as we made our way in. In the afternoons, children made necklaces out of the empty shells left by the crossfire.

We got inside and the place was dark. Light was streaming from the few windows, making it hard to see, as we made our way up the stairs. Flores' little brother Rick was waiting for us at the entrance. Flores lived in on the second floor. Carlos wasn't looking too good. His face had turned all puffy and grey like someone had pumped him up with air. I didn't know much about medicine but I knew it wasn't a good sign.

"Carlos, stay with me, OK, buddy. Stay with me, you hear?"

Rick was no more than 16 years old, but he was a strong kid and he helped me carry Carlos inside. We laid him out on the floor of the apartment. He was the medic, but he couldn't take care of this one.

Felicia and the other women were in the other room helping out with the birth. Rick, Grandpa Jim, and I got down on the ground next to Carlos. His eyes were closed and he looked like he'd lost a lot of blood. I didn't know what to do. We removed his shirt and cleaned out the wound with some fresh water and a clean cloth. I saw that the bullet wound was narrow like a slit, like an eye opening and closing. Each time he moved, the eye opened and more blood came out of Carlos.

"The bullet is still in there. We got to get it out," I said.

Grandpa Jim gathered sweet grass and burned it in the four corners of the room. I knew that sweet grass was burned at burials to keep the spirit from tempting his relatives to come with him. Grandpa had filled his pipe with tobacco. He was smoking it and letting the smoke out from his lungs in a circle of life.

Carlos' body was no longer moving. I placed my hand on his throat in search of a pulse and found none. Grandpa Jim and the others had already known that Carlos was dead. Everyone knew except me.

I saw that Grandpa was carrying a sacred hoop symbol made out of a willow frame in the shape of a circle with a cross representing the four winds. He left and came back carrying his pipe.

In the other room, I heard Flores screaming in pain. She was pushing life out of her body, the way Carlos had pushed the last breath out of his. One end of the circle to another, we were part of the sacred hoop.

Grandpa Jim handed me a cloth and told me to wrap Carlos in it.

"One *šicun* arrives, another one leaves," he said raising the pipe to the sky. The *šicun* was our soul energy given to us at birth and returned to the universe at death.

Grandpa Jim knelt by Carlos' side and cut a lock of hair from his head. He wrapped it in a piece of cloth and set it aside.

"I will act as the boy's father during this time of mourning."

Carlos had lost his parents when he was a child. He had grown up with relatives, and left home at the age of 16, when his family realized he was gay. He had never returned to his family's home since that day.

In the other room we heard the sound of a new life being born. Felicia came out smiling. Her face dropped as soon as she saw Carlos' body wrapped in a cloth. Grandfather Jim spoke in a serious tone: "We must remove the body from this place at once. It is not good for the *wanagi* ghost of Carlos to stay close to the child." Grandpa Jim went into mourning as if he were his own father.

"As the father during *wašigla*, the period of mourning, I may not hold a child, I may not touch a weapon, I may not run or make any violent gestures," Grandpa Jim explained to me.

He had gone into a period of mourning and nothing should disturb it.

I remembered the Calf Woman in the lodge handing me the rites. Now I knew that the ghost keeping ceremony she had mentioned had finally come. I wondered when the other rites would be realized. We held a brief ghost keeping ceremony called *wakicagapi* for Carlos the next day. Usually, the ceremony would have lasted days to allow the spirit to be released. Normally, Grandpa Jim or Carlos' real father would have carried out rituals for four days before inviting everyone to have a feast. At that ritual, Carlos' family would have given away all of their belongings and asked people from the village to bring them new ones. But Carlos had no blood relatives and we were at war. We feasted on beans warmed on a sterno and released his *šicun* spirit east into the wind.

Chapter 28 – Owl

After Carlos was killed, Felicia and I retreated into a cocoon. I don't know if she wanted to be away from the others as much as I did. But I felt that if we could just disappear into our own world everything would be OK. We hid ourselves into the museum where the camp stored some of our dwindling supplies.

We walked into the tiny museum in search of ourselves. We were searching for our past, searching for our present, searching for our future in the walls of the building I'd come to know so well. I must have stepped in here a dozen times and never once did I look at the artifacts or pictures around us. I tried not to see them. Tried to push 'em out of my mind. This wasn't something I thought about clearly. It was something I lived.

I held Felicia's hand in mine. I could feel the softness of her skin. We didn't have to talk. We didn't have to use words. I remembered the night we'd shared in the car facing the massacre site. That was the night when we had first made love, the night when I'd first seen a piece of myself in that massacre site.

Back hundreds and thousands of years ago—back when we were free—our people traveled our land without being bound by one place. All the men were warriors then. We would take our women and our children to the open plains of the black hills in the spring and we'd come back to the foot of the hills in winter. Whitetail Deer was right about the strangeness of time. About the way time in the prairie doesn't walk in a straight line. The wind moves through the reeds in the middle of summer carrying seeds hundreds of miles to the place where they will grow. Time does not walk in a straight line. When

Tunkašila watched over us, he watched over the dead and the living. We were all together in one place, at one time, without fences.

Outside, I heard shots being fired. I wasn't afraid. I could smell the brush fire of the flares being tossed to encircle us. Here we were again, being pushed into a shrinking circle of land.

Felicia and I walked along the edges of the wall looking at the pictures. A white man with his hand on his hip was standing in a ditch filled with our bodies. Dozens of bodies piled outside the ditch waiting to be thrown on top of the others. The man looked young, he looked calm and determined, like he had a job to do and nothing was going to stop him. The job was piling the bodies of women and children, some still holding each other by the hand. Babies in their mother's arms. Young boys, who tried to outrun their enemies. The man was wearing a hat and no coat despite the obvious cold with remnants of snow on the frozen ground. Tossing bodies into a ditch could keep a man warm.

I didn't want to look no more, but we were here. This was why we were here. Another picture showed frozen bodies scattered along the flat ground of the massacre site. White men in horses making their way around the bodies examining the result of their work.

Sammy was right about the museum. It had been owned by two white families for decades. Here it was, this decrepit museum calling us to see the desecration of our people. The place was run down. Artifacts were dusty in dirty cases. Clothing worn by our killed ancestors were tossed any old way in a pile in a dusty case. They were trying to make a buck off the misery of our people. But Grey was right about the balance of life being thrown off every time one of us killed or got killed. Couldn't the Gildersleeves, the Jones and the others feel their own balance coming undone?

"Look!" Felicia called out to me from the far corner of the museum. She was standing by a large framed picture of a man, a white general wearing his finest suit. He must have represented some kind of standards of beauty, a handsome man with his elegance and the force in his eyes. He looked no more than 25 years old. In his arms, he was carrying a little girl, an Indian infant girl with her hair sticking straight up like it was trying to find the sky. She was dressed in the finest white dress a baby could ever have. Felicia and I stood frozen in front of the picture. We couldn't speak. She held my hand in hers. This time, I heard her reading aloud the caption under the man's picture: "General Colby and his daughter Clara, also known as "Lost Bird."

Lost Bird, Lost Bird. I thought about this baby girl raised by whites. Felicia continued to read the caption.

Lost bird was an infant child found on December 29, 1890 by General Leonard Wright Colby from the United States Seventh Cavalry. She was rescued from the hands of her dead mother after the Wounded Knee battle and raised by the General Colby and his wife Clara.

A strange feeling came over me. I wanted to puke. And then I thought of my gun and the number of bullets I had left to shoot when I'd go back to the firing line.

That night, Felicia took our bedrolls and we slept behind a case of dried bean cans. I held Felicia tightly that night. So tightly she said she couldn't feel herself breathing. When I drifted off to sleep, I had a dream.

I was standing by the side of a creek, more like a lake, a large reflective pool of water. I saw myself standing there, at first alone, inches from the water's edge, only I couldn't see my own reflection. I walked closer and closer and closer until my feet were in the water. I looked down and saw myself. Behind me were many people, children, men my father's age, grandmothers and grandfathers. Women holding infants. I thought I saw Felicia and turned to find her standing behind me, alone. The people were gone. Felicia was holding a newborn in her arms, a tiny infant with a little red hat. I tried to go to her, but I couldn't reach her so I retreated into the water's edge. When I looked at her again, blood trickled from between her legs onto the earth. And each time a drop fell I heard the sound of a baby crying in the distance.

I looked up into the sky to find my way and saw the spotted eagle flying above me in a circle. I called to him. He came and landed on my shoulder and whispered in my ear. "Tunkašila. Tunkašila is here for you." Now the sky was full of birds. Magpies, swallows, meadowlarks, and sparrows.

The meadowlark spoke to me. "I'm your messenger."

I searched for Felicia but she had gone. I saw a young man standing on the other side of the lake. He was alone and crying. I walked away, leaving him alone in tears. I walked to the edge of the forest and saw many eagle feathers scattered on the ground and trampled like there had been a stampede of horses. Night fell and the wind from the west rose. I heard thunder and I knew that it had come from the great eagle flapping his wings and that lighting was the flash in his eyes.

In the distance, blue light lit up the sky. I searched for the company of others but I knew they were on the other side of the forest. I walked into the thickest bend among trees and saw that many creatures were living there. I heard the howling of wolves in the distance and when I did, it gave me great strength and I leapt through the forest and came out on the other side.

When I arrived, the sun had risen again and I came upon a clearing with many butterflies. I could see the residues of their cocoons scattered on the ground as I walked towards the sun. I came upon a tree. The largest tree of the black hills; its roots pushing deeply into the ground. I sat at the foot and when my feet touched its roots I heard it whispering to me: "We're all here. We're here inside the tree with you."

There were many voices in the tree. Voices of children and the cries of babies. Voices of men talking and women singing.

The tree sang me a song in its many voices and it went something like this:

The red man lives in the branches
The white man sings in the branches
The black man sees in the branches
The yellow man dreams in the branches
And their hearts live in the roots

When I woke, I saw that I had tears on my cheeks and gladness in my heart.

**

Our camp was running low on supplies and there was no way we'd make it through if some of us didn't go out and get what we needed. On the sixtieth day, I volunteered with Jerry to leave camp and pick up a load of supplies left for us by our many supporters outside the camp.

"I'll be back," I promised Felicia.

"You better, she said rubbing her belly in a circular motion." She leaned forward and placed her lips on mine one last time. "I'm proud of you," she said before I turned around was off in the night.

We left the camp at night when the firing was heaviest. It was the only way. Leaving in daylight only meant being seen and running the chance of getting shot point blank or get stopped by the Feds. The first line of fire was covered by goons. It was harder to make our way through that line because we were up against guys like us. Guys who knew the land as well as we did. The Feds had better weapons and toys but we outsmart them when it came to the land. The problem with goons is that they had the weapons of the Feds but the mind of an Indian. If you made it through the line of goons, and then the Feds, there were still the ranchers in the hills ready to shoot us like coyotes.

We walked the four miles and made it past the first government roadblock next to the Cluster housing. The same roadblock manned by the guys who had shot Carlos. It took us hours to get from one point to another, because we were working real hard not to be seen. Jerry was good at turning himself into a snake. He'd crawl in the smoldering grass and hide for hours, not moving an inch. Jerry was fearless and the truth is he had nothing to lose. That wasn't true for me. My mind would get in the way. I'd think of Felicia in her blue dress and the fear would come again. We'd have to stay still for hours motionless in the grass, or behind a boulder or in the gully or a ditch and wait for the positions of a single Fed to change. Sometimes, they'd turn to light a cigarette or they'd switch posts. It was in those few moments of change that we found ways to move forward.

By morning, we reached the hills right outside of Porcupine, eight or nine miles away from camp. We knew we weren't free to get around. Having the face of an Indian gave you rights to an automatic criminal record. On the outskirts of the city, we walked through the hills to get to the other side of town without having to cross it. We came upon a ranch in the hills, home of vigilantes.

I saw a meadowlark circling a nearby tree. I remembered the phrase in my dream: "I am your messenger." I knew something was wrong.

Jerry was ahead. He turned to me.

"Get down," he said. Just a few feet away, two ranchers came right out of the house carrying rifles on their way somewhere. I heard one of them say to the other: "There're no Indians at Wounded Knee, just a pack of niggers, spics and Cherokees." They both laughed.

We made it into town scot-free where we met a man named Jack, a Brulé who had stashed a load of supplies for us in an abandonned shack on the edge of town.

"Hey man, thanks for helping out the movement," Jerry told Jack when he saw us. I took one look at the massive 80 pound load of supplies and started laughing.

"How the heck are we going to carry this back to camp?" I said looking at Jerry.

"Beats me but we better start figuring it out."

The load was divided into large military packs we each strapped to our backs. With each step forward, I felt like I was about to topple back and lose my balance. Jerry and I had a good laugh about how stupid we must have looked with that much crap on our back. We left town through the hills again. This time it was a lot harder to hide when we came upon the enemy. Jerry was always ahead. And to this day, I wonder what would have happened if I'd been a little faster, if I'd been born a little smaller like Jerry.

"Freeze! Put your arms up in the air!" I heard the cop yell in my back. I was done. I looked ahead to see if I could see Jerry but he'd managed to hide before the cops could see him.

They took me to the station. The whole time I thought about Felicia and the promise I'd made to her.

"I promise I'll be back soon. I promise I'll be back."

Chapter 29 – Owl

I'd been in jail 60 days when the sky opened up in a raging storm. The less you see the sky, the more you think about it. Hadn't seen a whole stretch of sky since that night with Felicia when we lay down under a blanket on my last night on the res. I heard the thunder, thunder and lightning and I moved over to the window.

Sammy, the Jamaican, said, "What ya doin' man?" He always finished his sentences with *man* which made us name him the Jamaican. Sam was no Jamaican. Born and raised—as much as the system can raise a boy—in Rapid City, 110 miles north of Pine Ridge.

His mother died on the day he was born and his father never knew him. He was raised in foster homes. Twenty-two to be exact. He liked to say, *after a while, man, all those cracker families sure looked the same to me.*

We liked to have a good laugh over this one because we'd heard the same thing all our lives: "a nigger's a nigger's a nigger. Niggers and Indians, all the same."

I could see a tiny stretch of sky from the place where I stood by the window. If I pressed my cheek against the rough surface of the wall and looked up, I could almost see a triangle of sky cut out by the sides of the window and the angle of the building. The sky lit up and raged. Streaks of light tore up the clouds opening up like vaults from a bank. That's when I saw it. I saw the meadowlark come to my window.

It came to me, came straight to me and landed on the side of my cell. I could feel the presence of Tunkašila watching over me. The bird just sat on the side of the window without a song. She looked at me, her tiny eye blinking every once in a while like she was trying to get a real good look at me. I didn't move.

Didn't want her to go. I didn't want to speak and tell Jamaican not to come over. But if he came, she would be gone. I just sat there waiting. I waited for a long time. We sat there together she and I listening to the rumbling of the sky. And then she hopped, hopped once to the middle of the window ledge and stood there. I saw that her wing was hanging loosely, the feathers pulled out of line, touching the edge of the window. Her wing was broken. We looked at each other one last time, she blinked then she was gone.

I knew something was wrong. Something was wrong with the babies but there was nothing I could do except sit in this cell and talk to Tunkanšila.

**

First day I came to Grand Mal Penitentiary, I overheard one of the guards say to another: "Only two Indians killed over there? What's the matter with those guys? Give me an automatic and 71 days to do it and I kill every last one of 'em."

I heard their laughter echoing from all around our cell and I was grateful I couldn't see either of them. Later I found out the guard who said that was Custer. We named him Custer, cause of the way he liked to think we Indians were weak and could be broken. Some of us had been killed in jail, some of us had been beaten and bruised but none of us, not a one had been broken.

The trick to surviving in jail was not to make eye contact with the pigs. The smarter ones would notice and they'd push you to look at them. Some of 'em didn't know why they were mad but they were mad 'cause you weren't looking at them and they'd try to make you do it. Never look at a rabid dog. Never look 'em in the eye 'cause they'll lock right in there with you and never let go.

After 90 days in that shit hole, they let me go, which never happens.

"The Jamaican said: the jails are full man, they're making room for better criminals than you."

They let me out on a Monday without a dime in my pocket. I looked into every cell as they escorted me out to the exit. I looked at every face in there and committed them to memory. If freedom is what I was going to find out there on the other side of these walls, I was going to live it for our whole band of brothers locked up inside.

"Walk nigger, walk!" The guard said to me on my way out. It was the same pig who'd spat at me on my way in. Those pigs had made us all niggers and them crackers. In the last cell on the last cell block on my way out, I recognized Marty, Crazy fucking Jimmy's little cousin.

"Hey, Marty," I yelled. "Hey," before the guard whopped me upside the head. I saw Marty look around to see how on earth someone making his way out of that god-forsaken hole could possibly know his name. But before he had a chance to see my face, we'd already turned the corner.

I walked for two hours south in the direction of Colonia Pine Hills until I hit a stretch of highway that would take me straight into Pine Ridge. When the sun hit the highest point, a truck stopped and picked me up.

"Where you headed?" He asked.

"Pine Ridge."

"I'm headed that way, hop in."

The driver was a Brulé Indian named Lenny who'd taken a job as a trucker. Later, I thought about him, traveling the land of our ancestors with "the mighty bull." That's what he called his truck and it made me smile thinking of him traveling our lands, watching over the hills.

"I got two babies on the way," I told him.

"Your first?"

"Yeah, my very first babies."

"Ain't nothing like it," that's for sure. The first time you hold that small little body in your great big hand and think *I made that*. Ain't nothing like it, I tell ya."

I told him about the jail and how the worse thing was not being able to see the sky, to touch the earth with my feet. I'd never been free but I'd always been able to stay connected with mother earth with my feet. But when I was locked up, they took that away from me.

Lenny didn't look like an Indian which is how he'd gotten the job in the first place. I knew he was Indian from the moment I met him because of the way he didn't look me in the eye. I knew 'cause of his skin tone. He wasn't white, wasn't red neither. He had that glow, of the mixed bloods, skin the color of the inside of an almond.

We drove in silence. I didn't want to talk much. I liked looking at the road, looking at the sky opening up ahead of us. When you drive in our neck of the woods, you can see the sky forever—one infinite line that opens up, getting lost in the prairie.

When we got there, it was late afternoon. Light was shifting, sun falling behind the hills. The house looked smaller than I had remembered. There was no car in the driveway. I'd promised Felicia's father I'd buy him a new truck but I was years from reality. I thanked Matthew and jumped out.

I stood in front of the house, my heart racing. I could almost hear it in my throat, holding me in one place. The house was unusually quiet. So quiet it reminded me of the song-less meadowlark at my window in jail.

I heard her before I came in. Heard her voice wailing into the air. The cry of my baby lifted into the air where everything else was silent around her. When I walked in, Felicia's mother came to me. Even though I had never spent much time looking at this woman who had nurtured and raised my Felicia, I noticed that her face seemed worn, older, as if she had aged a decade in just three short months. Without touching me, I could sense that she wanted me to wait.

"Owl, it's good you're back. It's real good you're back."

I heard a baby again. Its single voice, her cries filling the room beyond the entrance.

"Wait, there is something you need to know," Felicia's mom Marie said grabbing a hold of my arm.

My heart sank. I knew in that moment that something terrible had happened to my Felicia. I pushed past Marie and past the cloth that separated the entrance from the rest of the room. Grandma Ihanblapi was sitting in a rocking chair giving a bottle to the baby. When she saw me, she smiled as tears welled up in her eyes.

"Where is Felicia?" I could barely get enough air into my lungs.

Marie had made her way next to Grandma Ihanblapi and the baby.

"She's gone, son. Felicia is gone."

Time became still the way winds die down before a raging storm. I wanted to crawl into the darkness of the earth and be swallowed whole. I wanted the earth to ingest me so I could disappear and never return. Felicia was no longer of this earth. My mind searched and searched in the four corners of itself for the possibility of accepting that my Felicia no longer existed anywhere on this earth. My mind tried to understand that my angel wife was no longer breathing. That I would never set eyes on her face again. That I would never hear voice. That I would never place my hand on the nape of her neck or let her lips grace mine. I could feel the weight of my rapid fire thoughts circling onto themselves, entangling me like a buck being taken down at rodeo. I fell to my knees and began to weep.

"When?" Was all I was able to say in between the cries pushing their way out of me.

"When did she go?"

Marie knelt down by my side and wrapped her arms around me. A woman rarely touched a man, unless he was her husband or her son.

"A month ago, son," she said. "Our Felicia passed a month ago."

"Who did this to her?" The grief gave way to a mounting rage that threatened to push me out into the world in search of destruction.

"Who hurt my Felicia?" When I said *my Felicia*, I felt the grief settle inside me again, battling rage battling grief, like a crazy cadence of demons.

"Sit down son. So we can tell you everything we know."

Grandma Ihanblapi stood up with the baby in hand and gently placed her in my arms.

"Your daughter," she said as I laid eyes on my Maya for the very first time. My daughter began to cry. I scanned Grandma Ihanblapi's face for direction. She simply smiled and nodded. Maya's face creased into a scream, her skin turning beet red.

"You shake and walk, shake and walk," Grandma Ihanblapi said smiling again.

Maya's eyes reminded me of Felicia's, perfect almonds. Her cheeks were round like Felicia's and her nose a tiny version of her mother's. As I held this tiny bundle in my arms I felt the hope and the pride Felicia had brought me in the short time we were blessed with each other's love. She was gone now, but I could feel her presence as I held Maya in my arms. I remembered the song Felicia had taught me on the night she had told me about the babies in her belly and I began to sing it to my daughter, calling the spirits to be here among us and hold us true to the legacy of our people.

Tunkasila
Wanmayanguye
Tunkasila
Wanmayanguyelo

Ikce wicasa tacannunpe
Wan yuha hoyelo
Mitaye ob waniktelo heyaya
Hoyewayelo

Maya's cries stopped and she watched me intently as I rocked her to the rhythm of the song of our ancestors. Grandma Ihanblapi joined me and we sang the song a second time in unison, calling the spirits to be with us.

Grandfather come and see me
I send a voice with the people's pipe,
So I may live with my relatives.

The baby became still as a rock. I pulled her to me to see her tiny face resembling a small animal, with its eyes like crevasses and its puffy red cheeks.

"What happened," I asked, looking at Marie and Grandma Ihanblapi. I waited for their words feeling like I'd placed my hand on a damn about to break.

"Babies were born in a storm. Very bad storm. Rain, thunder for days." I listened to Grandma Ihanblapi talk about the day of the birth and I remembered the storm on the day the wounded meadowlark had come to see me.

"Her contractions started at dawn. We took her to the center of the house and made her squat in the way of our women," Marie described the moment Felicia went into labor.

"Babies no come. Babies no come. Then sun set. Night outside. Very dark and one baby come." Grandma Ihanblapi and Marie took turns unraveling the tragedy of Felicia's last days.

"It took 35 hours for Felicia to give birth to the first baby," Marie explained.

"The first baby?" I gasped. Their recounting of the births was the first time the presence of two babies had been confirmed by something outside of Grandman Ihanblapi visions.

"Yes, Felicia gave birth to babies, two girls." Marie said with tears in her eyes. "But After 35 hours, they were still not coming and Felicia was worried they were dying inside her. We tried to tell her, everything was OK but you know how stubborn Felicia can...could be," Marie said with a sad smile on her face.

"Babies OK. I know babies OK. But Felicia cry, Felicia scream."

"Maya was born. We waited another two hours waiting for the second baby to come. But Felicia wanted to go to the hospital. *Don't let my baby die,* she kept saying, *don't let my baby die.* So after another hour we took her to the hospital." Marie was wringing her hands as she relieved the pain of her daughter.

Grandma Ihanblapi became agitated and got up to light the sacred pipe. She raised her hand up in the air. "*Wowahtani* is here, evil." She waved the smoke around the room and passed the pipe to me to smoke it. Hesitant, I looked to Marie for guidance, who nodded in agreement. I took the pipe in my hands and took a drag leting the smoke release into the air.

"At the hospital, they took Felicia away and we stayed in the waiting room for hours and hours." Marie continued.

"We wait long time. Long time. They say go away. Go home. Baby not ready yet." Grandma Ihanblapi added.

"After another ten hours, a nurse came out and told us to go home. They said Felicia would not be ready for a long time. She said something about *complications* and how Felicia would need a lot of rest. We refused to leave. We stayed all night and the next day and the next day after that. They still wouldn't let us see her. But on the third day when morning came, they let us see our Felicia." Marie looked down and began to cry.

"When we walked into the room, she was sleeping."

"Sleep of darkness," Grandma Ihanblapi called it.

"They gave her a lot of drugs," Marie clarified.

"*Where is the baby?* I said to the nurse when we sat down by Felicia. *When can we see the baby?* You see we were smart and kept Maya with family at home while Felicia was still giving birth to the second baby. The nurse just looked at me and said *what baby? She did not give birth to a second child.* And she walked out of the room.

She had been drugged so she could sleep. They asked to see the second baby but the nurse there was no second child. Felicia had given birth to one child, they said, not two.

"They took the baby away." Grandma Ihanblapi looked at me and I saw that she had tears in her eyes.

"We talked to nurses. We talked to doctors. They all said the same thing. On the third day, they let her go with heavy medication. They gave us papers we didn't look at until Felicia came back to herself.

"Felicia told us she remembers giving birth to the second girl in the hospital. *A perfect girl,* she called her, *just like the first one.*" Marie explained to me. "And then after they took the baby to clean her, Felicia never saw her again. They gave her heavy medications that kept her sleeping like a rock." Marie added.

Even after she came home from the hospital, it took days for the drugs to wear off completely and let Felicia think straight again here at home.

"When the drugs wore off, Felicia lost her mind with sadnesss," Marie said holding back the tears. "She read the papers they gave her at the hospital."

They say the largest mountain can split under the force of a single drop of water. Centuries of rain falling on the rock and then one day a single drop will split it open. This is what happened to my wife.

"*Sterilization—removal of ovaries* were the words she read on the paper," Marie finally said.

I wanted to scream. I wanted to fly to the hospital and grab hold of the doctor who had butchered my wife's body and taken her last chance to create life ever again. I wanted to destroy the person who had lied to our family and stolen our child. I was beginning to understand what had killed Felicia.

"After days of silence, Felicia began to speak again. She held Maya every day and nursed her and she kept repeating the same thing over and over again *they took my baby away.*

"Felicia knew she'd birthed two babies. A woman knows those things," Marie said.

A knot formed in my throat. I should have been there to protect my family. I hadn't been there to protect Felicia and the babies. I hadn't been there and they had opened her up and butchered her like an animal for slaughter so that she couldn't give life no more.

"Every day she was weaker and weaker," Marie told me. And then she got sick. I think she wanted to leave this earth because she stopped fighting. The doctor said it was an infection. But she woudn't even drink water to stay alive."

"The doctors, they kill her soul," Grandma Ihanblapi said strenly.

That night, Felicia's parents made their cot in the other room leaving me to sleep with the baby. I woke up every few hours and gave her a bottle Marie and Grandma Ihanblapi had prepared for us in the evening. Maya was a strong baby, she was a baby who could feel the heartbeat of the world. And when her mama died, she became sad even before she could speak a word.

Marie told me that Felicia named our baby Maya for the way she held herself, like a Mayan queen. I remembered how Felicia and I had talked about the unity of all indigenous people, after meeting Carlos on the res. We had both understood that the Mayans and the Aztecs, the Brulés, and the Oglalas, we were all one.

I didn't need to know the facts to understand that Felicia had been broken. In all my years on the res, I'd seen and heard about people breaking. I'd seen the wino in the corner of the village, coming back from the bars off the res, his teeth missing, his skin dried up by booze, making 'im look like ancient elders when he was still in his 40s. I'd seen girls going off into the city to sell themselves so they could make money for their children. I'd seen young boys go mad circling round and round on the res, I'd seen girls forget their beauty and wither before they had a chance to bloom. But all these years, I'd never known anyone I loved slip away from me like Felicia had.

For a long time, I tried to find out about the other baby. If I couldn't be there to save Felicia, I wanted to find our child and bring our family back together. I returned to the hospital several times only to be threatened with arrest. We had no proof and no money to hire a lawyer and as the years went by, we drifted into settled grief.

Part VI

25 years later

Chapter 30 – Owl

Pine Ridge Reservation, SD, 1998

At the police station, the cops took me down to the morgue so I could identify Maya's body. The pig with the cropped hair pushed the metallic door opened and let us into a large, cold room that smelled like the hospital where I searched for my baby. Above us, I heard the buzzing of the neon lights up on the ceiling and felt a chill in my back.

"Number 27," he said stopping in front of a series of metallic drawers. He pulled the large handle and slid the drawer open. He unzipped the body bag, exposing a purplish face with swollen eyes and a mouth partially opened.

"This is not my daughter," I said my heart leaping out of my chest.

"This is not Maya Owl Feather?"

"No, this is not my Maya."

"Well, it's got to be somebody's Maya," the cop said zipping the bag back up. "I guess, you're not out of a daughter after all."

Maya was not dead! They had tortured me to believe that my last remaining child had been taken away from me but this was not true. They showed me to the door and let me walk home. This a tactic they like to use to remind you who's boss. Outside, the sky was turning shades of purple and gold, like old bruises or crushed plums, like the wild violets that push their way against all odds, through the earth each spring. I thought about the way the white man had tried to break us through the years. I thought about the virus of the hatred they had tried to pass on to us through the generations. They had tried to destroy us. They had killed our people and stolen our land, they had taken all of our natural resources, they had taken our sovereignty and killed our leaders replacing them with puppets like Washington in the hopes that we would rot at the roots. And when we had no land, no food and no leaders, then they took away our language and our children. Conqueror, I can see you in my mind's eye now. You can kill us, but you can't erase our memories of the ancient ways. You can take our children, but you can't make our love for them fade away. You can strip us of our ability to speak in the tongue of our ancestors, but you can't stop us from connecting with their spirits. For more than one hundred years now since you massacred our men, our women, and our children on the sacred land of Wounded Knee, you have tried to destroy us.

I listened to the sound of wood frogs calling out their mates and I remembered that even if Felicia was dead in body, she was present in spirit. I could hear her in the Buffalo grass rustling in the wind. There isn't much of it left anywhere on this res, but you can't erase the memory of the ancient ways as long as we continue to share it with one another. I could feel Felicia and the others in these sounds of spring giving way to light and I felt myself coming back to myself. I thought about the life force that returns each year. The call of the heart. Always returning to what it knows: the earth. Everything comes from the earth and everything returns to it. As I walked alone along this road, I thought about the strength of our people. I thought of the dead as well as the living. And I rejoiced in the fact that I am still here. We Indians are still here and we will always be here, on the land our ancestors.

Chapter 31 – Elbe

When they turned onto US Route 18, both Joey and Elbe knew that their road trip was coming to a close. Dawn pulled at them magnetically, drawing them both to all of the mythical places they had each imagined they would release on this trip. For Joey it had been his absolute maleness, the way he had drawn his body in the soft dark corner of his mind. The angled sinews of his muscles, the depth of his voice, the hard push of his body out into the world. But it was also, the letting go of what he had discovered with Jennie Stevens, his mother. The way he knew now that he had to let her go. He could measure the loss he had carried inside all of these years since that fateful morning when the blinking lights of the ambulance had made their way through the trailer windows. He could finally understand the breadth of all that he had lost on that morning. Past the yellow hue of Jennie's dress when the doctors carried her out of her bed. Past the darkness of the partial morning when the little girl Michelle he had once been cried in the silence of his mother's absence.

Elbe also carried around her own myths with her. Soon, they would need to be discarded. How lurid dreams become when they are confronted with reality. How untrue and imperfect, how deformed and terribly wrong little kids' dreams look in the harshness of daylight. Elbe knew on some level that she would need to learn to dispose of the invisibility of her own image. She would have to learn to redraw herself, from the inside, without anyone's salvation. No matter what or whom she found in Pine Ridge, she would need to let go of the self she had falsely constructed.

They came upon a sign that read *Welcome to Oglala Nation – Buckle Up! It is OUR law!* Here they were. They had arrived.

The landscape was stark, desolate with miles and miles of prairie grass. There were so few houses, Elbe wondered if this place was actually inhabited.

"Where are the people?" she asked visibly worried.

"Here and there, I guess."

They drove by a series of broken down and abandonned trailers.

Elbe pulled out the piece of paper where she had transcribed Maya's address. She had memorized it, read it so many times she did not need this anymore and yet she could not let go of it. Like a map, the paper made her feel safer, more grounded.

"There is no way I can just drive up to the address right now. Let's go find a place to stay and regroup and then we'll head over. What do you think?"

"Absolutely. If that's what you need, that's what we'll do." Elbe could feel her heart constricting. *Why am I doing this?* She asked herself. *I've gone this far without them, why do I need to meet these people?* Why was she so sure there was more than one person? She wanted answers. She did not want them. They drove to the nearby town of Allen where they found a motel on the edge of the world.

Elbe wished she had found natural beauty instead of the desolate landscape that surrounded them. She had invented a magical place of poppies and blackbirds flying around the peaks of the black hills. She had wanted to find all of this imagined splendor instead of the austere empty, dusty roads and this motel on the side of a barren road. They walked into the musty mustard deserted lobby. *Ring here for service,* read a small sign on the counter. Elbe pressed it, shyly. She did not want to disturb. Joey pushed it again, this time with more insistence. A man came from behind a plastic curtain that he pushed aside slowly. When he saw Elbe, he nodded, and smiled faintly ignoring Joey. Elbe noticed his toothless grin. It was difficult to say how old the man was or whether he *looked*

Indian. Elbe thought how the man and she did not look like they belonged to the same people and yet she had felt his recognition in the way he had eyed her. This was the first time in her life Elbe had felt claimed. He had *seen* her. Instinctively, he knew she belonged here.

"We'd like a room, please," she spoke responding to his recognition.

"We have a $39.99 special," the man said, looking at Elbe calmly.

"Good. We'll take that. As long as there are two beds in the room."

"What? You don't want to cuddle with me little lady?" Joey snuggled up against her. Elbe found both comfort and embarrassment in his words. She wondered whether her body *knew* this place, the way the man behind the counter had *known* her. She wanted to believe she was genetically wired to the somberness of the black hills pushed back behind hundreds of miles of burnt prairie grass. What if everyone were genetically wired to one geographic location? Were there places where we truly belonged, even if we had never been there or carried any memories of the imprints left there by our ancestors? Elbe wished this to be true. She wanted to belong not just to a people but to a place as well.

They climbed to the second floor of a series of outdoor entrances to the rooms. They pushed open the rickety door to their room. It was dark. The sound of trickling water sounded from the closed door of the bathroom. Elbe waited by the door as Joey fumbled for the light. A bare bulb ignited exposing two parallel single beds next to each other.

"We could push them together and cuddle." Joey smiled again.

"Enough with your cuddling. I'm not one of your conquests Joey," Elbe wasn't sure whether she was serious or not. Joey was not either.

"You know I'm kidding right? You don't actually think I want your nasty pussy, do you?" They both laughed.

Elbe remembered the scars she had seen on Joey a couple of days earlier in the previous hotel room. She pushed the thought away.

"Can I read it to you?" Elbe finally asked Joey as she propped up the pillows on her bed.

"Read what?"

"Maya's letter." Her heart was doing this strange flip-flop of a twist in her chest.

"Yeah, read it!" Joey screamed like a kid on his birthday.

"Dear LB." Elbe paused. "Oh, she wrote Elbe with letters, as in *L* and *B*, Weird, right?"

"Why would she do that?" Joey asked.

"No clue," Elbe answered.

"OK, Keep going."

Elbe started over.

"Dear LB, Receiving this letter is probably as strange as writing it I'm sure. I recently found out about your existence by accident. You and I are sisters. Not just sisters. Twins. Yeah, I know, it's weird. I can't wrap my mind around this one either. Thinking of you out there, another one of me. Well, you're not me, but you know what I mean, right?"

Elbe looked up and smiled at Joey. Secretly she thought about how the phrase *another one of me* had been the exact words she had chosen to refer to her twin sister when her mother had given her the letter.

"She's kinda funny. Well she'd have to be to be your sister," Joey laughed.

Elbe kept reading. "You can reach me at this address. I know you live far away, but maybe we could meet? Please write OK? I have waited for you my whole life." Signed "Maya."

I have waited for you my whole life. That was Elbe's favorite line.

"I wonder what she does for a living."

"Hey, at least you know what she looks like," Joey laughed again. Elbe looked at him sitting cross-legged on his bed. He seemed uncomfortable and smaller somehow. Suddenly Elbe felt that Joey could not really help her get through this moment and journey. Maybe no one could.

"We'll drive to the address in the morning," Elbe finally said, putting the letter away. That night, Elbe tossed and turned in her small motel bed thinking about the moment when she would see her twin sister for the first time. Each time, she tried to picture it, she saw herself staring back at her own image in the bathroom mirror, the way she had done her entire childhood. Soon, Elbe would see herself.

**

The end

Acknowledgements

My heart opens in gratitude to the many incredible people whose energy and magic contributed to the birth and culmination of this book. First and foremost, I would like to thank the late Heather Lewis for her brilliance, generosity and friendship. A big thank you to Akiba Onada Sikwoia for opening the portal to the beautiful Lakota culture. Gratitude to Celia Colmerauer for loving and healing me during during those early years. Thank you to my partner Eva Clemens for allowing me to share all that I have healed and relearned about love. Gratitude to Ginny Root for mentoring me in those early years. Thank you to Wendy Root for bringing me back from the dead, and to Chris Root for a lifetime of friendship. Thank you to Luisah Teish for plucking me out of thin air on LinkedIn, and for introducing me to Harvard Square Editions. In gratitude to Louise Hammonds for her generous editorial input. I am grateful to Megan McDonagh for her expert cover design skills. And most of all, thank you to my ancestors, and family, including my mother Kalu Fernande Pollefort for the legacy of my roots. There are countless others to whom I am forever connected in gratitude for their contributions, but whose names do not appear here. To all, thank you.

More books from
Harvard Square Editions:

People and Peppers, Kelvin Christopher James

Gates of Eden, Charles Degelman

Love's Affliction, Fidelis Mkparu

Transoceanic Lights, S. Li

Close, Erika Raskin

The Beard, Alan Swyer

Living Treasures, Yang Huang

Nature's Confession, J.L. Morin

Upper West Side Story, Susan Pashman

Dark Lady of Hollywood, Diane Haithman

Fugue for the Right Hand, Michele Tolela Myers

Growing Up White, James P. Stobaugh

Birds of Passage, Joe Giordano

Parallel, Sharon Erby